OPEN SPACE

OPEN SPACE

NEW CANADIAN
FANTASTIC FICTION

edited by
Claude Lalumière

Red Deer Press

Published by
Red Deer Press
813 MacKimmie Library Tower
2500 University Drive NW
Calgary Alberta Canada T2N 1N4
www.reddeerpress.com

Credits
Edited for the Press by Claude Lalumière
Cover illustration and design by Jean-Pierre Normand
Text design by Erin Woodward
Printed and bound in Canada by AGMV Marquis for Red Deer Press

Acknowledgments
Financial support provided by the Canada Council, the Department of Canadian Heritage, the Alberta Foundation for the Arts, a beneficiary of the Lottery Fund of the Government of Alberta, and the University of Calgary.

National Library of Canada Cataloguing in Publication Data
Open space : new Canadian fantastic fiction / editor, Claude Lalumière.
ISBN 0-88995-281-7
1. Fantasy fiction, Canadian (English)* 2. Short stories, Canadian (English)* 3. Canadian fiction (English)—21st century.* I. Lalumière, Claude.
PS8323.F3O63 2003   C813'.087660806   C2003-910483-4
PR9197.35.F35O63 2003

5 4 3 2 1

Contents

INTRODUCTION

Step on everyone's foot in a crowded elevator until someone apologizes—that's how you find a Canadian in a crowded elevator.

Two (one to change the lightbulb and the other to go to Manhattan and make sure lightbulbs are still cool) is how many Torontonians it takes to change a lightbulb.

We're a nation of apologizers, a genreful of shoulder-checkers, overshadowed by the pushy States and the CanLit mafia that may dole out the occasional arts grant but will never put us on the Governor General's shortlist. We're told that we're not as brash as our American cousins with their muscular adventure stories, and we're told that we lack the delicate touch of a proper Canadian *"fantasist"*—an Atwood or a Davies or a Kinsella whose wistful words are as heart-wrenching as a snatch of Leonard Cohen song escaped from the steam-wisped closing door of a Montreal café when it's so cold on the streets your snot freezes in your nose.

We're neurotically betwixt and between, and we've got our ghetto humour as pointed as a Borscht-belt self-deprecator's stand-up routine. We've got our cons, awards, and clubby writers' workshops. We've even got our stupid scandals and nasty gossip, and our thugs and our saints. We've got legendary Merril, we've got expats Spider and Gibson, we've got native sons and daughters writing and living abroad in strange Californian climes (no, I don't mean me—I mean Sean Stewart).

Our internet bubble did not inflate to the Biggie Size yanqui standard, and our crash was more of a slow hissing deflation. Our music-video station is naive-retro enough to actually show *videos*. Our cities support multiple newspapers, and even the talk-radio Morning Zoo types hold out enough hope of working at the CBC that they tend more to the Gzowski than the Limbaugh.

The CanLit establishment's been badly wounded by the Chapters/Pegasus debacle—the one time that most Canadians would have *loved* to see some tax dollars spent on governmental antitrust regulation—and the American future's deflating along with its bubble and its economy and its Constitution, in an Ashcroftian nightmare of debt-driven military adventurism and terrorist witch-huntery. The American story's pointing inward, all inward, in a kind of provincial orgy of self-examination, the hyperconcentrated news oligopoly telling the embedded story that emanates straight from the Oval Office, and our American cousins who turn to the internet to get the story from abroad find themselves isolated pariahs for choosing to listen to the kooky, non-credible auslander media.

The fantastic and the hopeful and the future are all looking foreign to me today. They're betwixt and between, stories told from the perspective of people whose identity is made up of equal parts compulsive politeness and nagging self-doubt, people who have *owned* those traits, *honed* those traits, used to them to avoid the pitfalls of hubris and arrogance.

Canadian fantastic writers—and Britons, and Aussies, and all the polyglot writers of Spain and France and the ashes of the Soviet Union—are writing the stories that resonate in the twenty-first century. We're telling stories that inhabit the middle ground between the swashbuckling Continental Rabble and the anemic, maudlin wistfulness of the CanLit establishment.

We're telling stories like the ones in this volume, unflinching and clear-eyed and still hopeful—even in bitterness—and pointedly funny without being broad or mawkish. We're telling stories that call for something better than a world united under a super-duper-power and for something better than a world balkanized to ethnic flinders.

We're telling these stories, the ones between these covers. They're damned fine—they're even cool in Manhattan. (And we've got nothing to apologize for.)

Cory Doctorow
April 2003

GROWING UP SAM

Melissa Yuan-Innes

TODAY JACKIE BRING CAKE. "It is your birthday, Sam Ian! You are three years old."

We eat cake. It fruitcake. It taste good.

Jackie bring present. Shiny. I see my face in it. Smile. My teeth scary! I yell. She laugh.

She bring daughter. Séverine two years old. She have smooth brown skin, fuzzy black hair, big brown eyes. Like Jackie. We look. She comb through my fur with fingers. This is best present.

TOM GET MAD TODAY. Tom try teach me sign language. "Come on, Sam. You use the computer. Now you have to learn the signs."

I try, but it hard. I like portaspeak. Push keyboard, synthesizer make sound. Talk for me. Fun.

"But Sam, this is more visually interesting. An homage to Koko. Now come on."

Tom use big words. I try. I learn *apple, water*.

Jackie come in. She say something to Tom. She hug me. She pretend give birth and holding baby. Then she show me sign, *mother*.

I point at her.

She smile. Look sad. "I'm not your real mother, Sam. Well, I guess I fulfill that kind of role, and I did help make you. But I'm not your biological mother."

Sometimes Jackie talk big words too. I wish someone hold me and groom me again.

TODAY SÉVERINE BIRTHDAY. Six years. I ask her watch Jackie Chan. Car chase good. She clap hands. We like old movies. Fun. Jackie like show me nature holos. She sigh but put movie in and make popcorn. I chew and show Sev popcorn in mouth. She does back to me. We laugh hard.

Outside, I hear bang. "What that?"

Jackie get up. "You two stay here."

She gone long time. Movie over. "Was it good, my loves?"

"Yes!" we both yell. We laugh. Séverine ask, "Mom, where you going? Was it the bad—"

"Shh. I'll tell you later."

"Okay." Séverine look serious. I poke her. We laugh.

TODAY I CLIMBING IN GARDEN WHEN SÉVERINE COME BY. I jump down when I hear her call. She hug me.

"Hi Sam. I'm on my way to school. Grade seven. Can you believe it?"

I point at her hair. She have long braids now, down to bum.

She laugh and spin around. "Hair extensions. You like them?"

I pull on one.

"Ow!" She laugh. "Sam, you're always the same. Don't change." She hug me. She smell funny. Too sweet. She laugh. "You're my brother."

"Why this funny?"

"Oh, you know."

I punch words in portaspeak keyboard. "No. You tell me."

"Because you're an ape!"

I turn up synth volume. "Not ape."

"Oh, you know what I mean. Half ape. Priman. Whatever. But we grew up together, Sam—"

I turn my volume to yell. "NOT APE!"

"Yeah, of course, Sam." She smile and turn to groom me. I duck. My hands in fists, my breaths little grunts. I never been so angry at Sev. I run through garden to steel room and my computer. Better language software. When she come in room, I boom at her. "I am not ape! I am not little kid! You treat me better or you not welcome here!"

She stop. Her mouth open. She start to cry.

I sorry now. I walk over and touch braids. She cry more. I start grooming. I run fingers through hair, pat back, soothe face. She stop crying. "I'm sorry, Sam." She start groom me back. I let her. After long time, we sit together quiet. Then she press kiss on head and go.

I sit. Not feel like do anything. Tom come in for language. I throw pillow at him. He look at me, then press keypad. Steel door open and he leave.

I sit.

Jackie come in. "It's okay, Sam."

"Not ape," I mumble.

"No, you're not." She stroke my hair too. "Séverine's just getting to an awkward age. She knows it all, but hasn't done very much. And she's jealous."

I open one eye. "Me?"

She keep stroking me. "And me, too, maybe. I'm not very good at all the mother–daughter things, like clothes and hair. We don't understand each other all the time any more."

I reach and stroke her hair. She sigh and let me. I groom and then we sleep together.

Tom TELL ME MY GRAMMAR BAD. "You could do so much more, Sam. You want to be made fun of for the rest of your life? People are imitating the way you talk. They think it's funny. Don't you want to show them up?"

I shrug. Jackie show me Sam fan websites. There even a translator that turn their words into samspeak. Funny. "Some people like."

"Yes, the seething mass of illiterates and the bleeding hearts who feel so guilty about bonobo extinction that they'd be charmed to hear you fart. I think you're holding out on us. I've talked to all the other Missing Link linguists, and they think so too. Come on, Sam. It's so basic. You have to have a verb in every sentence, and the object has to agree with it, and make sure you use articles like 'the' and 'a'—"

I yawn. Make sentence on my computer to boom at him, "TOM IS A BIG DRAG."

I still laughing when Jackie come in.

Tom turn to her. "I still have five minutes left!"

I type "Tom is a angry man" and flash screen at her. She smile.

Tom see and turn red. "I am not! And it should be 'an angry man.' Remember to use 'an' before a word that starts with a vowel!" He shake head. "I give up! Forget it!" He stomp away. Steel door close behind him.

My mouth open, laugh without sound.

Jackie smile. Stroke my head. She put on nature video and watch me watching. I like. Bonobo chimpanzees in jungle. Pretty good. I pick up knife and start peeling apple.

"What do you think, Sam."

"I like how they all family together. I like how they sex maniacs." I laugh. I have spell 'maniacs' out. Not auto-programmed. They not want me use word like that, but I save afterward.

Usually Jackie not like sex talk. This time she ignore. "Sam, do you recognize any of them?"

I shake my head, start chewing on peel. Funny. Can chew long time, going round and round, if long peel.

"Sam." She point to large female. "This is your mother."

I stop. Peel fall from mouth to floor. I freeze video and walk up to touch her face. "My mother?"

"Yes."

I forward through video to dominant male. "He my father?"

Jackie shake her head.

"Who?" I print 3D picture of mother. I touch face. "I not look like her."

"You do, a little."

I look at my face in mirror. Yes, black hairy face. But less hairy, nose bigger, jaw smaller. "Who my father?"

She sigh, blow hair out of eyes. "You don't really have one, Sam. We took your mother's frozen eggs and . . . changed them and fertilized them with changed human sperm. Then we put them in an artificial uterus to grow. Do you understand?"

I know Jackie geneticist. Hard word, hard ideas, but I try to understand. "You not my mother?"

She stroke my hair. "Your adopted mother."

"Who my father?"

She shake her head. "Well. We don't really know. All the sperm donors were anonymous, and we didn't really think any man would want to be identified as having an ape baby. It took a lot of tries to get you right. Just you, Sam Ian."

I am quiet. Then, using not keyboard, but hands, I sign, I love you.

She get tears. I know this mean happy. And she hug me tight and say, "Sam, I love you too."

ONE DAY, I CLIMB ON JACKIE'S LAP AND PRESS KEYBOARD. "I want girlfriend."

She laugh. "Séverine's not here today, honey."

I shake head. "No. Real girlfriend. Hybrid."

She get quiet. "We're trying, baby. Believe me."

"What problem?"

"Well. We just haven't been able to. Our chances are less than one in a hundred just to get to a fertilized embryo, let alone successfully implant one . . . and the Christianoids are winning the public relations battle . . . and some of my colleagues think that we should be concentrating on other life forms instead of the ape, easier, less controversial . . . but we're trying, Sam. I promise."

MY STEEL ROOM FILLED WITH PEOPLE IN WHITE COATS. Scientists. Jackie not there. I press against door to garden. But it not open for my thumbprint. I press keypad. Door still closed.

Tom say, "Not just yet, Sam. We want to talk to you about keeping you safe."

People all smile and nod. I go to computer. Screen saver is picture of Jackie. I feel better. I snarl. "I safe here."

"We think so, Sam. But, well, not as many people are as nice as we are. We need to keep track of you at all times. The cameras and infrared detectors just aren't good enough. We're going to give you a chip." He hold up green plastic chip.

"No! No chip."

"It won't hurt. We'll put you to sleep. It's like an operation."

Black woman step forward. I wonder if they choose her to make me think Jackie. She say, "Like if you needed your appendix out. This will save your life, too. We'll put it in your brain, and that way we'll know where you are all the time."

They smile. Nod again.

I want scream. I keep down. Humans not like scream. Make them think I am animal. I hit keyboard. "NO."

"But—"

"NO. This is my body. You not touch me. You not operate me. I refuse." I shaking. They can knock me out. They use drugs. Machines. No one know. No one believe me. "YOU TOUCH ME AND I SUE YOU."

Door open. Jackie run in. "Sam! Sam!" She grab me. She wrap arms around me. She shaking too. She yell at them. "How dare you do this without me! You knew I was in Houston." She turn her back to them. Speak low, in my ear. "Sam, do you know what they want to do? What do you think of the spy chip?"

I reach one hand to tap on keyboard to repeat. "YOU TOUCH ME AND I SUE YOU."

She turn and glare at them. "Then it's settled. Sam is a sentient being as ruled by the Supreme Court. You have to get informed consent, and he refuses."

They stand there.

She glare at them.

"Alright then," Tom say, "you heard the lady." He walk over to keypad and press code. Door open. "That's it for today."

They walk out. Slowly. Stare at us. We stare back.

When they gone, I break Jackie hug. She hurt. I jump up, climb wall, knock cameras away. Then I hug her. She hold me like her heart breaking.

TWO WEEK LATER, I SEE JACKIE ON NEWS. They want me watch ape documentaries and Disney, but I use internet to see other.

Man with wrinkle face say, "It's an honour to have Jackie Routhier here. She's Sam Ian's 'mother' in more ways than one. She was the head of the genetics team that created him, and now she's bringing him up! Come on out, Jackie."

Applause. Jackie come out on stage. She look beautiful, but I know she mad. Eyes hard, fake smile, back too straight. She not want to be there. I wish she here too. Sometimes, she sleep here. She say I too old, but I say, Sev has sleepovers. Why not me? She laugh and stroke my hair.

Now, Jackie say, "Thank you, Warren. I think of myself as a geneticist who helps to raise Sam Ian. It's a team effort."

They play hologram of me and Jackie. Me learning sign language.

"Jackie, what do you say to the people who claim Sam Ian is an 'affront to the laws of God and morality'?"

"Warren, I'm glad you asked that question. Sam is a very lovable, wonderful little creature who likes to watch movies and go on the internet as well as play with holograms of bonobo chimpanzees. If you knew him, and I hope you do through the holos and films we've made, you would know that he is no more an affront to God than any other thirteen-year-old."

Man give fake chuckle. "Jackie, you called him a 'little creature.' What do you call him? Human? Ape? Both? Have you raised him to see himself as a hybrid?"

Jackie no smile. "We call him a priman, as in 'primate-human.'"

"What is the point of your 'priman?' I mean, why are you spending millions, or billions—may I ask how much—"

"No. The Missing Link, which funds us, is a private organization and does not publish its numbers."

"Had to ask, didn't I." Man have big teeth.

She shake her head. "Warren, you ask what the point is. I could justify it, the way I have so many times, as well as in our mission statement, that the bonobo chimpanzees are wonderful, family-oriented creatures worth saving."

"Ah. Then why not save the bonobo and leave out the mixing with humans?"

"Because we have tried that. And tried again. We have to save their habitat, first of all, and the human African population keeps growing and is increasingly unwilling to put aside forested area. The so-called First World refuses to put any real time or effort into helping them. The Missing Link does work towards conservation. But they also wanted to try a completely different method, which is to make a new creature that could take the wonderful bonobo and make it into a creature that could survive in the only world that's left: our world."

"The priman."

"Yes."

"And all you have to show for it is Sam Ian."

Her shoulders are stiff. "So far. And if you knew him, you wouldn't say 'all.'"

"But he's just one little hybrid, Jackie. What about the death threats from the Sons of the Apocalypse, the Human Purity movement, and Save Our Souls. If they succeed—"

"It would be a loss to everyone. More than they will ever know."

I feel funny in throat. But man keep talking.

"Wouldn't it make more sense to make more of them? Right now, he's been compared to a donkey because he's a hybrid who's sterile."

Jackie press lips together. "We don't think he's necessarily sterile. But he probably can't breed with a human—or a bonobo, even if they still existed. They're different species."

"So why don't you make him a girlfriend?"

"We're working on it."

"I heard that it's difficult, something about the X chromosome—"

"Well, if you remember your biology, females have two X chromosomes and males have an X and a Y. Not as much genetic information is carried on the Y, so in a male, the X always expresses itself—"

"Whoa! Males have less genetic information? Is that why we're so basic?" He wink at camera.

"No, not at all. We all have the same number of chromosomes, but the Y is a smaller chromosome and has fewer genes. Let's say, if it's a card game, that girls have doubles of everything, through the double Xs, and males have one and a half. So a girl would always have a spare, but a boy wouldn't. So for certain genes in boys, the X 'card' will always be played. That's why certain genetic diseases manifest in boys but not girls. That's an advantage for girls.

They have two Xs. If each cell is a card game, one X gets played and the other one has to be turned off or put aside. We call that a Barr body."

"You mean that girls have too much going for them?" Another wink.

"No. Being a hemophilia carrier instead of a hemophiliac isn't 'having too much going for us.' But we're having trouble with that in our lab, because half the X comes from the maternal ape and half from the paternal sperm, and when you inactivate a different X in each cell, well, the results are a little unpredictable."

He pretend to shake. "You mean you end up with monsters?"

"Oh, no. But I won't say anything more. It's confidential information for the Missing Link. But it's a big challenge for us—"

Man give big smile and cut in. "Well, thank you for coming in and talking about this controversial topic, Jackie. Coming up next, on Scary Science: scientists in India have more evidence that drinking your urine every day may, in fact, be good for you. Back in a moment."

JACKIE NOT COME SEE ME. Séverine neither. No one come for two days.

I bang on the wall. No answer. I press call, call, call. I email. I mime in front of camera until Tom come. "Hi Sam." His voice wavy.

"Where Jackie."

He blink hard. "She, uh, can't come today, buddy." He clear throat. "She might not be able to come for awhile. You want to play?"

I fake casual. "I play on computer. 'Bye." He go. I log on.

Humans lie. Bad. But also too stupid to realize I use computer like this. Before, I look for porn on net. Now I start search engines for news on Jackie.

Bad. Her name everywhere. *New York Times, World News, MS News* . . . my hands shake when I see headline for Save Our Souls News Bulletin.

MONKEY MAKER'S DAUGHTER SHOT! See it on Real Time! Captured by Her Own Security Cameras!

I click on it.

Colour screen pops up. Showing someone in white coat, I think Dr. Gilden. Jackie saying, "And then we'll really show them!" Dr. Gilden laughing. Then hear pop, pop. Jackie turn and scream, "No!" She run, camera bouncing.

Camera autofocus when Jackie stop. See girl's brown legs lying on floor, skirt tangled. Then bloody T-shirt. Jackie's hands, trying to stop blood. "Help! Somebody help me! Call nine-one-one! Call the police! It's my daughter! It's my daughter!" I see Séverine's face. Eyes closed. Pale. Then Jackie's hands again, covered in blood. "Help! Please!"

I scream and scream. Before they come, I shut down computer and hop around, pretend I bored with no Jackie. They believe me. I get them groom me.

Then I search more.

Tom want teach me language more. He crazy. I spend hour with him, keep him happy. Then I email Jackie. I do again, again. Finally, she link with me. "Hi, Sam." She no smile. First time she no smile for me.

"I love you. And Sev."

"I know." Something flicker in eyes. Then dead again. Whole face droop.

"How is she?" I try extra hard. Good grammar.

"She's alive. They got her arm back on."

I clap hands.

"But she's very sick. We're worried that they coated the bullet with some sort of superbacteria. The worst part is, that makes us wonder if it was really a Christianoid who did it."

I sag. "I know. It is on internet."

She reach hand to me. Stop. "My poor little monkey. I love you. But I have to be with Séverine now. Goodbye."

I say bye. She cut off link. I not have chance to ask, "What can I do?" But I know what. I wait for Tom to come. He pretend happy to see me.
I smile back. For once, not fake. "Tom, let's make bet."

"What're you talking about, Sam?" He guffaw. Look at camera to share joke with watchers.

"A bet. You want to?"

He interested.

"Let's play chess. If you win, we do language. All day. For a week."

His eyes hungry. I always stop after one hour. Then I throw pillows at him. "And if you win?"

"If I win, I get news conference."

"Deal." We shake hands.

I win.

I HAVE PREPARED SPEECH. I replay on computer for them. With pictures of Jackie and Sev. And my real mother. They record it, but bored. Their eyes light up at question and answer.

Short blond woman call out, "Do you regret being alive? Do you feel guilty that Dr. Jackie Routhier helped make you and now her daughter's at death's door?"

"No. Not my fault. Christianoid killer."

They smile. "Is that what you call them? Christianoids?"

Maybe I make mistake. Blond woman go on. "They wanted to attack Dr. Routhier because she made you."

"No. They attack because they love to hate."

"So you think Jackie did the right thing?"

"Of course." She make face. I type out more. "You think Jackie wrong. She play God and create. You play God and kill her. Which is wrong? Which is worse? Which is forbidden by Bible?"

Man with glasses stand up. "Sam, do you believe in God?"

"I not know." I retype, trying good grammar. "I do not know. Maybe He exists. If he does, he is not happy with the killers."

"Maybe he's not happy with Dr. Jackie, either."

I shake my head. "I am not trying to judge. I am not human. I am not bonobo. I am not sure what I am. But I have family. Jackie. Séverine. Even Tom." He give me forced grin. I finish, "Hate me if you want. But don't kill my family."

After, I watch the number of hits on websites and check surveys: "Sam Ian. Monkey-man. Love him or leave him?" They love me. They not really love me before, through holos. So I go out and do more news conferences. I talk at schools. I talk on talk shows. I am big hit.

Sometimes I miss my steel room. I miss Jackie. I miss Sev.

Tom calls me. I forbid him to be my travel companion, but he still call. I link. He is already yelling. Eyes small. "What if someone kills you, Sam? For God's sake, come back, we'll take care of you, Séverine's getting better, Jackie will come see you every week, just come back..." The Missing Link not want me dead. Too much invested.

"This all I can do."

"What? Get killed?"

I shrug. "If I killed, we win."

"How can we win?" Tom yells. Spit at corner of mouth. Jackie would wipe off. I shake head and spell it out for him, since no word auto-programmed: MARTYR.

"For God's sake!" he yell again. I wish he stop talking like that. I delink and block his ID.

I type my next speech. This is my job now. I get paid. I give half of my money to Jackie and Sev, keep half. If Missing Link disowns me, I need money. Or maybe I fund anti-Christianoid guerillas. Gorilla's guerilla. I laugh at my words. I am funny. I fight with words. I fight until the Christianoids kill me. Or until Jackie and Séverine come home. They are tough. They can do it. Every night I dream that I am in my steel room. The door opens. They come in, laughing. Beautiful. Alive. We groom and groom until we fall asleep together.

LEAVINGS OF SHROUD HOUSE: AN INVENTORY

Richard Gavin

THE HOUSE ITSELF

THE FOLLOWING DOSSIER IS CULLED FROM MANY SOURCES; thus it contains the whispers of various disparate souls. Its only unifying element is the fact that all these eerie testimonials relate, in a manner that is at once both intimate and vague, to a demolished sixteen-room Victorian farmhouse in the town of Chatterton.

Shroud House. Long before its walls were razed, and before the reclusive family that inhabited the house and lent to it their name faded into the fog of history, Shroud House was lush with mystery. Its very appearance was the stuff of our most tantalizing nightmares, for the house did not merely stand, it loomed. The multigabled roof lent the house all the majesty of a mosque or temple dedicated to some unnamable spiritual practice. The tinted window glass shimmered like constellations of diseased stars and the splintery beams of the porch were so very much like the jawbones of a prehistoric beast.

And its interior?

A veritable museum of occult materials.

These materials were drudged out from the house's shadow-encrusted rooms almost immediately after the last member of the Shroud family departed this mortal coil. Items better left to the night side of the universe were cast out into the sunlit mortal world for the most lurid and shallow reasons. Men in tailored suits divided the most intriguing or lucrative objects, like a cluster of seedy undertakers pilfering the pockets of the recently dead.

Shroud House's leavings were divided into auction lots or became charitable donations. Other items were hocked to any collector of arcanum that was willing to accept the cost, both fiscal and spiritual.

Time passed.

Stories flowered.

And from them I learned that the ghosts of Shroud House cannot be confined to the past. Nor do they require the shelter of their fallen sanctuary in order to weave their insidious magic upon the world.

THE PHOTOGRAPHS

THE METRO ART GALLERY launched a new exhibit one snowy Friday evening in January. It consisted of twenty-four photographs, all of which had once been the property of the Shroud estate.

Waltz of Shadows was the exhibit's name. The corridor of the main gallery was lined with the photographs, twelve on either wall. Each photo had been professionally matted and was displayed in a sleek silver frame.

The curators piped funeral music through the sound system and had the lights at the dimmest possible setting that would still allow the patrons a decent view of the exhibit.

The photographs themselves were in a sepia tone. All of them were afflicted with blotchy stains, tattered edges, or vein-like creases. But such flaws were expected of a collection that was as old and as peculiar as this one.

The queerest feature, the one that had captured the attention of the Gallery executives several months prior, was documented in the *Waltz of Shadows Guidebook*, which is quoted below:

> There seems to be two unifying characteristics for all the photographs in this collection. The first is that each photo features only a single member of the Shroud family. The second (and most unusual) characteristic is the fact that not one of the subjects is facing the camera. Though each picture displays an adept level of skill in the areas of composition, lighting, and mood, the viewer is left to speculate as to why the photographer decided to photograph each Shroud from behind.

THE PATRON WHO DISCOVERED THE HORRIFIC ANSWER to this mystery was an art student. Her initial impulse was to dismiss her finding as nothing more than an optical trick, or as just another flaw in the crumbling photograph. But others quickly began to cluster around the picture. Soon there were pointed fingers, gasps, murmured theories.

That particular photo depicted an elderly woman seated at what looked to be her dressing table. She was dressed in a long, dark gown. Her silver mane had been wound into a tight bun (which was very prominent, for its placement in the picture was where one would normally find the subject's face). On the table before her sat perfume bottles and various other cosmetics.

There was also a mirror.

The camera had mistakenly (?) captured the old woman's reflection. The visage that peered out from the looking glass was closer to that of a crypto-zoology specimen than to the face of a woman. A pair of sewer-dark eyes were embedded much too deeply in a blob of withered flesh. It was so much like a monkey's face. The elongated, needle-thin nose resembled the beak of an ibis. It drooped down as though deflated. The subject's mouth was no larger than a coin—a tiny, yawning circle of blackness, like an anus, or a wormhole.

WEDDING GOWN

(Episode #443-CI of the BBC program *Man & Magic*)

DRY ICE SWIRLS ABOUT A DARKENED STUDIO that is decorated to resemble an antiquated study. The study door creaks open and a gaunt figure steps into view. He introduces himself as Dr. Otto Valzer. He proclaims himself a world-renowned expert on the paranormal. He welcomes the viewer to join him on another excursion into what he calls "the shadows that challenge the bound-aries of human reason."

Opening credits roll, accompanied by eerie synthesizer music.

Fade in to a close-up shot of a Victorian-style wedding gown. Age has yel-lowed its white silk. The lace trimmings are beginning to look threadbare. In a voice-over, Dr. Valzer informs us that on the surface this gown is just like any other. It was hand-sewn by a distant relative in the hopes that it would be passed down through generations of young brides. But this particular gown is no ordinary gown. And the family it belonged to was no ordinary family, for they were the mysterious Shroud family of Chatterton.

Cut to a home video of a chubby twenty-four-year-old girl seated in a very suburban-looking kitchen. The young woman begins to talk about how excited she is regarding her upcoming wedding. She says that she's been imag-ining the ceremony ever since she was a little girl. She'd always imagined her-self to be a princess; and when she finally met Tom she knew she had found her prince.

The mysterious Shroud gown, purchased for the young bride-to-be at an antique clothing show by her aunt, seemed to be the ideal dress for the fairy-tale wedding.

The wedding date arrived, and, as another home video clip reveals, the young bride went down the aisle wearing the Shroud gown, which had been cleaned and tailored so as to look new. But even on the poorly shot videotape, it is clear that the bride's face is a sickly ashen colour. She staggers.

Dr. Valzer's voice-over states that all day long the bride's family had been commenting on how sickly the bride looked. Her father had gone so far as to suggest postponing the wedding. But his daughter was insistent, refusing to yield to anything that might tarnish the long-awaited ceremony.

We now see the cake-cutting. The father of the bride does his best to film the reception with a steady hand, but is unsuccessful. Because of this poor camerawork, we are offered only a brief and blurry glimpse of what may be the bride's face transfiguring into a withered, corpse-blue visage. We can see a figure in a bride's dress crumpling to the floor and can hear several gasps and cries from the wedding party.

The home video's most notorious clip, one that was published as still photographs in tabloids around the globe, was the shot of the bride lying lifeless beside her banquet table. Her husband, shrieking for help, bends to help his lifeless bride. He takes her hand in his and screams when her appendage sifts through his fingers like ash. The young man flings the veil that had fallen over the bride's face. Blue-grey dust silts off of the pearly arches of an ancient skeletal face.

The segment of *Man & Magic* runs through further interviews with relatives, doctors, tabloid journalists, and experts on spontaneous human combustion; yet in the end no conclusion is given.

Dr. Valzer's closing monologue is performed before a large photograph of Shroud House.

"Vengeance from beyond the grave or a home-movie hoax?" he asks us. "In the end, it is up to each of us to decide. For as Shakespeare once observed, *'There are more things . . .'*"

There is a brief close-up of the host. His eyes shimmer darkly behind his glasses. Then the good doctor steps back into the smoky shadows.

End credits roll.

THE GARDEN GATE

(Clipping from an October issue of *Gardener's Globe* magazine)

"Ghosts in the Garden"
by Rudy Morrell

(The photograph that appears just beneath this headline features an elderly man and woman posing as the archetypal couple from the painting "American Gothic." But instead of clutching a pitchfork, the couple holds an ornate wrought-iron gate between them. The gate is composed of eight spiraling posts set inside an arch-shaped frame. A carved face leers from the centre of the gate. Mossy green blotches obscure its finer details.)

JEROME AND ALICE LANCE seem to embody the very essence of grandparenthood. Both of them are spry, genteel, and generous almost to a fault. This generosity is exhibited the minute we are ushered into the cozy living room of their cottage-style home, where Alice has taken the liberty of setting out tea and homemade marzipan cakes.

It is truly chilling to think that such a lovely couple, now just four months shy of their Golden Anniversary, was subjected to a horror story beyond the imaginings of Hollywood filmmakers.

Their story begins innocently enough: with the Lances discovering an antique gate at a local home and garden show.

"It was just so beautiful and unique," Alice gushes. "We both knew it would be perfect for the garden."

The dealer at the garden show claimed to be unaware of the gate's history and also claimed that he had found the gate in a scrapyard near his home.

Although the gate was in perfect condition when the Lances bought it, it became horribly tarnished within hours of being attached to the fence that frames their tidy perennial garden.

They assumed that the piece was faulty, but since the dealer had a strict "no refund" policy, the Lances were forced to make due. Little did they realize that the loss of two hundred dollars would be the least of their troubles.

"The first thing we noticed that was out of the ordinary was a whole lot of fliers for lost dogs and cats being posted around the neighbourhood."

The mystery then hit even closer to home when the Lances lost their beloved Labrador retriever, Rex.

"He woke us up at about two in the morning," Jerome recalls. "I went downstairs to see what the problem was, but nothing seemed out of place. When I opened the back door, Rex took off. He went tearing across the yard, right towards the gate. I ran out after him, but before I could grab hold of him, he squeezed his way between the bars. I opened the gate and looked all around the garden for him, but he was nowhere to be found. I could hear him barking but couldn't see him. At the time I figured it was just because it was so dark outside."

Jerome has to pause to dab the tears from his eyes. "But then there was a loud yelp, and that was the last I heard of him."

The next day Rex's picture joined the tapestry of fliers around the neighbourhood.

The final, and most harrowing, incident occurred a few weeks later, during a family barbecue at the Lance house. Some time between Jerome's hamburgers and Alice's homemade apricot pie, Ella, the Lance's three-year-old granddaughter, wandered off from the picnic table.

It was Carrie, Ella's mother, who first noticed the child toddling towards the garden.

"Carrie was calling for Ella to come back to the table because she didn't want her tearing up any of my flowers," Alice recalls. "When Ella didn't respond Carrie got up to fetch her. That's when she said she heard Ella talking to herself. Just saying one-word answers like 'Yes,' 'No,' 'Maybe.'"

Alice stops momentarily. Her hands are trembling so severely that the teacup and saucer she holds begin to clatter. She sets the dishes down on the table before continuing.

"That's when it happened."

The "it" Alice is referring to is the opening of the garden gate.

"No one touched it, nobody was even near it," Jerome assures me. "But we all heard the latch pop open, and we all saw the gate just swing open all by itself. Once it did that, Ella took off running straight for it. Luckily Carrie went tearing after her and caught her right before Ella stepped inside the garden. Then Carrie started screaming. She kicked the gate shut and kept shouting 'Leave my baby alone!'"

"We all ran over to them," Alice adds, "and I looked through the gate, but for the life of me I couldn't see what had gotten Carrie so upset. All she kept saying was that there were all these . . . well, deformed people standing inside the garden. And they were all trying to pull Ella inside with them."

Jerome removed the corroded gate that very evening. The next morning Alice awoke to find her beloved garden in ruins.

"Everything was all black and brittle, like it had been burnt," Alice tells me in a slightly defeated, if bewildered, tone. "Not one plant was salvageable. . . ."

MISCELLANY

THERE ARE MANY OTHER INSTANCES of Shroud House's perpetual haunting of humanity. I could detail the legend of the enormous black cat that is thought to be the totem of Gabrielle Shroud. Rumour in the town of Chatterton claims that the cat still roams the streets on overcast days, studying the townsfolk, plotting vengeance. It is said that at night Gabrielle shapeshifted into teratisms that defied description.

I could tell you of the phonograph records that contained dozens of voice recordings made by Shroud ancestors, long deceased. According to one of my informants, who claimed to have listened to these discs, the recordings were actually a form of soothsaying: omens of the terrible kingdom that awaits us all upon death.

Then there is the old woman in England who sold her story to local tabloids. Apparently (if one can trust such lurid journalism) the old woman began receiving a regular flow of postcards with her daily mail. Each card contained a blurred photograph of what the old woman thought to be an extraterrestrial lifeform stepping through a half-open door. The cards were inscribed with brief and cryptic messages like "Find the Well & Wait for the Visitor" or "The Cellar has become the Chapel. Come."

Indeed, I could go on with a great many tales. But time is of the essence, so I will instead move on to the final two items that close the circle around my involvement with this phantasmagoria.

THE SPECTACLES

PHINEAS SHROUD LIVED TO BE EIGHTY-NINE. A mysterious disease had rendered him an invalid for the final arc of his life, and he spent his twilight years holed up in the musty attic of Shroud House, with its crooked beams, its groaning mortises, and the ghosts of dead generations. During the few hours when he was well enough to leave his bed, Phineas would perch his gaunt body in his wheelchair and sit before the large attic window. One can only speculate as to the weird visions that could have entranced the old man night after night. . . .

THE SPECTACLES CAME INTO MY POSSESSION during an otherwise uneventful business trip overseas.

"These were designed according to Phineas's specifications," the proprietor explained as he held a small tin case out to me. We were standing inside a small boutique called Visions. The store was overstocked, claustrophobically small, and poorly ventilated. Most of the tiny showroom was cluttered with boxes of varying sizes. Many of the cartons were labeled, but even without reading the labels their contents were obvious to me—eyeglasses. Thousands, or perhaps even tens of thousands, of eyeglasses, many of them antiquated or just discarded. Visions was a specialty shop. Its exclusive stock-in-trade was spectacles, particularly antique ones, or ones that possessed some queer aesthetic quality.

As I watched the little shopkeeper pop the tin case open I wondered how one could ever earn a living off such a peculiar trade.

"He planned to be buried wearing these," the man explained as he carefully lifted the delicate glasses from their tarnished container. The lenses were not circular, but were slightly oval in shape, and they were set in a very plain wire frame. The lens glass was the colour of brandied wine.

"These lenses are not prescription." He pointed at the shimmering egg-shaped glass with his pinky finger. "They were actually cut from the attic window that Phineas loved to stare through. Legend has it that Phineas had hoped to take that beloved view with him to the grave."

I was reaching for the spectacles as the shopkeeper made this statement. I hesitated.

"To the grave? You don't mean . . ." I trailed off, unsure of the most genteel way to phrase my question.

The shopkeeper intuited my ghoulish suspicions, and he began to chuckle.

"No, no, no," he said, "you needn't worry. These eyeglasses weren't swiped from a cadaver's face. Phineas was never buried with them. In fact, he was never buried at all. Supposedly the old man simply vanished one night, just disappeared off the face of God's green Earth. I was told that the Shrouds searched for many months, but the only trace they ever found was these spectacles, which Phineas had commissioned a local craftsman to make. Merwyn, one of the younger and more mischievous of the Shroud children, discovered them sitting on the attic windowsill in front of an empty wheelchair. The fate of Phineas remains a mystery to this day."

When I reached for my pocketbook the shopkeeper actually licked his lips with greedy anticipation.

MY HOTEL ROOM WAS ON THE FOURTEENTH FLOOR (which was in actuality the accursed *thirteenth* floor; it is titillating when superstition overpowers logic). It was inside that immaculate little room that I first prepared to try on the Shroud House spectacles.

Night. I was standing before the room's large window. A harvest moon poured a milky sheen over the tight cluster of skyscrapers in the distance. The spectacles were resting on top of an oak desk. A small lamp shone down upon them like a spotlight. This dim cone of light was the room's only source of illumination. The open tin box and the handwritten receipt from Visions both sat outside the lamp's halo, for the light was meant for the spectacles alone.

I stood before the window for some time, waiting for some cosmic or internal cue to instruct me. When none came, I waited until everything felt suitably calm and serene.

Then I reached for the glasses.

I hesitated when they were halfway to my face.

The peripheral details of the room still appeared normal, but the small portion of the room that was filtered through the brandy-coloured glass was anything but.

I believe that what I stared at through the spectacles was the armchair that was set in a corner of the room, but through the lenses the chair's contours seemed fluidic, its edges blurry. The entire chair had been reduced to a bewildering storm of wood and coiled steel and fabric stuffed with padding the colour of gunmetal.

Of course when I peered over the rim of the spectacles the chair was at it should be—an inanimate, tidy furnishing. But once I glanced through the glasses, the very concept of "chair"—as a distinct, inanimate *thing*—felt wholly alien to me. I could not separate myself from the chair. The furnishing seemed as sentient to me as that strange biological spasm we reverentially refer to as the "soul."

This feeling of dislocation led me to conclude that the spectacles were not suited for the chaos of a modern urban setting. I returned them to their tin case and carefully packed the case in with the rest of my luggage.

My choice as to where I would next try on the spectacles? Alas, there really was no choice to be made.

Eleven days later, when I was back on my native soil, I made a pilgrimage to the ruins of Shroud House.

With a sack containing all my Shroud tokens—the gallery guidebook, various news clippings, and, of course, my spectacles—slung over one shoulder, I stumbled through the chunks of smashed foundation until I was situated roughly in what used to be the centre, the diseased heart, of the house. Once there I slid the spectacles onto my face. . . .

THE SKELETON KEY

THE KEY MATERIALIZED ON TOP OF A CINDERBLOCK JUST OFF TO MY RIGHT. I made several tests and discovered that without the spectacles the key was invisible, but, with them, the key could not only be seen, it could be touched, and utilized.

Like the key itself (whose appearance can be likened to the skeleton of a fish, or perhaps that of a small reptile), the door it was designed to unlock could only be apprehended though the shards of attic glass.

The door stood in the middle of the woods; a dark monolithic slab with a handle that glinted like a jewel.

The key slid easily into the door's complex lock. Once the lock was unlatched the door autonomously opened.

Can you fathom my reaction when I saw the alien door open to reveal the interior of my own apartment? That is to say, the apartment I looked into certainly *resembled* my home in every conceivable way. Perhaps it was this veneer of familiarity that pushed me across the threshold so swiftly.

I closed the door behind me and immediately began exploring each of the rooms. In doing so, two facts became clear to me. The first was that the similarity between this apartment and my Earthly home was purely superficial. Something, a current or invisible force, was seething beneath the skin of apparent normality.

The second realization did not crystallize in my mind until much time had passed.

And that was the fact that I was not alone.

The realization began as nothing more than an uneasy feeling that there was someone (or something) following me. And no matter how quickly I moved, my stalker always managed to lurk right behind me. I was never able to catch so much as a glimpse of that which pursued me.

I carefully inspected the apartment, but my investigations turned up nothing. My uneasiness blossomed into fear, and that fear fermented into dread. The passing of time drew the stalking presence nearer to me.

I gradually came to intuit that my stalker's intentions towards me were anything but benign. This was not the result of any overt act on the part of my stalker, but was due more to a growing sense of my impending extinction.

But I created a stalking game of my own, a feeble form of retaliation against an enemy I could not see.

There is no doubt in my mind that my attempts to discover the identity of my haunter served only to amuse it. For every time I crept into the soft darkness of a vacant room, I could sense my stalker looming over my shoulder. Tried as I did to ignore the raising of my hackles and the quickening of my pulse, my terror always overpowered me and sent me back to the half-comforting stillness of the armchair.

By this time I had grown so accustomed to the spectacles that I no longer removed them. The one instance where I did momentarily peel them from my face, the details of my strange new home immediately mutated into the bewildering chaos I had experienced *with the spectacles on* when I was in the hotel room.

I wondered if my eyes were beginning to fail me. Perhaps, to see in this inverted world, the Shroud spectacles were the only eyes I needed?

So I keep the spectacles on, and I wait.

My stalker is becoming more daring. Just today I was awakened from a much-needed nap by the sound of a door slamming shut. I leapt up in time to see the small cloud of steam evaporating from the surface of the mirror that hangs above the chair where I now spend all my time. The residue of my haunter's breath was the first tangible proof of its existence that I have seen. But this too was fleeting.

My thinking now is that if this entity came while I was sleeping, perhaps it will return if I create the *illusion* of sleep. Thus, I have decided to remain motionless in my chair so that I might learn the truth behind this nightmare. A nightmare so vast I now realize that the Shroud family is but a small facet of it; their house is but one gate amongst many.

This will be my last entry. This journal will be placed in a small wooden chest along with all the Shroud House memorabilia I collected during the course of my life. I will open the door one final time to toss the chest back to your world. Once this task is completed, I will destroy the skeleton key and I will perch myself in this chair. I no longer need the relics of Shroud House, for my investigations have led me much closer to the source of this horrible phenomenon.

I hope the clues I've bequeathed to the world serve to inspire you to continue to unravel the mystery of the endless haunting of the human race. For myself, I feel that I am very close to revelation. Day by day I can feel the truth seeping into this strange realm. In this chair I remain as still and as receptive as Phineas Shroud did before me.

I wait.

Wait for an encounter with this lurking force. I pray that in time I will finally learn the secret behind the haunting of our species—and discover the hidden intentions of the grand Haunter who alone holds the key to our shadow-laden fate.

The Traumatized Generation

Murray Leeder

LAND SNIFFED AT THE AIR. He felt a kind of peace out here, so different from the city thick with industrial fumes and soldiers. The prairies sprawled in every direction, wilder and more overgrown than they had been in more than a century, and the Rockies were lost in a pink haze to the west. All of it sent Land back to a childhood spent traipsing around the countryside, when he didn't need to be worried about what might be hiding in the wheat.

He rapped on the front door. Eventually a woman came to the door in her nightgown, slightly older than him and glowering at him. She knew what was happening, and Land's heart sank when he realized what he was about to do.

"Mrs. March? I'm Michael Land, Paul's home-room teacher. I'm here to pick him up for today's—" He hesitated. "Today's field trip."

"I didn't give permission for any field trip," she snorted, and Land put his hand against the door to stop her from closing it.

"I'm afraid the school board doesn't require parental permission when the field trip has been made mandatory by the government of Canada."

"The government," she said. "You mean the military, don't you? Either way, I'm not about to send my son away to be traumatized by your bloodshow."

"Mrs. March," he told her. "In that car is the sergeant they sent to escort me up here. If Paul doesn't come out of this house in ten minutes, she'll have to come and talk to you herself. Nobody wants that."

There was desperation in her voice. "Mr. Land, you and I remember a time before the military controlled our lives. You're an educator—how can you stand idly by and—"

"Just get your son, Mrs. March. Please. Just get Paul."

Mrs. March breathed in deeply. "Wait here," she said. "I can't believe I'm doing this."

She returned a few minutes later with the round-faced, serious little boy, dressed in unfashionable clothes and shoes that so often made him a target for jeers.

"It's good to see you, Paul," Land said, and the boy half-smiled up at him. Land knew the boy all too well; smart, shy, sensitive, and far too vulnerable for this world. Just like the young Michael Land, back when CNN reported that the dead were rising from their graves.

The car door opened and Sgt. Hazelwood walked over to the door just as Paul was slipping on his coat. She was blond and beautiful, but Land disliked her intensely. She was just the kind of rhetoric-spouting career army type that Land had encountered too often during his own tour of duty in Alaska. "All ready to go?" she asked, wearing a false smile that Mrs. March did not return. Ignoring the sergeant's presence, Mrs. March dropped to her knees and embraced her son.

"Remember not to be too scared," she said, and Paul nodded uncertainly.

"Do something for me," Mrs. March said to Land. "Promise me you'll sit by him. Try to keep him from being too scared. He has a weak heart."

Land nodded, but before he could speak, Hazelwood interrupted. "Then we'll just have to strengthen up that heart a bit," she said, ushering the trembling boy towards the car.

As Land looked back at Mrs. March, watching the doorway as her son went away. He wanted to look in her eyes and reassure her that everything will go alright, whether or not that was true, but found that he could not.

THE HUGE CHAIN-LINK FENCE ENCIRCLING CALGARY was intended to keep the zombies out, which it did, but it also served to keep the people in. The rule of law didn't need to enforce this, for few wanted to leave. Officers waved Sgt. Hazelwood's transport through the military checkpoint at the city's north gate, and they continued down the vacant Deerfoot Trail, bound for the Saddledome. In the distance, Calgary's downtown was silhouetted against the morning sky, postcard pristine, like a snapshot from Land's childhood.

Paul was quiet the entire time. His parents certainly taught him to avoid talking to anyone in a uniform. Land felt like he was ferrying a prisoner to an execution. He always hated this day, the worst of any school year. Nothing he'd seen up in Alaska bothered him half as much as the sight of ten thousand schoolchildren, all screaming for gore.

Yellow school buses dotted the Saddledome's parking lot, and Hazelwood wove through the crowds of kids before they found Mr. Land's grade-seven class. Land hoped they'd arrive first, to spare Paul the humiliation of arriving under military escort, but no such luck. Built for the 1988 Olympics, the Saddledome had served for years as sports arena and concert venue. Now the military had appropriated it and remade it into their modern-day Coliseum.

"You get out here," Hazelwood said. "I'll go park in the barracks and join you inside."

"What?" Land said. "Isn't your duty here finished?"

"No." The sergeant flashed him an unreadable smile. "I'm with you for the whole day."

Land coughed in disgust. She probably thought he'd let Paul slip away from the show at the first occasion. She was probably right.

The rest of the class caught sight of them as they stepped out of the military vehicle. Land saw Bruce Tomasino say something to Jason Barrows, and they sent their whispers all along the line.

"Don't worry about them, Paul," Land said softly. "Just take your place in the line."

His student dutifully shuffled over to the uneven row of students. Land addressed them: "I don't want to see any shoving or shouting. When we get the signal, I want us to go in a straight line inside and take our seats. Any questions?"

"I got a question," asked chubby Jimmy Conway. "Is it true . . . I mean, we heard a rumour that Zombie Bob will be here."

Please, no, Land thought. That would make it even worse; the presence of a TV celebrity would change this field trip from a military demonstration to a rock concert. Robert Smith Harding went with a camera crew behind the lines in lost cities and in infested countryside, found zombies, and inevitably killed them in daredevil ways. His weapons of choice ranged from a jackhammer to a katana. The kids loved him, wore his picture, talked about him constantly. Land watched Paul's face grow grimmer still at this news.

A whistle blew somewhere across the parking lot, and the rows of students started proceeding up the concrete stairs and into the Saddledome itself. A uniformed officer waved Land's class ahead, and he took up the end of the line to watch they kept their course. Amid all the noise of kids gabbing away, he could barely hear Bruce and Jason talking about Paul. He made out one sentence: "That corpse-hugger's going to wet his pants when he sees this."

Land was always impressed by how little the Saddledome had changed since his childhood. This wasn't a real surprise; though the military owned it now, it was still a sports arena of sorts. The floors were still sticky and the plastic seats still painful. The Jumbotron was still there too, left over from hockey games. Now it flashed messages like "ENJOY THE SHOW" and "THIS IS FOR YOU KIDS."

The most visible things changed from the old days were the sideboards. The protective glass now went up much higher and needed to be cleaned nightly of splattered blood and brain meat. As usual, the arena was covered with a layer of freshly tilled dirt. At one end there was a raised platform with a few microphones, and at the other there was a black velvet drape, which hid the zombie cage. A trained crew with cattle prods were ready to send them out into the arena on cue.

When the students took their seats, Land called for Paul to come over and sit by him by the aisle. He wished he could have done this more subtly—Paul didn't need to be a teacher's pet on top of a zombie-lover—but he'd agreed to sit by the boy. As the other students chatted away, he asked Paul: "What do you think of all this?"

"I don't know," the boy said. "I've never been anywhere like this before."

"Your parents didn't want you to come here," Land said. "You know that."

"But they made you get me."

Land nodded. "The military thinks it's important that you be here."

"Why?"

The question caught Land by surprise. It was a good question—why? Why did one child deserve all this special attention? He stammered, searching for an answer, before one was provided.

"Because someday you'll be called to the service, and we think it's best you know what it's all about." Sgt. Hazelwood stood in the aisle, grinning down on them both. She had changed from her green field outfit into a brown dress uniform that accentuated her curves.

That's not a real answer, Land thought, but he couldn't say anything here.

"Got room for one more?" Hazelwood asked.

Land looked at the empty seat next to him and tried to think of an excuse to keep her from sitting there, but could not. "Sure," he said. "Have a seat."

"No." She shook her head. "You sit there, and I'll sit on the other side of Paul."

Land went to protest but thought better of it. He stood, and as she slipped past he felt her body against his, her holstered pistol rubbing against his thigh.

She took her place next to the boy and smiled at him. "Your parents don't let you have a TV, do they?" she asked.

Paul shook his head.

"Then you don't know who Zombie Bob is?"

"Well, I know who he is because the other kids . . ."

"Oh good," she said. "It just so happens that I'm a friend of Bob's, and after the show I could take you to meet him backstage."

"Well," said Paul, "I don't really know if . . ."

"Just you, out of all these kids." She gestured at the thousands of school-children around them. "That could really help you could make friends, Paul. They'll want to know you for sure after that."

Land shot her a disapproving look, but she only grinned. Fortunately, the lights began to dim. He heard Hazelwood whisper, "We'll talk about this later," as a hush settled over the Saddledome.

A spotlight sprang into life, illuminating a lone figure on the platform. It was a silver-haired man in a brown dress uniform, metals dangling at his pocket. His image appeared, a thousand times larger, on the Jumbotron above.

"Howdy, kids," he said. "I'm Colonel Patrick Simonds. I recently got back from directing the troops on the coast, and the top brass asked me, 'Pat, you've just done such a great job in Vancouver. When you get back, just you name it and it's yours.' And I said, 'I want to be the one who talks to the kids at the Saddledome.'"

The colonel wore the same politician's smile that he was never seen without. Affable and grandfatherly, Simonds was just the kind of public face that the military needed as it pressed its endless, costly war against an enemy that neither thought nor planned.

"Yup," Simonds, went on, "that's my favourite duty, because it's so important for the future. Once we recapture Vancouver and Toronto, then the real challenges will be open to us. New York, *Lost* Angeles . . ." he paused briefly as some of the audience of the chuckled at the popular pun, "maybe even London, Tokyo. That's where you kids will be fighting the zombies. You should think of this day like a 'thank you' in advance. I think the very least we can do is show you how to do it."

Another spotlight suddenly cut through the darkness, spotlighting the black drape at the other opposite of the arena. Out stumbled a putrescent walking corpse, flailing its arms and awkwardly making its way forward. Its jaw was slack, its tongue lolling out in anticipation of its next meal. A collective sigh filled the arena.

"Look at it," Simonds said. "I bet most of you kids have never seen a zombie on the loose. That says something about how far we've come. It's hard to imagine, but there was a time when zombies even walked the streets of Calgary. But thanks to the vaccine developed right here in Canada, none of us will ever be zombies. Remember that: kill a zombie, and that's one closer to killing them all.

"That disgusting creature you're looking at was somebody's brother or father or son once. I'm not going to lie at you about that. But he isn't no more; in fact, he's not a 'he' at all, but an 'it'!"

The colonel pulled his service pistol from its holster and carefully aimed at the brightly lit target before firing. It sounded little more potent than a cap gun, but Paul twitched in his seat anyway. The bullet struck the zombie's shoulder, and it barely even noticed as it kept shambling forward.

"Ah, I didn't quite get him, did I?" Simonds said. "I've seen zombies lose all their limbs and keep on going. Their brain and their hunger drives them forward. They want to eat our flesh. That's all they want. And they never hesitate before they strike."

The zombie lurched steadily forward, having made it almost halfway to the podium. Many children clenched their teeth with the tension, but Land knew that it would take a minor miracle for that zombie to actually reach the colonel.

"Now," said Simonds, "there are some who say that because these things were once our loved ones, that means we shouldn't be allowed to kill them. We all know people like this. These zombie-lovers say that zombies are trainable, that maybe we can toss them the odd steak to keep them happy and teach them to fetch our slippers. But I challenge anyone to look in the eyes of the dead and see anything worth saving. Fellas, can we focus in on that?"

The Jumbotron zoomed in until the zombie's twisted, drooling face filled the screen.

"No life. No intelligence. In humans we see some kind of spark of life; I don't know what it is, but it's always there. You don't see that in zombies. That's what zombies are: humans minus a certain spark, and that's what makes them a perversion in the face of God. There's only one thing to do to them!"

Simonds fired again. This time it struck the zombie square in the head, a perfect killshot. There was a splash of bright red blood, and the creature fell. The Saddledome erupted with cheers and shrill whistles.

The house lights came up. "Pretty cool, eh?" whispered Sgt. Hazelwood to Paul.

"Now before I bring out a very special friend of mine," Simonds said, "we should all rise for the singing of our national anthem." An organ started up with "O Canada," and, as they stood, Land extended his arm behind Paul's back and nudged Hazelwood.

"Sergeant," he whispered. "We need to share a word outside."

"But Mr. Land, it's disrespectful—"

"*Now*," he said, just a little too loud, and he started away from the arena. She placed her drink at her feet and stomped after him. He led her right outside onto the Saddledome's front steps, and there she began to snap at him.

"Who do you think you are that you can—"

"Who do you think you are to mess with my student like that?" Land shouted back at her. "God, a military pick-up, you hanging over his shoulder. . . . Do you think this isn't hard enough for him anyway? The other kids will never let him hear the end of this."

"Good," Hazelwood said. "I don't want him to forget today. I want him to be traumatized as hell. He'll thank us for it later."

"When? When will he thank us?"

"When he's been dropped in some hellhole and told to kill." There was an absolute conviction in her voice.

"He'll be a man then, and better equipped to handle it than these kids are," Land argued. "Listen to them: they're whistling and cheering! It's just a show for them. That's just how you want them. They don't consider things. They don't think about things. The military doesn't want them to. I don't know who's more braindead, zombies or soldiers."

"How dare you!" Hazelwood cried, her throat hoarsening. "This isn't our world any more! It's theirs! We let our guard down, and they tear our throats out! Society *must* be prepared, prepared in every way, for war! It is the only way!"

Land shrunk back at the force of her argument. "Do you remember," he said, his voice cracking, "when they used to say that watching violent movies was desensitizing, and that was a bad thing?"

For a long time there was silence, and then Hazelwood said, "You've been wondering why all this special treatment for this one kid? What makes him so important?"

Land nodded.

"That was my idea. When I heard about Paul from your school's liaison office, I thought about the way I was before the zombies. A quiet, rural life. No TV. I'd never even witnessed violence. Then I watched while a zombie tore my father's head off while he was working the fields. You know what I did? I didn't run, I didn't scream—I just shut off. The shock almost killed me. But that made me who I am.

Hazelwood was trembling slightly and clenched her fists where she stood to steady herself. "Maybe you're a zombie-lover too, but you earned that right by fighting for humanity up in Alaska. Mr. and Mrs. March never served, but their son will have to. Maybe it was noble once to be a conscientious objector, but now it's lunacy. The more they shelter Paul, the more they try to protect him, the more harm they do." She paused briefly, looking oddly embarrassed.

"I know you have stories like mine. We all do. We are the traumatized generation. A bit older, and maybe we could have been better prepared for what was happening. A bit younger, and we'd never have known a world without the zombies. If we are to spare the new generation what we went through, they must grow up impervious to trauma. Understand me. I value innocence. That's what Paul has. But in this world of ours, innocence kills." There were tears in her eyes. "It seems wrong, I know. Sometimes I spend whole nights crying into my pillow. But it's the only way. Let them cheer when zombies die. Better they cheer than they scream."

Land turned away from Hazelwood and gazed at the skyscrapers of downtown Calgary, built so many decades ago and standing there like silent memorials to a dead world. "I wasn't made for these times," he said.

"None of us were," she answered.

Land wiped his eyes and turned back to face her. "They've probably brought out Zombie Bob by now. We should get back to Paul."

"Yes," Hazelwood agreed. "He needs our support."

Inside, the Saddledome pulsed with rock music. Land recognized the Doors' "Peace Frog," which, thanks to the tastes of a certain general, became something of a military anthem. To its steady beat, Zombie Bob, dressed in full western garb with a white Stetson, wove his way between ten or so zombies, a roaring chainsaw in his hand.

It was part of Zombie Bob's appeal that it seemed like he could die at any moment.

Colonel Simonds was still on the platform, now protected by a half-dozen guards with submachine guns, offering commentary as Bob played the clown, always making it look like the zombies were just about to get him, before getting them instead.

"Careful Bob, there's a another deadhead behind you," said Simonds. Bob did a cartoon double-take and slid the saw around to his back. Then he slid backwards on the dirt, driving the saw through the hapless zombie's midsection. Bob did a pirouette, slicing the zombie mostly in two before slamming his weapon right through its neck. A thick plume of blood shot out.

Land winced at the display. No one he had known in Alaska would attempt anything remotely like Zombie Bob's antics. He and Hazelwood slid back into their seats on either side of Paul, and Land asked the boy, "How are you doing?"

Paul March sat there in wide-eyed, stunned silence. "I . . . uh . . ." was the best answer he could manage.

"Remember," Hazelwood whispered, "there's glass between you and the zombies. They can't get you."

Zombie Bob's opponents seemed selected for maximum diversity; an old granny, a slender college girl, a middle-aged Chinese man, and so on. All that was missing was a child zombie. The media always shied clear of those.

"Wow, look at that, kids," Simonds said. "Remember, you can see Zombie Bob's adventures every Wednesday at 3 PM on CBC."

"Peace Frog" ended and the music switched gears to a whimsical country waltz. Bob took awhile to forget the zombies and offer a few dance steps, tipping the white hat now splattered with blood. Bob pulled away from zombies for a moment to wave to the crowd, eliciting laughter as the zombies lurched up on him from behind. Then he sprang into motion, running circles around the zombies, causing them to bump into each other, trip over each other, fall down. The crowd roared with laughter.

Paul made a fist of his hands and squeezed until his knuckles were white. He was trembling hard, unstoppably. Land put a hand on his shoulder to try and steady him, and he felt the reverberations through to his bones.

In this confusion Bob rushed forward with his chainsaw swinging at chest level. He caught two zombies right next to each other and forced the saw through bone and flesh, slicing through both of them. Their legs collapsed, useless, but their upper torsos were not dead and pulled themselves across the dirt with their strong arms. Bob pulled away, ignoring them for the time.

"Two at once, Bob!" Simonds declared. "You've outclassed yourself this time. I don't see how you can top that."

The crowd went mad, screaming, whistling, stomping their feet, sounds echoing through the Saddledome's steel rafters. For a moment Land felt like he was a kid again, listening to a crowd cheering for a wrestling match or a fight in a hockey game. Paul started making noises like little yelps. Land and Hazelwood looked at each other.

"Are you alright, Paul?" Land asked, looking into the boy's eyes. They were beginning to look glassy. Paul grasped hard onto his forearm and squeezed. Land cried out.

Zombie Bob slipped among his remaining foes, so that they lurched at him from every side. Most weeks on his show, he performed some variant of this, positioning himself directly in the densest collection of zombies and fighting his way out. It was a crowd-pleaser with any weapon, and the chainsaw was best of all. He swung it at the zombie in front of him, smoothly slitting it through the middle. On the Jumbotron they could see smoke billowing out of the chainsaw. As he retrieved it, it seemed to sputter and die.

The camera caught the expression on Bob's face. It was real panic. This was not that unusual; the TV cameras often found Zombie Bob running for his life.

"Uh-oh," said Colonel Simonds. "Looks like ol' Bob's got himself in trouble again."

Somebody cut out the music just in time for everyone to hear Bob release a stream of profanity. He threw the dead chainsaw in the face of the closest zombie and dove past it, his Stetson tumbling off his bald head in the process. He kicked up dust as he raced away from the remaining zombies, but had the misfortune of tripped over something, landing face-first in the dirt. Before he could run, a strong zombie hand clamped down on one of his legs. He looked back at a half-zombie, one of those he'd sliced in two earlier, its entrails dragging through the dirt behind it. It squeezed tighter on his leg, shattering bone and pulling away a handful of flesh. Bob's scream hit the steel roof and resonated through the Saddledome's every corner.

"Fuck!" shouted Simonds into his microphone. There was no doubt now— this was not part of the show.

The smell of fresh blood spurred the other zombies on to greater speed. Zombie Bob tried to pull himself to his feet, but they were on him in no time, ripping, tearing at his clothes and his flesh. The entire Saddledome could hear his screams. Piece by piece they devoured him, stuffing human meat by the handful into their mouths. So here it was at last, the death of Robert Smith Harding. Everyone knew he'd die violently, himself most of all. But nobody expected that it would be witnessed live by ten thousand schoolchildren.

This would be remembered as the great trauma of a generation. The kids weren't screaming in excitement now. They were screaming in terror.

Land felt Paul's hand go limp on his arm.

"Fire! Fire! Fire! Fire!" Colonel Simonds shouted the command like a mantra, and his bodyguards loosed a hail of bullets into the mass of zombies. Many of the bullets struck their targets, but those that didn't impacted against the bulletproof glass, ricocheting through the arena and off into the crowd. One of these stray bullets caught Simonds in the chest, and he collapsed on stage, barely noticed amid all the pandemonium.

Children and adults alike crawled over each other, fuelled by the most primal surge of adrenaline, frantically seeking to escape the danger. Bodies swamped the exits and fell from balconies. Land grabbed Paul, ready to carry him out of the Saddledome, but found him limp and cold. He reached for Paul's jugular but felt no pulse.

He has a weak heart, Mrs. March had told him. She must have meant it. This shock must been too much for poor sensitive Paul, and his little heart gave out. Hazelwood looked at him open-jawed, and amid all this chaos noise and chaos everything suddenly seemed so still and calm.

Then Paul's eyes jumped open.

Thank God I was wrong, Land thought first, but then he saw his eyes. He could never explain this to anyone who hadn't seen it for themselves, but the eyes of the dead were different. Simonds was right; they lacked spark, life. This was true even of the freshest zombies.

Paul sank his teeth into Sgt. Hazelwood's forearm, biting down hard. Her legs kicked involuntarily, knocking against the seat in front of her. Her mouth opened to scream, but no noise came out as her eyes glassed over and she sank back into her chair, growing increasingly inert as Paul gnawed through to raw bone. Land grabbed Paul by the hair and yanked back, but even a child zombie possessed inhuman strength, and Paul wouldn't release his grasp on his prize.

The Marches, Land thought. *They live outside of the city. The inoculation drives must have missed them somehow.*

Damned zombie-lovers—they didn't even inoculate their own kid against becoming one of them! How irresponsible can they be?

Land slid his hand down Hazelwood's thigh to her holster. He pulled out her service pistol, drove it into Paul's chin, and squeezed the trigger.

HOLD BACK THE NIGHT

Colleen Anderson

FIREWORKS WENT OFF CONSTANTLY LIKE MACHINE GUN BLASTS. Chandi opened the blinds and stared out. Through the window, bright lights—white, red, green, blue—littered the sky like a battlefield. Diwali: the festival of lights—to stave back the darkness of the turning year, to hold back Kali's dark embrace.

Kali, the Black Mother of time. Kali the destroyer. It was in Kali's service that Chandi still lived. A devoted follower those many years gone, a priestess.

Chandi sighed and let the curtains drop. She felt uneasy being back in India. There were far too many memories. But the film festival in Bombay, and boredom, had propelled her from New York. As a film critic she had a good reason for coming.

Frowning, she swirled her scotch and drank the last drop, then donned her wrap and left her apartment. She should have known that being in her homeland would trigger thoughts of her origins.

Born in Calcutta—Kali Cutt to the locals—Chandi had been dedicated at a young age into the sect of Kali. She had held the goats, washed them down, and garlanded them for the sacrifices. As she grew older, she said the sacred rites, anointed the goats, and took the blood to the great statue of the Black Mother. Eventually, she drank the blood in Kali's stead, she slit the throats of murderers and thieves. She had given her life to Kali. In turn, she was given a long, long life to serve Kali faithfully.

She had not been Chandi then, only Kirwa. A lowly, ugly name: Worm. Given to her in hopes that demons would pass her by. In fact, they had not.

She had been taken in Kali's service and deeper into a sect so secret few knew of its dark sacrifices. The demons had made her their own, and, though she changed her name later, it was a worm they had made her. Never again to see the sun; instead, to travel in subterranean blackness and be the lowest form of life. To never know true warmth again.

There had been little reason at first to love or be loved. Carry out the rites of Kali. Carry on as priestess as she had done for decades. And she had been content with that, believing that the rites were all that mattered. Though Kali lived on, the world around her priestesses changed. Times changed, and Chandi changed her name from Kirwa. A lethargy and boredom set in so that eventually she left her homelands to travel far. But no matter how much distance she put between herself and India, she knew she was still Kali's servant. Chandi Kalidas—fierce slave of Kali.

She had loved twice in all those centuries, but the lovers died too soon, giving her a loneliness that gaped like the abyss. She wished she had had the courage to take her life, to end the torturous long days. But the worm of time continued to carry her on its back.

Chandi had been many things through the years, dancing a masquerade that never ended.

She met up with an old friend, and they went to see a movie, a musical. As the swelling soundtrack filled their ears they left the theatre, discussing the film's barely hidden attempts to extol the caste system. In the bright lights and press of so many people, Chandi didn't see the petite woman until she had nearly knocked her over and had to reach out a hand to steady her.

Papers cascaded in chaotic abandon; a couple of books toppled. Chandi heard a muffled "Oh." Then, where she would have expected a curse or a sharp word, the woman turned instead and said, "Are you alright?"

"Yes, but I'm the one who should be asking you if you're alright. I'm very sorry. Let me help."

The woman, who didn't even come to her shoulder, looked in Chandi's eyes, then stopped as still as the warm winter air. Chandi was not surprised. Most people did stare, and in the long years of her life she had seen few of any race with eyes like hers.

"Like a tiger," the woman breathed. "Your eyes are beautiful—tawny gold." Then she caught herself, smiled briefly, and apologized. "Oh, I'm sorry. Really. I didn't mean . . ."

"It's alright." Chandi laughed, a bit surprised at the woman's candour and reaction. She had grown accustomed to the looks askance, the steps backwards, even in the most modern cities. She gathered some of the fallen papers and handed them to the woman. "I'm used to it."

Her friend called to her, "Chandi, I must leave. Call me tomorrow, alright?"

She nodded absently as she helped the woman. Chandi noticed the petite woman's wavy hair, cut to shoulder length. A pixie chin and classic dark brown eyes, but they were larger, more liquid, with green flecks around the pupil. Peace seemed to flow from her and envelop Chandi.

"I'm Chandi Kalidas."

"Padma Rhaduri. Really, you don't need to help. I can gather these up myself."

"Nonsense. I didn't look where I was going. It's the least I can do." In the humid air, a few papers hung limply from Chandi's hand as she handed them to Padma. *The Survival of Matrilineal Society in Modern India* read one sheet. "This looks interesting. Are you filming this?"

And the conversation had grown wings of its own, had flowed into drinks and a kinship that stunned Chandi in its unexpectedness. Padma was looking for funding for her documentary film. An anthropologist interested in matrilineal societies, she had begun her research as an escape from a bad marriage, arranged when she was twelve. Not unusual for India, but her husband Ashok flaunted the custom and brought street prostitutes to their house.

"I hate him," Padma said fiercely while holding her chai tea. "He treats me like I'm one of his possessions. All he wants is someone to cook and to clean." Then she looked up, startled. "What's got into me? Here I'm telling a complete stranger about my personal problems."

Chandi, smiled tenderly, feeling a thawing of her dark heart. She reached out and patted Padma's hand. "Perhaps you needed to let your feelings out, and who safer than a stranger?"

An expression crossed Padma's face that could have been worry or fear. "I don't think you'll be a stranger for much longer."

There were too many forbidden thoughts and secrets for Chandi to reveal them. Yet, this small intense woman woke something in her, and she knew that they would meet again to talk.

CHANDI ENDED UP EXTENDING HER STAY, although she did not like being in India for too long; too much history welled up. Padma was busy during the days, researching and seeking funding. Chandi made her own excuses for being occupied. In the evenings, when it cooled down slightly, they met for dinner and to talk.

Passion seemed to spark from Padma's eyes as she talked about anthropology, ferreting out where traditions began and how they evolved. The air itself seemed to lighten, to be revitalized when her soft, birdlike voice touched it. Chandi felt drawn into her light. The inhumanity that threatened Chandi's world as the years had spun by moved a little farther into dark recesses.

One night, Padma waved her hands about saying, "Even though the heart of their culture is being threatened, the Khasis men insist they want to change the ownership rights. They don't even understand their own traditions."

Chandi replied ironically, "Well, sometimes traditions have gone on for so long that no one knows how they started or why." She poured a tumbler of imported scotch and passed it to Padma.

Padma curled herself onto the couch and sipped, both her small hands grasping the wide tumbler. "Mmm, this is so good. I love this stuff, but it's so hard to get here." Her eyes held a light that reflected her enjoyment.

Chandi smiled and sat down, crossing her long legs, looking briefly at the full curve of Padma's hips and legs outlined by her thin silk sari. "Well, I'll leave you a bottle when I go back to New York."

A frown clouded Padma's face before she looked down into her drink. Softly, she half-whispered, "You're leaving? I thought . . ." Padma shook her head, then took a swallow of the oily looking alcohol, not meeting Chandi's eyes.

"You thought what?" Chandi sat beside her, pulling the soft curling hair back from Padma's downturned face. "Padma?" Her finger brushed Padma's cheek, sending warning flares along her own skin. Padma shuddered and turned to look at Chandi.

Sincerity and scotch added a hint of huskiness to Padma's voice. "I thought . . . you liked me."

Warmth, which usually only suffused Chandi when she drank blood sacrifices, melted her resolve to remain apart. Unable to look away from Padma's shiny eyes, she ran her finger down Padma's cheek and throat. "I do. I do very much."

In an interval that was interminably long, yet as quick as their breaths, Chandi's lips brushed Padma's. Tasting slightly of the burnt tones of scotch, Padma's firm, supple kiss answered Chandi's own.

"I like you a great deal, Padma. You're the fire that holds back the night."

Padma sighed into the kiss, sending a butterfly of heat and longing into Chandi's mouth, permeating her with a thrum that electrified her from head to toe. Slowly, Padma leaned back.

"I . . . like you very much, Chandi, but I must return home now. It is very late."

Chandi stood, helping Padma to her feet. "I insist in walking you home. I'd hate for anything to happen to you."

Padma smiled shyly, adjusting her burgundy sari. "What about you? You'll have to walk back by yourself."

"True. But I've learned many . . . self-defence tactics that have been helpful in New York." She could not yet mention to Padma the real reason she would be safe, if she ever could.

They could have taken one of the many rickshaws or taxis, but neither mentioned it and they moved quietly together.

They did not touch as they walked, but their closeness was more than flesh. Padma moved slowly, rolling into each step, her arms crossed, and a small smile flitting over her face, then replaced by a tiny frown.

"Why do you stay with him?"

Padma looked up at Chandi. "Because, we formed a sacred bond."

Chandi couldn't keep all the scorn out of her voice. "Sacred bond? You've told me yourself how much he honours that bond."

"Yes." Padma hesitated then stopped. The warm night air blanketed them in stillness. Chandi had, through the years, come to understand the different nuances of silence. "But I honour the sacredness, the vows we have made. I try to uphold the tradition even if he does not. And I will not stoop to his tactics." A sigh escaped before Chandi could hold in her exasperation. "That tradition will get you killed. You could come with me to New York."

"I can't."

"For a while, at least. A vacation?"

Padma shook her head. "I can't. Not . . . yet. I have to finish my research first. And it's easier to do it here at the source. She began walking again, and they moved in silence until they reached Padma's door.

Chandi's fingers traced the plane of Padma's cheek. "Well, don't rule it out. We can talk further about it. I could help you find funding."

The door flew open. "Where have you been?" demanded the balding man in the doorway. He glared at Padma and pulled her towards the interior. "You never told me you were going out."

"She was with me," replied Chandi calmly. She held out her hand, more to delay Padma's leaving than to actually get to know this man. "I'm Chandi."

He just stared at her until Padma said, "This is Ashok, my husband. I met Chandi at the film festival."

"I don't care. Get inside." He started to push her through the door but she turned to say good night to Chandi. That's when Ashok's meaty palm slapped her face. "I told you, get inside now."

Chandi's hand was around his wrist in an instant. "Don't you dare hit her again."

He wrenched his hand free and snarled, "What I do with my wife is none of your business."

"Yes, it is." She glared down at him and did not move back. "She is a human being and my friend, and she does not deserve your abuse."

"She is my wife." His darkly shadowed gaze did not leave her face. "And you know nothing of what she deserves."

Chandi let some of the hunter flare in her golden tiger's eyes. Ashok started slightly but held his ground. "I know very well what she deserves. Don't hit her again."

Padma pushed in between them. "Ashok, Chandi, it's not enough to fight about. I'm home now, and it's late. Let's go to bed," she said to Ashok and pulled him into the house. She pointedly looked at Chandi before she went inside. Ashok continued to stare at Chandi but then looked away.

After the door closed Chandi stayed quietly in the shadows for a while, listening for the sounds of fighting. When all remained calm through the hour, she finally left.

Two nights crawled by until Chandi saw Padma again, but she was well and said she had just been busy. Over the next languorous week, they talked and strolled through the brightly lit streets. Though they grew closer, Chandi had done no more than kiss Padma, afraid to dive deeper into the unknown future. Chandi had all the time in the world, but the proximity to the temples of Kali began to weigh on her. It was time to leave.

She tried in vain to persuade Padma to move to New York with her. There were more chances of finding funding there, but Padma refused, not until her research on the documentary was done. It was easier to finish it in India. "It's important to preserve the culture and to make sure certain traditions aren't lost. It should only take another six to eight months," Padma replied.

Her hands splayed out in front of her, and Chandi said, "And what of the tradition that leaves you in Ashok's clutches? It's bad enough that you don't even love him, and even despise him, but that you're still his wife and possession is intolerable. He's beaten you, Padma. He'll continue to do it too. That's where tradition gets you, caged by outmoded ideas."

Padma's lip trembled, but she stubbornly continued, "Weren't you ever married? You said you were born here. Didn't you end up as someone's possession at some point too?"

Chandi bit her tongue, then turned and stared out the murky window that overlooked smog-shrouded Bombay's evening lights. "Yes," she replied. "To Kali."

Taking a deep breath, she turned and looked at Padma. "I have secrets to tell you, but please don't leave until I'm done."

Padma looked surprised, but only nodded. Chandi bit her lip and wondered why she wanted to open up to this woman. It was partly, she knew, to try and help Padma, but also because there was a strong attraction taking hold. In the incense-laden air, Padma sat quietly and listened, drank her scotch and then poured another. Chandi let everything out, from how she had made her way through the centuries to why she needed Padma. For love, for even one of Kali's dakini needed love.

When she stopped, Padma was still there, and she began to speak so quickly that Chandi could barely answer fast enough. But the words were not the ones she'd been expecting. No, "You've got to be joking," or, "I don't want to see you." No, "Will you kill me now that I know the secret," or, "How could you?" Only, "What was it like?" and, "How did it feel?" and, "What did you see?" and, "But you seem so human."

Sadly, Chandi replied, "I am human, of human blood, but yet so different. Both more and less."

Padma rattled more questions at her until finally, shakily, Chandi held up her hands. "Wait, wait! You mean you're not . . . horrified at what I am?" She tried to make light of it, but her mouth pulled down. She still couldn't quite believe that Padma hadn't yet condemned her.

Padma answered, "Horrified? I love you."

Then Padma's fingers unbuttoned Chandi's blouse, and Chandi's hands burrowed beneath Padma's sari. Clothing slithered to the floor. Their lips brushed each other like ephemeral wings brushing the air. Chandi's cool amber skin had broken out in a sweat as Padma's hot tongue trailed shivers down her shoulder and then her thigh. In a cascade of silk, Chandi's fingers revealed Padma's chai-coloured skin. Her deep chocolate-coloured nipples invited kisses. Chandi worked her way down to the cleft between Padma's legs. More kisses. Her tongue roved along silken contours till Padma shuddered in her arms. A blending; a marriage of honey and cream. A swirl of love and being one that moved beyond what called Chandi or what drove Padma.

Pulled into a vortex of feeling, Chandi murmured, "You are my light, Padma. You are the fire that drives back the night."

It was morning when Padma left.

THAT EVENING, CHANDI ROSE WITH A SMILE ON HER FACE. She dressed more carefully, slower, feeling the daze of happiness suffuse her. Padma would be with her again tonight.

At a quarter past eight, Chandi began to worry. Padma had wanted to see a movie, a cultural exposé on a small tribe in southern India. She'd talked about it constantly for the past week. Yet, she was now a half-hour late.

Apprehension growing, Chandi disappeared into the softened shadows of evening and moved quickly to Padma's home. She knocked on the stained door. Then she knocked louder. "Padma! I won't leave until you answer." Still no answer, but, when she tried the handle, it gave—with a bit of force.

No lights illuminated the interior, and the furniture mattered little. Chandi didn't need light to see; she moved from room to room until she found Padma laying on the bed and crying softly. Relieved that Padma was at least alive, Chandi hastily made sure that Ashok was not in the house. Then she returned to Padma.

"Pad?" She sat beside Padma and touched her shoulder.

Her muffled voice replied, "Just go, Chandi. Just go."

Gently but firmly Chandi turned her over and swept the hair from in front of Padma's face. Padma's hands flew up, but Chandi held them away and saw what she had expected. "Oh, Padma."

Padma's bruised face shone with tears and blood.

Rage rose quickly, flushing Chandi's heart to molten. She stood and pulled Padma to sitting position. "He'll pay for this." Turning, she went to the chest of drawers and opened drawers until she found Padma's saris and cholis. She started tossing garments on the bed. "Get a suitcase. You're staying with me."

"But I can't."

Chandi snapped, "You can. There is no *honoured* tradition of beating one's wife. He'll kill you if you stay. You know that. And . . ." Chandi choked up, but went on. "And I have just found you. I will not lose you." She kneeled and gently kissed Padma.

Fiercely they embraced, Padma murmuring into her hair. "He knew I'd been gone all night. I told him I loved you. And I do. I have never loved anyone like I have you, Chandi."

Once they had packed Padma's clothing and papers, they left.

CHANDI SETTLED PADMA INTO HER APARTMENT knowing that Ashok knew nothing about her or her whereabouts. She fed Padma scotch and bathed her wounds, then put her to bed.

In the middle of the night, Chandi went on the hunt. "Kali, Black Mother, I make you an offering this night."

She picked up his scent from their home, then followed it down the streets and alleys wet with indescribable lumps and oily rivulets. Unsurprisingly, his smell, acrid like souring lentils, led to a brothel. Boldly moving through the ramshackle place, Chandi did not care who saw her. Some might think she was a worker, others would not care or notice.

In a room curtained with a frayed, thin piece of cotton she found him, just getting dressed. He zipped his pants beneath the sagging belly and reached for his shirt. But his hand connected with her arm. Ashok started to laugh, to say, "I thought you'd had enou—" Seeing Chandi, he said, "How did you get here?"

She looked at the prostitute on the bed just rising to protest. "Out."

"But this is my room."

"Out!" Not caring, she confronted Ashok and punched him in the gut. He grunted and crumpled over his ample belly. But Chandi gave him no reprieve and grabbed him by the throat. The prostitute scrambled from her bed and ran from the room, probably for help.

Chandi's hand clamped on Ashok's throat, but he still managed to gasp out, "B-bitch."

Her hand dropped as her other hand came up in a fist and smashed into his face, not as hard as she could have or his face would have caved in. "How does it feel? Do you like this, Ashok? Do you think that Padma has enjoyed the pain you've given her? Have you ever even shown her affection? If you had she may never have needed love elsewhere." She slapped his face twice.

She heard raised voices on the floor below, moving closer.

Ashok gasped out, "Go ahead, kill me. If you do, you'll lose her for sure. That I know."

Several more times, Chandi slapped and punched him, punctuating her words with her hands. "Oh, I won't kill you. You don't deserve such an easy release. But if you ever go near her again, I will." She stopped, in control, not breathing hard. The fear in his eyes made them glitter like black stones.

The voices were outside the room. Chandi said, "Don't ever go near her again." Then she moved in quickly and kneed him hard in the groin. He went down, and she leapt to the window and was gone as the first person entered the room.

PADMA WAS QUIET FOR THE FIRST TWO DAYS, unwilling to talk, but eventually she let her grief and pain out. Chandi soothed her, holding her close. "Padma, I'll stay as long as you need to finish your research. But when you're done, come with me. Please." Chandi bit her lip, wondering how strong Padma's sense of tradition was. Would it keep her in India forever?

Then Padma just nodded, sighing.

Chandi closed her eyes, not daring to speak.

THE CALL CAME EARLY IN THE MORNING, when she was groggiest, already nodding off from her book, and barely able to lift the receiver.

"Padma has honoured Sati, as was her right."

"Who is this?" Silence. Chandi looked around the suite, and dread clutched her gut. No sign of Padma. Then she saw the note. Padma had gone home for some forgotten research. "Ashok? What have you done? Where is she?"

"In the hospital. Don't bother going to see her. Let her die in peace. She's mine, not yours."

Fear nearly choked her and made her breathless. "I will get you for this."

She could, too, any time. He just laughed and hung up. For all her words all she could do now was wait until evening and hope Padma still lived. Cursing her limitations, she lay down to sleep.

AS THE LAST RAY OF DAYLIGHT WITHDREW, Chandi raced from her door, had in fact already been pacing for hours, waiting until she could leave. In the streets, Chandi heard people shouting and laughing, heard the discordant snatches of music as they celebrated Diwali. Paying little attention, she ran all the way to the hospital, dodging cars, bicycles, and cows.

Bursts of ghostly radiance flickered through the drawn blinds in Padma's room. The lights were dimmed, though Chandi could see well enough. Did the nurses do it to soothe the damaged patient or to lessen the horror for family?

Yet, it was family that had caused this. Ashok stood there blandly staring at Padma's unmoving form. He started at the sight of Chandi at the door. She towered over him, willowy, yet strong as a taut bow. Ashok backed up a step.

Then he shrugged and shook his head. "I told her to be careful. But those kitchen fires, so uncontrollable, and no one was around."

"You. Miserable. Impotent. Worm." She advanced a couple of steps. "You could have just let her go."

"She's mine," he said, and glanced about, sweating heavily in the warm evening air. She could see his bluster falter when he realized that they were alone. "She had no right to leave."

"You didn't want her. You never loved her."

Ashok mustered his courage and flipped his hair out of his eyes, then puffed out his chest. "There's nothing you can do. She was my wife; she'll stay my wife until she's dead. Get out."

Chandi swallowed back her fury, held it in check. "I suggest," she said, letting the fire rage in her voice, "that *you* leave before you leap from the window in your grief." She moved in close, very quickly, before he knew she had.

She used everything she could to drive in that intimidation, and her tiger's glare made him look away. He tried a laugh that failed. "There's nothing you can do," he repeated, but it was he who left.

And what could she do? In all her years, so many she had lost count, she had never been able to really heal the ill or bring life. She could only bring death. In that, there was little difference between her and Ashok. He too had brought death to Padma, but not merciful, swift, and painless death.

Chandi went over to Padma, who still lived, if a burbling mass of melted skin and hair immersed in a burn tank could be called living. Burns to sixty percent of her body, the nurse had told Chandi in the hall. She could live if she made it through the next twenty-four hours. Whether there would be any life of quality was the question. But there was shock. Shock could kill. Chandi had seen it happen enough times before at her own hands, but, please, not to Padma. *Shiva, Kali, please, not Padma.*

It had been a long time since Chandi had manifested Kali, but the urge was strong in her this night. However, nothing she did now could reverse the events that had made Padma a charred, reddened thing. Cherished Padma. Without her, there was little light left for Chandi. And yet, it was light, or rather fire, that had taken everything away.

"What sacrifice, Kali, what sacrifice do you want?" Chandi whispered fervently. No answer, except for the hum and beep of machines that monitored Padma's life systems.

All Chandi could do was get the best care for Padma, a private room, but moving her to another hospital was out of the question. And this, like so many other Indian hospitals, left much to be desired in cleanliness. The walls held indefinable stains, the floors showed the dirt that clung to everything.

Chandi waited, praying, feeling helpless.

The hum and beep of the machines, their neon green and red lights watching, sang an odd counterpoint to the festival of Diwali raging outside.

"CH-CHAN . . ."

She lifted her head quickly and moved to the burned thing that was Padma. "Pad?" Her hand reached out, but there was no part of the woman that she could touch.

A wet rattle emerged from Padma's lips, then she whispered, ". . . love you . . ."

"And I love you, my f—" Chandi choked on saying *fire*; fire had burned away everything good and brought back the night. She chewed her lip fiercely, drawing the sweet, coppery tang of her own blood. Leaning in close, she whispered, "Padma, I can save you. You know I can. I can only do it twice at most— I've never—Padma, let me save you."

For a brief moment Padma's eyes opened and met hers, then they shuttered. "No. That road is yours, not mine. . . ."

Padma faded back into unconsciousness. Chandi's nails bit into the heel of her closed fist. The hum and beep, the shouts and fireworks outside, all faded away. Familiar with silence of all types, she knew this one brought death. Padma was delirious, and she wouldn't thank Chandi, but a life was better than this sort of suffering. Any life. And there were always ways to end it. Chandi leaned closer.

"Isn't she dead yet?" Ashok stood in the doorway, no emotion showing on his pudgy face.

Chandi spun, snarled, and in three quick steps had hauled Ashok by his collar into the room; she shut the door, then pinned him against the wall. "Why?" she gritted out, not much caring if he saw her fangs or not.

Ashok trembled, but his voice was all bravado and scorn. "It was my right," he spat. His shirt pulled taut over his hairy belly. "She's my wife, not yours. She was cheating on me, and with the likes of you."

Chandi twisted his shirt collar a little tighter. He had no idea what the likes of her really were. "You brought home prostitutes. You bruised her. Why?"

He refused to answer. Her hand tightened, and he started thrashing for air. She loosened her grip slightly. The whites of Ashok's eyes showed.

"So I can remarry, alright. It was the only way. . . ."

Chandi threw him to the floor. "It wasn't the only way. There were many other ways. Do not let me see you here again, ever. If I do I'll rip your throat out with my hands."

Ashok scuttled away from Chandi's predator glare. She noticed dawn encroaching then. It was nearly time to leave. Before she did, she bribed the staff to keep Ashok away.

SHE SPENT A RESTLESS MORNING TRYING TO SLEEP AND, when that didn't work, got up and tried to read. It ended with Chandi pacing back and forth in the curtain-shrouded apartment, waiting until the sky darkened enough to go out. The heat weighted everything to stillness, as if foreboding pressed upon her shoulders. She would not have left Padma's side at all, had it been possible for her to stay.

What gnawed at her stomach was more than hunger; it was a grief and anger that threatened to consume her. Still, she could not put off any longer that she needed blood. Bombay was a fairly modern city, but there were still temples to Kali throughout and, yes, it was time for a manifestation.

Once it was dark enough, Chandi ventured out. Women in saris as bright as tropical flowers, yet muted by the heavy air, walked through the streets. Men in modern Western dress, and a few in Nehru jackets, strolled along, chewing sweetened betel nut or smoking. Chandi made her way through the crowd to the closest temple, gave the words that admitted her into the innermost chambers.

Through a lattice screen of carved-wood flowers, she saw three goats, washed, garlanded with orange marigolds, and waiting blissfully unaware near the scrubbed marble of the sacrificial arena. Turning away, Chandi dropped her clothes and anointed her brow and limbs. The great Black Mother, Kali Ma, stood before her in sculpted relief. Skulls and limbs beringed Kali's neck; fangs sprouted from a mouth chewing on the entrails of Shiva even as she mounted him. The mother of all, giver of life and the destroyer who devours all things, even time itself. No-one escapes her embrace in that final black ocean of creation and blood.

Chandi had often performed the sacrifices for Kali Ma: taking thugs, thieves, and murderers—she had torn out their throats, or beheaded them. She had drunk their blood in dedication to Kali and for her own sustenance. Everything became a part of each other. All would melt back into one in Kali's embrace. Chandi embodied Kali, and she danced the divine dance.

The ritual chants poured from the sacrificial arena and flooded her ears. She waited and prayed to Kali. Something sparked deep within Chandi's mind—vengeance. Soon, she would bring another to Kali's embrace.

The priests appeared with the bowls of blood. Chandi lifted one and poured, drinking, letting the blood run over her body, a flesh-and-blood image of the Black Mother. When she looked at the priests, even they stepped back from the fire they saw in her eyes. The blood tasted sweet. She was used to its clotting thickness, but there had been times when it was all she had been able to do to gag it down. Now, letting the trance take her, she nearly dropped the bowl. It was removed and another put into her hands. She drank, smeared the blood over her breasts and limbs, and danced.

She danced as if time stretched across a vast expanse of night, for it did. She danced as if wound in the entrails that Kali gnawed, as if spun out and drawn back in again. She danced out the darkness, making the night one with her, knowing that it all came to this, that in the end all returns into the great encircling clasp of Kali Ma's arms. She danced and let the inky despair lap out, touching all in the temple until a great wailing howl rose from its walls. She danced, whirling, twirling, and spinning with the cosmos until she was lost among the stars, the white, grinning skulls, and the flowerbursts of Diwali.

Eventually, there was an awareness of hands reverently sponging and drying her body—dabbing soothing oils upon her skin, wrapping her in soft silk—and a liquid other than blood being brought to her lips and lacing her veins with fire.

She found herself outside the stone temple, people parting around her like water around a river rock. Cleaned and dressed again, she couldn't remember the trance, but that had happened so often before that it mattered little. It mattered only that Kali had not forsaken her because of all the time she had spent in North America. She had work to do.

She saw the doctor waiting for her. "Sit down, Miss Kalidas," he motioned to a chair in a little waiting room. The walls were a pale shade of greenish grey blended with ageless dirt. The hospital was one of the better ones in India, but the halls spoke of neglect and insufficient funds.

Chandi sat and closed her eyes for a moment. Then she opened them and said, "Is she still alive?"

The clean-shaven man looked down at his watch and said, "She is, but I'm sorry, we don't expect her to make it. Her injuries are just too severe. And the shock to her system has been too much. I'm sorry. We've done what we can to ease her suffering." He hesitated under her intense gaze, but added, "If she lived, she would lead a crippling life, always in pain. It is better this way. I'm sorry."

He left Chandi sitting there, staring at nothing. How many times had this happened before? Not so many that she couldn't remember every person she had cared about. Not many could bear to be with a servant of Kali, or be trusted with the knowledge of what it meant. As Chandi sat there letting the darkness swirl in her mind, she knew she had loved no one like Padma. Padma completed and complemented her.

She managed to go to Padma's room; the silence was such that it was almost as if death had already settled there. The only sounds were the murmur of machines and their beeps. Something greater than anger and hunger balled itself in her stomach and pulled at her throat. Nevertheless, Chandi moved to Padma's bedside and looked down. There was a hollow growing inside her. She wanted Padma to live, to be able to laugh and make love again, but she dared not pray to any god to let Padma live in the state she was. If she lived she would be crippled and in pain until she died. Yet, Padma knew Chandi could save her. The cost would be dear, but she would heal.

Chandi found herself gnawing her knuckles. Wetness slipped over her cheeks, and she realized that she was crying—something she had not done since she was a young girl, freshly dedicated to the sect of Kali. She reached forward, determined now to give Padma the kiss of life. Chandi was not sure she could live without her.

A sudden change in Padma's breathing halted Chandi. "Padma," she whispered softly. And Chandi hesitated. Could she stand the anger, perhaps the hatred, Padma would have for her if she lived through Chandi's touch?

"Chandi." It was like a long sigh. Padma's eyes didn't open.

"I love you, Padma."

"Chan—don't kill . . ." The words were barely more than exhalations. Chandi leaned as close as she could, thankful for her heightened hearing.

"Don't kill? Padma, I must—"

"No. Ashok."

Chandi had misunderstood; she wanted to scream at Padma, "You won't let me heal you, and now you take away my vengeance too," but she didn't. In the long run, Padma would not know what Chandi did.

"Promise."

It was hard to get the words around the lump that blocked her throat. A sob escaped before she nodded her head and said, "I promise, Pad." She blurted out, "Please let me save you. Please. I need you."

"No."

Chandi cried but Padma would not change her mind. Then Chandi noticed her breathing deepening. "Padma, please don't go. . . ."

"Love you. . . ." A long sigh escaped her and no more. Kali Ma had welcomed Padma home.

Chandi turned away, consumed by tears she could not hold back, feeling as if the darkness would swallow her until she disappeared.

IT WAS THE DARKEST PART OF NIGHT. Nothing stirred; even the ever-present rats seemed to be sleeping. The warm night air held no breeze, and everything seemed to hold its breath, waiting for the light, or for a cool wind. Soon the monsoons would begin.

Neither insects nor cats heard her move into Ashok's house, glide over broken floorboards, around sparse furniture, and into the bedroom. She was sitting on his chest before he woke, her other hand covering the mouth of the woman sleeping beside him. The woman struggled and beat at Chandi's hand but could not remove it. Ashok woke with a start and a muffled shriek at Chandi's cool hand around his throat. The whites of his eyes shone brightly in the room.

"She's dead," she growled, "because of your pettiness and greed." Her hand tightened on his throat until he gagged.

Chandi lowered her face within an inch of Ashok's. The woman beside him stopped moving, her body trembling. Chandi's fangs gleamed in the sickle-moon's light, which bled through the curtains. "You are lower than a worm, for a worm is still part of this Earth. I am Chandi Kalidas; know that name, for it is your fate. I am a dakini, and you have provoked the Black Mother's wrath. Some day I will strike you down like the rat you are, but you will not know when, you will not know where." She slid one sharp nail an inch along his neck, opening a fine cut from which blood trickled. Her fingertip dipped in the blood and she raised it to her mouth, then spat it out in his face. "Even your blood is sour. I'll be watching you, Ashok." She smelled the sharp tang of his urine, and smiled. "You will not know when, but you *will* feel Kali Ma tear into your entrails and you will feel every bite."

She left as silently as she had appeared. It would be a long while before he or the woman dared to even move from their bed.

Some day when she felt that her promise to Padma had been fulfilled, that Ashok had lived in terror long enough, she would sacrifice his blood to Kali. For now, she would honour Padma's last wish.

Her body was wrapped in the sacred saffron-coloured shroud, marigolds adorning her bier like bright eyes in the dark. They carried her body through the streets, torches lighting the way. People moved out of their path, or disappeared, not wanting to be part of the funereal atmosphere in the last days of Diwali, the festival of lights. They wound up the hill to the burning ghats. There, everyone departed, friends and family, except for the priests who would preside over the cremation. Chandi stayed and none dared remove her, for she wore the blood-red and black robes of a devotee of Kali.

She watched as the priests chanted, and as they slid Padma into the purifying fire. Like a phoenix she would be reborn, and maybe Chandi would be lucky enough to recognize her in her new incarnation.

As the flames licked up the marigolds and began to devour the shroud, tears wetted Chandi's face. She never moved throughout the cremation. Padma's body disappeared, enveloped by red and yellow flames and by white-hot tongues of heat.

Chandi whispered, "You are the fire that holds back the night."

THE BANSHEE OF CHOLERA BAY

Jes Sugrue

THE SEA ROCKED THE SHIP, gently at first, then impatient as a ma with a fussy child. The wind and the waves played a lullaby that became a might bit fearsome for those in the belly of the boat. The weak. The sick. The dyin'. Hangin' on to life, they were. Not givin' up hope. That's the way it was the mornin' the sea swallowed up me Daniel and made me a widow.

Said me Daniel fell overboard and put the lie in that book they keep their records in, an accountin' of the days at sea, of the comin' of babes and the goin' of corpses. The gospel accordin' to British liars and thieves masqueradin' as the ship's crew and officers. No better on sea than on land for the way they treated us. Made it sound like an accident, they did, or somethin' me Daniel might have done to escape the sickness. But, as God is me witness, it wasn't at all like that. I seen it with me own two eyes.

They weren't supposed to be tossin' bodies overboard so far up the river, I heard told. Not ones dead of consumption or, worse yet, the typhus. And not live ones either, to be sure. And me Daniel still had life in him. And hope. I'd swear it on what's left of me ailin' pa and ma in Ireland, Sweet Mary, Mother of Jesus. And on me sisters, God rest their famine-weary souls.

THE CAPTAIN MUST HAVE FIGURED I was sleepin' when he came for Daniel, he and his sorry excuse of a first mate. T'wasn't the first time they tossed bodies into the sea, gettin' rid of disease any which way they could afore the inspectors came aboard. Didn't want the bother of bein' turned in at the quarantine. So they took 'im.

There was I, afore the sun rose, nursin' wee Sean on the one side and stickin' a finger in Pearl's mouth on the other. Dryin' up, I was, from the lack of food on board and the lack of fluid to build up me milk. What rations they gave us were salted to bring on a thirst. Tryin' to gouge the last of our coin by sellin' us water, they were. And those who couldn't pay went without, or got water worse than the likes of what was in the buckets we pissed in. So we did without.

The captain gave me babes the once over, on account of how much they were fussin'. His pokin' and prodin' only made matters worse, and I was fearin' for their wee lives.

It's the hunger, I told him, that was makin' 'em cry, not the sickness. Sure or he would have given them both a watery grave afore we reached the new land. But they took me Daniel. And what if he was near dead? They had no rights takin' him afore his time. No right at all. Not under God.

"His skin's dead cold like a corpse," the captain said.

"It's just his fever broke," said I.

"His eyes are far off gone," he said.

"Dreamin' of Ireland and kin," said I. "Not seein' Heaven yet, to be sure. A wife knows these things."

The captain wouldn't listen. Wouldn't let me hold him. Not even one last time. Kicked me like a ragin' bull, the first mate did, when I tried to hang on for a moment more. Pain shootin' through me leg, me hand graspin' at a patch from Daniel's coat. Graspin' for somethin', anythin' to remember the scent of 'im by.

I FOLLOWED 'EM, I DID, THROUGH THE DARKNESS OF THE HOLD. The only light bein' a lantern flickerin' slowly on the verge of death, bringin' more shadow than light. I followed past all the beds. Beds atop beds on wooden legs. Beds filled to overflowin' with bodies sleepin' aside other bodies. Some on the mend, some waverin' between life and death, bathed in fever and skin blisterin', lips crackin' from thirst and dry vomit and bile.

I followed 'em up the rickety stairs that led to the deck, past the buckets of human waste and what was on the floor on account of the buckets bein' full and the crew afeared of dumpin' 'em. The stench was too familiar to be worthy of complaint.

I'd left me babes with the mam who'd just lost her own wee lass, so I could see me Daniel off. And they let me, just so long as I kept silent. But the silence felt like betrayal, and the horror of it set a fire burnin' in me sorrowed eyes. Me heart rose up to cry itself heard.

"Shut yer trap, woman," the mate screamed at me. Threatened to kick me again. "Irish dog," he said, just like that, snarlin' like a dog 'imself.

And when they swung me Daniel up in their arms and over the side of the ship, I saw his eyes close and open again—and his fear in them.

I almost jumped in after him, I did, to be spared the need of sayin' goodbye. Only he'd be goin' to Heaven and me to Hell if I did. But I might 'ave still, if it weren't for the babes.

"Slán leat, mo mhile grá. God speed me to you."

HE WAS A GOOD MAN, me Daniel was, a husband to put all others to shame. And bless his soul, he didn't want to leave Ireland, but did so for the love of me. Promised Ma and Pa he'd take us away after the eviction. After the landlord had the cottage tumbled and burnt to the ground. Alongside it was everythin' we had in the world that we couldn't carry. It was the boat together, or the workhouse alone, we knew, for there they split families apart. Even husbands and wives who might perish from the need to hold the other, like nesting spoons. Like Ma and Pa. Like me and him, not that I let on near enough. Would that I could have shown him better that I loved him.

Couldn't bear to have me taken from his side, he said, by day or night and so, even though he was fierce afraid of goin' near the water, he found us passage. Love me he did to gift us with such a hope. And Ma and Pa through us. And Pearl with Daniel's grey-blue eyes and Sean with his skin so flour-dust fair.

I didn't want to leave Ireland. Not with the sureness of knowin' I would never set eyes on it or on Ma and Pa again. And it was a sureness, for none from these parts that had left for the new land had ever come back. So it was a final goodbye till Heaven, I knew. As final as could be short of a funeral.

"Slán agat," I whispered, me face against the bones of me mother's face, me lips against me father's whiskers. "And forgive me for leavin'."

ALL THIS WAY ACROSS THE SEA, and there we were, night fallin' fast, and us at anchor twenty ships from the island's shore. A quarantine it was, with too many sick and dyin' to make room for us. Not allowed to set foot on land out of turn, and the threat of cannon fire to keep us from sailin' to another port. And so it was for another day and night, and then another.

By daylight came the steady drone of buildin', the back and forth of saws, the poundin' of nails. Wood takin' on the form of hospitals and beds and coffins, we heard told. By night came the sound of sufferin' from shore and other ships, of foul-mouthed workers cursin', drinkin', matin' even, on the rocks for all to hear. And while we waited in this purgatory, between death and life, and old and new, those able-bodied were enlisted to ready the vessel for inspection. Me hands joined with the hands of other peasants, and, on promises of bread, we scrubbed the deck till our flesh was raw and our joints swelled and our backs gave out when we tried to stand. For every hour I worked, I aged a year.

It was desperate some were to feed their bodies, for many kept their ration to themselves instead of sharin'. Not with friends or kin. But I gave a portion of me portion, first to Pearl and to the mam who cared for her and Sean, and then I softened bits inside me mouth and scraped the paste inside of Sean's wee gums. And it sat there while I prayed his tongue to find it, his throat to swallow. As the wind rose and the rain fell, I stood vigil and willed his infant chest to rise and fall the same.

PERHAPS IT WAS THE SHEER NEARNESS of land that made kin turn one on the other, but so afraid the livin' were to touch the dead, that they used fish hooks instead of tenderness to haul the bodies from out of the hold. The hooks pulled at tattered clothes and dragged the bodies like mops across the floor. And those without a stitch of coverin' they bound with rope and treated much in the same way. And God 'ave mercy on their souls, and mercy more on them that sat and watched this bein' done to those they loved.

Just before dusk and storm, the splash of oars announced the approach of company. It was as promise-filled a sound as birdsong on the eve of spring. Several men came aboard and one of them a doctor. He was kind and respectful in his manner, but his words I could not understand. He'd come to carry out the inspection, but he mustn't have been happy with the state of things for no sooner had he gone than a priest was sent to bring us prayer, and with 'im a nurse for our comfort. Though, as surely we needed both, we needed food and doctorin' more.

If we were fit to stand, we were sent up on deck for airin' out. It was a plot, I feared, to 'ave us catch our death by chillin' us to the bone. When the first mate came round and shoved blankets in our faces, suspicion left me.

"Thank you," said I, "for the blanket."

"Doctor's orders," he said, "though I'd rather see you all locked down." Then, not so's any but me heard, he said "locked down or dead." And I knew he meant it.

The mam next to me shared her blanket with Pearl and I with Sean. Would have given him the blanket for himself if I'd a thought it would save him.

"Short on everything includin' coffins," the nurse said as she ran a tender hand over Sean's brow. Countin' on the new day for supplies, she was. She paused and made the sign of the cross over Sean. "Tomorrow," she said, her voice rich with compassion, but it sounded more like a wish than a fact.

I closed me eyes and held Sean to me heart, wishin' I had milk left in me to feed him. I breathed in the salt air and whispered out prayer after prayer, imaginin' me rosary in me hand and me fingers markin' each Our Father, Hail Mary, and Glory Be. I prayed for Sean to hold on till the nurse's tomorrow and thanked God his dear sweet face was coolin' after its heat. Then me eyes beheld a smatterin' of fine red spots among his freckles. And it was more than me broken heart could take.

I took Sean from the cold down below into our bed. Smaller than me marriage bed, it was, and so empty without Daniel and Pearl. Poor Sean, whimperin' for not knowin' why he felt so poorly, and all the others, moanin' and groanin' with the sickness, knowin' they were at the end. Some cursin' their fate and wishin' they were back in Ireland, others wantin' to speed death along. All I had to give Sean now was the familiar of me voice and so I sang to 'im and rocked 'im in me arms. *"Mo mhile stór*, me thousand treasures, good night, good night, *oiche mhaith*, me love."

When I finished singin' there was a heaviness in his body that wasn't there before, a heaviness that comes when the lightness of the spirit leaves. But his spirit hadn't gone far. I could feel his presence with me, and so I kept his body in me arms and hoped he might return. That's what I told 'em the next evenin' when they tried to take me son.

"No, no. A thousand nos," I cried as we waited turn for the rowin' boat to take us ashore.

"Think of Pearl," the mam beside me said, "she'll be needin' you all the more."

"Is cumma liom," said I. I wanted no one but me Sean.

"You can't keep 'im, woman," the captain insisted. "The dead go on another boat."

"Not all the dead," said I as Sean was ripped from me arms, for the part of me that was dead was stuck with the part of me that would live on.

The longest night of me life came, with a moon so full, it lit the way for the island men to row the dead ashore, and me Sean with them, headin' for an unmarked grave without a mother by him for the final tuckin' in.

COME FIRST LIGHT, I was woken by a mighty commotion on deck and, with no lock on the hold, several of us went up to see what the fuss was about.

I looked overboard as a myriad of bodies floated by, as silver-eyed and bloated as dead fish. I didn't know what to think except that one of the ships anchored further out had grown tired of keepin' their dead on board, or one of the rowboats, laden with corpses, had overturned. Not the one that carried me Sean, I knew, for me eyes had followed that one safe to shore.

These were the bodies of other mothers' children, young and old, and me heart was heavy for them. It made me count me blessings, at least the one remainin' that I had. Me Pearl. And so I went below to fetch her from the mam.

It was as though the lass knew that I'd turned her away when Sean died, the way she turned from me and into the other woman's bosom. That, or she blamed me for her father and brother bein' gone.

"I'll have 'er now," I said to the mam, and put me arms out, but the mam held fast and turned away. I grabbed her shoulder, tremblin' with the comin' together of fear and anger. "I'll have me daughter, and thank you for the care you've given."

The mam began to cry, and Pearl cried with her.

"Hush now, little Mary," the mam said, and she stroked her hair and jiggled away her tears.

"She's not your Mary, she's me Pearl," I said and peeled the woman's one hand from Pearl's backside and the other from around her shoulder, guilt fillin' me all the while as though I was doin' them both a grievous wrong.

"There you are, Pearl of me heart," I whispered when she was safely in me arms. I scattered kisses by her ear, the way her pa did to cheer her. "'Tis you and I now, darlin', and I'll not leave you again while there's life in me bones."

Her little hands reached round me neck, and she lay her cheek on my shoulder and sighed. An immense sigh, far too large for a child of her wee size and her three years.

SOON AFTER THE DAWN of the next morn the captain was given orders to send the sick ashore, and so the worst were lowered into boats that set off in a procession. With no one to greet them on the dock, the sick were left to bake under the sun. The swelterin' skies cast down a heat the likes I'd never felt in Ireland. For as much as I had craved the feel of land beneath me feet, I was content to bide me time rather than join 'em. Eventually the least sick were landed and guided by the islanders to handle the worst, to drag them past the fever sheds, towards a field of tents, and out of sight.

One of the boats returned with provisions to take the bite off our hunger. There were makings for weak tea and enough bread to go round. Together we imagined how it smelt straight from the oven, and how it might have melted in the mouth. Only what was set before us hadn't seen the inside of the oven long enough to cook it well. Though it was hard as nails and golden on the out-side, the middle was, by far, too over-soft. I ate it all the same and with a haste that set me belly achin', an ache that brought me to my knees regrettin' I'd not prayed the food be blessed. I prayed this new discomfort was the food not set-tlin' well and not the typhus settin' in. A wasteful prayer, I feared.

Rumour reached the shore that we had illness still aboard, perhaps because so many took to throwin' up their bread over the sides. A boat was sent, dis-patchin' orders to remove the sick, and so the captain set out to rid 'is vessel of the weakest and poorest, the later havin' naught to pay 'is bribes.

There was an irony in 'is doin' the choosin', given that he looked worse off than some of those he'd singled out. I kept me peace as he safely passed me by, only the mate came to stand at me side and called 'im back.

"Have you forgotten this one," the mate asked the captain. "Likely to have the sickness, this one, given that 'er husband and the boy took ill. And remem-ber all she's seen—"

All that I 'ad witnessed came back in a rush of fiery pain as the embers of me loss were fanned by this cruel man. I knelt before him and pulled Pearl closer still.

"It's not for us to tell the future," the captain said, and he walked away with an anger in his voice that came from bein' told his duty.

"Makin' predictions may be all that gets us away from this forsaken place, Captain. But if you're happy anchored—"

The captain doubled back and looked me over. "She's fine enough," he said, and then he looked at Pearl who'd suffered through an awful night. "She's fine," he said pointin' at me, "but the girl goes."

The mam stood nearby and lunged at the mate. "Don't touch me Mary," she screamed, still in her delusion.

The captain grabbed hold of her and gave her a push towards the group goin' ashore, then he looked back at me. "The girl goes. You can take 'er there, or stay behind, or go to Hell for all I care."

Pearl started cryin' and pullin' on me arm, as though afraid I'd let her go. I held her more closely, and her tears stilled. Then we descended into the hold for one last time, and gathered what few belongings we still had: mine and Daniel's rosary, given to us by the priest the day we wed; the children's names and birthdates on a sampler of me mother's stitchin' to hang upon a wall in our new home; Pa's pipe, handed down to Daniel who'd long since lost a father of 'is own; Daniel's mother's spankin' spoon; a change of clothes, except for Daniel, who travelled light; wee Sean's favourite blanket; Pearl's linen doll.

Not near enough to build a life with, but more than some.

I placed our family treasures in the threadbare bag a neighbour from the village gave us, and with each piece I yearned to be back home. So like the bag, the hope our dreams were carried in was frayin' at the seams. I felt as weary as the threads. And then I looked at Pearl, and, for her sake, I prayed me hope would mend.

I SAT PEARL ON ME LAP, dead centre in the boat, and held me breath as our boat was lowered through the air on ropes. We swayed with the breeze while the oarsmen shouted for us to keep still, or so I gathered from their tone and gestures. The smallness of the boat I didn't notice till we came nearer the waves, and I looked up at the cursed ship and those who manned it. "May God's justice be equal to your mercy," I said.

Even from the water I could tell what sorry excuse the island had for a dock and me apprehension grew as we drew nearer. One of the men who brought us safely in secured the boat and helped us up. When he set his hands on Pearl, he smiled at her so big and bright it warmed me heart and put a smile on her.

We made our way across the slippery surface of the battered dock, mindin' the hazards of loose and rotten boards. When we were halfway in, I heard an awful groan from underfoot, and as the next wave struck somethin' gave way and the dock lurched. I stumbled over on me side and as I did, Pearl tore loose. I screamed as she fell towards the deep and watched an oarsman jump in to save her,

"C'est pas ta p'tite!" the other shouted. "Reviens!"

His strong arms fought the current, and he raced to snatch her body from the frothy waves and rocky shore. I held me breath as he gasped "Mon Dieu!"

The mam cried, "Mo Dia!" and the world turned black.

I DON'T KNOW HOW LONG I WAVERED BETWEEN LIFE AND DEATH, I only wish that death had kept me. As in a dream I felt me body bein' carried from one shed to another and, like the Virgin Mary, bein' turned away.

And then Daniel findin' room for me in a tent.

A torrent of a rain poundin' against the thinness of a cloth roof and walls, and water seepin' in under the straw, under me bones. Me knees knockin' together keepin' time with the rattlin' of me teeth.

And Daniel sittin' at my side with Sean in his arms.

A drought inside me mouth and throat the likes of any desert, and pain with every word I tried to speak. And still I asked for Pearl.

"The girl is gone, sweet thing."

Heat risin' from me brow like vapours, minglin' with the stench of human waste. The vapours fallin' down again like a dark cloud over me face.

And Daniel callin', his voice growin' distant.

I dragged meself across the straw, crawled out of the tent into a night lit dimly by the moon and lantern glow. I crawled across the grass, and then the gravel of a road, bits of rock and buildin' splinters embeddin' in me hands and knees. Still I followed his voice towards the bay. Sheltered it was, its water cool and sweet. I stopped but for a moment for a drink and then I noticed Daniel in a golden boat driftin' away.

"Wait for me," I cried and went in further. Water risin' to me knees, me thighs, me waist. I pushed me body forward 'til I was neck deep and within reach. And when I was so close our fingers almost touched, me Daniel gave me the saddest look.

"And where is Pearl?" he asked, and then again more desperately.

"I thought her with you."

"And I with you," he said.

I looked towards the shore, so distant now, then back at Daniel. "I must find her."

"No, come now," he said. "We'll wait for her together."

"I must find her," I said and started for the shore. Daniel had Sean, and Sean his father. Pearl was alone. "I promised her I'd never leave her," I tried explainin', but he looked so hurt.

"Mo beatha," he pleaded as I turned from him. My life.

"Pearl," I screamed, again and again, drownin' out his mournful call. Water rushed into me mouth and filled me up and weighed me down. I kept on callin' even as I felt the pull below.

I thought of Daniel and Sean and knew them together, gone from here, but I never would have found hereafter peace had I left Pearl behind. I'll have no paradise without her, me heart cried out. No paradise.

The bay pulled me body down and away towards the sea and left me soul behind to search the quarantine. To drift through time, a ghost, with grief and rage the likes of which gave me the name of Banshee.

Banshee of the island and its shores and all who land here, alive or dead. I am the Banshee from the depths of Cholera Bay.

MARCH ON THE NEW GOMORRAH

Mark Anthony Brennan

NIGHT CAME QUICKLY OUT ON THE PLAINS. As Christopher watched the orange globe sink below the horizon, his heart sank with it. He shuddered, mostly from the sudden chill but also out of fear.

Christopher hunched his shoulders and scanned the sky above him. He listened carefully for that telltale flutter of leatherwings. They came out to hunt just after sunset. The men in the camp would laugh at him for being afraid. Grown men had little to fear from the flying beasts, but Christopher knew that a leatherwing could easily snap the head off a child his size.

It was a good thing he had started the fire well before sunset. He now had a roaring blaze going. In fact, he'd had to move the tripod holding the cooking pot away from the centre of the fire because it was too hot. Christopher reached over and threw another chunk of olgawood onto the flame and then stoked the fire with his stick. The crackling noise and the sparks that rose up into the night air were comforting. Leatherwings shied away from fires.

"That's quite a fire, son."

Christopher jumped at the sound of the voice. He hadn't noticed his father approaching him out of the gloom. Carpenter was grinning at him through his beard, his eyes dancing in the firelight.

"Are you trying to light up the entire plain?" Carpenter was still smiling as he crouched next to the cooking pot. "And you have the stew ready, I see." He reached over and patted his son on the cheek. "You're a good boy, Christopher."

Carpenter removed his broadsword from his belt and laid it on the ground. He then sat down on the ground next to his son.

"And I've prepared our beds, Father," said Christopher, nodding to the spot where their travelling blankets were laid. Underneath the blankets were stuffed bundles of prairie grass that Christopher had gathered.

"What would I do without you, son?"

"Well, you always travelled alone before now." Christopher laughed. "I'm sure you managed."

"Ha. I suppose I did. But it's good to have you with me. Tell me, how does it feel to be on your first campaign?"

"I'm not sure really. Not much has happened yet."

"No," said Carpenter, glancing over towards the main fire in the middle of camp. "Not yet. This is important for you though, son. Now that the priests have said they'd be willing to take you in as an apprentice you have to impress them. This campaign is your chance."

Christopher's stomach lurched with a pang of fear. He'd never been more than a day's hike outside of Nazareth in his life.

"Father," said Christopher quietly, "what are the other villages like?"

"They are called settlements, son. There aren't many of them, as far as we know, but they are all godless, evil places."

"But are there no villages like ours? Are there no men of God, like our Great Seers?"

"Perhaps. Perhaps in the settlement that we are heading to." Carpenter sighed. "That is what we are about to find out. It is possible there are prophets there. Men like Abraham and Isaac."

"Father, do you think I will be a priest someday?"

"You will make a fine priest, Chris," said Carpenter, looking his son in the eye. "I have always known that." He slapped his thighs. "Now, let's get the bowls out and have some of your stew. I am as hungry as a slithercat."

As Christopher's father ate he fell silent, all the while peering out over the camp. Nearby the priests' horses were tied up to a row of low, stumpy olgatrees. The horses shuffled back and forth but made little noise. Further over, closer to the main campfire, the women were shackled and chained together in a group. With their head bags on they bumped blindly into one another, which caused the occasional scuffle.

At first there was very little happening over by the main campfire. Then, just as Christopher was scraping the bottom of his wooden bowl, some of the acolytes brought out the crucifixes. They propped them up against a makeshift fence set up on the far side of the campfire. A few minutes later the priests came out of their tents and positioned themselves on the crosses. Then the ringing sounds of the acolytes' hammers pierced the night air. The priests screamed out in agony as their hands and feet were nailed to the wood.

Some simply yelled out, "Jesus!" over and over. Others chanted, "Jesus, my Lord, I feel Your pain. The sweet, sweet pain. Thank You, oh Lord, for the pain."

The acolytes unshackled the women and led them over to the crucifixes. The head bags were removed once the women were positioned in front of the priests. Despite the distance, the priests' erections were visible in the glow of the main campfire.

As the women's heads began to bob up and down at the priests' crotches, Christopher turned to his father. "Father, why are women evil?"

"Because they are the daughters of Satan, son." Carpenter did not turn to look at Christopher. His face was drawn into a scowl. "Jesus discovered this when He was crucified. As the bastards of Rome flayed His flesh, His disciples ate the flesh as it fell. To feel His pain. But there was a woman among them— the Whore. She would not eat. Instead she . . . touched Jesus, as only a woman can touch a man. Just as God had sent down His only son to save us, Satan had sent his spawn to defeat Jesus on the cross. Woman, you see, is the beast. She is the demon that must be vanquished."

"But, men have . . . relations with women. Why?"

"Well, son, we must, of course, have children. And sex is, in fact, pleasurable. The pleasure you feel is the joy of conquest. The sexual act is the vanquishing of the demon. You are holding down the beast, keeping it at bay."

"So that is why we keep women around?"

"Yes. Until they are past childbearing years. Then we dispose of them. They are no longer any use to us."

"Like mother?"

Carpenter dropped his gaze. He sat staring at the ground by his feet for several seconds. Then he frowned and muttered, "Yes."

The next day Carpenter and his son broke camp early. They had everything packed and had their rucksacks on their backs before the morning prayer. The sun had just started its climb into the vastness of the blue sky, but it was already warm. The day's march would be a hot one.

Everyone kneeled, including the priests, when the Great Seer, Abraham, emerged from his tent. The Great Seers of Nazareth were not normal men— they were a breed apart. Even their clothes were cut from a different cloth. They did not wear the leathers and furs that most men of Christopher's village wore. Their tunics were crisp and clean and incredibly white. But more than anything it was the eyes that set them apart. They always seemed to be looking beyond this realm, into that other place.

Abraham raised his hands to the sky as he stood before the men of the camp. "Oh Lord," he bellowed, "I stood in Your presence in the Void. I saw You force the Whore into submission. I have witnessed Your might. Hear me now and help us. Help us in this holy campaign against the beast. Your prophets, my brothers, have been killed at the hands of the unholy. Help us, oh Lord, to rain down Your vengeance upon those that would strike out against us. Just like the Gomorrah of old, this nest of evil must be eradicated. Help us wipe out the minions of Satan. The lovers of women."

"How does he know?" asked Christopher once they started walking. He had come to realize that this part of the campaign was not a lot of fun. It was hot and dusty, and the plains seemed to go on forever. The landscape hardly ever changed. Aside from the rustling, dry prairie grass there was very little vegetation, just the odd stunted bush. The ground was almost entirely flat, punctuated only by the occasional small outcropping of rock.

"How does he know what?" Carpenter and his son were well back of the main group. At the very front were the priests and Abraham on horseback. Behind them were the priests' acolytes with their backs well loaded. Then came all the rest of the men carrying whatever they needed for the journey. Carts and pack animals were not taken on campaigns.

"How does Abraham know that other prophets were killed? And how does he know where they are?"

Christopher didn't quite understand the Great Seers. He knew they were not ordinary men. For one thing they lived for many generations. In fact, prior to the death of Moses, it had been assumed that they were immortal. And they had extraordinary powers given to them by God. But how did they work?

"Son, the Great Seers have eyes that see beyond this mortal realm." Carpenter squinted as he looked up to the sky. "In the time of your great-grandfather we came to this place from beyond the Void. The Seers guided us. Only *they* could see the way through. In a way, the Great Seers remain out there, in the Void."

"But," protested Christopher, "they are here, with us."

"Yes, of course, son," said Carpenter, smiling briefly as he glanced down at Christopher. "They are here in the flesh. Their bodies are mortal. But in spirit they still exist in the Void, that place where Heaven and Hell meet. Through that portal, they can see virtually anything. Anywhere."

As Christopher watched his leather boots kick up dust he had an awful thought. What if Abraham watched *him*? Watched him do all those embarrassing things in private. But surely Abraham would have better things to do. Thank God there was only one of them along. Isaac, as usual, had stayed back in Nazareth to rule the village. Then again, if Christopher's father was right, Isaac could be watching him anyway because distance was meaningless for the Great Seers. And then there had been a third Great Seer. Moses had died several winters ago, but if the Seers were so powerful then couldn't Moses be watching him from beyond the grave?

Later that day they came across a herd of bovux. These lumbering giants of the plains were usually hunted for their thick, black hides. Right now, however, the men were interested in getting some fresh meat for their journey.

Carpenter ordered his son to stay back with the supplies and the shackled women while the men went in to hunt. Christopher knew it was for his own protection. A stampeding bovux, with its six horns jutting from a body the size of a barn, could be a deadly thing.

Not far from the pile of supplies was a large expanse of dryweed, a tall, thick prairie grass. As Christopher waded through, the stalks around him crackled in the parched air. Once he was well into the thicket he flattened out an area and stretched out on his back. The air wasn't much cooler in there, but at least the dryweed blocked out the afternoon sun.

As he lazily gazed up at the blueness above the stalks he thought about his apprenticeship. Was his father right? Was he really meant to be a priest? Christopher just couldn't picture himself in that role.

But, of course, the priests had undergone the sacrament of the leaves—that's what set them apart from normal men, from commoners. The waxy leaves of the trutix plant were sacred, only the priests were permitted to partake of them. And the priests chewed on the leaves almost continuously, in order to remain under their influence. Christopher's father described the trutix leaves as "hallucinogenic," which Christopher assumed meant something to do with divinity.

"Under the influence of the leaves, can the priests see into the Void?" he had once asked his father.

"No," was his father's reply. "Only the Great Seers can see into the Void. Only they have been touched by God. But through the sacrament of the leaves, the priests are able to have some sense of the wisdom."

"Wisdom?"

"Son, the Void is the place where Heaven and Hell meet. Where flesh and spirit touch. Where good and evil coexist. It is the source of all wisdom."

Christopher's attention was drawn to two round objects drifting high above the dryweed stalks. Floaters. The long, wispy tendrils that hung down below their gas sacs were well off the ground. They must have caught the scent of blood, however, because these floaters were on the move. That meant the hunt was probably over.

Christopher stood up and headed out of the stand of dryweed. Over where the herd had been was now a huge cloud of dust. There was a low rumbling noise. That would be the herd stampeding away. Presumably they were not heading Christopher's way, or else he would have seen them. It would be safe to go in now and help carve the meat for packing.

As Christopher wandered over to the dust cloud he spotted several more floaters heading in the same direction. He wished he had his slingshot with him. It was a popular sport for boys in his village to shoot rocks at floaters and deflate the gas sac. Once they fell to the ground it was amazing how small their shrunken bodies were. You had to watch out for the trailing tendrils though— they stung if they made contact with your skin.

The floaters that were sailing above Christopher's head would start to descend once they got close to the dead bovux. They would get low enough to allow their tendrils to scrape the ground. The tendrils would pass over the remains of the bovux, absorbing the blood and other bodily juices.

As Christopher got closer, the dust started to clear. The black mounds of the bovux corpses appeared before him. The men had killed about ten of them by the looks of it. Acolytes ran back and forth between the bodies. Several of the priests were hunched over the hindquarters of the beasts. Christopher was young, but he was old enough to know that these priests were copulating. Some were chanting, "Jesus! Jesus, we dominate the beast. We vanquish the beast in Your name."

Christopher spotted his father off to one side and trotted over to him. Carpenter was wiping his soiled broadsword with a cloth, all the while staring over at the priests with a frown on his face. Christopher followed his father's gaze. The sight of the bloodied priests vanquishing the beast was both repulsive and frightening. And yet this was holy work that Christopher would one day have to perform himself.

He opened his mouth to ask his father a question, but Carpenter silenced him with a wave of his hand. Carpenter looked down at his son in sombre silence. Finally, he pulled out a large carving knife and handed it to Christopher. "Go about your work," he growled.

The next day they could see the peaks of a mountain range far ahead of them. As they approached the range the terrain began to change. They rose from the flats into a series of low, rolling hills. The dust of the plains gave way to rocky ground. After three days the range stood before them like a massive wall—the smaller foothills in the foreground, with the much larger craggy peaks behind.

They had reached the head of a small rise. Abraham held his sword up high to halt the men. Below them the ground swept gently down to a small valley. At the far side, the ground rose abruptly into the foothills. In the centre of the valley was a settlement. They had reached their destination.

As the men broke into small groups to discuss strategy, Christopher helped the acolytes gather the packs and supplies and secure the women. Before long, the men were ready. Christopher was to stay behind with some of the acolytes who were too young for battle.

The acolytes looked at Christopher with contempt. They weren't much older than Christopher, but they didn't mingle with commoners. They were acolytes to the mighty priests—he was just the lowly son of a craftsman. Christopher shrugged and wandered off on his own. He sat down next to a boulder at the edge of the rise and surveyed the scene below. He swatted at the irritating tiny flying snakes that flitted around his head.

At the centre of the settlement was a large structure. Christopher recognized it as being very similar to the burned-out, rusting ruin outside Nazareth. People referred to it as the "old ship." No-one was permitted near it, as it was deemed to be unholy. This structure before him was different though. It was whole and complete, and it shone proudly in the midday sun. Around it were dozens of huts of various sizes. Even at this distance Christopher could tell that they were unlike the buildings of his village. They were bright in colour and seemed remarkably smooth and featureless.

The men of Abraham's campaign made their way across the floor of the valley. Abraham and his priests led the way on horseback, the other men followed on foot brandishing their swords and spears. When the men reached the edge of the settlement they stopped. After a minute or so, the horses split into two groups, one group heading to the right, the other to the left. Every so often a horse would stop and stay in place. The horsemen were surrounding the settlement.

Once all the horsemen were in place, there came a roar from the men on foot. They charged directly forward into the heart of the settlement.

Christopher could make out scuffles. He saw blades come down, spears thrust. Several people tried to escape from the settlement but were quickly hacked down by the priests. A couple of times, a group of people bolted. It took several horsemen to chase them down, but they didn't get far.

Christopher could hear the battle better than he could see it. Abraham's men roared in battle rage. But it was the screams that rang out louder than anything else. Screams of terror and screams of agony. The screams cut right through Christopher and chilled him right down to the bone. He sat there trembling but could not tear his eyes away from the carnage below.

The battle did not last long. Soon the shrill screaming subsided to wails and moans. The horsemen and footsoldiers disappeared from view as they converged in on the centre of the settlement. Christopher looked back towards the young acolytes who were sitting, shoulders hunched, among the mounds of supplies. They looked pale and scared as they sat in silence. They avoided Christopher's gaze.

Over the next hour or so nothing changed much, except that the moaning down below became quieter and quieter and then stopped. Christopher did not move from his spot next to the boulder. Except for the clinking of the women's chains and the drone of flying snakes, there was no sound to disturb the eerie stillness.

Finally, a single figure emerged from the settlement. Even though he couldn't make out the man's features, Christopher recognized the figure approaching as that of his father. When Carpenter was close enough, Christopher stood up so that his father could see him. Carpenter's face was grim—grimmer than Christopher had ever seen it. His broadsword was covered in blood, as were his hands. There were spatters of blood all over his leather bodycover, and even some on his face.

Christopher knew it was irrational to be scared of his own father, but Carpenter cut a frightening figure before him.

"Shall . . . shall, I clean your sword, Father?" Christopher stammered.

Carpenter slowly shook his head. "No. Later. Come with me."

Christopher didn't dare speak a word as the two of them crossed the valley floor. Before they reached the settlement, they passed a number of bodies strewn on the ground. Most were decapitated and dismembered. All of them were hacked up with their guts pouring out onto the bloodstained ground. Christopher's stomach churned with rising nausea. He desperately wanted to turn and run back to camp. But he couldn't. He couldn't.

Inside the settlement the scene was even more gruesome. Every building was splashed with blood, and there didn't seem to be any break in the red stain on the ground. Bodies and body parts were everywhere—bodies of men, women, and children. Even bodies of babies. The lifeless heads stared dully. Christopher had to watch where he was walking to avoid stepping in gore or tripping over body parts. Waves of nausea overtook him. It took all of his efforts not to vomit. He couldn't show his father that he was weak.

It was abundantly evident that these people were unarmed and had been taken completely by surprise. Christopher's head began to spin. He felt detached, as if he were dreaming. In a daze he struggled to keep up with his father, who was striding briskly forward.

Towards the centre of the settlement they came upon a throng of Abraham's footsoldiers. They were stuffing bits of bloody flesh into their mouths. Their faces took on the appearance of ravenous slithercats.

"The pain, Jesus. The sweet pain!"

There were poles stuck in the ground with severed heads impaled on the tops of them. The images before Christopher began to swim. He didn't know anymore whether the images were real. Priests were copulating with the decapitated bodies of women.

"Jesus! In Your name we vanquish the beast."

Christopher's legs went rubbery. Just as he was sure he was about to faint, his father hustled him through the doorway of a building. Christopher's body was washed with relief. Carpenter led him down a corridor that was brightly lit, although Christopher could not figure out where the light was coming from. He also absently noted that the walls were made of a strange substance. Not wood or hide. It looked like rock, but it was too smooth and shiny to be rock.

They entered a room. It reminded Christopher of his village's clinic. There were several cots in the room, and the tang in the air was unmistakably the smell of medicine. Christopher assumed that the equipment along the walls had to be medical, although he could not recognize most of it. He was taken aback by the sheen of the unblemished surfaces.

In the middle of the room was the Great Seer, Abraham, and several of his priests. On a cot next to them, there was a body laid face down with the hands bound behind the back. The feet were also bound, and a dirty rag served as a gag over the mouth. Although the tunic was badly torn and bloodied, there was no doubt that this was a member of the settlement and not one of Abraham's men.

"Ah, Carpenter, there you are," said Nabokar, one of the priests. He had that glassy-eyed look and the constant half-smile common to all priests. "We are about to leave. Abraham is going to address the men. But you will stay and keep an eye on the prisoner." Nabokar nodded at the body on the cot. "Abraham has plans for this one."

The prisoner was alive? From what he'd witnessed, Christopher had assumed that everyone had been slaughtered. Christopher looked up into the face of Abraham. What did the Great Seer intend to do with this godless sinner?

Although Abraham didn't utter a word, he dominated the room by his presence. Upon his face was an unfathomable expression—his state of mind was nothing that men of this world could understand. Although he was clearly aware of everything that was happening in the room, his eyes focused on no one. As always, he was looking *beyond*.

"Plans, holy one?" asked Carpenter, addressing Nabokar.

"This is the one primarily responsible for the murders of the prophets, the brothers of Abraham. It is not God's wish that she be thrust into the arms of the Whore, her mother, too quickly." Nabokar looked down at the prisoner in disgust. "We will acquaint her with many forms of agony before she slowly passes through the gates to Hell."

A *woman*? Christopher glanced over at the prisoner in disbelief. Her body was covered in wounds—deep gashes, gouges, puncture marks, bruises, and even burns. Her face was badly beaten and was puffy from bruising. Given the tunic and the short hair, Christopher had naturally assumed that this was a man. What kind of a woman was *this*?

Abraham and his priests left, leaving Christopher and his father alone in the strange room with the prisoner. The prisoner groaned and occasionally screwed up her face in pain. Christopher tried to avoid looking at her and busied himself looking for something to clean up his father's battle stains. He found a cloth in a drawer and a metal basin with running water. He dampened the cloth and proceeded to clean the blood off his father's hands, face, and clothing. His father stared down at the ground, the whole time seemingly in a trance.

Christopher was just rinsing out the last traces of blood from the cloth when he jumped as his father's voice broke the long silence.

"Give the prisoner some water."

Christopher found a small bowl, filled it, and brought it over to the prisoner. He hesitated before removing the gag. He looked up at his father. Carpenter closed his eyes and nodded.

The prisoner took the water in loud gulps. It seemed painful for her to swallow. Most of the water ended up spilt on the cot. Christopher filled up another bowl. After the second bowl the prisoner grunted and moved her head to face in Carpenter's direction.

"Your pilot . . ." she said in a rasping voice, "the pilot is in charge?"

Christopher wanted to ask what a "pilot" was, but he knew better than to say anything. He braced himself for an outburst from his father, who would be angry at this woman for speaking out without permission.

But Carpenter merely scowled. "You mean our Seer?" he growled. "Yes, he is in charge."

"God help you," gasped the prisoner. She moaned as a wave of pain hit her.

"Who *are* you, woman, that you address me this way?" demanded Carpenter.

"I . . . I am Council Leader Catherine Green." The prisoner blinked. Her eyes were bloodshot. "But . . . I . . . I don't understand. Your women . . . don't . . ." Her voice trailed off as she closed her eyes, panting for air.

Council Leader? Christopher was confused—how could a woman be involved in the affairs of the settlement?

"You don't have seers to guide you?" asked Carpenter.

"Our pilots . . . tried," said the prisoner falteringly. "They are powerful men . . . and many found it hard to resist them. But we managed to . . . keep them under control. Keep . . . them isolated. But lately . . . they became worse. We had no choice. Their influence was too great . . . their following was growing. Had to kill them. To protect ourselves. Good god . . . your pilot is in charge?"

Carpenter took a deep breath. "Woman, what do you mean? About these . . . pilots."

The prisoner narrowed her eyes. "Don't you know what happened to them? The passengers and the animals were fine. They were in suspension the entire flight. But the pilots weren't." The prisoner paused to take a few deep breaths and then continued. "By necessity they weren't in suspension, even though the trip through normal space took several years. They were awake, they were aware. Even when they made the leap." The prisoner grimaced in pain. Her body convulsed several times. She let out a sigh when the convulsions stopped.

"Go on," said Carpenter.

"During the leap, in the void, they saw something, experienced . . . something. It changed them . . . they were changed . . . mentally. Maybe physically too. They had . . . enhanced sensory abilities, but they were . . . damaged. They became . . . unhinged. Demented. Good god, you follow them? How can you?"

The prisoner grimaced again. Again the convulsions racked her body. This time they wouldn't stop. Her body was shaking uncontrollably. She looked over at Carpenter, her eyes pleading.

Carpenter looked down at the broadsword in his hand. He paused for several seconds. Then suddenly he was on his feet, his sword raised high in the air.

There was a quick swish and a thud, and then the prisoner's head was falling to the ground. Several streams of red shot up into the air. Christopher flinched as he felt a warm splash on his cheek.

The body on the cot arched backwards, jerking obscenely. But the face that rolled around the floor looked to be in peace.

Carpenter stepped back. His broadsword clattered as it fell from his hand. He collapsed into a chair, his shoulders slumping forward.

Christopher quietly stepped over and knelt down next his father. He looked fearfully over at the headless body on the cot. "You were supposed to keep her alive, Father," he whispered. "The priests will be angry."

"I will tell them that this . . . woman . . . spoke blasphemy. I couldn't stop her. I couldn't allow her foul words to contaminate your young mind. I had no choice. That's what I'll tell them. They'll understand."

"So, what she said isn't true?"

Carpenter was silent for a while. Then he shook his head. It was as if his eyes had been cleared of a fog. "No! No, this is nonsense. Son, listen to the Seers. Forget what you heard here."

Christopher looked at the blood oozing from the prisoner's neck, soaking the white sheets. Then he remembered the horror that awaited them outside. The spasms of nausea returned.

"Father," he said softly.

"Yes."

"This . . . work. I don't think I can do it. Will I ever get used to it?"

"You won't have to."

Christopher turned to look at his father. His brow was wrinkled in puzzlement. "But my apprenticeship . . ."

"You will apprentice, son. But not in the priesthood." Carpenter slowly pushed himself out of the chair and looked around the room. He wandered over to one of the walls and ran his fingers along a seam, peering intently at the gleaming surface. "This craftsmanship is like nothing we have in Nazareth. There is much we can learn here."

Christopher caught his breath at the sound of the word "we." He had never dared to hope but it had always been his secret wish to apprentice under his own father, to learn the family craft.

"Carpentry should be a family business, Christopher," said Carpenter, walking along the wall, feeling its smooth lines. "There is much to be done. I will need your help."

"Of course, Father," breathed Christopher.

Carpenter turned and looked over at his son with a smile. "And what we learn together we will pass on to *your* sons."

His smile faded at the sound of splashing liquid. The sheet on the cot was now drenched, the blood dripping noisily to the floor.

"Just promise me one thing, son," said Carpenter, his eye on the red mess in the middle of the room. He paused, taking a deep breath. "Give me only male grandchildren. No granddaughters. Dear god, no granddaughters."

Postcards from Atlantis

Catherine MacLeod

WANTED

Sentenced to twenty years' imprisonment, desperate, chained in an underground cavern, Maga listened to the river. It ran through the cave, fed by the ocean nearby. At high tide, salt water ran over her feet.

The first time the merman came to her, she thought he was only exploring, that he'd been caught in the current, but he returned on every tide. They became lovers. He brought her rare blossoms, and wooed her in his soft clicking language.

At the end of her sentence she was dragged from the cavern screaming—how would the merman find her now?

As he closed the door behind them, her jailer glanced back at the river. The skeleton of the cave's last occupant gleamed wetly, sheathed in seaweed. Then the bones clattered down the bank as the tide carried them out again.

OUT IN THE WASH

Bored with housework? Craving life on the edge? Walk this way and watch your step—the laundromat's busy on Monday.

Look past the usual tired housewives, at the not-so-usual student doing his thesis on the relevance of shrunken heads in a cannibalistic society. His clothes make this strange clunking noise in the dryer, and, sure, it *could* just be a set of heavy buttons.

See the woman who says her husband ran off with the waitress yesterday, washing blood out of her jeans. Okay, she's menopausal, she's stressed, but that's a *lot* of blood.

And this quiet man, whose backpack you accidentally kicked, smiling as a tiny blond braid flops out. "A doll for my daughter," he says. Does he look as if he could afford a doll with real hair?

You want thrills, the laundromat has them.

Just don't let them catch you looking.

EMERGENCE

LIDA WATCHED THEM FROM HER BED: five-star generals pretending they were ready for the invasion. And avoiding her while they did it, because you always hate the messenger.

She'd seen the UFO first. No, she said, the aliens *weren't* friendly. She'd definitely been in the wrong place at the wrong time.

All the armies of Earth were waiting. They said they were prepared, but she doubted it. She wasn't, and she was on the front line. Hell, she *was* the front line; she expected to be the first casualty of war—who knew how this alien scout would react?

They were about to find out.

She said, "It's time," and passed a hand over her stomach. The first soldier of the invasion kicked itself into position, and she howled as her water broke.

REMEMBERED

OLIVIA WAS AFRAID OF BEING FORGOTTEN. She had no family to carry on her name; she'd never written a book, won a prize, or gone over Niagara Falls in a barrel. She wanted to be remembered for *something*.

So in her eightieth year she took up gardening, growing roses that were perfectly formed, richly hued, beyond exquisite. Their scent carried for blocks. Even the rare mite was healthy and fat. The owner of the local greenhouse followed her planting instructions perfectly, but his flowers were merely beautiful. When asked why, Olivia said she put her heart into hers.

And so she did, at night when nobody would see.

Her arms under long sleeves were marbled with needle marks. Her watering can was washed daily so the blood wouldn't crust. She was patient and serene in her craft. Someday people would say, "Oh, I remember her. Those roses—who could forget?"

COLD HEART

CONSIDER THE GODS OF THE ICE: Tes, Ymir, Iia, securing the merest reference in any book of myths. Daese? One line, if you can find him at all.

Daese was a minor god who one day chose to create life.

But he learned from his mistakes and never did it again.

He made his son Roh out of falling snow, which could explain the child's cold-heartedness. At the age of ten minutes he staggered to his feet and tried to kill his father.

Chilled and grieving, Daese still couldn't bring himself to destroy his son. Instead, he imprisoned him, freezing him deep in the polar ice where no one would ever find him.

Global warming is a bigger problem than you think.

HOLY WATER

"WAIT! COME BACK!"

Mrs. Riley grimaced as the vampire hunters pounded out of the church. She heard their truck go squealing down the street, and considered the bucket she carried ruefully. Too late. They would have been better off getting supplies in a church with a bigger budget, she thought, or at least a sturdier roof. This one leaked something awful when the snow piled up.

Well, she was only the cleaning lady, not a carpenter, and there wasn't much she could do about it, was there?

Though perhaps a prayer wouldn't hurt.

She moved the baptismal font away from the leak and replaced it with the bucket, then whipped a cotton rag from her back pocket. She'd clean the font now. Father Thomas could fill it later.

SUGGESTIVE

Finish your drink, dear. You've already swallowed so much of the venom a little more won't matter.

Pardon? It makes you vulnerable to suggestion.

Head spinning? Limbs heavy? That's to be expected. But I *told* you I poisoned your cocktail. It's not my fault you didn't believe me—any more than it was my fault you cheated on me while I was at night school. You were so anxious to get me out of the house you never asked what I was studying.

I *was* taking a cooking course. When I heard about Leila I switched classes.

Making Zombies, dear. No, I'm not joking about that, either.

I understand the attraction. Leila's a beautiful woman. I'm sure you could just eat her up. Yes, she *was* a mistake. So was not taking me seriously. But I'm willing to be fair.

You can have her.

After you finish your drink.

EXPIRY DATE

Instant rice, instant coffee, instant gratification: staples for a just-add-water society.

Dehydrated potatoes, evaporated milk: goods that keep in storage until you want to be bothered with them.

Coming soon to a store near you: Relationship-in-a-Box. Contains one companion, reasonably priced. Limited shelf life. Heat, drain, refresh, enjoy. Keep unused portion on ice.

JOB SATISFACTION

Gremlin was an agent of the Lords of Probability.

He was also the best worker at Sal's Car Wash: employee-of-the-month three months running. He was a squashed-looking little guy in baggy pants who sort of shrunk into the background, but he put in a solid eight hours. He drove the cars through the buffer, a job no one else wanted.

Causing mechanical trouble was Gremlin's real job, and he'd never found a better place to do it. He could sabotage a customer's front brake lines between wash and rinse—front *and* back if they wanted hot wax—but he needed privacy.

Sal's was *it*. Nobody put security cameras in a car wash, and cops never suspected the peons who polished the grille. Both Sal and the Lords admired his diligence, but Gremlin just believed in getting the job done.

Those statistics weren't going to make themselves.

RAINMAKER

A ring around the moon is a sign of rain to come, says the oldest superstition. It's true because you believe it.

And because it's a sign for me to dance.

Rainmakers were born in the first ocean. We're invisible—except to those few who feel an erratic power and dance in unknowing homage to us.

Sometimes we dance with them.

Sometimes we outstay our welcome.

My mother, perpetually angry, danced tsunamis and storms. My grandfather, long senile, danced rains of fish and frogs. I've danced floods when the spirit caught me. We bring the rain; we don't control it. When the moon is ringed, even we tremble with anticipation. We know how dangerous it is to dance.

But believe me, you don't want us to stop.

THAW

SPRING CLEANING: WAS THERE ANYTHING MORE TEDIOUS? Paul wiped out the fridge and put a fresh box of soda in the crisper. Did he really want to defrost the freezer tonight? Well, no; but he didn't want to leave it, either. The hamburger was okay. The fish had to go. The three coeds packed in the bottom *definitely* had to go, and preferably tonight.

Since they'd been frozen it would be impossible to set a time of death; and because there was still ice in the river the cops would think they'd washed down with the early thaw. The trick was to dump them before they got freezer burn. There was no excuse for shoddy housekeeping.

Besides, he needed more freezer space.

WATER MUSIC

TODAY'S JOB WAS A LEAKY BATHTUB FAUCET. Jack Caswell opened his toolbox and pulled out a wrench and a set of earplugs. Even out in the hall he could hear the sirens singing, which meant they were probably in the water main.

Well, he wasn't the only one who heard them. Most accidents happen in the home, but he guessed the number of Harperton toes stuck in the tub drain, fingers down the garbage disposal, and drownings in the toilet were above the national average. And he supposed when discussing them no one admitted hearing women harmonizing in the pipes.

He *could* say this little seaside town just breathed grace and intrigue, but no one cared to hear from Harperton's resident plumber and cranky old fart. He stuffed in his earplugs and went to work, smiling.

Funny how a little romance made people nervous.

INFILTRATION

IF YOU COULDN'T SEE THE GHOSTS YOU DIDN'T FEAR THEM.

Maggie did both. And she dreaded the rain, because that's when they got you.

She was racing for the house when the first drops hit, and cursed the ghost on the roof. In mid-stride she grabbed a brick from the rock garden and pitched it overhand. The spook vanished as the brick passed through it, probably out of sarcasm.

Go figure, she thought, and ran inside.

The coroner listed the cause of her death as *heart attack*. He saw nothing strange except that her hair was wet when they carried her in—she'd died sitting in a chair under a leaky ceiling.

The beat cop checked it out anyway. The rain had leaked through an old shingle split by a brick thrown on the roof.

Go figure, he thought, and walked away.

BAITED

MERLE REELED IN ANOTHER TROUT. His brother Bernie had never told him this river was so peaceful. The son-of-a-bitch had always told him it was the best fishing in ten counties, though.

It wasn't enough Bernie was Mom's favourite, the one who made it to Dad's bedside before he died, an all-around great guy—he just *had* to be a champion fly caster. Fishing was the only thing Merle really loved, and he'd spent sixty years hearing Bernie did it better.

He'd never told anyone how to find this place, but at the end he'd given his secret up to Merle. And that was as it should be, Merle thought. Blood was thicker than water, after all.

He baited the hook again. There was still a piece of Bernie's fingernail on the lure, but, hungry as the fish were, he didn't think they'd mind.

ACOUSTIC

EVERY SEASHELL CONTAINS A SOUL.

Listen.

That's not the ocean you hear inside. It's the whisper of a life-that-used-to-be. Place the shell in the sunshine; the dead have been a long time cold. Polish it softly; they've gone long without a gentle touch. If your child gathers it as a keepsake, understand—they want to be remembered.

Just listen. They've waited a long time to be heard.

LETHE

EVIE THINKS THE WINTER'S BEEN TOO LONG. She can't remember a time when she wasn't chilled, when she didn't wish for spring, when frost like old lace didn't silver the windows.

Evie can't remember a lot of things.

This same hard frost she finds so lovely has cracked her well pipe, heaved her cellar wall—and diverted the river Lethe. For a week now this dark water has been leaking through the fissures, along with things that keep forgetting they're damned. Evie's shoes are perpetually damp, and her tea tastes funny. The damage to the basement is grim. The smell is even worse.

She keeps meaning to get that fixed.

DIVINED

EGAN WAS A DOWSER WHO LOVED HIS WORK, growing willows with a tenderness he'd never shown his wife. Rianne lived with his indifference.

But his vanity frayed her nerves.

"I'm the best because I have faith in myself," he said once too often. "I could find puddles in the Kalahari."

Rianne, who knew he *was* that good, said, "Then why haven't you?"

Egan was stunned: how dare she speak to him this way? That day he took a willow branch into the desert, vowing to find water—and put Rianne in her place.

Egan's remains were found years later, the dried branch still twisted through his ribs. It had found the only water in a hundred miles, just as he'd promised.

At his wake a friend said, "You know, I don't think anyone could've predicted this."

Rianne lowered her eyes modestly and said, "Indeed."

SOLACE

Time travel and grief, Alyssa thought. Both were exacting. You always knew where you were going and what you mourned. Her hand parted the rain like beads. She stepped into the field and looked for the house. Right on target: it was here Seth's heart had given out.

A bolt of lightning cracked nearby. She saw the house and sprinted for it. The child inside was alone and screaming, her parents off somewhere partying. Alyssa had to find her fast.

And say what?

Starting tonight, storms will terrify you? Forty years from now you'll watch your husband die in the rain because you're too scared to go to him?

She stumbled through the door towards the child she'd been: one who didn't know a broken heart was worse than this. Alyssa gathered her close, and the screams became sobs.

"It's okay," she whispered. "You're fine. Shhh—it's only the rain."

THE IMAGE BREAKERS

John Park

TRAVELLING ON FOOT, the neohominid named Katana descended the mountain passes towards the site of the landing. She had spent two days in the mountains, heading for the ship she had seen arrive from beyond the moon. The rest of her praetorian unit had become unfit to serve, and she had left them in the disabled time vault. She could not remember having been alone for so long since her first training.

She did not know this world, this ruined future the time vault had released her into. Here she had no one in authority to guard, and therefore no purpose. Though she might have cursed those who had built into her such a need to serve, she knew that cursing them would not remove the hunger they had given her. She would find the arrivals, whoever they were. If they were human, she would offer her services. Then, if she was accepted, she might feel free to curse.

At the mouth of a valley, a crippled fighting machine challenged her in a language she struggled to understand. After she failed to answer satisfactorily, it fired on her. She leapt away from the blast and destroyed the armoured turret with a shot from her rifle. When she found no signs of human life in the wreck, she went on.

The remains of a road wound out of the valley. Stone columns lined either side. Some had fallen and were wreathed in briars. Each was topped by a white stone cage curved like a tulip bloom, and inside each bloom lay the remains of a human skeleton. A crow flapped to one of the standing columns, bearing food to its young. It turned and croaked at her as she jogged past.

ON THE THIRD DAY, SHE CAME TO AN ESTUARY. She pulled down her helmet visor and adjusted the lenses to scan the far shore. Low cliffs ended in a headland surmounted by a white column. Her direction-finder for the landing pointed ten degrees inland of the column.

She was on the crest of a sand dune covered with coarse grass. Along the shore she counted eight pieces of driftwood, none much bigger than her arm.

She weighed the burden of her armour and weapons against the effort and time needed to assemble a raft and against the hunger that drove her. Behind her, the sun was setting, and now it seemed she saw thin trails of smoke rising from the headland. The prospect of finding humans made the decision for her. She ran down the dune and plunged into the waves.

Once, when it seemed she was alone in an endless night and an infinite ocean, she heaved her face clear. She rested, treading water in near darkness, and an icy full moon peered down at her—the strange moon of this disjointed age.

Memories from her march rose in her mind. A platoon of sprawling human skeletons, three with firearms, the rest with spears or hatchets. A vixen leading her cubs across the rusted hillslope of a fallen air freighter.

Water forced itself into Katana's throat. She flailed back to the surface, choked and coughed until she could breathe, and swam again.

Finally her feet touched bottom.

The column on the headland gleamed in the moonlight. It was a statue, a white figure in armour, staring inland, its mouth opened to cry out.

She made one last effort and surged onto the rocky beach, whispering commands and flashing hand signals to the rest of her unit, until she remembered she was alone.

The moon seemed to fill half the sky with its brightness. It began to move in slow, wide circles, and she realized she was shivering, about to fall.

She found a cave, hidden from both the moon and the statue. Numbly she went through her weapons check, cleaned her armour, set sensors. She turned around three times, invoking her sentinel mode, curled up on the stones, and slept.

She thought she heard cries of mourning and opened her eyes to find the cave white with moonlight. She had begun to reach for someone near her, perhaps Athamè, her lover, who was dead.

The waves lapped and whispered outside. Minutely, the moonlight shifted over pebbles on the cave floor. Her sensors were undisturbed. With a familiar effort she stilled her mind and slept again.

At dawn two men attacked her. Wakened by her reflexes, even before the sensors trilled, she was waiting as they stepped into the cave. The first pointed some kind of rifle at her face. She leapt as he fired and took the shock on her chest armour, then plucked the weapon away and broke his arm. The second swung a heavy sword. She slipped past it, knocked it to the ground, then threw him on his back and held him, her claws just piercing the skin of his throat.

Her armour smelled scorched, and she could feel heat on her breasts.

"Look at me," she said. "Do you understand what I say?"

One after another they jerked their heads, which she took as an acknowledgment.

"Had I wished it," she rasped, "you would both be dead now. Tell me where you come from and why you attacked me."

The two glanced at each other, then at her. The one she was holding shook his head. Neither spoke.

"You are alone," she said. "You carry weapons but no packs; your gear is clean. Therefore you have a base nearby. Who commands you?"

She moved her hand from the man's throat, extended her claws, and flexed her fingers in front of his eyes. She bared her fangs. "I strongly advise you to tell me."

"Leave him alone!" The one with the broken arm tried to sit up, his lips white. "What are you? They told us their women didn't fight."

"In your terms, I am not a woman—as you can surely see." She paused. "But I'm not from the spacecraft, if that's what you meant."

"Then what are you?"

"My questions first," she said, then considered. "Better: I'll help your friend splint your arm, and the two of you will take me to whoever sent you."

WITH HER RIFLE LEVELED, Katana followed them along the beach. They climbed a rough path up the cliff and reached a causeway surfaced with stone slabs. Deep ruts had been worn in it, leading to the headland and the statue. To her left, the land was only about five metres below the level of the causeway. Among stands of willow and oak were pastures and fields of crops separated by hedgerows. Lambs nuzzled ewes. A newborn calf stumbled to its feet.

I almost drowned, she thought, *coming here. I almost gave up.*

Ahead, the causeway was joined by a ramp leading up from the fields, and the widened path climbed to the headland. Beyond a grey stone wall with an iron gate Katana could see the roofs and upper storeys of buildings apparently grouped around the statue. White and gleaming in the morning light it gazed over her head, silently crying out towards the shore.

Boats were drawn up on the beach below. Two men coiling fishing lines stood up and watched her. One shouted. Ahead of Katana the gate slid open and half a dozen men in leather uniforms started forward, carrying pikes and one rifle. They stumbled to a halt when they got a good look at Katana.

She unslung the weapons she had taken from her prisoners and tossed them at the guards' feet. "I'm returning these two fat fish alive," she said. "In return I want food and information. Bring me someone in authority."

The guards hesitated and looked at each other. Katana raised her rifle and, on minimum power, blasted a handful of stone from the top of their wall. "I come in peace," she said. "Don't test my patience."

One of the guards ran back inside the gate. After a while, a white-bearded old man in a shabby grey robe appeared in the gateway. He was holding a partly eaten chicken leg. He stopped short and stared at her, then swallowed and wiped his mouth. He turned to the guards and Katana's former prisoners and held a whispered discussion. The injured man was led inside.

The old man took a step forward and jabbed the chicken leg at Katana. "Creature," he said in a scratchy baritone, "I am Nestor, the appointed elder and chief servant of the Basilids. You injured those men."

"I defended myself," she said, and found herself adding: "That's what I was made to do—defend myself and the ones I serve. I am praetorian Katana."

"Wait." Nestor turned and spoke to the other man again. He gnawed at the chicken bone, peering at Katana, while they replied. Finally he returned to her.

"It seems they felt we needed a hostage," he told her. "They would not have harmed you, if you hadn't startled them, but they'll be more careful in future. We do not normally greet visitors this way." He chewed and swallowed. "On the other hand, none of our visitors came brandishing high-power weaponry—until recently. You claim you're not from the spacecraft. Should I believe you?"

"I'm travelling alone," Katana said. "And I gather their females do not bear arms. If that's not enough, believe what you want."

Nestor regarded her without speaking. She grew aware of sounds inside the wall: doors opening, running feet slowing to a halt, the whispers of a crowd gathering, listening. And, coming from one of those opened doors, metallic-sounding voices that chanted and were echoed by the voices of children. Above her, a seabird screamed like a creature in fear.

Katana tensed, then put up her rifle and slung it over her shoulder. "I should not have fired," she told him. "If you wish, I'll leave and go on my way."

"You said you were created to serve," Nestor said, and frowned. "If you're not from the ship, what brings you here now?"

"I saw it land, and I came to find it." Once again she found herself adding more than she had intended: "This is a strange world to me. It has already cost me much, and I haven't found a community I can join and serve." She shook her head. "What do you know about the ones in the ship? Are they human?"

"Human enough," Nestor said slowly. "At least in appearance. Some of them came to us in small flying craft. They said their ship had landed more than a day's march away. . . . You are a guardian, a protector of some kind? And you want a community to serve?"

"I need to protect—I must . . ." She shook her head. "Where are they now, the ones who visited you?"

"Back at their ship, considering their next moves, I imagine. It seems they came with a purpose—returned from the stars, they said—and we are not congenial to them, or their purpose." He chewed on the bone, looked at it thoughtfully, then tossed it away. "You must have had a difficult journey. Let me offer you our hospitality."

She lifted her hands. "I should move on."

"One night's stay. While you rest and think. Come in. Let us show you around."

The guards stood aside, and Katana followed him through the gate. "Enthusiastic, our militia," Nestor said in an undertone. "But we've lost our military traditions. They really need someone with experience to lead and train them."

Among the low buildings the statue on its dais stood like a tree among weeds. The children were still chanting, and Katana realized that the smell of roasting meat had been in her nostrils for some time.

She drew a breath and turned to Nestor. "To lead and train them? One night's stay, you said. And I haven't agreed."

"But you have come inside," he said with a smile, and waved her forward. "You're travelling alone, you said? Have you come very far?"

"Yes. A long way in time as well as distance." She explained about the malfunctioning time vault that had held her in stasis until a few weeks earlier. "I don't know how long we were trapped. Everything here is strange. I had to leave the others." She hesitated. "It would help me if you could tell me something of your history. What is the statue? It seems very important."

"Of course. We are the servants of the Basilid, the Prince."

"Servants? You mean you worship it?"

"We serve his memory and try to preserve his values. In turn it he guides us and watches over us. Our ancestors gathered here when this summit was still an island—before the moon was moved to adjust the tides. When the sea began to fall, our forefathers built the causeway." He peered at her. "You really haven't heard of any of this—of us?"

"No. How long have you been here?" she asked, thinking of the rutted causeway.

"Much longer than any actual memories go back. Unfortunately we've lost many of the records of our earliest days."

They crossed a square of stone flags and entered a building ornamented with white columns. Nestor led her to an inner chamber where he called to a small, dark young woman wearing a brown tunic and leggings.

"Anis. This is Praetorian Katana. She will be our guest; please get her some food and drink and a place to sleep, and introduce her to our records."

The woman picked up a very small child, started to put it in a sling over her shoulders. Then she looked at Katana and stared. Her face paled, and she handed the child to another woman, whispering something. Unfamiliar with very small human offspring, Katana was struck by the child's large head with its fine, dark hair and wide eyes, by the glimpse of pink gums in the toothless mouth.

Slowly the woman came forward.

"Anis?" said Katana. "I will not harm you if you are honest with me. You have no need to fear." She found herself oddly uncomfortable and added, "I would not harm your child."

Anis turned quickly and led her outside to a long low building. "Our guest house." There she showed Katana to a small white-walled apartment and demonstrated how to command the doorlock. Katana checked the window, the furniture, and the plumbing. Anis showed her how to illuminate the room from panels in the wall. Katana put her pack in a closet, considered, then unclipped her helmet, removed the power cell from her rifle, and placed weapon and helmet on the top shelf over her pack. "The rest of my armour stays with me," she told Anis. "We have traditions too."

"You want to study our history?" Anis asked timidly.

"Certainly. But first I need sustenance. Show me where I can eat, and I need not trouble you again. I can eat most human food." She added, embarrassed: "I have not eaten fully for four days."

KATANA WASHED AND ATE IN THE ROOM SHE HAD BEEN GIVEN. With the door locked, she pulled off her armour and examined the breastplate where the man's weapon had burned it. The inner layer was still smooth and white, undamaged. The outer carapace had been partially ablated. She wiped away the blackened residue, then cleaned and anointed the burn. At its centre, the underlying fibres were exposed, glistening, but seemed mostly intact. It would take the armour about a day to fully regenerate.

She fastened the breastplate on again and made her way to the building Anis had shown her.

In the main chamber, a dozen children were seated, facing what Katana recognized as a kind of deepscreen. Blurred images moved in it. From where Katana stood, they were almost indecipherable among sudden shafts of darkness and bands of mist. The accompanying sound was better preserved, but still all she could be sure of was the regular refrain: "The blood of the Basilids is not to be shed." The children echoed this each time it sounded.

The walls should be white, Katana thought suddenly. Then, looking at the children, who were apparently engrossed in the display: *Why are they so old?* She exhaled harshly, then glanced down and retracted her claws.

In a back room, Katana found the material Anis had picked out for her: scrolls, memory cells, bound volumes. She listened to speeches, songs, lectures, dramas, and squinted at hazy images, both flat and solid. But the chaos of names and events was impenetrable. She needed a guide.

Finally she put back the scrolls, turned off the display units, and went outside.

It was late afternoon. Under a grey sky, wind was driving waves against the beach and shaking the trees on the other side of the causeway.

At Katana's feet, steps cut into the cliff went down to the rocky beach. And there, almost below her, Anis sat, apparently examining rubble that had fallen from the cliff. A couple of paces away, her baby lay sleeping, swaddled in a thick brown blanket.

Katana descended the steps and approached.

Anis looked up, and her eyes widened. She shifted between Katana and the child. Katana stopped and knelt a few steps away.

"I didn't mean to interrupt you," she said. "Continue what you were doing. Please."

"I'm looking for fossils," Anis said after a moment. She held up a small silver instrument like a broad-headed hammer. "The bottom of the cliff is much older than the causeway. It erodes and the rock falls here. Sometimes it contains pieces of life's past." She picked up a grey slab and peered at it from different angles.

"And you're the keeper of the past."

The infant stirred and blinked; a dark wisp of hair was tugged by the wind.

"For another couple of days," said Anis. "I won't have much time after the elevation."

"I don't understand."

"Nestor didn't tell you? I've been accepted into the Elect. The ceremony is the morning after next. I'll be taking him too. Derran. It's a great honour."

Katana looked at the baby, sleeping again.

"You'll be serving the statue, the Prince?" she asked. "And your boy—tomorrow will decide his life, all his life?"

Anis nodded. "We're lucky to be chosen."

Katana listened to the waves rustling up the beach behind her, chirping among the gravel, sighing back towards the sea. Derran stirred again, blinked and rubbed tiny fists against his eyes, then yawned and went back to sleep.

White walls, Katana thought again, uneasily. "He's lucky he'll have his mother with him," she said at last.

The waves sounded in the silence between them until Anis said, "Sometimes in the elevation, the ceremony, the Prince speaks. I'm hoping he will for us. It would be a wonderful omen."

Katana looked at her. "It speaks? The statue speaks? You've seen this?"

Anis bent over another slab of rock. "I have a memory from when I was very young. It might have been at another elevation. The Prince looked at me and cried out. Or maybe I dreamt it. There's something in the records, but it's not clear. Nestor might be able to tell you what happened exactly."

"Well, actually, I came to you because you know the records. I couldn't make sense of what you left for me. I need something simpler at first, an overview, less detail." She flexed her claws in frustration. "I wondered if you could help me yourself. Tell me about the statue, for instance—where it came from."

"Just a moment." Anis lifted the rock and squinted along its surface, then placed the silver tool against one edge. There was a sharp buzz, and the rock split. The top layer slid to the ground. Derran blinked and gurgled, waved fists like clusters of pink flowerbuds. In the rock Anis held was a dark twisted mass, the hard residue of a life. "Good," she muttered. "I've been looking for you." She twisted the handle of the tool and drew it along the rock. Stone crumbled to fragments around the fossil and fell away.

"The Prince," she said, leaning forward to blow dust from the fossil. "The earliest records are lost—the eyewitness reports. But he was a great leader. He saved the world from ruin. He changed the climate, moved the moon, held back the sea. And now he watches over us here, and sometimes he intervenes, guides us. Usually he sleeps, but, when a real threat appears, he'll wake and return, and then be with us forever." She caught Katana's look and spread her hands defensively. "That's what the records tell us."

She turned and peered at the sun, a dull silvery disc in the clouds. "It's time we went in." She packed her fossils one by one into a bag that stiffened around them, then swung Derran onto her back.

Katana followed them, the child's oddly large eyes gazing at her in apparent fascination.

Katana found herself accompanying Anis to a building beside the records centre. "I'd like to see your fossil collection," she said when Anis stopped at the door.

"Certainly. Let's meet tomorrow." When Katana did not move, she added, "This is our home. I have other things to do now."

"Of course." Katana shuffled back a pace.

Watching her, Anis said, "I couldn't help noticing the way you keep looking. . . . Have you lost someone recently? A child?"

Katana jerked her head at Anis. "I have mourned him. Not a child. I am on active duty." She snapped her teeth. "Children are only for those unable to serve."

Anis flinched and backed away from her. Then she whispered, "That's so sad," and left Katana staring.

THAT EVENING, Katana found herself crouched on the end of her bed, in the dimness of an unlighted room, listening.

The sounds of sea and wind reached her ears. Children shouted in some game and were called away and quieted. There were footsteps, a called greeting, muffled conversations, chanting. Piercingly a baby wept and was comforted. Katana pictured Anis and her son.

She was alone, alone in a white room, and for more years than she could count, she had not been alone. Her lover was dead, her companions lost.

She realized she had found out nothing about the political alliances, military resources, or weaponry of the world she was trying to join.

Her muscles had begun to shake, minutely and rapidly, like the frame of a beaten drum. Her joints ached as though her body was trying to tear itself apart. She listened to a mother murmur to her frightened child, and the shaking continued.

THE NEXT MORNING she made her way back to the records chamber. She had slept badly.

Anis was waiting with Derran. She started leading Katana through their history, with Katana struggling to remember names and occasions, trying to judge where events she remembered from her own time might fall in this strange narrative.

"I know that name," she said at one point. "People were still recovering from his oppressions a generation later."

"No. That must be a different ruler," Anis said. "The Liberator—he was one of the Basilids' inspirations. We still venerate him."

"I'm sure of the name," Katana replied, then added placatingly, "But perhaps you found out things about him we'd forgotten."

"Perhaps. Was that something you learned as—when you were young?"

"No, it was part of our final preparation, it came later." She stopped, but Anis was waiting for her to say more; so after a moment Katana went on. "In infancy we were not treated like human offspring. We are not human, and we had to be shaped—our minds as much as our bodies—to fit in among humans." She paused, eyes narrowed, remembering. "Our handlers evidently found it an arduous task." She jerked her head. "Let's return to the document."

Later she watched groups of children sitting in classes listening to ancient recordings, marching, playing games with sticks and inflated balls.

"We educate some of the locals from the mainland as well as our own few," Nestor told her. "In these times, we have an overriding obligation. We must keep the past alive, to serve a failing age. We are the guardians of an era when great men could become gods. We hold open the way for such a one to return and lead us back to greatness. That's why we insist on the recordings—we want to speak the language of the ancestors, to understand them when he brings them back."

In the afternoon Katana watched Nestor stand on a dais at the statue's base. He heard disputes and gave judgements, sometimes going to the statue and kneeling to press his forehead against its base before pronouncing. He blessed a man and his pregnant wife, asked for a bountiful crop on a wheat field, and prohibited the use of some kind of automated cultivator.

Katana noted all this, and then watched as the crowds filed back along the causeway to the mainland. She did not know why she was staying behind.

Nestor came down from the dais. "Anis is with her child," he told her, "meditating in for tomorrow's elevation. You said you'd stay for that."

Katana looked across the woodland towards the hills and the hidden spacecraft.

"Yes," she said quietly, "I'll stay for that."

THAT NIGHT IN THE MOONLIGHT she strode across the square. The community was asleep; even the guards at the gate were dozing. But, above her, the statue gazed at the land, rigidly alert. She broke into a run, forcing herself into fast laps around the square, around the buildings. The guards stirred and watched her uncertainly. She ignored them and drove herself harder.

As she ran, the moon orbited the head of the statue, was eclipsed by walls and roofs. The estuary she had crossed glimmered, then the open sea, then the cultivated polder with its clumps of trees, and the dark hills beyond. Out there the spacecraft and its crew waited. Katana ran on through a repeating maze of buildings, moon and water, land and air, under the fixed white gaze of the statue.

Exhausted, she stopped, braced her hands against the base of the statue, let her breathing slow, and began to stretch her leg muscles. Too much stress on her body, too little care.

The stone felt strange under her hands. It was smooth and warm and seemed to throb. The ground beside it was ordinary synthetic stone, cold and gritty, stained and cracked with age. She peered more closely. There was a narrow gap between the synthetic stone steps and the dais, as though the statue had been placed in a socket that didn't fit perfectly.

She rapped the dais with her talons, then put her ear to it and listened.

She became aware that someone was observing her; she stood up.

"I have my age to excuse sleeplessness," said Nestor. "But I would have thought you needed rest, after your journey. Did you hear anything from the Prince, just now?"

"I heard the sea and the wind," she said. "Perhaps something more. The statue is hollow, isn't it?"

"Perhaps. There are several mysteries about it. Is it important to you, what the statue holds? Is that why you can't sleep?"

"I can't sleep," she said, "because I don't understand this world or my place in it."

"You could have eaten with us this evening and stayed for the hymns instead of retiring to your room. Give us a chance, and we will do our best to make you welcome."

She shook her head. "I'm not sure. . . . I don't know if I can stay with you."

Nestor said nothing.

"I came to find the ones from space. I didn't expect—I didn't know—"

She was stammering, unsure of what she was trying to say, or why she should be revealing such weakness to an old human male she barely knew. She turned away.

"Praetorian Katana," he said, "you agreed to say until Anis's elevation. I hope you will keep your word and see more of what kind of community we are. But, tonight, I think you should sleep."

"I will," she said, "when I'm ready," and went pounding around the buildings again.

THE NEXT MORNING, while seabirds shrieked and croaked and the first arc of sun sent shimmers of crimson across the grey water, Katana watched the acolytes gather beneath the statue. They were dressed in shabby, patched robes she had not seen before. Some of the crowd had walked over the causeway before dawn.

Nestor arrived and made a short speech extolling the Basilids and their legacy of peace and order, which his acolytes strove to preserve.

Then Anis emerged with Derran in her arms and climbed the steps to the base of the statue. She wore a flowing yellow gown. A corroded metal harness held a complicated device of metal coils and fins to her back.

The birds had fallen silent. From somewhere out of sight, a drum tapped rhythmically, a flute sounded long low notes.

Nestor spoke a few more words, a hidden trumpet called three rising tones, the device on Anis's back hummed, and Anis and her child lifted into the air.

Just above head-height, the device gave a sudden grating whine and Anis stopped and swayed in the wind. The crowd hissed, but the whine had already quieted. Anis and her child ascended smoothly to the statue's head.

Anis took a circlet of flowers, almost invisibly small from where Katana stood, and placed it on the brow of the statue. Then she lowered until she was level with the open mouth. She gripped one upper incisor and carried her child inside, crouching between the jaws.

The drum made a crescendo, the trumpet blared, the flute shrieked. Then everything fell silent. Katana sensed the crowd had stopped breathing. The ultimate test of acceptance, she thought, to enter that white stone cave willingly; and she wondered if those jaws had ever been known to close. She was holding her own breath, she realized, and made herself exhale.

She had counted slowly to twelve when Anis and Derran came out of the mouth and settled slowly to earth.

The crowd palpably relaxed. Anis knelt before the statue, whispering, then rose and backed away before turning to face the crowd. Her face was radiant.

Katana wondered why the crowd was still silent, then she realized this would be when the statue spoke if it was going to.

Waves rustled on the beach below her. A bird screamed. Derran stirred sleepily, stretched out an arm.

From inland, beyond the statue, came another sound. Katana guessed what it was; then others in the crowd began stirring, peering at the sky.

With a whining roar, three broad-winged craft appeared over the woodland and drove towards them. Their shadows passed over the crowd as the craft circled the statue, then hovered and landed in the square. The acolytes pressed back from them but did not flee. Caught up among males a head taller than her and half her strength, Katana wormed to where she could see, but decided to remain inconspicuous.

A door opened in each craft. Ramps lowered, and figures in black and silver marched out. Helmets and visors hid their faces. Each guard carried a rifle; Katana counted thirty-two. From the centre vehicle a single man then strode down. He was small and slim, dressed a pale grey, hooded robe. She focused on his face: swarthy, dark-eyed under a single thick brow. He carried a silver rod in his right hand. As he reached the foot of the ramp he gestured with it, and the guards formed up in an arc facing the statue.

This was display of force, Katana judged, rather than a demonstration of military expertise. They were daring anyone to intervene.

The officer marched the far end of his arc of men and pointed his wand at the statue. The guards levelled their rifles at it.

The man faced Nestor across the square. "This representation of our persecutor has been proscribed," he said in a precise but amplified voice. "You are here to observe its destruction."

Nestor shook his head, a response Katana was not sure the newcomer understood. Nestor began to walk towards the steps, arms outspread as though he meant to shield the stone with his body.

The robed man paused for a moment, then said to Nestor's back, "I am not impressed by your offer of self-sacrifice. I have a task to complete. I should prefer it not to involve bloodshed. But if blood must be shed, I shall shed it."

Nestor kept walking.

Again the other waited briefly; then he lifted his wand to eye level and pointed it at Nestor. There was a sharp buzz and a flash. Just short of the bottom step, Nestor cried out and pitched forward. He writhed, his face against the stone. His legs twitched and spasmed, like a broken insect.

With Derran strapped her back, Anis ran to him.

Katana noted where the guards' rifles were aimed, watched Anis struggling to get him to his feet, then shoved her way through the crowd and sprinted to the steps.

She pushed Anis aside and slung Nestor over her shoulders. "Get your child away from this!"

They ran to the side.

The robed man waited a moment longer, then gestured with his wand. The guards fired.

The air cracked and thundered. Shouting, the crowd started to back away; some started to run. The statue seethed with crimson and purple flashes.

The robed man barked a command, and the firing stopped. A thin haze drifted away, and the statue re-emerged. Red-hot patches blurred and faded. The figure itself, white and impassive, remained unmarked.

The robed man gestured and barked more commands. On the three shuttles, weapons pods rotated towards the statue. The guards aimed again.

Again the air roared. This time the steps at the base of the statue glowed white and shattered like glass. Men screamed as fragments struck them. Grey smoke boiled up.

And the statue moved.

The raised arm lowered, the head turned, a knee bent.

Ponderously the statue stepped free of its ruined plinth. It was like watching a great tree walk or a cloud come to life. It stepped past Katana and strode towards the guards, who were still firing. As it went, its movements became faster and more fluid. It bent forward, arms swinging. The robed man shouted, and the guards fell back. One was caught by a stone hand, and crumpled redly.

The statue went on, turned towards the shuttles.

The leader shouted more urgently, and the guards funneled back into their three craft. Ramps still retracting, the shuttles lifted away from the statue's hands.

The craft made a half-circle, gaining altitude, and flew back the way they had come.

The statue turned as if to watch them, then started towards the nearest building. It punched one arm through the side wall, sent rubble flying, then swung towards the causeway. It smashed through the gate and went lurching off into the woodland.

AFTERNOON CLOUDS DRIFTED ACROSS THE SUN. Katana paced by the breach in the wall, then drew a breath and waited for some of the chaos to subside. Militia with vacant eyes and wet cheeks were trying to organize teams to shift the rubble of the smashed building. *Hopeless*, she thought. *They have no idea what to do.* She could collect her pack and go. She paced again. A family ran past her, then stopped in the ruined gateway and stared at the familiar land-scape as though it had become monstrous. A child's wailing sawed at her nerves. The statue was nowhere to be seen. *Their world has turned against them, and they're helpless.*

A stone pillar had fallen into the damaged building. She watched three men fumbling to work it clear. Finally she cursed and went over. She moved two men to the other end of the pillar, wedged a rock under it, and had the third man wedge in more rocks as she helped the others lever it up.

When they seemed to understand what they were doing, she went into the building where the injured were being treated. Neither Anis nor her baby was there.

Nestor was, pale-faced but conscious, lying on a pad of blankets. He blinked and peered at her, started to point at something, then let his hand fall back and closed his eyes. Katana thought he had forgotten she was there, but then he whispered, "Thank you for helping just then."

She shook her head. "It seems your icon does not appreciate your genera-tions of loyalty."

His eyes opened. Then he looked away from her. "Yes, it appears so."

She gave a bitter, barking laugh. "Of course, we might be misinterpreting his actions. Hardly anyone was actually killed, after all."

He said nothing.

"What will you do now?" she asked.

He peered about vaguely, his mouth working. "Keep watch, I suppose," he said finally. "I'll order the masons to begin the repairs. We'll rebuild. Soon." He swallowed and looked at her with a faint smile. "It seems we may have more need of your protection than we thought."

"Yes it does, doesn't it?" Katana took a step away from him, came back, shook her head. "I can't provide it, though. I can't stay with you."

His chin lifted, his eyes focused. He waited for her to go on.

"I am made to serve authority," she said: "the strong, the winners. They are the ones who have to get my protection and obedience."

He nodded, still watching her. "You'll go to the visitors."

She leaned over him, baring her teeth. "I have less choice in this than you had in serving your stone master." She snarled at him. "We cannot undertake to serve the weak."

Nestor sighed and raised himself on one elbow. "If you're waiting for me to dissuade you—to coerce you into staying—I must disappoint you. You've cho-sen. I'm sure any change now would only increase your unhappiness with us."

Katana swallowed and drew a long breath. "And we couldn't have that, could we?" she whispered. "We couldn't have that." She went to collect her rifle and pack.

THE FOLLOWING DAWN, the wind was rising and a wall of cloud masked the sun. Katana judged she was less than half a day's march from the spacecraft. Just as the sun's scarlet edge broke clear of the cloud, one of the shuttles appeared ahead of her. It circled and landed. Weapons focused on her, and an armed officer waved her aboard. In the loading bay she permitted her own weapons and helmet to be taken. A few moments later a bright image of the robed guards officer appeared seated before her.

She identified herself, and he introduced himself as Hierocrat Zehn. "If you come as an emissary," he began, "I must tell you we are reconsidering how to deal with the image of the persecutor and its acolytes."

"No," she said. "I come to offer my services."

"Indeed." Zehn squinted at her and then at something she could not see. "And what services might they be?"

"I am trained to guard and protect. I am effective against most non-mechanical weaponry and capable of opposing light mechanized armour."

Again he looked away from her. "I have the analysis of your weaponry. I believe you. But we don't get many recruits offering themselves like this. Why should I trust you?"

She jerked her head. "The way I am made, I have little choice."

"Interesting." This time he stared at his invisible data source for several heartbeats. Finally he smiled. "We found some records a couple of days ago. It seems you should be extinct, but here you are. And what an ambitious project you all were. They thought they could manipulate anything—maternal obligations, pack instinct—with hardly any crippling conflicts at all." He peered at her. "So, then, you will obey. . . ?"

"Any command that does not endanger you or unnecessarily endanger me."

"And yet you're reluctant," he said. "You understand I would not command you myself. I would merely make manifest a Will that you would find ineluctable if you recognized its existence and its purpose."

"I don't care about your beliefs," she said. "I don't understand them; I don't imagine I would like them. But I'm not required to."

He nodded. "The truth has no obligation to be pleasant or easy to accept. It is merely true. And once recognized, it is inescapable." Zehn leaned forward a little, fixing his gaze on her. "I accept your doubts. You will pay a price, but so do we all. Don't think we undertook this task lightly. Our ships are wonderful, but the decision to return and reclaim our home cost us almost everything. We spent a week after launch preparing ourselves, while we watched our world shrink to the size of this fingernail. Then we entered the chambers and slept. It seemed no more than a long night's slumber, but when we awoke, our world, our cities, our rivers and mountains, our families, our shrines—all were aeons behind us. Many of them will be dust by now; all will be utterly changed. And none of us will see them again. Such is the Will," he said. "Great is the Will."

He paused and regarded her. "You think you don't like us, but you must have seen the remains of traitors caged on stone pillars and left to starve and rot."

"I've seen something of the kind, though it wasn't recent. I don't know who was responsible."

"It might easily have been your friends, the statue-worshippers. The practice was traditional for some time, and quite widespread. If you look, you may find it still happens."

She said nothing.

"Katana, the Will moves in you, as it does in all creatures and all things. That it shows so clearly and strongly in you, by opposing your own desires, marks you as a chosen one. I'm sure we shall be honoured by your service. Your first task—consider it a demonstration of commitment, if you wish—is to eliminate the last of that misguided, malicious sect."

Katana snapped to attention, teeth clenched, breath held. Then she stepped back, bowing.

"As you wish."

SHE FOUND NESTOR had posted sentries at the head of the causeway. The moon was hidden in clouds. Thunder growled and rain began to patter. Her movements masked by the sounds, she crept to within an arm's length of a skinny, middle-aged man clutching a rifle as though it were a pitchfork. She considered how many ways she could kill him, then slipped past and headed for the gate.

Most of the rubble had been cleared from where the statue had broken through. Inside, fires burned on the steps of the empty plinth and in the square. Katana levelled her weapon and walked into the encampment.

Two teenaged guards cried out and froze against the wall. A woman gasped and dropped a cup she was bringing to a child. People backed away from her, staring, rain dripping over their eyes. Under the eaves of the hall of records, Nestor lay on a palette beside one of the fires. He blinked and started to push himself up, but fell back and watched her approach.

Katana stopped in front of him. "You're a feeble, narrow-minded old man. This community is a rotting, stagnant relic. You have no claims on me. Understand? No claims whatsoever." She was shivering.

Nestor gazed at her, then gestured at the palette, inviting her to sit beside him. Rain spattered on stone, hissed among the leaves below the causeway. Thunder rumbled again. When it faded, he asked quietly, "Why have you come back?"

She remained standing, breathing heavily. "To tell you—you must go."

He looked quickly past her at the darkness over the mainland. For the first time he looked apprehensive. "Gather up everything and leave? Why?"

"I have accepted orders to destroy you all."

His gaze fixed on her again. He drew a deep breath, watching her without blinking. Finally he nodded. "And you could do that, by yourself?"

"Given my armour and weapons, quite easily."

"Then, I repeat, why are you here?"

"I don't know!" She took a step forward, her head lowered, her shoulders hunched. She whispered, "I find—I prefer not to carry out those orders." Sheltered by the eaves, she still felt as though the rain were lashing her body.

"Then leave the visitors. Join us."

She snapped her teeth, lowered her head further. "Out of the question," she whispered, and shook the rifle helplessly. Lightning glared, was followed by an explosive crack. The downpour increased.

"But you are willing to deceive them?" Nestor asked. "You'll tell them— what?—that we defeated you, you couldn't find us, or you really did slaughter us all, and hid the bodies in the water? I hope you can be more convincing than you seem now."

Katana ground her teeth and said nothing. Her hair bristled.

"Or will you tell them the truth—that you violated your orders and we are still alive?" He looked at her and shook his head. "If you go back to them, what have you achieved?"

She jerked forward and snarled, "You'll have time to hide!"

"And you?"

She hissed, then drew a breath and looked down. She retracted her claws, lowered the rifle. "I have very little control over that," she whispered. For a moment the firelight dazzled her. The rain sounded like a river.

On the causeway, someone yelled.

A white stone arm swung down out of the darkness. Bricks and plaster crashed around Katana. Acolytes screamed and fled. The white body swept away the corner of the building and strode out of sight. Nestor was unharmed, staring into the dark, but a baby was shrieking. The whole side of the building looked about to collapse. Katana ran inside, saw the child at the entrance to an inner room and threw herself over him as the timbers fell.

Then she found she could not lever the beams from her body and still shield the baby from the weight. She choked on fumes from burning wood and plastic, but dragged air into her lungs and bellowed for help.

Some of the weight was lifted off her.

Holding the child under her body with one arm, she crawled out. Awkwardly she stood, held him in front of her. His face was scarlet and crumpled with weeping. She traced his cheek with one finger, the claw rigidly retracted. Tiny fingers came up to grasp her own single one.

"Bless you for saving him."

Katana looked up. Anis was standing in front of her, small and terrified.

"You should not have left him alone," Katana said tightly.

"He was only across the room. The wall fell between us."

"*You should not have left him alone.*"

"I know. I'm sorry. I won't do it again. O—please, please don't take him."

Startled, Katana thrust Derran into his mother's arms. "I have no use for your children," she snapped. "I was checking for trauma. I told you, I'm not of the child-rearing caste; I am . . ."

Abruptly she turned her back.

Outside, three guards were peering through the rain towards the mainland. Lightning flickered, and she glimpsed the white figure flailing through the trees. Its head was thrown back, and she imagined its open mouth turned to the sky as though trying to roar.

She went back inside.

Nestor peered into the night and muttered to himself. Katana stalked to the edge of the firelight, peered into the night, came back. "I can't stay with you," she said, and spat. "You understand? If you stay here—I won't be able to defend you. You don't know who else might burn and smash what's left here. Burn and kill. If I try to help you, I'll change. I'll start to hate you. And then none of you will be safe from me. . . ." Nestor peered into the night. His mouth twitched. He said nothing. "Fool!" she cried. "You're a fattened pig, ignoring the open gate when the wolf is behind you. You could all die here. Here and now. Every one of you—your *children*."

He looked past her again, then shook his head. "It's not me you're angry with," he muttered. "You understand that, don't you?"

"That's enough," she cried. She unslung her rifle and blasted stone from the ceiling. "Hear me!" The shout filled her throat and burst from her. "I can see in the dark. After midnight, any of you still here, I hunt down and kill. Now leave. Take what you can carry and get out!"

NESTOR LEFT, BORNE ON A LITTER. He met her gaze briefly and then was carried away with his head bent and his eyes lowered. One of the last, Anis, carrying her baby, stared at Katana, who hissed and bared her teeth. "Don't presume on me. If I see you again, I'll kill you both."

The rain had stopped. Gaps opened in the cloud, and moonshadows fell across the square, and suddenly she was alone.

Katana opened her mouth to the moon and howled.

IN THE MOONLIGHT she began to tear off her armour. If she continued to live, she would have to find a new name. Her fingers were weak; they fumbled with the fastenings. And her eyes blurred. Even close to the fire she shivered. But the armour was dishonoured and had to be removed.

Then it lay beside her, like the remains of a giant mollusc. She held her helmet in her hands. From its visor, the moon stared into her eyes. She looked up at that distorted face and suddenly understood how it had changed. It had been rotated a quarter turn, so that much of what she now saw had been hidden, and what was familiar had been wrenched into a new perspective. They had twisted the moon's face as though they had wanted to break its neck.

She hurled the helmet across the forecourt. It hit the remains of the plinth and clattered onto the steps, a blank-faced parody of a skull. She snatched up the rifle and fired at it. A yellow flash flung the helmet into the air. Her second shot glanced off it in mid-flight and blasted the base of the plinth. Shards flew, while the helmet dropped into the space beyond and vanished.

Then she blasted at the armour—the limbs, the hollow thorax. She watched the blooms of light open and fade.

And she stopped. She remembered the guards firing on the statue. The same colours at the impacts, the same smooth fading. She remembered the feel of the stone.

She spun towards the empty dais, staring. "What are you?" she whispered. "Why are you wearing my armour?"

She started forward and remembered the flash from the wall when she had fired at the helmet. Bursting across the surface of the stone, the light had turned tiny protrusions into sparks, had flung shadow into the smallest pits and hollows, into grooves . . . markings . . .

Before her was a rough wall descending into a pit of rubble. The plinth was a hollow square, as she had suspected. In the twisted moonlight she peered at the face of the outer wall. The markings were real, but badly eroded. They looked like writing, and they continued below the rubble. The steps must have been added after the markings were almost gone.

A moment later she was in the pit, heaving stones away, flinging gravel onto the steps. Pack instinct, Zehn had said. Whatever her makers had put into her, she thought bitterly, it liked to dig.

Then she was in a narrow space, with moonlight falling on the wall in front of her. And white walls close about her. Her breathing rasped. Alone, in a place like this, she realized, most of her mind had been shaped.

She ran her fingers over the inscription in front of her: images and a script she could begin to decipher.

Gradually she pieced together a story.

A dynasty of autarchs. They built walking statues of themselves, one grandiose gesture among many. For generations, they ruled without mercy, and they went mad.

Finally an uprising. Overthrow. Some kind of tribunal.

"You were the youngest," she whispered, "so young. Were you the only one they could take alive?"

Retribution. But the blood of the Basilids must not be spilt. So, instead, a variation on the old punishment for treachery.

Confinement in a tiny cell on a stone column. As vengeance and a warning, they froze the statue.

The Princeling must have slept much of the time, but woke or was woken often enough over the ages, as stories accreted around it. . . .

Katana sat back from the inscriptions. Above her, the moon had shifted more than she had expected. Wearily she turned and clawed her way back to the top of the steps. There she sat and stared at her empty armour. Her mind was filled with the thought of something trapped inside white walls, slowly shriveling, aching to get out.

The world blurred.

Tears. Human lachrymatory fluid. Whatever she was now, she was no longer a warrior.

She slumped against the ruined plinth and wondered what Zehn would do to her.

The moonlight vanished. She spun to her feet, disturbed that she had not heard the shuttle motors. Then she realized she had heard the approach and had chosen to ignore it—the crash of branches, the crunch of stone.

The statue's head eclipsed the moon. A white arm like a band of solid mist was sweeping towards her. She grabbed the rifle and heaved herself from the plinth and into its shadow. She landed on both feet and was sprinting before the masonry crashed into rubble behind her.

"I'm not yours to kill," she snarled. "They have priority."

She stumbled down a moonlit gully, caught herself against a dead tree in a spray of mud and gravel, and the shadow fell across her. Stone fingers rasped through the undergrowth as she dived headlong. She ran.

"Ho! Stone-boy! Hey, fossil!" she cried. "Trapped in a pebble! Want to know what's happened to the world since you last looked out? Step lightly, stone-boy. Skip, skip. Let's see you dance."

Then she was stalking it. "Hey, stone-boy. Look behind you. See me? No? Look again. I'm the one you can't see, waiting for you in the dark. You know what I want. You know what I'll do. If you don't do it first."

It lurched around in the moonlight, came after her. And she was leading it back towards the plinth. She circled the square and stopped in the shadow of a building.

The statue followed, hesitated at the ruined plinth.

"Hey, stone-boy. How well do you see in the dark, little one? Can you see this?"

She set her rifle on full power and fired.

Under the statue's feet, rock bloomed blue-white and erupted, the ground fell away. The statue tottered on one leg, leaned, lost its balance, and fell.

It struck thunderously; stone flew to pieces and the ground split open. The statue flailed one arm, twisted its head towards her, and slid into the chasm.

Katana went to the edge and looked down.

In the moonlight, the statue lay among ruined machines. Now its icy surface was netted over with fine lines. A chip fell away, then another. Chunks the size of bricks split loose, rattled into streams of bright gravel. An eye rolled up, became dead stone, and shattered. The head split open; the torso crumbled. Dust and thunder filled the air, and a dry smell like dead leaves.

A small dark shape remained in a nest of tubes and wires. It was wrinkled, as though it had shriveled, with thin stunted legs and a goblin face. Clawlike hands hid its eyes from the moon.

Katana sighed and began to work her way into the pit. Let Zehn and his men find the remains and puzzle over them. She freed the shriveled creature, cradled it in her arms. Its eyes were feral, its teeth sharp. She sighed again, held it so it could not bite.

"Hello, Princeling," she whispered to it. "Meet your new monster. Let's find you something to eat."

She started back up. Soon it would be dawn.

OF WINGS

Shane Michael Arbuthnott

JACOB IS NOT MEANT TO WITNESS THE MIRACLE. He is one of the forgotten, the fallen, the crumpled masses at the foot of heaven. He is nothing. But he is there when it happens.

He sees the man in the tired trenchcoat, broken down, wandering the pavement. He sees the briefcase hanging open at his side, spilling its papers like blood out onto the ground behind him. He sees the rain gripping the man in its covetous fingers, insinuating itself into his skin. He sees the tears the man is crying.

He is not unusual, this shambling figure that makes his way across the mouth of Jacob's alley. He is another fragment of failure to add to the overflowing pool of this city. He is a broken toy in a graveyard of children. Yet his grief plucks at the part of Jacob that is still human. The man's keening rises through the cloying storm and rends at his ears.

He watches the man as he slows on failing legs, stops, and turns his head to the sky. He watches the briefcase as it finally falls from the man's grip. He sees the man shuck his jacket and leave it on the ground.

For a moment, the man is a painting of sorrow; his red eyes search the starless sky, his arms spread slightly, imploring the vastness for an answer. His trembling knees go still beneath him. Jacob watches the man with hidden sympathy.

There is no flash of light, no heraldic chorus to frame it. It is a casual, offhand impossibility, fallen accidentally before the eyes of the unworthy. Jacob watches as two vast white wings burst from the smooth back of the weeping man and stares on as they spread and carry him upwards, away from the world and deeper into the embrace of the cold storm.

Jacob does not cry hallelujah. He does not crow the glory of God. He does not drown in the wonder of it. He rolls back, away from the mouth of the alley, and lies awake, knowing only one thing:

Jacob is not meant to witness the miracle.

THIS CITY HAS NEVER SLEPT WELL. It tangles itself in sheets of cold regret, awash in nightmare and bleak retrospect. It heaves its bulk, groans through its bridges and streets as it tries again and again to find its way into rest. It is a tortured, guilty soul.

But if you listen, on the days when the drunkards and the drug-heavy have found their ways home to sleep off their stupors and the cacophony of cars has settled to the distant idling of engines, then there is a moment, perhaps once in the turn of the moon, when the tired beast breathes deep and eases momentarily into peace. It does not last more than an hour, but, in that infinitesimal gap, this city is beautiful.

For the first time in his life, Jacob is awake when it happens. He has lived and wasted here for fifty-three years without the slightest hint that there is anything more to this place than a diseased carcass. He has never once thought of it as a home; to him, it has always been a grave.

Now, watching the play of red lights over the greasy waters of the bay, he is not so sure.

It has been three days since he saw the man with wings. It has been three days since he has slept. He wonders now, watching the sleeping grace of the city, if he is beginning to go mad.

An otter breaches the surface somewhere to his right, and then dives back down into the polluted depths. It pauses only momentarily to examine him with eyes the colour of ebon. Inside his cocoon of troubled thought, Jacob does not notice.

Within the rare silence, a few meagre sounds rise. Here the pale, echoless cry of revelers, there the ambling of distant wheels. They are the vulnerable mutterings of the city's dream. They do not seem real. Jacob should turn away, he knows. In the alleys, in the gutters, it is better not to know the secrets of the souls around you. He is used to turning his back in the moments of weakness.

But he cannot help but hold his breath and listen to this. It is like music; it is like the beating of wings. Even if the city will make him pay for it later, for now he will listen.

He wonders idly what has happened to the precious blankets he has hoarded for so long in his alleyway home. Surely they have been taken by now, to be used as lining in some other nest, to keep some other skin warm. He lightly fingers the trenchcoat that hangs from his shoulders, the strangers' jacket he plucked from the ground, and considers the trade a good one.

He thinks again of wings, but the mystery is too deep, the implications too profound, and his mind turns to flee from the recollection. Like a babe he mewls quietly, then finds his way down to the pebbly sand of the shore and curls into it, resting in the cool quiet of the night.

HE IS WOKEN BY THE TAPPING OF A BOOT ON HIS SPINE. He looks up to the familiar sight of a uniformed man, half-heartedly glowering at him.

"Can't sleep here," the officer says. There is no malice in his voice. Jacob nods and rolls up to his feet, moving to join the stream of people on the seaside walkway. He turns east to begin the walk back to his alley and only makes it a few feet. His sudden stop raises a loud curse from the rollerblader who swerves to avoid him. He mutters an apology, but the woman is already gone, lost in the monotonous reverie of her motion. He checks for more traffic, pauses to allow a mother and stroller to pass him, and then turns west.

As long as he has been here, Jacob has never gone inside the park on the western edge of downtown. There are groups of homeless who live within the forest, he has been told, but he has never sought them out. He has just now decided that was a mistake.

The walk there is a long one. Stares follow him as his uncertain legs carry him along. He does not smell it anymore, but he knows the stench of crumbling humanity still follows him. He coughs roughly into his sleeve, and the ragged emptiness of his stomach turns his breath into moans. He is used to scorn, but today it seems to bite a little deeper.

He tries to keep his eyes to the water. In the grey morning cloud, it looks like silver, cut randomly by the prows of boats and stones thrown from young hands. In the daylight no life stirs within it. A heron briefly brushes along its surface and then is gone again, great wings taking it past the curve of a bridge. Watching it go, he realizes he is the only one who has seen it.

Every eye is turned forward. Joggers run by with stern, set jaws; students trudge along under the burden of their backpacks; would-be actors stride confidently past him in expensive sunglasses to shut out the light. None turned their necks to look at the waters next to them. Until Jacob's offensive odour rouses them, they exist somewhere distant. He turns his head again to the bay and watches, this time in a silent protest.

Slowly, he makes his way west. The trees of the park begin to peer over the low tops of apartment buildings. They would be grand, save for the towers of concrete and glass that dwarf them. The city robs them of their glory and replaces it with none of its own. It leaves the landscape monotone, dull. Jacob ignores it and keeps moving.

THE PARK BREAKS SLOWER on the consciousness than it does on the landscape. In one great, staggered line the trees steal the land back from the pavement, leaving the western pocket of downtown, ringed with water, as a sanctuary for the natural. It is so sudden that Jacob's eyes do not take it in. The uniformity of the city has corroded his awareness to only its slightest capacity, allowing him to see when the road turns, the traffic lights change, but nothing more. It takes time for his mind to allow the colours back in and let him know he has reached the park. By then he is already deep in its greenery.

He tries to recall if he has ever been in a forest. He has seen so many pictures it is hard to remember which are his own experiences and which are snatched from he covers of magazines. He doesn't think the memories that rise now are his own; he has never left the city.

He stops where the grass of the open field gives way to the thicker trees. He sits for a moment, runs his hands through the fresh-cut blades. Somewhere behind him a riding mower still hums, traversing the green expanses and robbing them of their complexity. Jacob doesn't like cut grass, but the lush smell it brings up and into his lungs disarms any resentment. He considers idly why the blood of grass would smell so sweet.

He wonders suddenly why he is thinking this way. Beginning to connect things. In his mind, the awareness is linked somehow to wings, and to the subtle breath of a dreaming monster. He gets up and moves on.

In the trees, he is lost within seconds. He knows corners and crevices, not the meandering, patternless curves of the forest. He wanders without a point of reference. He doesn't care.

He realizes, with the dazzle of sunlit leaves in his eyes, why he has come here at last. He is not searching for nature. He is searching for wings.

He knows somehow that the miracle he saw, the man and his wings, are not connected to this. The birds he will find here do not hold the answer. But it is the image of curving feathers, the resting of a body on the wind that holds him, and the closest he can come is in the simple flight of sparrows and jackdaws.

He is scanning the branches hungrily now, watching for his minor miracle. Squirrels, upset as they feast on apple cores and unfinished chocolates, chitter angrily at him. The rare skunk or rabbit peers from its burrow, both frightened and enticed by the aroma of urine that leaks from him. But this is all he sees. The birds are there, but they are too fast to follow. He can track them only in the swaying green they leave behind.

He sighs, uncertain if he is disappointed, and sits to wait.

THE MAN, WHEN HE COMES, MAKES NO SOUND. He is ragged and torn like the newly dead, and smells of old sap and sewage. He moves through the green like he's just another wind in its leaves.

Jacob has never sought out company. He has considered it and decided that he has enough scars to keep him warm already. At times there is a camaraderie between the homeless; he has never shared in it.

But he does not turn away as this man moves towards him. He nods and shares the glimmerings of a smile with him and looks back to the trees. He sees a flash of black feather as he turns, and then nothing.

The man is still moving towards him. This close, his rank musk is overpowering, forcing Jacob to acknowledge him again. The man strides up and stops directly in front of him. His eyes follow Jacob's upwards.

"Nice here, huh?" he says.

Jacob grunts his agreement.

"Bit cold today, though. I think it's just waiting to rain."

Jacob shrugs. The man twists his mouth in something between a smile and a grimace and seats himself next to Jacob. They both stare upwards.

"Haven't seen you around here," the man says. "Welcome to the park."

"Thanks. Just got here."

"You need a place to sleep then?" Neither of them looks down as they talk. Jacob shrugs.

The man, with a low, clear baritone, hums to himself. It's beautiful, Jacob decides, though he is not one to judge. It has been months since he's heard music. When the song stops, the man looks over at Jacob.

"What are we looking for?"

"Birds."

Without pause the man stands. "We're in the wrong place, then. Come on, I'll show you." He extends his hand to where Jacob is resting.

Jacob, slowly, brings his eyes down from the treetops. He stares at the man, taking him in for the first time. His eyes are indefinite, seeming both grey and vivid blue at the same time. His beard is ill-shorn and pitch black, only slightly darker than his skin. He seems tired.

After a moment's hesitation, Jacob stands on his own, ignoring the hand, and then follows the man as he leads into the woods.

"BOCEPHUS," THE MAN SAYS AS THEY WALK. He doesn't shake hands as he says it.

"Jacob."

He still can't tell where they're going. The trees cut out the horizon, leaving no landmarks but the twisting trunks and roots.

They cross and recross paths, staying mostly to the inner halls of the trees. Bocephus moves without the slightest impact; he is there, and then he is gone and everything is as it was. Jacob feels like a locomotive, tearing his way through the tangle. Everything is broken where he has walked.

The day is close. Bocephus is right; it's just waiting to rain, and the air is thickening in anticipation. Just before the cold waters fall, it becomes almost unbearably warm. Jacob thinks of shedding his jacket, but, as he slides the cuff between his fingers and remembers what it once contained, he decides it will remain on. It is his way to stay near the wings.

Here and there inside the trees, Jacob is beginning to see the signs of the park's population. Next to the candy wrappers and used condoms of the more affluent visitors are the ashes of night-fires and thrown-together shelters.

It looks nice, he thinks. He wishes it weren't so alien.

Bocephus, without warning, leaves the ground. Jacob catches a vanishing pair of legs in the corner of his eyes and follows it upwards. For a moment there is nothing, and Jacob thinks perhaps it has happened again, and he has missed it. Then a grinning face finds its way between the leaves, and Bocephus is leaning down towards him.

He sees now the low branch, strange in this forest with its towering, bare trunks, and the precarious path Bocephus has taken.

"Come up," Bocephus says. "You'll see them better up here."

Jacob looks up, tempted, but then shakes his head.

"I can't climb," he says.

"Just try," his guide prods him. "It's not so hard."

Jacob breathes deep and heavy, and then reaches up.

The branches are sturdy, but their bark is flaking off like snow from a pole. It's hard for Jacob to keep his hands on them, and even harder to do it without cutting himself. In a few places, fresh red blood is welling up and out of his skin. As he pulls, every one of his fifty-three years make themselves felt in his muscles. It hurts. It's nice.

The branches are a little too close together, making it feel like he'll fall at any moment. He doesn't. He keeps climbing, and Bocephus is grinning down at him.

The only time he really comes close to falling is when they stop. Once he's not moving—no longer focusing on his next hand-hold—he can feel how tired his old legs are. He wobbles on the wide branch, and then falls clumsily, landing hard on the branch beneath him and gripping it tight. He does not let go. A hand from Bocephus comes down to steady him.

"Alright there?" he asks. Jacob nods. He is scared, but he is steady. He cannot remember why he started climbing.

"Good," Bocephus is saying above him. "You're done. We can see from here." A dark, scarred finger curls out from a hand, and Jacob's eyes follow. In another tree, metres away, is a nest. Around the nest, like a fractured halo, wings. He remembers now why he came up here.

But it is not as it should be. The wings curl and jag. There is no sweep, only an uncanny wildness. Jacob's wonder shudders to a halt, and he sits in the tree trying not to cry.

"What's up?" Bocephus asks beside him. He cannot answer.

Bocephus does not press. He only nudges Jacob gently into climbing back down.

THERE IS A GREEN BLANKET, hung from broken branches to make a tent. There is a basin of rainwater. There is a gnarled root that can be used as a bench. There is nothing golden, not even the slightest hint of glimmer, in this man's home.

"You ever slept under the trees?" Bocephus asks him. Jacob is still not talking. He writhes in his cocoon of disappointment. "It's rough, the first while in winter. Then you get to like it." He splashes rainwater on his face and lets it drip down into his shirt.

Jacob sits, and then stands again. He finds a corner, against the thick bole of a tree, and tucks himself inside.

He is thinking of wings again. His eyes are on the ground.

Bocephus is nattering. He speaks, and paces, and runs his fingers through hair so thick they get lost inside. Jacob pulls the stranger's coat tighter around him. Words mean nothing to him; the coarse touch of fabric is the only language he can speak.

Bocephus reaches down and breaks his introspective prison. His hand on Jacob's shoulder is warm, even through the coat.

"It's soft here, if you want to sleep," he says. His face folds when he smiles.

"Thank you," Jacob replies. His voice sounds strange in his own ears, as if it is not quite real.

He could sleep, he realizes. He is aware that if he only closed his eyes, he could dream. Perhaps of disappearing beyond the clouds. He chooses not to. The wings draw him on, and consume him, and terrify him beyond reason. He does not want to see them, but his heart will not beat again until he does. He feels he has woken from a too-gentle dream. The world grates against him now. He hates the dream for bringing him happiness.

Bocephus pulls himself below the blanket-tent. The sun is only beginning to set. It will rain soon.

JACOB SEES, BUT HE IS NOT SEEN. He feels like a memory; his own skin is gone, he cannot feel the cold drops that are soaking through his jacket. There is only thought now, only sight. And so he watches.

He has never seen anyone sleep so calmly as Bocephus does. Nothing stirs him. Even his breath seems to fade. He looks like Jacob's mother did, the night she died.

He was five, he recalls, when that happened. He does not recall how old she was.

For a moment, he can see it: the gutter, the glowering sky above. His mother's face, thick and tired, framed by a torn sleeping bag they had found in a dumpster. And then it all melted. Her ragged breathing cooled, the lines etched long into her face stretched and then vanished, and she was still. Even there in the alley, surrounded by all the markings of her poverty, she was beautiful.

Then Bocephus rolls in his sleep, and it is broken. He is in the forest, and, sitting next to this new man, he is alone.

He stands, stretches lightly, and digs into the brush.

It's not so thick as he expects. This far inside the trees, the light is strangled by leaves and branches far above, and the foliage cannot feed. The ground is a litter of twigs and the occasional sparse bush, nothing more. In the darkness, roots curl up to snatch his feet. He feels hunted, but he stumbles on.

The forest holds him uncomfortably. It is gentle, but his skin is too full of concrete, and it does not know how to care for him. Its noises and shiftings stumble awkwardly over him.

He pauses for a moment, and relaxes when he hears the sound of cars, not too distant. Horns blare, drunken laughs rise. He is soothed, and he is saddened.

The city is a drug he cannot go long without; it kills him as it keeps him sane. He turns his back on the light it bleeds into the sky, and he keeps moving.

If he were more than a memory he would feel the rain grow harder. He would feel the hail striking his skin like blades. But he is gone, and he feels nothing.

The trees around him fade, and the scrub turns to stone. He is standing on a cliff. Below, in ghostly twists and twines, lays the seawall that surrounds the park, empty now except for dark dribbles of water. Below the seawall is the ocean.

The tide is out. From the wall a great stretch of rock and glassy shards extends itself. The soft, restless tide pulls at it in the darkness, trying to steal its stones. Out in the black the northern expanse of the city winks at Jacob, giggling in the voice of streetlights. Somewhere to his left there is the hum of the bridge.

The city is not sleeping, but it is close. It lies tangled in its blankets, too diseased to sleep, but beneath its pockmarked surface there is something else, pure and pained. It's so obvious now, Jacob wonders why he never saw it before. He sits so he can watch it better. The night flows past him.

In the vicious stillness he hears something breathing. It is vast, it is slow, and it is fading. He looks for its source in the darkness.

The sound mixes with the tide, sounding like another ripple along the shore, but it is too ragged to be that. It is slowing as he listens. He focuses, censures the echoes of the forest until he only hears the breathing, and looks down.

Far below, on the wide rocky beach, there is an orca. In the darkness it is nothing but pale patches of white, rising and falling.

Jacob cannot breathe. He is staring like a child. This is the largest living thing he has ever seen. His mind searches for a source of reference, and can only come up with the image of a half-ton truck, parked idly at a corner. But a truck has never trembled as this creature does.

"I didn't think whales came here," he whispers into the night.

"They don't," the night answers in the voice of Bocephus. Jacob turns, and the old man is behind him. "They stay out past the island. It's too shallow for them here, and there are too many boats. But it's here."

Jacob turns back and stares at the whale. Its abstract white patches shift silently and then lay still. He thinks he hears a keening, as subtle as the dawn.

He looks down. The rocks below him are steep, perhaps five metres high. They pierce the darkness like daggers and then fall back before the pavement of the seawall walk. With one heave of his arms, Jacob jumps.

It is not what he expects. What seemed like rock, so threatening in the shadows, is only soil, soft and yielding. He slides down, breaks his skin only twice on harder patches, and collapses at the base of the cliff. It hurts, but it is alright. He stands and limps across the walk and down the steep steps to the beach.

This close, the whale's attempts at breath surround him, echo off the grey brick and cliffs and descend like the rain over his head. He takes the tentative steps to its side and stops.

He can see it fully now. The white seems rougher this close, but it still glows against the midnight body of the orca. Its eyes are tiny starless skies that stare up at him. He cannot remember why he came down. Maybe to see the whale die. But now, staring in to eyes that encompass him, swallow him like water, he knows that is wrong.

He looks up, and Bocephus is here with him too.

"What do we do?" Jacob asks. Bocephus shrugs his narrow shoulders.

"They usually dig a trench so the water comes up, and roll the whale into it. But I don't know if we can do it alone."

Jacob doesn't hear the last. He is staring now at Bocephus. There is something like the whale in the old man's eyes, something that he cannot read but can only know in the vaguest sense of the wonderful. He breaks the gaze before he is swallowed. He bends down.

There are no tools to help him, and the rocks slide as stubbornly as water, filling the gaps he makes with his hands. Bocephus stands by, does not help. Jacob's fingers shatter like glass on the stones; he is bleeding beneath his fingernails in seconds, and seconds later his knuckles are stained red to match. But he grabs at the stones and throws them aside.

The whale is whimpering beside him, so quiet he only hears it when he is bent low, ear next to the great body. It sounds like a child lost. His bleeding hands dip again, grip the slipping stones.

Around him, there is nothing of the city left. His eyes are low; he cannot see the lights. The whisper of wheels is eaten away by the grinding shore and the murmur of tides. There is only himself, and the old man and the beast near his side, watching as he tries to dig a hole large enough to hold a titan. He feels lost. He keeps digging.

It is like pushing at oil. The rocks move, but only vaguely. The hole is a smudge, a stain filled by shadow. In an hour's work, the trough is as deep as a finger. Jacob cannot feel his hands. He thinks only of the dark line beneath him, listens only to the whine of the great child at his side. He looks up and finds the dark eyes still on him. They urge him on.

The dawn seems to flee like some frightened beast. Fragments of colour rise over the eastern trees, seeming to signal the day, but they fall back into shadow before Jacob raises his eyes again. Hours pass, and hours, and hours, and there is no light. Jacob does not see; he can only see the stones giving way beneath his numbed hands.

The water is black when it comes, like tar, like polish. It slides in over his shoes, his still-moving hands. It is cool, and it is dark. Jacob is a passing dream on its surface, a reflection never quite formed.

He steps out and sees the trough he has made. It is wider than he can remember digging it, but its edges are stained with his blood. The whale hangs on its edge like the possibility of an avalanche. Its eyes are still on Jacob. Its futile breath is almost gone.

Bocephus is standing, smiling at him with his rotted teeth.

"Now what?" Jacob asks him.

Bocephus shrugs.

"Try something," he says.

Jacob stands awhile, and watches the breath fade from the whale. He is imagining himself pushing that weight into the water. He remembers a story someone told him long ago; Atlas, carrying the world. It's the same, he thinks. But he is not Atlas.

He looks at his hands. They can't take any more. He can't feel anything, except a dull throb in the bones. He watches the veins struggle to carry the blood, watches the rain and hail take it away where it leaks from his cuts.

The hem of his jacket is cracking against his legs like a whip. The rain tries to find its way into his eyes. He blinks it off. He is wondering what happened to his blankets. He can't remember what they look like anymore.

Slowly, his feet slide from their rests, and he moves to the other side of the whale.

He can hear nothing now, no keening, but as he lays his cheek to the creature's black skin, he can feel motion, slower than the turning of the moon. It is like the city; outside it is dead, inside it is only dying. He digs his feet into slippery stones, braces his arms, and pushes.

There is no grace in the struggle. There is sweat, and there is the rain, and there are his hands bleeding on the slick skin of the beast. And there is progress, Sisyphian in its speed. Dawn continues to tease the eastern sky, never advancing, never falling back. And then, with arms numb, feet breaking against the rocks, there is a slide of stone and skin, and the whale is in the water.

Jacob numbly guides it down the channel. Its tail thrashes, deathly weak, breaking up the rocks beneath it. It moves solemnly down towards the greater ocean, pauses once, and then is free. Life bursts back into its veins as it swims deeper, stomach scraping the stony ground. Jacob collapses into the surf, does not see as the whale joins the deeper tides. He sees darkness, and breaking waves, and a moment later feels Bocephus's hand on his back.

It lifts him. The arm is stronger than Jacob could have imagined from something so old. It raises him out of the water, and in the distance his eyes fix momentarily on a fin, a dark form lifting from the surface, and then diving again, impossibly deep in the shallow waters.

"Nice work," Bocephus says.

Jacob does not hear. He is watching the place where the whale vanished.

Bocephus bends down to Jacob's ear.

"Beautiful," he says. Jacob nods. He watches the ripples disappear from the ocean surface.

"You want to follow, don't you?" Bocephus asks. He nods. "Then go."

Jacob looks up into the dark face, smiling through the underbrush of its beard. Old eyes glimmer in the half-light of the forming dawn. He looks out to the ocean and waits for a fin to rise out of the water. It never comes.

He looks up once more, to the sky above. Through the sickly city light a few stars struggle, piercing the orange haze with white. He watches for a moment, and then, without standing, he slides into the water and begins to swim.

Behind him, the morning breaks over the forest branches.

THE OCEAN IS DARK AND ACIDIC; its pollution stings Jacob's eyes, burns at his lungs. He spits the water out in acrid gouts.

He does not know how to swim. He thrashes through the water like an eruption, like a whale's spume. He cannot stay afloat long enough to see where he is going; he can only press himself desperately through the ocean, his long, waterlogged coat pulling him down.

In the water, he cannot think. Each concept is interrupted by the leaden swing of an arm, the weak kick of a leg, the feel of oily water running down his throat. He prays that he is not moving in circles.

When the shore comes, he grinds against it like a shipwreck. His hands jar on stone, his knees drag along the sudden surface. He scrabbles, frantic, up the stones and on to land. He breathes deep and vomits up the ocean he swallowed.

He looks up and out. For a moment, all he can see is a blur of stars, and it seems he has thrashed his way up into the sky. But slowly the pollution clears from his eyes, and he sees that the stars are streetlights, the comets only passing cars. He has found his way to the northern expanse of the city. He is nowhere new.

He lies down for a time and weeps, wondering why he wanted to escape. This city is his skin, his breath. He is a thing of concrete. He has never been anything else.

Yet still he rolled through the waves, chasing the whale, the world he held on Atlas's shoulders for a brief moment.

And it led him here, to the city, to nothing but the same, over and over.

He is weeping, and he does not know why. He stands slowly, legs shaking, and moves slowly in, towards the streets.

"You want to go farther, don't you?" a voice says above him. He turns his head skyward. Bocephus is above him, hanging from a streetlight. He does not cling to it; he sits atop it, as if the narrow steel was a bench, and the distance below no more than a few inches. Jacob looks up at him and nods.

"Then go," he says. He is smiling like the newborn sun.

"I don't know how," Jacob tells him.

Bocephus nods. "If you did, you would be gone already. So learn."

"How?" Jacob asks.

The old man shrugs. Shadows from the streetlight dance over his face, play inside his beard. "Just try something."

In the streets of the city, traffic begins to wake itself and flow with the mad desperation of blood through veins. Cars slice through the air next to Jacob, set his jacket swirling in the wind. He does not notice.

He looks past Bocephus, past the blinding glare of the streetlight and the blue haze of early morning. Above, a few whimpering stars can still be seen, pale and dying. They groan and glower. They shimmer like his mother's eyes. He stares into their scattered white, through the darker surroundings.

He is remembering his blankets. He is remembering the feel of granite beneath him. He is remembering the burn of bourbon as it slides into his stomach.

His memories lose their shape, become dumb shows of themselves, mutely playing out their actions void of any meaning. They roll down, one behind another, too many sad, too many broken, and then become a dull background to his mind. And as they wan, the stars wax, pull themselves through the blue of day to stain the sky white. He watches, and his tears collect on the pavement below.

"Try," Bocephus whispers from above. He sounds distant, as if he and the streetlight have risen until they met the stars, joining the celestial glimmer and waiting for him in the sky. With every part of himself, every cell in his body, he yearns to soar up with them.

And he wonders suddenly what his holding him here. The lights dim on his memories, his cravings, his dull and witless need to survive. They vanish, and he is left alone with the sky, with the sounds of the street echoing around him. And he does not want to be here. He does not want the stink of concrete on his skin anymore, he does not want the wheels echoing in his ears. He wants to follow the whale, to swim up to the sky, to go so far that he cannot find his way back home.

He reaches up as if the sky will take him and coddle him in its arms. He hears a swirl behind him, a great symphony of air and wing bursting from his back, and then he is rising, rising.

He thinks of looking back once, to see the streetlights one more time. But the stars hold his eyes until he is blind, until he sees nothing but the dark and light of heaven. The city flows away into the washed-out world, and he is gone.

Emily, sitting quietly on the beach, watches him wing his slow way to the sky. She is not meant to witness the miracle. She is one of the forgotten.

THE WOMAN WHO DANCED ON THE PRAIRIE

Steve Vernon

ON THE PRAIRIE, THE HORIZON IS A FOREVER-LONG TAUNT.

Damn!

I keep walking. Sending my left foot after my right. Following footsteps laid down two hundred and seventy-one days ago.

One long reeling jig of vengeance and desire.

Desire because I want vengeance. Vengeance wanted because I could not forget desire.

Damn you, Tyler Cooting.

Damn!

The intervals are closer.

The baby is coming.

I keep walking. Walking's heavy work. Especially when you're loaded with an unborn child.

The shovel swings like a rifle in my hand.

Light in weight.

Freighted with duty.

It isn't that bad. My extra weight rolls me into a ball of momentum. The pregnant walk. That side-to-side saddle gait, part waddle, part waltz—this whale-walk suits the roll of the prairie.

And the prairie does roll. I know you wouldn't guess it, not by just looking. Strangers look at the prairie and see nothing but tombstone flat.

Just another reason for never talking to strangers. They don't know a god-damn thing.

Sometimes it don't pay to trust your friends either.

Ask Tyler Cooting.

Only he ain't talking.

Damn!

The prairie keeps laughing at me, and I keep walking.

Walks are long on the prairie, but they ain't flat. Flatness is just a mirage. The prairie arcs a long, slow curve. Each footfall strokes the belly of my mother, the Earth.

That's prairie talking. Prairie thinking. Prairie people speak in roots, rather than route. The long dry vastness just begs for digression. Wander talk. Wonder talk. A conversation on the prairie starts somewhere half past tomorrow, damn near yesterday. It can land you smack in the lap of an ancient ancestor or feet first in the heart of a rocketship barrelling towards an undreamed future.

Keep walking.

It's July. Grasshopper weather. The prairie is a hot yellow laugh of sunshine and sunburnt straw. Daisies dance with the whispering wind. Black-eyed Susans hang on stubbornly. Devil's paintbrush stick out like a thousand hammered thumbs.

Everything's the colour of fire. All red and yellow and miles of unsudded blue. The wind rolls like a song torn from a whiskey-smoked voice.

I sweat from walking. It fogs my back. Sticks my shirt to my belt line. Feels like salty fungus, rankling my armpits and deeper places. I feel sticky and poisonous. The water in my belly is boiling hot.

This land is as dry as a Baptist picnic. The dust kicks up tiny ghosts that haunt down like a handful of wind-tossed dandelion dandruff.

I been walking a long way.

Damn!

This morning, just before breakfast, my Daddy shook his dust-grey head over a plate of eggs and salted ham.

"Been sixty-three days since our last rainfall."

My Daddy was a counting man. Counted the days like it was some kind of magic. Like if he reached a secret number his wishes would come true.

I'd been keeping my own count.

Two hundred and seventy-one days since Tyler Cooting left me.

Daddy said he would. Said he'd up and go when the spirit started talking.

And wasn't Daddy right? Just as soon as Tyler's seed took root he stole his uncle's rust-red pickup and headed west for the Rockies.

Least that's what folks tell me, and you'd figure they'd know. Lots seen him go. Said that truck looked like a wind-stirred dust devil, aching for the call of sunrise. Said he never stopped. Just kept on rolling, bound for the western coast.

My, my. Don't people love to talk.

Anyone asks, I tell them I hope Tyler Cooting's brakes fail going over the far side of the Rockies. Hope he rolls that pickup right through Vancouver and straight off a dock. A long dock. Long enough to give him time to think about what he did to me, as he sails himself straight into a shark-filled ocean. Hope he keeps on going. Hope he wraps that pickup truck around a telephone pole in downtown Tokyo.

That's what I tell them. What they want to hear.

I tell them I hope Tyler Cooting screams all the way.

He did, too.

Damn!

That's vengeance talking. Vengeance is what I want.

Vengeance is a woman thing. Men just seem to get what they want for the asking. Women get taught real early to wait for whatever comes along.

Like a prairie, like an ocean, we just stretch on forever.

Just waiting to be asked.

Only Tyler didn't ask. Tyler Cooting tipped me up and drained me like a bottle of stolen whiskey.

Should have known better, but damn he was beautiful. A big beautiful bastard. Made me hot and wet just looking at him. Work-hardened and lean like a stalk of wind-stirred wheat. Crowned by a sun bleached shock of untamable cowlicks. A grin like a sickle. Kissed me hard and fierce.

My God, I miss him even now.

Hope he burns in sunburnt Hell.

Wonder if he misses me? If he called my name one last time. Called it into that fierce grin of the horizon as the prairie wind blasted skin from his bones.

No.

Probably didn't.

I would have heard him if he had.

Damn!

It's coming soon.

Three times this week Daddy offered to drive me to the city hospital.

Three times I told him it wasn't time yet.

Three times I lied.

I lied, even though it tasted like a glassful of piss.

I lied because Daddy can't afford a hospital trip. Not with the way the drought's been burning the crops.

Second time in my life I lied to Daddy. First time was Tyler Cooting. I lied when I said we weren't nothing more than honest friends.

Daddy seen that lie grow in my belly like a dirty seed.

Damn!

Pains get closer, every time.

Just got to go a little further. As far as I can, like one of those old Eskimo women. Walking out of the igloo and into the wilderness to die.

Only I ain't going to die. I'm just out to have my baby, out in the eye of the sun. Make some old magic. Prairie magic. Vengeance and desire magic.

Shovel magic, too.

Got to dig a hole and dig it deep.

Not for me, though. I ain't out here to die.

Don't matter. What I'm aiming to do might kill me anyway. Kill me from a broken heart, and hearts broke twice never heal.

Maybe it'll be alright.

I can picture my bones lying out on the prairie like castaway dreams. The sun will parch them kindling dry within a week. If Daddy takes too long to find me I'll have dried away into bone dust.

Don't mind. Long as the magic works.

Damn!

The little piece of girl squirms in my belly. I feel the tickle of her fingers on my rib bones like they were plucking the strings of a dead moaning harp.

I know it's a girl. That's part of the magic. How a mother always knows.

I'm going to name her after my Momma, just before I put her in the hole.

Damn!

My Momma died out here. Out on the prairie. Was the winter. Snowing, and she stepped out to look for the cat. Hadn't bothered waking Daddy. He was sleeping off the rye and ginger he drank after a long day of plowing wintered-over highways. Was the only work he could get, besides farming. And with the drought the farming wasn't doing much, so the highway had to pay the bills. We were in debt most of the time.

Funny how debt sounds so much like death.

So he plowed, even though he hated it. And afterwards he'd drink. Man's got to do something, he'd say, even when there's nothing left to do.

That cuts twice as deep for women, once you get down to the bone of things.

"I'll be out on the porch," Momma said, just before stepping out to look for the cat.

Don't know what happened then. Maybe the wind caught her. Lofted her like a seed pod. Didn't find her body until spring thaw. Was a lonely mile and a half from the farmhouse. Wrapped around a broken pine root, like she'd been trying to tie herself to the prairie floor.

"A body can wander a long way in a prairie snowstorm," was what Daddy said, and maybe he was right.

I was three when it happened. Shouldn't remember, but I do. I blame the baby on my Momma. If she'd been here to set me straight I might never have fallen for Tyler Cooting.

That's what I tell myself.

Daddy found the cat sleeping under his bed. Picked it up and wrung its neck like he was trying to wring grief tears from his hands.

We buried the cat in a snow drift. A wild dog must've dragged the body off, because by spring the cat was gone.

Daddy buried his rye bottle with the cat. He was a great believer in sacrificing for your sins. Expiation, he called it.

Until last week I never seen him take another drink.

Damn!

I'm nearly there.

There's Tyler, right where I planted him. Neck deep, staring blind into the unforgiving prairie sun. Skin's dried like onion peel, loose against his skull bone. Nearly rotted away.

Wasn't too hard to get him out here. Men are like dogs that way. Little pink leashes slung between their legs. Told him I wanted him, one more time. Just once for the road is how I put it. Just once, on the prairie, naked together.

Wasn't hard at all.

Took him out here and left him neck deep, with nothing but the knot on his skull the shovel left behind. After I planted him snug, I pissed on his head to wake him up.

Let him talk awhile. First he cursed me. Then he begged me. Then I took my jack knife and peeled his eyelids back for the sun to shine through. Sang the old songs and danced like my Momma taught me.

Old magic.

Prairie magic.

Vengeance magic.

Now, standing over what was left, I had to laugh like a heated-up loon. Didn't look so big, buried neck deep in prairie sod.

I hefted the shovel like a broad axe. Took a short practice swing.

"Hey Tyler!" I hollered.

He might have moved, or maybe that was just my imagination.

I swung the shovel down and hard. Wanted to take his head off. Only it wasn't so neat. Broke his skull like a chunk of rotted fungus.

That wasn't part of the magic. That was spite, pure and simple.

Just didn't want his head, dead or not, staring up at me while I laid my baby under.

The wind whipped up like a woman whisking children with the hem of her skirt. Caught the pieces of Tyler Cooting's shattered skull and swept them skyward like confetti.

I had a feeling the prairie understood.

I planted the shovel blade into the dirt, so it stood over me like a tombstone cross.

Then I laid down into a little grassy cradle of prairie, just perfect shaped for my pregnant body.

Damn!

Another pain, only worse.

I lay still.

Damn!

Listened to the prairie wind coaxing me to breathe deep and slow. Riding the birth pains like a bird rides the wind.

Damn!

I ain't saying it was easy. I ain't felt such pain since Tyler Cooting tore out my heart.

Damn!

The sun yelled down like a sheet of red pain.

Damn!

I yelled back up. The prairie started digging at me. Opening me up to the sun and the sky. I felt the grass kindling like a fuzz stick in an open flame.

Damn!

I felt Tyler's grin bone nuzzling my cheek. Felt the earth talking to me, the sun talking to me, the prairie singing to me.

Damn!

A white buffalo thundered past, hard on the heels of runaway legend. A Cree hunter clung to its back in one last mad gallop. The flames licked my thighs like hot hungry wolves.

I think about Momma. About Daddy. About my baby being born out here on the prairie.

Love and death swim round like half a hundred ghost fishes.

It's old magic.

Woman magic.

My Momma dances before me. Her bones blasted clean with the frost. Each step raises a hundred buried snowflakes. Her laughter is the mournful song of cracking glacier hearts.

She sings and her voice is the winter wind that kisses buried grass. Her feet beat rhythms of the Ukraine, of the Cree, of the Blackfoot. Of all the nameless women who danced on these prairies, and the nameless ones who came before them.

There's a million ghost women dancing on these prairies, and I feel each stomp reverberate in the boiling birthwater buried deep inside me.

Damn!

Damn!

Damn!

A pain peels from between my legs. Birth piss splashes and sops into the sun-dried dirt of the prairie.

My Momma whirls with all those other ghost women, working old woman magic. In the whirl of her wildflower skirt I see thunder clouds rolling over dry prairie fields. The sky opens up like a woman weeping for joy.

My baby's screaming sheer hard life, and all I can do is hold her, tears running down my cheeks and splashing her greedy open mouth.

I hold her, running my tears down my cheeks and splashing on her greedy open mouth.

The shovel I'd planned to kill and bury her with rusts into the blood-coloured dirt. A sacrifice is not necessary.

Everything around me is dancing. Even Tyler Cooting's husked-out bones laugh and clatter with helpless joy as my baby screams thunder and rain pours down upon the prairie.

Then all the colour fades away. All the magic and the mystery fades away. I hear Daddy calling me home as he stamps a heavy lumbering jig through the muddy fields that can finally drink and be reborn. Momma's voice swims like a soft echo beneath Daddy's joyful whoop, and I am just a girl walking home on the prairie, my newborn baby wrapped tight in my arms, taking one more risky step in life's mad dance.

THE CURSE OF THE SCIENCE FICTION WRITER

Ahmed A. Khan

THE KING OF SARNIYA WAS A TYRANT AND A SADIST. He had no end of fun torturing anyone who dared raise even the tiniest of voices against him. His dungeons were vast and filled with state-of-the-art torturing devices, many of them invented by the King himself.

One day, the soldiers captured a science fiction writer and brought him before the King. The author had written some stories about an imaginary land that was ruled by a benevolent king. This was, of course, subversion of the highest order.

"You are a science fiction writer, are you?" The King smiled. "I love science," he said. "Let us a try an experiment, shall we? Let us see how long a man can live without water." He turned to his guards. "Take him to the dungeons. Feed him as much as he wants, but do not give him water or any other liquid."

The science fiction writer searched in his mind for the most potent curse he could think of. "May God punish you by putting you into a time loop," he said, as the guards dragged him away.

A few days later, the King of Sarniya was sitting in the garden when, out of nowhere, a long black pole made of plastic swung through the air and hit him on the head and then vanished. The blow on the head jarred the neurons of the King's brains, and, for a few seconds, its synapses went whacko and the neurons started sending wild signals to each other. Suddenly, out of these random signals, a pattern emerged, and the pattern gave birth to an idea in the King's brain, an idea about faster-than-light motion.

A few days back, the King (who was quite erudite for a king) had come across a book on angular motion.

According to Einstein (thought the King), *nothing can travel faster than light. Well, that's true in case of linear motion, but what about angular motion? Suppose there is a pole that can move with one end as its pivot. When I move this pole, the linear velocity of a point on the pole near the pivot is much lesser than the linear velocity of the other end of the pole. Now, suppose I build a very long pole, such that a small impetus at the pivot would result in faster than light motion at the other end? Is this possible? And, if this were possible, would the nether part of the pole (the part that was moving faster than light) really travel back in time, as some scientists suggest?*

The King ordered his engineers to build just such a pole. It took two months to build the pole. The King performed the experiment by pushing on the pole near its pivot.

And what do you think happened?

The pole moved.

The linear velocity at the far end of the pole surpassed the velocity of light, and the far end of the pole travelled backward in time and hit the King on his head while he was sitting in his garden two months ago. The blow on the head jarred the neurons of the King's brains, and, for a few seconds, the neurons started sending wild signals to each other. Suddenly, out of these random signals, a pattern emerged, and the pattern gave birth to an idea in the King's brain, an idea about faster-than-light motion.

The King of Sarniya went mad thinking through the resultant chain of causes and effects. The commander-in-chief of the King's armies took over the throne and proclaimed himself the new ruler of Sarniya. To gain the favour of his newly acquired subjects, he handed over the former king to their mercies . . . and there is no rule whatsoever—written or unwritten—that it is only kings who can be cruel.

A GIFT OF POWER

Janet Marie Rogers

I WAS COMPLETING THE EIGHTH WEEK OF A DIET. I was determined to lose the extra fifteen pounds I had carried around with me since adolescence and worn like a protective layer around my reproductive parts. It showed on my face too, as bloated cheeks and heaviness under my chin. Ah, the joy of inheriting my ancestral characteristics. Besides the cocoa-tinted skin and dark almond eyes, a healthy paunch was a common telltale sign of a modern-day Native North American—or Indian, as I preferred to call myself.

With the loss of nine pounds, I found myself spending more and more time fantasizing about my new figure or, rather, the power my new figure would add to my life. I looked forward to the reactions from the other plump ladies in the community, especially those who were teetering on dislike for me, who would now be pushed right over into full-on hate once they got a glimpse of my new slimmer hips and deflated belly. My motive to stay off the sugars and reduce carbs may be cruel or petty, but it provided me with a much-needed incentive to get through the next few weeks.

I was heading out on a walk downtown, bundled up to fend off the ocean winds that can crack you across the face in February. A warm wool hat, regardless of the coiffure-damaging effects, was also a necessity. I passed by the female speed-walking duo. The guy on the bench with the walkman headphones stuck in his ears staring out over the harbour's activities. The families who were hosting visiting relatives, openly bragging about the temperate climate on our west coast during the winter months. And the usual dog owners making their way along the boardwalk, practically wearing their pets as accessories. Made me wonder who was walking who.

I was just trying to break a sweat and burn off some of the peanut butter and rice cakes I had eaten mid-morning. As I passed by some trees along the walkway, I saw a man. He was pruning the low hanging branches of the arbutus trees and carefully stacking the off-cuts into neat triangular piles, pyramid-like. He wasn't wearing the customary city-issued uniform. There weren't any fellow crew members around. He worked alone. My steps automatically slowed as I passed him and noticed the air had a warm quality to it. He was snipping away effortlessly at the arbutus, a hard wood with unpredictable twists and knots, like it was made of twigs. What was his intention with those wood piles anyway? I couldn't begin to guess. The experience stayed with me for the remainder of my walk.

While I was rewarding myself with a steamed soy milk at a trendy coffee shop downtown, a friend of mine walked in. Mike is the kind of guy you would describe as loose, like easy to be around, a comfortable conversationalist. Mike was part of a powwow drum group. Our school called on him and his group to do welcome ceremonies sometimes. I could describe to Mike in putrid detail my menstrual discomfort, and he wouldn't be phased except to express sincere sympathy. I began to tell him about the strange experience with the tree pruner on the walkway.

"It was like, when I noticed him, everything seemed to slow down, the air became warm and things just felt really strange for a while." I explained. It was then that I realized that, although I had stared at him the entire ten seconds it had taken to pass him, I could not describe him—light or dark hair, full or thin face, nothing. "Flashback," he offered. "You know, any kind of drugs we did gets stored away in fat cells, and you've been taking it off pretty good, Rhea. You know, maybe it was a little bit of leftovers in your system getting reactivated by your diet."

"Really?"

"Ya, lots of people get that, like acid flashbacks, stuff like that."

"No, I mean you can tell I've lost weight?"

"Sure, you're gorgeous."

"Keep talking like that, Mike, and I'll let you see my stretch marks."

Mike laughed, but I wasn't kidding. I had lost weight, and I wanted to celebrate by showing off my new body between the sheets with someone.

"Well, I better get going, I got drum practice in the west end." He rose from the table.

I asked, "You walking?"

"Ya, my truck is sick again, broke down last week. Nothing a hundred bucks and a new starter can't fix."

"I'll walk with you."

We made our way along the ocean path exchanging bad Indian jokes.

Mike said, "So there's this rich white guy, and he wanted a mural painted on his living-room wall. So he calls up this Indian artist and says: 'paint me something historical that depicts the beginning relations between Indians and white men. I'm going away for three weeks, so here's my house keys. When I come back I look forward to seeing the finished mural.' After three weeks, the guy comes home and sees a painting of a big turd with a halo over it, and around the turd is men and women Indians, and they're all copulating. The white guy says 'What the hell is this, I wanted something historical!' and the Indian artists says 'When the white man first came to North America, his first words were "holy shit—where did all these fucking Indians come from!"'" We both burst out in laughter.

We were approaching the man on the path, and I gave Mike a soft nudge in the ribs to take notice.

"This your guy?"

"That's him." He was still cutting branches and making pyramid piles from the off-cuts.

Mike's eyes narrowed to get a better look at him from afar.

"Looks normal enough to me, Rhea."

"Mike, he's been cutting those branches since before I saw you downtown and those trees don't look anymore thinned out than before."

"Okay, that's weird," Mike admitted.

When we approached the area near the man, I noticed the same warmth in the air, the slowing of our steps, and this time there was a sweet scent in the air, like spring flowers blooming. Without cueing each other, Mike and I stopped in unison in front of the busy gardener. Unable to move or form words, we just stood there, while the man quickly assembled a three-dimensional pyramid from the freshly cut branches that stood about two feet high. The path was empty of the usual pedestrian traffic, and all was silent. Without breaking the rhythm of his work, the man spoke to us. Rather he communicated to us, without verbal language. He said:

I have promises to keep, so I have come here, to do this work, to touch those who are touchable and can take the ripples from my finger on the water to create waves of change from the inside out. Take the structure before you and use it as a tool. Birth new visions within it, visions for a better day, a brighter tomorrow and promise for centuries to come. Take it now before it's too late. It starts with you. Take the structure and use it as a tool.

Mike leaned forward, took the wooden pyramid, and off we went. We walked in silence to the end of the path. Finally, I said, "Still think it was a flashback?"

Looking down at the carefully crafted arbutus branches, he answered, "No. No, I don't."

Since we were close to my house, I suggested we bring the thing to my place to have a better look at it. We entered through the back door and placed the pyramid on the kitchen table. We plunked ourselves in chairs opposite each other and stared at it with a million questions racing through our minds at once, but not attempting to verbalize any of them.

Mike jumped up. "Hey, I got that drum practice! Those guys are gonna can me if I miss this one."

"Mike, you're not going to leave me alone with this thing are you?" Fear began to set in.

"Sorry, Rhea, but it's not like I can swoop into drum practice, prop it up on the drum and say, hey guys, look what I have here, got it from this cool guru dude who spoke to me with his mind. I don't think that'll go over too good, ya know."

"So take it home with you."

"I don't want to be alone with it either, Rhea. What if it starts buzzing or glowing or something, then my landlord finds me unconscious next week, with my brains missing and some weird symbols branded into me. No thanks!"

"Wow, it's not an alien mothership, Mike." I laughed.

"We can't be sure of that. So what do we do?"

"I don't know."

We both sat back down and stared at it, hoping it would give us some answers. As I refocused my gaze, I spied Mike's eyes looking back at mine through the slots between the stacked branches. They were warm, soft, and sexy. I wondered if he was looking at me or something inside the structure. I looked back into his eyes, enjoying the flex of green in his brown pupils. My heart suddenly felt as if it would burst. My breathing quickened, and I was overcome by a strong sensation of brightness, hope, and love. Through the tiny spaces between the wood, I was seeing into Mike's soul. It was beautiful. It felt like freefalling backwards into a pool of pure crystal energy. Heat and cool sensations flowed through me. Then I heard him speak my name, which brought me back into the room.

"Rhea," he repeated. "I love you."

"I love you too, Mike."

We said it like we had been saying it to each other all our lives. Without prompting of any kind, we simultaneously rose from our chairs and came together in a sweetly sexual open-mouthed kiss. We were in love in an instant. We were lovers, about to make love. What had just happened? Who was the man on the path, and what kind of magical thing did he give us? It didn't matter, love was born. A new energy entered us both. One of surprise and delight. As we embraced, a warm electricity passed between us, shifting from one to the other, moving in waves. We spent the entire night making love. It was new and yet familiar at the same time. Our union had none of the awkwardness new lovers experience when exploring flesh, sexual nuances, and body movements. We proved to be old pros at pleasing each other. The sunrise was our cue to the end of a magical night and the beginning of a beautiful new day. As we lay intertwined among rumpled sheets, I could suddenly recall the appearance of the mystery man on the path. Much to my surprise, he was familiar to me.

"Hey, you know, now that I think about it, that man on the path, he looked like my grandfather on my father's side. A big burly man with a full head of salt-and-pepper hair. Thick lips and a good strong Indian nose."

"Ya?" Mike looked curiously at me. "Because the guy I remember was the spitting image of an elder fella I knew from back home. Old Nicky Morely, 'cept he had a real slight build, frail and bent over most his later years. He had a head of thin white hair and stubble on his chin. Old Nicky passed away last fall. But when I think about it, the guy looked exactly like Nick."

"Really? That's weird."

"Is your Gramps still living?"

"Died two years ago."

We looked at each other with more questions racing through our heads. Then Mike said, "What say we get some breakfast into us before we try to solve this mystery. We been working up a good appetite, my love." Mike squeezed me and headed to the kitchen. Me, I wasn't hungry at all. I was still buzzing from head to toe, all over and inside too.

Mike shouted from the kitchen, "Hey, where's your bread? I can make us some toast."

"Sorry, no bread," I shouted back. "Too much carbs."

"Well, how about some coffee with milk and sugar?"

"Coffee with soy milk and sweetener is all I can offer you. Sorry, it's the diet thing."

Silence.

"Well, what d'ya got?"

"How about a boiled egg and an apple?" I suggested, feeling like a bad hostess.

Mike appeared in the bedroom doorway looking as excited as a little boy at a fair.

"Rhea, you gotta see this!"

He led me back into the kitchen

The wooden pyramid was hovering above the table.

"Oh my lord," I found myself saying.

"Pretty cool," Mike said, beaming me a smile.

"Mike, this thing is too big for us. I mean, what are we supposed to do with it?" I hated sounding like a cliché worried girlfriend, but, considering the circumstances, this was my truest reaction.

"I know, I know." He brought his tall frame over, enveloping me in a comforting embrace. "Shhh, slow down sweetie. This is magic. We made magic together. My people say never to be afraid of magic; it's all part of the natural universe. Whatever this thing is, it's done some pretty good things so far. Remember, that guy told us it was a tool, a tool that can help us do some good for the people, for the world even. I think this thing just helped us to find the love between us that was already there. Maybe it's like an amplifier of positive energy."

He was making sense out of something based in anything but sense. Still I couldn't help but feel overwhelmed. And besides, the man's instructions were so vague, so brief, and the thing didn't come with a manual.

I asked, "How are we supposed to know how to use it properly?"

"Well we can try looking into it like we did last night," Mike suggested. "Think we should tell anyone about it?"

Still in his arms, I looked into his face and asked, "You mean about this spooky triangle floating in my kitchen or about us?"

"About the triangle," he responded without hesitation. "You know Indians, everybody probably already knows about us."

I laughed and agreed and gave him a reassuring kiss square on the mouth.

"I might have some oatmeal in the cupboard. I'll cook some up for you. But we'll have to eat in the living room."

"With that soy junk?" He grimaced.

"'Fraid so, my man."

Mike retreated to the living room, while I got to work in the kitchen, trying to ignore the pyramid hovering over the table.

Over the next two weeks Mike and I learned many things about ourselves, about each other, and about the magic T, as we came to call the pyramid. "T" for triangle. We rose early each morning, just as day was breaking, to begin our new ritual. We covered the magic T with a cotton cloth and trekked it out to a piece of grass that over looked the ocean, about a ten-minute walk from my place. Once there, we faced each other and brought the magic T between us, holding it up to heart level. Within a few seconds it began to generate its own vibration, enough to float independently. Soon it would rise to our eye level, where we would lock our gaze into its centre. And the visions would begin. Prior to leaving the house in the morning, Mike and I would agree on a community issue we felt could use some help. Things like improved housing for the people on the reserve, greater harmony among the workers within the Native agencies in the city, strength needed for those still caught in substance addiction, things of this nature. One particular day we woke up and had the same idea. Since Mike was part of a drum group whose membership was wavering and inconsistent, we thought it would be beneficial for the community to come back to the drum to improve community unity.

We locked eyes through the slats of wood and began to see the lights inside. They collected and shifted apart to make images. We saw the drum; it was larger in size than the one Mike usually plays on. Then we saw the drum sticks surrounding the drum, and there were more than I could count. And then something new happened. We heard music. It was a slow drum beat, serious and honourable. Then we heard a chorus of singers. Deep men's voices at first singing in operatic tones, in a purposeful chant. Then women's voices, then children's voices. The haunting chant was sung in tones that filled our souls. Healing tones that made us see beautiful colours and balance our energies. Neither of us could recognize the song. It was a very ancient song, from a time so long ago, it had almost been lost forever.

That night, Mike had a drum practice at the community hall, and I decided to join him. We pulled up in front of the hall with our blanket-covered mystery tucked between us in the front seat of Mike's truck. Some of the guys were already seated around the drum, waiting for the remainder of the group. They didn't seem as surprised as I thought they would be when I followed Mike in.

Randy greeted me. "Rhea, hey girl, look at you! Looking good Rhea. You're not hanging around this skinny Indian are ya? You could do a lot better. Come and sit by me tonight."

"Where's your old lady, Randy?"

"Ahhh, you know."

Then our package was noticed.

"What the heck you got there, Mike, a crab trap? Ain't the season man, you know that."

Mike addressed them in a serious tone. "Guys—" he broke off looking for the right words.

"What we have here requires an open mind." With that vague introduction, I raised the blanket, revealing the pyramid. The drummers looked unimpressed.

"Let's start drumming," Mike suggested.

Everyone placed tobacco on the centre of the drum, offering up a silent prayer. The lead drummer began to beat out a soft rhythm. I stood beside Mike and tried to recognize the song. When all the drummers had joined in and they settled into a steady beat, I raised the magic T over the drum where it suspended itself a foot above the drum. The drummers looked up and at each other in amazement without interrupting the song. The song then began to change. The men's voices dropped and took on more harmonious tones. My heart began to beat in time with the drum. I found I knew this song, deep in my memory and in my heart. That is where I sang it from. I supplied the high tonal accents. As we continued to sing, the magic T rose higher. It stopped near the ceiling. I closed my eyes and allowed the song to work through me, enjoying the sense of giving over. I had never heard the drum sound like that before, so powerful, as if ten drums were playing together. I placed my hand on Mike's shoulder to make a connection. A subtle buzz of energy passed through us, moving from me to him, from him back to me, like the first time we had kissed.

When I opened my eyes, I noticed that more people had slipped into the hall, lured in by the irresistible song. They too began to sing. More and more people appeared—older people, boys and girls—until all the floor space was taken up. We all sang the same song into the early morning without becoming parched or tired. When the drummers finally stopped, the magic T wafted back down to rest over the centre of the drum. Everyone stood in silence, shuffled around a bit, feeling their bodies again, and without a word they all slowly began to exit the hall. Mike moved to place the blanket over the T, but his hand recoiled in pain.

"Ouch!"

"What is it?"

"It's burning hot, Rhea, way too hot to touch."

"Well let's leave it to cool down. Let's get some air, babe."

A heavy rain fell during the night, and it was just letting up when we walked outside. As we breathed in the fresh moist air, Mike asked, "What just happened? Did you feel the energy in that room? I think I went into a trance." Mike slipped his arms around me, and we shared a long kiss.

"You put me in a trance," I whispered.

Mike cupped his hand over the top of my head and let it drop to the small of my back.

"You are like a magic potion to me," he said, looking into my eyes. "My life and everything in it is more wonderful because of you, Rhea. I want you to be with me always."

I pulled my head off his big chest to look at him square in the face.

"Michael Brooks, is that a proposal?"

"It could be," he teased. "I propose we climb into my truck, then into a hot bath together, and make some more music, just you and me."

I laughed and gave him a squeeze.

"I accept," I said. "Lets pack the T away safely and get home.

Mike and I re-entered the hall, and right away something felt wrong. The drum was gone, the drummers were gone, and so was the triangle.

Mike shouted, "Where is it!"

"Lets get in the truck and see if we can catch up with whoever took it."

Panicking, we loaded ourselves into Mike's truck and drove without a plan or direction. Mike knew where most of the drummers lived, and together we decided to make a beeline to Randy's, the lead drummer and keeper of the drum. We'd been pounding on his door for five solid minutes, when Randy finally appeared, dressed only in a pair of *Free Willy* boxer shorts.

"Mike, man, what d'ya want? My old lady's on my case for being out all night."

We could hear her in the background. "Who the hell is that, Randle? Better not be that hoochie you were with last night!"

"No, woman, I told you I was drumm'n, now go back to bed."

Mike jumped in, "Okay Randy, where is it?"

"Where's what?"

"The pyramid, man. Where is it?"

Randy looked confused, "You don't have it? Man, I left after you and Rhea headed outside. I had to drive Nathan, Hank, and Pete home."

"What about Alyster?"

"Said he didn't want a ride, said he was gonna walk."

"But he lives across the bridge on the reserve, that's like twenty miles."

"I know, I thought it was a little strange too, but I figured the brother must know what he's doin'."

Randy's woman yelled again. "If you don't get back in this bed right now, Randle, I ain't cookin' you no more fry bread!"

"Alright!" Randy shouted back. "Hey, help me out, man, just come in and tell her we were drummin' all night."

"But we *were* drumming all night," I said.

"I know, but she caught me in a couple little lies, and now . . ."

Mike said, "Hey, that's your karma jar you're pulling those cookies from, man, it's got nothing to do with me."

And with that we turned back to the truck.

"Hey, thanks a lot, bro," Randy sulked after us.

"Randle!" came the final summons as he closed the door.

"Alyster," Mike said, more to himself than to me.

We headed out of town towards the reserve, where Alyster was staying with relatives.

"You know, both of his parents died last month in a house fire," Mike told me.

"Oh, I heard about that on the news, where the older couple perished, but they managed to save a little baby."

"Ya, that's Alyster's kid, three months old. She has bad lung damage from the smoke. She's been in the hospital ever since."

"Oh, Mike, that's terrible. I hope she'll be alright. What did they say the cause of the fire was?"

"The stove was left on. Alyster told us he was fix'n something to eat before drum practice and ran out of the house leaving one of the elements on high. They didn't charge him with anything 'cuz it wasn't intentional."

"He must feel so awful."

"Yah, can't imagine the guilt building up in that guy. Thing is, Rhea, he has no idea of the power of the T. Took us awhile just to learn how it works."

"Mike, what do you think Alyster wants to do with it? Why would he take it?"

"No telling. Could be for something good or something else."

It was still early morning, and the rush-hour traffic hadn't had time to build yet. The heavy rains still covered the streets in slick layers. Mike drove swiftly, but safely, out of town. I kept a tight grip on the door handle and the seat as we sped through intersections, keeping my eyes peeled for any signs of Alyster. As we took the turn leading up to the bridge, I spotted him.

"Mike, there he is. Slow down."

Alyster was a small guy, but the absence of other pedestrians made him easy to see. He had the pyramid slung over his shoulder like a bag of laundry.

He was standing on the bridge, nervously contemplating the fast-moving river below. Mike pulled over on the shoulder of the road, well before the bridge.

"I don't have a good feeling, Rhea. We better stay cool."

We walked towards the bridge, pretending we were just strolling and enjoying the fresh morning. He didn't see us approach at first. Alyster seemed hypnotized by the river's currents.

Mike greeted him. "Hey, Alyster, how's it going, man?"

Alyster didn't buy our casual act. He tensed up at the sight of us and backed away five feet. He maneuvered the T into his arms and cradled it.

"I need this. I'm taking it to Cynthia."

I assumed that was his baby girl.

"Alyster, that's cool," I said, trying to reassure him. "We're not mad at you. Come with us. We'll give you a ride to the hospital."

"No!" he shouted back. "Leave me alone!"

He broke down and sobbed. His grief was heavy, but he managed to speak.

"I killed my parents! They burned to death in the house my father built for us. What the hell kind of son am I? What the hell kind of father am I? I don't even know if my baby is going to make it! They have her hooked up to all those damn machines. She struggles just to breathe. She's just a baby!" He sobbed more.

Mike bent down to whisper to me. "I'm going down to the rocks below, just in case. You keep him talking."

Just in case, I thought. I didn't even want to imagine.

Mike kissed me on the lips and calmly made his way under the bridge. Drivers were beginning to take notice of the increasingly desperate man on the bridge. Cars were beginning to slow.

"Alyster, we can teach you how to use the T. Cynthia will get well—we just need to show you."

He suddenly became angry. He screamed at me, "It can't bring my parents back!"

I could see Mike below negotiating the rocks, positioning himself. Alyster made me wonder if the T could bring people back to life. I didn't doubt its power one bit, but resurrection, I wasn't so sure about.

The traffic volume was increasing, and it became more difficult to talk with Alyster. My natural instinct was to move closer. Alyster backed away, while raising himself onto the rail. He was still holding the T, dangling it from the crook of his middle finger.

Traffic stopped completely.

Alyster caught sight of Mike down below.

I reached towards him. "Alyster, please come down from there."

Someone must have called nine-one-one. When Alyster heard the approaching sirens, his sobbing stopped. His eyes turned clear. He stood straight up, hugging the T in his arms. Then, he looked down at Mike and waved.

Alyster let himself fall. The sirens stopped. Mike dove in the river after him. All I could see and hear was the rushing of the current. No-one surfaced. My heart felt as if it had stopped, and yet it was beating double time. Air, light, sound—nothing existed except the churning water. Then up popped Alyster, still clinging to the T, which seemed to float six inches above the water. Even though the river was running as fast as rapids, Alyster floated sideways towards the bank, where police hoisted him out. When they laid their hands on the T, it fell apart and the pieces rolled back into the river.

Where was Mike? My eyes scanned hard, but I couldn't catch sight of him. Suddenly, light bubbles began to appear on the water's surface, twinkling and bursting as they made a quick journey downriver. That's when I knew.

My family rallied around me for the next few weeks, plying me with casseroles, pies, and homemade breads until I had successfully gained back all the weight it had taken me three months to lose. I spent my days sitting at the kitchen table while a mountain of dirty dishes piled up at the sink. I thought about Mike and constantly replayed that last kiss on the bridge. Then, one day, I had enough motivation to go for a walk. I found myself heading towards the cliff where Mike and I used to evoke visions with the pyramid. I sat there and let my legs dangle over the rock edge. I began to believe it was right for me to end my life. I had known love, and I had experienced miracles. The rest was cruelty and hard lessons I didn't have the energy for any longer.

I noticed a man on the beach below gathering rocks. His actions were slow and methodical. As I continued to watch, my heart sunk. He was building stone pyramids. Then a young Asian couple came along and stood silently in the man's presence. He handed them a stone pyramid, and they turned without a word. Together, they carried their strange gift away. That was all I needed to see.

APPETITE

Nicholas Knight

YELLOW EYES. In the ditch. Rat's eyes glowed in headlights.

Car passed quick. Quick as my temptation. Not tonight. Fleeting temptation. Tonight, eating in style.

Two hours past dark. Three hours since last vehicle slowed. Only for a moment. Slowed then sped. Threw dust in my face. Saw me. Shirtless. Sped away. Away from the tattooed torso.

Tired of hitching. Stomach growled. Growled. Incessant. Incessant. Needed to get grub.

Looked to flashing lights. Across large field. Blasts of music. Intermittent. Flash. Blast. Flash. Blast.

Didn't know location. Slept the day away. Trucker's cab. Bleary-eyed when dumped. Jo-Jo's Gas and Gear. Five hours passed. All I knew. Somewhere in the Prairies. Near boonie circus grounds.

A circus. A carnival. Typical. Magical. Altogether laughable.

Irresistible.

Followed country road. Humid summer night. Remained shirtless. T-shirt jammed into jeans. Followed road to music. To a four-storey-high tent. Music punctuated by screams. Screams of awe. Screams of delight. Adults and children alike.

Didn't enter bigtop. Circus as expected. Rusty children's rides. Squeaking by on recycled oil. Duct tape. God knows what else. Interspersed with hucksters. Plying cheap toys. Rigged games. And sideshows.

Sideshows unsettled nerves. Played with the mind. Confused the soul.

Chuckled. Uneasy chuckle. Result of unsettled nerves. Passed sideshow signs. A four-armed man. A cyclops. A mermaid. An animate mummy. Played with the mind. Other unthinkable creatures. Played with the soul. Almost turned. Almost fled. Refused to believe. They didn't exist.

Didn't exist.

Walked away. Headed for food. Concessions. In fleamarket-type booths. Smelled grease. Pungent. Overwhelming. Long-empty stomach flip-flopped. Fingers rummaged pockets. Left: small fishing knife. Right: quarter-sized slug on string. Back: empty. No cash. No checks. No plastic. Take-out only. No dishes to wash. Nothing to trade.

Went straight. Did not hesitate. Straight to garbage can.

Full can. Child darted in front. Discarded half-eaten burger. "Just what I wanted," under breath. Casual movements. Quick snatch. Continued walking. Looked left. Weary parents. Wired offspring. Vacated picnic table. Hurried over. Empty tables in short supply. Adults cleared away waste. Eight-year-old lingered. Then left. Left behind unfinished juice. French fries drowned in ketchup. Grinned. Special value meal. Should've asked for super-size.

Tore off burger's bite marks. Still had standards. Munched on dinner. Marveled at crowdedness. Looked like every hick came. Everyone within twenty miles. Everyone showed up. Every last cousin along.

Time for dessert. Stood. Stretched. Walked towards busy booth. Mini-donuts for sale. Freshly made. Young boy crossed path. Carried overflowing bag of donuts. Tantalizing smell. Stomach growled. Recent meal forgotten.

Boy tripped. Hazard of untied shoelaces. Fell forward. Refused to let go. Death-gripped donuts. Hit hard-packed dirt. Smacked side of face.

Impact jarring. Bag's contents flew.

I paused. Eyed dusty donuts. Eyed about-to-cry child. Thoughts crossed my mind. Comfort the boy? Snatch up donuts? Ignored both instincts. Continued to booth.

Passersby trampled donuts.

Five long lines. Three harried cashiers. People jostled for position. Confusion. Made it easy. Easy for me. Scooped up tip jar. Off counter without notice.

Hole in jar top. Too small. Fingers didn't fit. Quick flip. Dumped contents onto hand. What the hell? Not just coins. Though coins aplenty. Also dumped water. Several ounces. Wet coins. Wet hand. Scowled. Slipped jar back. Cashier would be suspicious. Suspicious of wet money. Deposited coins in pocket. Turned to leave. Wanted out. Out of crazy lineup.

Didn't leave. Noticed bag of donuts. Unattended. Sitting on counter. Purchaser fishing in purse. Couldn't find money. Swore she had some. Grabbed treats. Hurried away. Ignored sign. Over cash register: "In God we trust. All others must pay cash."

Hurried away. Then stopped. Ate some donuts. Noticed tent. Bright yellow tent. Hand-painted sign. Hung over entrance. LIVE WEREWOLF - *BE AMAZED* AS IT STALKS *AND KILLS* ITS PREY. Underneath, small disclaimer: *Not for Children, Vegetarians, or the Weak of Heart.*

Contemplated entry. Worth a laugh? Nothing more. Walked the perimeter. Bright yellow tent. Fastened to ground. All around. Heavy pegs. One peg missing. Looked around. No-one watching. Lifted flap. Slipped inside.

Air smelled musty. Tasted musty too. Tent coated with mildew. Mildew molecules sucked in. Each breath tasted off. Tasted wrong. Stale. Musty. Tainted. Almost departed. Disgusted. Couldn't leave. Sensed something. Energy. Palpable excitement. Interest held.

Ate some donuts. Counteracted mustiness. Somewhat. Then moved closer. Amongst other spectators.

Paying customers. Wanted to see. Everything. Money's worth. Clustered around fences. Four large fences. Chain-link cage. Three sides accessible. Twenty-feet tall. Twenty-feet wide. Far side masked. Velvet curtain. Dirty red curtain.

Cage reminded me. Something. What? Wrestling match? Yes. Saw wrestlers in cage. Similar. Half-expected to see again. Has-been wrestlers. Maybe. Fighting. In costumes. Werewolf costume. Sheep costume.

Probably not.

Looked upward. Far left corner. Where cage abutted tent. Atop elevated chair. Perched man. Like a lifeguard. No red bikini. Thankfully. Dressed in black. All black. Like a commando. Gun and all. Holstered at waist. Held cheap megaphone. Pressed against mouth. Talking. Already talking. Rattling on. Something about legends. Werewolves? Yes, werewolves. Captivity rare. Very rare.

"As the more observant among you may have noticed," showman said, "there's only a quarter moon tonight." Acknowledgement murmured. "I can't say for sure if the moon thing's entirely a myth, but the fact of the matter is, *our wolfman* does not need a full moon to transform. Nosiree. *Our wolfman* can do it *at will.*"

Crowd oohed. Crowd aahed. Oohed and aahed.

"However," showman said. Pulled out gun. "This here pistol is loaded with silver bullets. Just in case things get out of hand. . . ."

Loud whispers responded. Audience deliberations. Speculating. Disputing. Laughing.

Nervous laughter.

"But enough talk." Showman sheathed sidearm. Audience quieted. "Ladies and gentlemen, prepare . . . to be . . . amazed!" Showman leaned forward. Pulled a rope. Drew up curtain. Dirty red curtain.

Truck bed visible. Behind the fence. Open-ended truck. Couldn't see inside. Not clearly. Large trailer. Too long. Too dark. Movement in shadows. Swift movements.

Showman pulled chain. Heavy chain. Connected to fence. Swung gate open.

Spectators gasped. Gasped as one. Jerked away. Away from cage. Like suddenly electrified.

My feet were stomped. Overweight woman. Backed up quick. Whiff of cheap perfume. Barely noticed. Creature in cage. Held attention.

Werewolf? No question. No doubts. Had to be. Real. Live. Werewolf. Monster.

Beast in cage. Stood still. Eyed crowd. Knees and elbows bent. Back arched. Head cocked. Tattered clothes. Covered groin. Almost. Covered torso. Somewhat. Body blanketed with hair. Pointed ears. Forlorn face. All covered. Blanketed. Except grimy nose. And grimy lips.

Cracked lips. Around crooked mouth. Mouth that snarled. Silent, frozen snarl. Teeth bared. Jagged. Yellow. Twice human size. Jagged. Deadly.

Blood-red eyes. Demon eyes. Studied crowd. Watched. Waited. For what?

Onlookers gaped. Fell silent. Fear? Awe? I pondered. Couldn't tell.

Creaking noise. Overhead. Everyone looked. Rusty door. Trapdoor. Top corner. Showman opened. Dropped something through. Live rabbit. Cute white bunny. Black spot on back.

Werewolf howled. Savage sound. Full of hunger. Echoed throughout tent. Savage. Hungry.

My bladder cramped. Nearly lost control.

Beast stalked rabbit. Timid rabbit. Didn't move. Stunned by fall? Didn't matter. No chance. Dead soon. Crowd inched forward. Pressed against fence. Wanted close-up. View of kill.

Werewolf growled. Pounced. Rabbit bolted.

Rabbit slammed fence. Crowd jerked back. Bunny tried again. Threw itself against cage. Repeatedly. Every few feet. No weak spots. Pitiful.

Werewolf lunged. Missed rabbit. Hit the fence. Hard. People screamed. Crowd stumbled back. Further back.

Werewolf paused. Stared at crowd. Growled. Three short bursts. Raked its claws. Along the fence. Curved claws. Raked fence. Sharp nails. Clackety-clack.

Shivered. Tiny hairs rose. Neck. Arms. Back. Hairs on end. Clackety-clack. Clackety-clack.

Werewolf tilted head. Howled again. Ear-splitting. Reverberated, throughout tent. Beast raised fist. Shook fist. Not at crowd. At showman. Then turned. Found rabbit. Cowering in corner. Beast growled. Rushed prey.

Rabbit darted. Too late. Werewolf anticipated. Leapt. Same direction. Caught prey. Sharp claws. Speared rabbit. Brought prey to mouth. Bunny's body twitched. Life lingered. Werewolf tore off chunk. Thick chunk. No more twitching.

Animal appetite. Another chunk.

I retched. Vomit jumped up. Throat to mouth. Acidic bubbles. Taste of burger. Swallowed back down. Looked away. Couldn't take it. Gruesome scene. Stuffed donuts in mouth. Sucked off cinnamon. Icing sugar. Purged awful residue. Didn't swallow. Spit out soggy donuts. Didn't trust stomach. Couldn't take solids. Not now.

Looked back at cage. Couldn't resist. Had to see.

Furry white rabbit. No more. Pile of bones. Few tufts of fur. Blood-soaked pelt. Nothing more.

Werewolf licked carcass. Savoured it. Satiated. For now. Glared at audience. Growled. Lumbered off. Returned to truck.

Gate swung closed. "And *that*," showman said, "is our show." Lips stretched. Big smile. "It's hard to say," he added, "just how many werewolves roam the country, but keep in mind that they normally travel in packs. So if you ever hear a werewolf's howl late at night, I'd advise you to run the other way. . . ."

Crowd murmured. Shocked disbelief. Departed en masse. Swept me out. Outside tent. Fresh air. Alleviated queasiness. Gobbled down donuts. Staunched lingering foulness.

Considered leaving. Hitting road again. Getting far away. Away from werewolf-thing. Far as possible. Considered. But didn't. Been thumbing too long. Needed cash. Had to line pockets. Before moving on.

Travelling circus work. Why not? Probably provided food. And bed in trailer. Decided to ask. Sought out owner. Asked broom pusher. Cocked thumb showed way. Nearby. Sort of. Straight path. Trailer a ways back. Behind yellow tent.

Dark behind tent. Too dark. Main grounds bright. Lights reached out. Almost enough. Sufficient guidance. Insufficient comfort. Trailer window lit. Beacon to follow. But too many shadows. Black patches. Hidden areas. Underneath the eighteen-wheeler. Hiding the beast. Flesh-hungry werewolf. Inside truck. So close.

What if . . . it tore through? Rusted floor? Could happen. Any second. Rusted floor. Savage beast.

Smelled me. No doubt. Tracked my movements.

Shivered. Warm air be damned. Imagined werewolf. Stalking me. From beneath the truck. Stumbled. Over what? Something on grass. A football. Picked it up. Thought of uses. Trade with a kid. For popcorn. A candied app—

Movement. Out of darkness. Werewolf flew at me. Attacked too fast. Gaping mouth. All I saw. Glistening teeth. Hurtling at me. Too fast. Couldn't avoid. Thrust out football. Shielded face. Animal slammed into me. Hit my chest. Knocked me down.

Kept football in-between. Between me and beast.

Werewolf's teeth sunk in. Punctured pigskin. Shook ball savagely. Growled deeply.

"Sorry about that," a woman said. Suddenly beside me. With a leash. Attached it to beast's collar. "My puppy is a little protective of his ball-ball." Petted animal's head. "Aren't you, baby?"

Puppy? Looked closer. Hard to see. Dim lights. Circus seepage. Multicoloured glow. Looked closer. Saw the truth. No puppy. No werewolf either. Full-grown dog. German shepherd.

"No harm done," I said. Didn't mean it. Wanted to say: "Muzzle. That. Damn. Thing!" Remained civil. Had to. Swearing at master. Bad idea. Upset dog. Big dog. Protective dog. Safety in silence.

I stood. Ignored outstretched hand. Brushed myself off. Jeans still dry. Even in front. Glanced at dog. Shot reproachful look. Walked away. Towards trailer.

Woman called out: "So sorry. . . ."

Didn't look back. Didn't respond. Unsettling encounter. Vicious dog. Cleared mind. Looked ahead. Rickety motorhome. An oasis of sorts. Pulled on T-shirt. Approached office. Small sign on door. Sign proclaimed: Dan *the Circus King* Cregg. Knocked. Aluminium door rattled.

Gruff voice from within: "It ain't locked."

Opened door. Stepped inside. Felt cool air. Fleeting. Rotating fan. Not refreshing. Blew body odour. Awful welcome. Eyed the room. Right: small washroom. Door ajar. Left: sheet partition. Hid rest of trailer. Straight ahead: rickety card table. Grey vinyl. Littered with papers. Mostly bills. Around the table: four folding chairs.

Behind the table: middle-aged man. Beige short-sleeved shirt. Unbuttoned over tank top.

Some "king." Almost snickered. Serious paunch. Food-crusted moustache. Circus King? Slob King!

Cregg eyed me. Warily. "Well? What do you want?"

I smiled. Fake smile. Work face. "I need a job. Can you help?"

"Not today. I've got enough mouths to feed already."

"Don't need much. Forget pay. Food and shelter. All I'm after."

"I said not today. Now, go away."

"Come on! I'll clean animal shit. Or—"

"Unless you've got some freaky skill that I can build a show around, I ain't interested."

I grinned. "Beer skills. Can drink a two-four. Nonstop. Without pissing."

Cregg's eyes rolled. "All the guys that run the rides can do that. Big whoop. I need something that'll sell tickets. A showstopper. Not something lame like burping the alphabet. And I don't want to hear about how many marshmallows you can shove in your mouth or how many strands of spaghetti you can floss through your nostrils."

Had nothing.

Cregg leaned forward. Looked at me. Thoughtfully. "How do you feel about raw meat?"

"That Sushi stuff?"

"Nah. More like rabbit or lamb, maybe even some pig guts."

"I've eaten stuff. Pretty rancid stuff. Old stuff. Rotten stuff. But cooked. At some point. Tell you what. I'll eat whatever. Any weird stuff. Monkey brains. Gizzards. Dog meat. Whatever. Just . . . not *too* pink."

"Pink?" Cregg retorted. Spat the words. Spit beaded his moustache. Spotted his papers. "Not too pink? No." Shook his head. Extra emphasis. "When I say raw, I mean *raw*—red meat, dripping dark red blood from some pathetic little critter's still-beating heart. *That* kind of raw."

"Oh." Didn't respond. Didn't know how. Wanted a job. Had eaten stuff. Repulsive stuff. For survival. But fireroasted rats. Barbequed squirrels. Never raw. Not like a freak. This slob's idea? Too sick. Not for me. Oh well. Hit the road. Again. A whiff of Cregg—stale perspiration—decided it. Time to go.

Didn't leave.

Cregg spoke first. "I don't suppose you caught the werewolf show?"

"Yeah, actually—No. You don't mean—That thing's not . . . not *human*?"

Cregg sneered. "You thought it was real?"

"Well, I . . . All that fur. The claws. And—"

"Not fur, hair—thick, human hair. Rogaine, or whatever that hair accelerant stuff is called, works like a charm. Just slather it all over the body in heavy doses. File the teeth into sharp points, superglue on some claws, add some rubber ears, and voila . . . you got yourself a bonafide werewolf."

"The guy let—"

Door banged opened. Man rushed in. Familiar man. The showman. From werewolf show.

Cregg laughed. "Hey, Sims. Where's the fire?"

"No fire," Sims said. Paced tiny office. Ignored me. "The stupid rabbit had rabies"

"Dammit. Is the freak gonna make it?"

"Shit, I don't know. But I doubt he'll be in any shape to perform any time soon."

Cregg grinned. Creepy grin. Pointed at Jake. "This fella's another drifter, looking for food and shelter. Think we can build his appetite enough by next Saturday?"

"Let's find out," Sims said. Next to me. Raised gun.

Gun smashed down. Blackness. Nothing.

WOKE UP. Later. How much? Didn't know.

Chained up. Inside truck. Large. Dank. Dirty blankets strewn around. Water bottles within reach. Blankets and bottles. Nothing else.

Truck bed stank. Smelled of decay. Death and decay.

Sims was sewing. Something rubbery. Sewed onto my ears.

"Won't co-operate," I said. Understood predicament. Horrified. Dire fate. "Won't howl. No wolf sounds. No way. I'll talk. Tell audience."

Sims laughed. "All the werewolf sounds are on tape." Laughed again. "And I still have the tongue of the last guy who asked the audience for help—got it in a jar. Want to see?"

Fell silent.

Circus King grinned. Evil grin.

Sims finished *alterations*.

"See you in a week," Sims said. "Try not to spoil your *appetite*."

They laughed as they left. Cruel laughter. Echoing. Echoing. Laughter filled my ears. Excruciating.

Truck doors closed. Darkness surrounded me.

My stomach growled.

Silent tears fell.

LA RIVIÈRE NOIRE

Leslie Brown

SHE BALANCED IN THE STERN OF THE CANOE and politely waved to the float plane pilot as he churned past her, gaining speed for takeoff. She watched him climb over the tree line at the far end of the lake and bank right for his return trip to St. Christophe-des-bois to the south. Between her and the float plane's destination lay two hundred and fifty kilometres of primal northern Québec wilderness devoid of human habitation. Even the trappers shunned the banks of the Black River, her only way back to civilization. The reason for this had been made graphically clear last night in the bar below her rented room in St. Christophe. She had inquired about the condition of the Black River. Was the water level high or low this year? And were there any unexpected obstacles to be found? Instead she was given vivid descriptions of monsters and demons that predated even the first natives in the area. She had heard about *la chasse-galerie,* the ghostly flying canoe steered, it was said, by the devil himself. And then there was *l'enfant maudit,* the damned child, which lured its victims with pitiful cries. She quickly ceased to be entertained by these stories and had been ready to leave in disgust when old Father Rosaire had touched her arm and asked her name in French.

"Rachel Sawyer, Father," she replied politely in her best high-school French and had to spread her hands in incomprehension when he continued in rapid Québécois. Speaking more slowly and carefully, the old priest asked her why she wanted to travel *la rivière Noire* alone. She looked at his arthritic fingers, which constantly caressed his worn rosary.

"My husband and his best friend drowned on the Black River last year, Father. I want to follow their route on the anniversary of their deaths. To say goodbye." It seemed so simple when she phrased it that way. No mention of the nights lying alone in their bed in the house they had designed together, watching the moonlight shine on the empty pillow beside her. Reading something interesting in the paper and looking up to tell the vacant armchair about it. Of losing interest in what had been their shared passion for architecture and watching their small firm lose business because she no longer cared enough. Of the money spent on grief councillors while Mark's wife Cheryl went on with her life and new boyfriend. There was much more involved for her than just saying goodbye. Somehow, she had to let go of Rob and find her way out of the pit that she had fallen into. She hadn't gone on that trip with Rob because of morning sickness and fatigue. He reluctantly left her at home and took Mark, never to return, not even in a coffin. She miscarried the child at three months. No, her explanation to Father Rosaire didn't even come close.

"My child," Father Rosaire said gently, "this is not a good idea. There are many bad things along *la rivière Noire*. These men," and his stern gaze caused most of the bar's customers to study their beer bottles closely, "try to frighten you for fun, but I am concerned for your soul. I will have a mass for your husband and his friend. You can say goodbye here."

Rachel shook her head firmly but smiled at Father Rosaire to take the bite out of an outright refusal. "No, Father, I've trained for this; I've bought the right gear so I can go it alone, and I've booked the float plane. This is something I have to do for the good of my soul. Do you understand?"

Father Rosaire shook his head sorrowfully. "My child, I fear for you, but your grief will not let you hear me. I will pray for your husband and his friend and for you too." He rose shakily, and Rachel quickly stood and placed a hand under his elbow. He caught her hand and clasped it in his own dry, twisted ones. When he let go, she was holding his rosary and crucifix. She looked up in protest.

"Father, I can't take your rosary. Besides, I'm not even Catholic!"

With a twinkle in his eye, he replied, "Then I will pray for you twice as hard." Quickly he sobered. "Be careful on *la Noire*, my child, careful for your life and careful for your soul. Keep this token of my concern for you." She watched him leave the bar, slowly and painfully, his back bent with arthritis.

A day later, she sat in her red canoe and patted the pocket of her shirt where the rosary rested. A year ago, she might have been frightened by Father Rosaire's warnings, but now, after the worst thing that she could imagine had already happened to her, she dismissed them as unimportant. Lac Wendigo stretched before her, silver white in the late morning sun. It was the headwaters of the Black River and merely the first step in her journey towards Rob.

Lac Wendigo proved a bit of challenge when the wind came up in her face, but the red canoe was easy to handle and very stable. Even so, fighting the wind and waves left her tired by the time she reached the indentation in the shoreline that marked the commencement of the Black River. She rounded a point and entered its waters. A trick of the light and the narrowing path of water made the river look black. Out of the wind, she was able to stop paddling and wet her dry lips and throat. Her face felt hot from windburn, or perhaps from the fever of elation. Here she was at last. Rob and Mark had passed by here a year ago this day. She imagined them ahead of her, their paddles flashing as they dipped in and out of the water. Their old green canoe would have been low in the water, not only because of ten days' worth of gear and supplies but also because Rob and Mark had been big men. The top of Rachel's head only came to Rob's chin, so she loved to kiss the place where his collarbones met. Rachel shook her head and firmly took her paddle in hand. She knew where she wanted to camp, and daydreaming would not get her there before dark. She would follow the guys' planned route, camping where they had, seeing what they saw until Devil's Bend. Devil's Bend, that set of rapids marked as unrunnable. That's where the Provincial Police determined Rob and Mark had drowned, trying to do the impossible. Fragments of the green canoe seemed to confirm their theory, but Rachel knew better. The guys were careful and responsible canoeists. Rob wouldn't have taken stupid chances with a baby on the way. She had no hope of finding out what happened, but maybe there would be some sort of understanding.

The campsite was where she had expected it to be. She landed the canoe next to the sandbank that stretched a third of the way across the river. Before unloading the canoe, she checked the site for recent evidence of bears and other campers. The fire pit had been unused for a long time. Rob and Mark might have been the last to have a fire here. There was no bear scat or clawed-open logs around, so she returned to the canoe and carried her gear up the bank. In short order, she pitched her tent, gathered firewood, and had her first dinner bubbling on the camp stove. She watched as the setting sun changed the patterns and colours on the surface of the river. A loon began its haunting call back in the direction of Lac Wendigo, and, for the first time in a year, Rachel felt the tight knot under her breastbone loosen a little bit.

The next three days followed the same pattern. Running a few small rapids and then scouting the abandoned campsites, some nicer than others but all devoid of animal and human signs. She hung her food anyway, out of the

157

reach of bears and raccoons, and read by the light of her small lantern until she was tired. So far into the trip, her sleep had been heavy and dreamless. So many times at home, she replayed scenarios of Rob's death in her sleep. She would wake herself up with her sobs. It must be all the exercise that brought her relief. If only she could paddle forever, not thinking of anything but the rhythm of her strokes and the obstacles in the river ahead of her. Tonight, however, her dreams were chaotic and distressing. She woke to the first light feeling more tired than when she had gone to bed. She was still not used to the profound quiet at dawn. In other places, birds would be calling loudly from the treetops and squirrels would be dropping pinecones on her tent. She unzipped her tent door just enough to stick her head out to judge the weather and temperature. There was a fine mist hanging over the river, already burning off in the sunlight. The day would be a warm one. She emerged from the tent and stretched luxuriously, casually scanning the campsite. She paused in her survey. Her cooking pots were not where she had left them, nested and in their protective bag by the fire pit. Since they were cleaned thoroughly the night before, they would have no attraction for animals. Therefore, their absence implied a human presence. There was no sign of the pots around the camp. Had some of the raconteurs from St. Christophe followed her down the river, playing an elaborate joke? There must be a simpler explanation. Raccoons could be quite ingenious with their hands. They might have dragged the pots down to the river. Rachel scrambled over the rocks down to the sand spit. Beside her canoe sat the three pots, removed from their bag and placed side by side along the water's edge. Each was filled to the brim with the gold-flecked water of the Black River. Rachel pivoted on her heels searching for intruders. The woods, dark and brooding at the best of times, took on a menacing air.

"Hello, who's there? *Qui est là?*" She shouted. The answer was loud flapping and outraged quacking. Startled, Rachel stepped back into the largest cooking pot and landed on her rump. She listened for malicious laughter but only heard the ducks flying down the river, still quacking in panic. Rachel angrily picked the pots up and dumped their contents onto the sand. She packed up quickly, chewing on a fruit bar as she worked. Her safest bet was to get out quickly and watch the river behind her for her tormentors. She fingered the knife at her belt. She had thought it would have been sufficient protection against animals and never considered a human threat.

She watched the river behind her all day but no one appeared. The peace she had begun to feel evaporated. She paddled further than she had planned just to make it difficult to catch up to her. She chose a spot to camp where her tent would not be visible from the river. By the time she had made dinner, she was quite angry. She had been forced to deviate from her plans to commemorate Rob's route and camp where he had. To top it off, her concealed location meant there was no wind to drive the mosquitoes away. When she lay down in the tent, she placed the hunting knife beside her head. She was furious enough to use it on someone, practical joker or not. She made a concerted effort to calm herself and clear her mind. Gradually her adrenaline levels fell, and she drifted into a restless sleep.

She woke suddenly in the middle of the night to the sound of a loon's call, echoing and re-echoing between the hills. She could never be annoyed at being awakened by loons, because their calls were too hauntingly beautiful and too integral a part of the north woods. She rolled over and tucked the sleeping bag under her chin. The distant calling continued, but the sound began to change. It sounded more like a child sobbing in distress than a loon's hoot. The point of origin seemed to be different now, too. The noise rose and fell. Rachel sat up, the hair prickling at her nape. It was an unworldly noise, one she had never heard before in all her years of camping. She drew her knees up to her chest, reluctant to leave her tent although the protection offered by a thin layer of nylon was dubious at best. The crying faded, and the night was silent again. Rachel unzipped the tent door and shone her flashlight out towards the fire pit. Everything looked undisturbed. Tonight she had put the cooking pots in the food bag, which was now hanging twelve feet in the air some distance from the camp. The practical jokers would have to find something else to play with if they had followed her this far. If they had been making that crying noise, they sounded far away and had probably lost her. The preternatural wailing was surely an attempt to continue to harass her at long range. She muttered, "Jerk-offs," and settled down, determined to get a good night's sleep.

The next morning was overcast, and she pulled out her raingear from the bottom of the clothes pack. Her food bag hung from its rope undisturbed. She lowered it down and wound up the rope neatly. She hauled the heavy bag over to the cooking area and opened the top. The place where the stainless steel cooking pots had nestled was empty. A cold finger ran down her spine.

"Damn," she whispered. She pushed her way through the dense brush to the river, stepping over her canoe hidden in the low bushes that grew on the banks. The three pots, full of river water, waited for her, each balanced on a separate rock, since there was no beach where she had landed. The rage awoke and boiled over again.

"Damn you!" she screamed. "Leave me alone! *Laissez-moi tranquille!*" She was shaking with rage and fear. What kind of people could find her camp, get her pots out of her food bag, and then rehang the bag, all without making a sound? Maybe she had heard something in her sleep that woke her up, only to be masked by the loon call and the strange crying afterwards. Her efforts to reason out her tormentors' methods calmed her, and common sense reasserted itself. The prank, although elaborate, was harmless. As long as events did not escalate, she could tolerate it. It would be best to resume her planned route and camp at the cleared campsites instead of in this prickly bush. She picked up her pots and drained them. She forced herself to make breakfast and pack her gear in a calm, unhurried fashion.

She had been paddling for an hour before the thought struck her. The weird crying could only be *l'enfant maudit,* the cannibal baby of the north. Yeah, right. She had been primed perfectly in the bar, with all the horror stories the boys in the plaid shirts had been raised on. They had told her that women were particularly vulnerable because of their soft hearts. A woman would think that the child was abandoned and when she bent to pick it up, she was consumed for her pains. What was next? A cardboard ghostly canoe hovering over her campsite on hidden wires? She laughed out loud and was taken aback by the unfamiliar sound of her genuine amusement. She hadn't found anything funny in ages. In their own twisted way, the boys in plaid were helping her forget the bigger problems. She sang defiantly as she paddled, hoping the sound would carry back to them.

Late that afternoon she carefully ran an easy set of rapids and pulled in to the campsite below. She had been five days on the water with five more to go. Tomorrow she would reach Devil's Bend, the impassable rapids where Rob and Mark's trip had ended. What if she felt nothing there? What if that place brought her no whisper of Rob's presence? She had no plans beyond the canoe trip, no idea on how to resume her life. The last six months had been spent working towards this goal, with the vague hope she would find some sort of closure. She paused in her unloading of the canoe and went to sit on one of the rocks beside the churning water. The other alternative had never been voiced, even in her thoughts. To end her trip where Rob's had. Let the police find the bits of red canoe downstream and shake their heads about the crazy Anglais who take the risks on the Noire.

Around midnight, she awoke to the peevish crying of a baby. The sound had mixed with her dream for a while, another recurring dream that she liked even less to think about. She was in their house, hers and Rob's. A baby was crying, and she ran from room to room looking for it.

What if the sound wasn't pranksters? Or not even some weird bird she had never heard of? What if she was going mad, thinking that she was hearing her dead baby crying in the woods? Best then to end the trip at Devil's Bend. The crying was close, right in the campsite. Rachel cursed and furiously unzipped her sleeping bag. Enough of being a victim. This was no hallucination. This time she would find her tormentors and face them down. She sprang from the tent, her knife gripped firmly in one hand and a flashlight in the other. As soon as she stood, the tone of the cries changed into the high-pitched wailing of a truly distressed baby. Despite herself, Rachel felt admiration for the skill of the mimicry. She cautiously walked towards the sound, using the light of the full moon to see by rather than giving away her position with the flashlight. Just as she thought she was closing on the source of the wailing, it suddenly came from behind, from the river. There must be two of them, trying to get her to run back and forth between them. She continued in the direction she had been initially going. The first noisemaker might still be there, waiting for her to be drawn off by his friend. She turned on the flashlight and ran it in a fast circle over the trees ahead of her. There was no movement, but the crying stopped behind her. Suddenly she felt oppressed by the dense coniferous branches around her. She backed away, her fingers cramping around the knife.

"Stop it!" she called into the darkness. "Father Rosaire would not be pleased with you for this. Just go home and leave me alone." An owl hooted from the other side of the river, and then the crying began again from somewhere just past her tent. She noted in a curiously detached way that the crier didn't pause for hiccuping breaths the way a real baby would. He just produced seamless wails that spiraled up into the night.

Rachel's nerve snapped. Down by the river, in the open, she would be able to see anyone coming at her. If need be, she'd get onto the rocks by the rapids. That might make it more difficult for someone to get at her. She sprinted towards the river's edge and her canoe, shining the flashlight on the ground ahead of her so that she wouldn't mistake her footing. She reached her canoe and paused to listen for sounds of pursuit. The wailing had stopped again, but, because she was nearer to the rush of water, her hearing was unreliable. She tucked the flashlight into the elastic band of her thermal underwear and picked up her paddle as an additional weapon.

Suddenly, from the direction of the rapids, came a noise she had thought she would never hear again. Rob's joyous whoop carried above the roar of the water, and, unthinkingly, Rachel dropped the knife and the paddle. She stood, hands to her mouth, straining to see in the uncertain silvery light. A dark green canoe appeared at the top of the rapids. Two shadowy figures inside plied their paddles skillfully in the torrent. The water looked higher than it had been that afternoon when Rachel had run it. Her numb brain supplied the answer: there had been more rain last summer. There was a fumble of some sort and the canoe hit a boil in the water. The nose dipped down and water rushed in on both sides. Suddenly the canoe flipped over in the white foam and two dark shapes swam. The bank on the far side darkened and flickered. A tree now hung out into the current. Its branches raked the water like fingers: a sweeper. A serious hazard in white water, because a swimmer could easily be pushed into the branches below the water and held there by the current. Rachel remembered Rob's instructions on what to do if she couldn't avoid a sweeper. The only solution was to swim hard directly at the sweeper and scramble up the branches, out of the water. She saw the two figures being swept towards the tree in spite of their obvious attempts to steer away. She witnessed the moment they decided to scramble and saw how the combined weight of two big men pulled the trunk loose from the bank. She saw how the bulk of the tree landed on them and pushed them under the water. She watched their arms flailing and clawing at the tree trunk that held them down. She stood with tears streaming down her face as the arms stopped moving and hung flapping in the current, as if they were shooing away the fish. Then the tree and the trapped men faded into the sandy bank opposite Rachel.

"So that's what happened, Rob. You didn't take any foolish chances, it was just a freak accident. I knew you wouldn't place risk-taking before me and the baby." The baby. She turned apprehensively towards the woods. After seeing a year-old drama played out again before her eyes, Rachel felt that nothing was impossible. Not even the damned child of the Black River.

She remembered the rosary in her pack, still in the pocket of her shirt. She had no other defence against the supernatural. She tucked her knife into her waistband and carried the paddle and flashlight in her hands. She cautiously climbed the path back to her tent. The woods were silent, but she felt eyes on the back of her neck. She fought panic and fixed only on her goal, the pack under the tarp beside her tent. She crouched beside it and fumbled with the straps. No more than three yards from her, there was a small sob. She wrenched open the top flap of the pack and yanked out its contents. One item of cloth had a hard lump in it, and she clutched it to her chest as she spun to face the source of the sound. Her eyes searched the darkness frantically as her fingers worked to free the rosary and crucifix. There was another sob from the same spot, and then the l'enfant maudit launched into a full wail. It rang in her ears and went on and on. Rachel screamed as loud as she could to break the other sound. The two cries blended and circled. Rachel's groping hand found the flashlight, and she flicked it on with her thumb. She shone it at the source of the sound. A dark form slipped behind a tree. She tried to follow it with the light, but it slid away from the beam. It moaned again, and suddenly it was behind a different tree. Rachel thought it might be afraid of the light and held the flashlight out in front of her like a shield. The light brightened and dimmed several times and then went out. She shook the dead flashlight and then smashed it against her thigh in a frantic attempt to get it to work again. She held out the rosary towards the dark shape sidling towards her. The wailing faded into soft panting. Rachel moaned and threw the useless flashlight at l'enfant maudit. But it was no longer there, and the flashlight bounced off a tree. Now it was coming at her from another direction, at times upright and at others on all fours. Why didn't it just rush her? Why this slow stalking? She threw the rosary at it. It didn't even bother to dodge. The rosary hit where Rachel thought its face might be, and the priest's gift fell to the ground, disturbing evidence of the creature's corporeality. She felt its breath on her face, a fetid blast of mould, wet moss, and earthy decay. She felt at her waist for her knife, but it was gone. Groping blindly behind her, she felt for the paddle, her only remaining weapon.

"Rob!" Rachel shrieked. "Oh, Rob."

Behind the creature, two shapes formed. They were featureless shadows in the moonlight and flickered in and out of existence as they moved. The creature stopped its slow advance towards Rachel. The new shadows darted towards it and then dodged back when it clawed at them. The damned child flailed after the new apparitions, and Rachel suddenly came to her senses. They were trying to give her a chance to escape. She fled towards the only source of safety she could think of: the river. She lost her footing on the bank and fell heavily on her hands and knees. She stood painfully and flipped the canoe upright. Her hands closed around the shaft of the spare paddle. A wail rose from the bush behind her, and she practically threw the canoe in the water. She splashed in up to her knees and then fell into the canoe. She felt the current catch her and sat up quickly to prevent herself from being swept close to the shore, where her pursuer waited. She paddled down the river keeping as best as she could to the centre. She could barely see. It was almost as terrifying as facing l'enfant maudit, this paddling down an unfamiliar river in the dark. She found an area where the river widened into a large pool, almost a lake. She paddled to the far shore and picked up a large rock. Returning to the centre of the pool, she anchored the canoe in place by tying the rock to the long rope attached to the bow. The canoe stayed in place against the weaker current. She looked back up river towards her campsite. The hair still stood up on her arms and now that she had a moment of respite, she realized she was trembling. Shock, she thought and lowered herself to the bottom of the canoe to shelter from the night breeze. She huddled there listening for the baby's wail. She fell asleep—although she had not expected to—her head pillowed on crossed arms.

She dreamed that she was sitting up in the canoe. The light had the quality of early morning. Rob rose up out of the water beside her and rested his hands on the gunnel of the canoe. His shirt was plastered to his chest and rivulets of water ran from his hair.

"Oh Rob," she said with unbearable longing. He smiled and turned his head upriver. He looked back at her.

"Don't forget to go get your stuff, Rache, it will be okay in the morning."

"Rob, I saw what happened. I know it was an accident. I lost the baby, Rob. I'm sorry."

He smiled at her again, and she saw he wasn't really responding to what she was saying. He looked upstream again, his attention on the spot where he had died.

"Sleep on the water, Rache, until you're out of here. You'll be alright." She saw his eyes had a watery film over them.

"What about you, Rob? Are you going to be alright? Are you trapped here forever?" He reached out and touched her forehead lightly with the tip of his finger.

"You're going to be okay, Rachel." He slipped down into the water, and it closed over his head without a sound.

She woke smiling. She noticed the light had the same quality of her dream. The canoe was still firmly anchored in the quiet pool. She pulled up the rope and untied the rock at its end, letting it drop back into the water. She paddled back to the campsite and smiled again to see the pots set out by the water's edge full of gold-glinting water and this time a few wildflowers. She lifted the blossoms out carefully and placed them between the folds of her map. She found the rosary on the ground near her tent. When the canoe was packed and ready to go, she lightly leapt to the highest piece of shattered granite overlooking the rapids. The Black River fountained high in the air and scattered droplets into rainbows. She held the rosary in her hand and ran her fingertip over the wooden beads smoothed by Father Rosaire's worrying hands. She flung the rosary high in the air. It spun in sweeping circles and fell into the centre of the boil where Rob and Mark's canoe had dipped and sunk.

"Yeah, I'll be alright, Rob." She jumped from rock to rock until she reached her canoe. She patted the map case with its pressed flowers tied to the top of the pack. Pushing her canoe away from the shore, she spun off into the river.

Chimère

Marcelle Dubé

Bittan did not need Leuk's coming to know Mother was dead.

She had known six days ago, known from the sudden thrumming deep in her centre, from the sudden knowledge that the god was now aware of her.

Her hikers slapped against the pavement, splattering water and echoing against the wall of the warehouse across the street. Puddles glistened under the haphazard streetlights.

Mother had described the god's constant presence as a comfort, sometimes a terror. But, for Bittan, the god remained a whisper, nothing more.

The wind blew cold and wet against her face. If she closed her eyes, she could pretend she was on the cliffs of Lulea, watching the wind-whipped gulf with her mother, learning the god's voice in the shrieking of the gulls.

The light over the front door of the converted warehouse beckoned her home. More light spilled through the half-open blinds of the upper-floor windows, comforting her. She wasn't alone on this deserted street. Michael—the owner and her neighbour—was home.

Her apartment was at the back facing the river. Perched on the parapet of the old church next door, Leuk would be watching for her.

Leuk. As bereft and out of place as she was.

With a sigh, she transferred her book bag to the other hand and fished in her coat pocket for her keys. What was she going to do now?

Then the sound of a footstep right behind her brought her head up in alarm. Before she could turn, a heavy blow caught her between the shoulder blades and sent her reeling. The canvas bag flew from her hand and fell to the pavement, spilling textbooks and tripping her. She landed painfully on one knee.

A line of fire sliced through her jacket and sweater, into the flesh of her shoulder. With a cry, she dropped to the ground and rolled. Fear-fuelled adrenaline shot her back to her feet. Breathing hard, she whirled on her attacker. He swayed before her—a tall, skinny man, holding a hunting knife in his trembling hand.

His stench reached out in coils, snaking around her, enfolding her in the sourness of his unwashed body and the reek of his fear. A glance at his skittering eyes confirmed it. Addict.

"Give me your money," he said, making no effort to lower his voice. A dark stubble covered his cheeks.

His need made him reckless, would attract Leuk. She had to get him to leave. "It is in my bag," she said in her accented English. She took a step towards it, only to jump back when he sliced the air in front of her.

"Don't move!" he cried shrilly. Only then did she realize how young he was.

"Please," she said. "You must leave—"

The front door burst open, and Michael leapt into the street, baseball bat in hand, bare feet landing with a splash in a puddle. He moved the baseball bat in tiny circles, holding the addict's attention.

"I've called the cops," he said quietly, his gaze never leaving the other man's.

For a moment, Bittan thought the man would back off. Then something in his crazed eyes telegraphed his intention. She swooped for her bag just as he lunged at Michael. She came up swinging the bag and connected with the back of the addict's legs. At the same time, Michael brought the bat down on the man's wrist. The addict dropped the knife and fell to his knees with a grunt of pain, clutching his wrist.

Then came the dreaded sound of heavy wings, accompanied by the dry dust smell of stone.

"No!" cried Bittan, looking up. The addict's eyes widened in terror. As Michael turned, a great stone wing brushed him, sending him sprawling to the wet pavement.

The addict scooped up the knife with his good hand and scrambled to his feet. He ran down the deserted street, waving the knife in the air and yelling hoarsely.

Bittan stared in horror as huge talons clamped onto the man's skinny shoulders, piercing flesh and muscle to fasten onto bone.

The addict's screams brought Michael lurching to his feet. He turned in time to see Leuk's powerful wings beating the night.

The addict's terrified shrieks faded into silence, leaving Bittan empty and aching.

"Jesus," whispered Michael. He straightened from his crouch. The bat hung from his fingers, trailing in a puddle.

"What *was* that?" he asked. The light above the front door turned his auburn hair the colour of old blood. His copper eyes looked black in his pale face.

The trembling in Bittan's belly spread to her hands, and she clenched them into fists.

"What?" she asked. Leuk—what had he done?

Michael turned an incredulous look on her.

"Are you saying you didn't see that . . . *thing* fly off with that guy?"

Bittan kept her face impassive while she considered an answer. Finally, she allowed one eyebrow to rise slowly while she looked at him.

"That is ridiculous," she said calmly. "He ran off." She picked up the bag and the books and turned towards the warehouse. Her shoulder throbbed with cold agony, and she felt queasy.

"Wait a minute!" Michael grabbed her arm, and she cried out.

"Oh, hell!" He wrapped an arm around her waist and grabbed her book bag, supporting her before her buckling knees could fail her.

"Come on," he said. "Let's take a look at that."

"What about the police?" Bittan leaned her good shoulder on him.

He shrugged. "I lied. I didn't have time to call."

MICHAEL PUSHED OPEN BITTAN'S DOOR WITH ONE SHOULDER. Her apartment was spartan, with very little furniture and a lot of empty space dominated by a huge, rectangular sisal carpet.

Across the room, directly in front of him, was a window. Their joined reflection stared back at them.

"First-aid kit?" he asked, tearing his gaze away.

"In the bathroom, under the counter."

He tucked her good hand in his and towed her to the bathroom, flicking on lights and leaving damp footprints in his wake. As they passed by the kitchen, a sudden movement caught his eye and he whirled. But it was only his reflection moving past the tall, narrow window that gave onto the church next door.

His back was beginning to ache. What had knocked him to the ground?

He glanced at Bittan over his shoulder, but her expression told him nothing. Maybe she hadn't seen that thing. But she'd been staring right at it. . . .

Unlike the rest of the apartment, the bathroom contained touches of luxury. Thick towels in brilliant jewel colours contrasted with the sea-green walls. A bouquet of freesias graced the counter and wafted fragrance over them as they entered. On the back of the toilet rested a tall, white pillar candle on a round brass coaster. Its shorter cousins were scattered on the wide tiled frame surrounding the bathtub. He had a sudden flash of Bittan taking a bath in candlelight.

Swallowing hard, he turned from the tub.

He flipped down the toilet seat lid. "Sit." When she hesitated, he placed a firm hand on her good shoulder and pushed. She sat.

"Can you take your jacket off?" he asked, his head under the sink. He emerged with the first-aid kit to find she hadn't moved.

Shock? No. He stared at her for a moment, caught by the sorrow in her expression. Her fair hair, usually worn in short spikes around her face, was flattened by the rain, giving her strong-boned face an air of vulnerability.

He set the kit down on the counter.

"I'll help." He unzipped her jacket and slipped it off. He was careful, but it must have hurt. She didn't make a sound. He helped her with the ruined sweater, and then she was down to a white T-shirt soaked down the side with blood.

Relief washed through him when he cut away the ripped sleeve and finally saw the wound. The knife had caught her on the meaty part of the shoulder. It was a shallow cut, three inches long, and the bleeding was already slowing down.

"How bad is it?" she asked, twisting to see.

"Not bad. A deep scratch. It's lucky you were wearing so many layers. I'll put a bandage on it, then I'll take you to a doctor."

"No doctor."

"You'll need a tetanus shot," said Michael reasonably.

"I have had one recently."

Michael studied her neutral expression for a moment. Well, he couldn't force her.

"I'll call the cops, then."

This time, he glimpsed fear on her face before she turned away. When she spoke, however, her voice was steady.

"I will call them. They will want to talk to me."

Michael cleaned the cut in silence. She wouldn't call. Did it matter? Montreal's finest weren't likely to rush over—not to this end of town—when the creep with the knife was long gone.

Why did she look afraid?

Maybe she was here illegally. Or maybe she had a criminal record back in Sweden.

He almost laughed then. She was a student at McGill University, hardly an international criminal. Still, he wouldn't call the cops, just in case her status in the country was a problem.

He placed a sterile pad on her wound and wrapped gauze around her arm. Her arms were slender and muscular.

"Hold this." He placed her finger on the gauze while he reached for the scissors. "Welcome to Canada," he said with a sigh. "We don't normally go around knifing people."

Bittan nodded gravely. "It is a good . . . land? Country. My mother approved of my decision to come here, although she found your god strange."

Michael secured the bandage with a piece of surgical tape, smoothing it against her skin.

My god is strange?

Then his fingers found the soft, tempting skin below the bandage. She looked up at him, her blue eyes darker, her cheeks flushed.

"Thank you for your help." She smiled, and, though it seemed brittle, there was real warmth in it. "You were very brave to risk yourself for me."

It was a dismissal. Gracious, but a dismissal.

He screwed the cap back on the tube of antibiotic ointment and replaced the kit under the counter. "Will you be alright? Can I call someone for you?"

Pain flickered across her face, but she only shook her head. "Thank you, no." She followed him out of the room, moving silently.

Just as well, he told himself. He needed time alone to sort out what he had seen, or thought he had seen. But Bittan . . .

"You shouldn't be alone," he said, stopping to look at her. "Do you have family here? Your mother?" The animation drained from her face and suddenly he understood. "Your mother . . . ?" he asked again, this time softly.

Her eyes closed. When they opened, they were shiny with unshed tears. "Six days ago. She fell from a cliff."

"I'm sorry," said Michael automatically. Six days ago. Jesus, her mom fell off a *cliff*. Impulsively, he took her hand and squeezed it. She looked surprised, then her eyes crinkled up in the corners in her first true smile of the night.

She stood so close he could feel the heat from her body. Without his willing it, his hand rose to stroke her bare arm. She leaned towards him. His fingers closed around her good arm, drawing her closer.

A loud crash outside startled them apart.

"That came from the alley," said Michael, pushing her behind him before heading for the kitchen window. A narrow, cobblestone alley separated the converted warehouse from St. Brendan's, the crumbling, abandoned church next door. He pushed the window open and looked down. A huge chunk of masonry had fallen from the church roof, smashing into pieces and gouging a hole in the cobblestones.

"Jesus."

"What is it?" asked Bittan.

"Part of the church eaves," explained Michael, pulling back to let her see. "I'll hate to see that old church go, even though it's falling apart."

"What do you mean?" asked Bittan, staring at him.

"The church is condemned. They're tearing it down." After two centuries of serving the parish, St. Brendan was coming down. Only preservationists— and architects like him—would miss the beautiful gothic building. He looked up at the belltower.

"What the hell!" He stumbled back, raising his hands in an automatic reflex.

"What is it?" asked Bittan softly, her voice coming from just behind his ear.

A grimacing statue crouched in a niche halfway up the six-storey bell-tower. Made of a rough, dark stone, it had bulging eyes and sharp teeth in a too-wide mouth. Its wings folded back to reveal long powerful arms ending in clawed hands. It gripped the edge of the opening as if ready to launch itself into the air. To Michael's intense relief, its eyes were closed.

It looked like the creature he had seen earlier, carrying off Bittan's attacker.

He could feel her behind him like a warm cloak. Her warmth contrasted sharply with the chill on his chest from the open window.

"What?" she repeated.

"Nothing," he said. He stared at the statue. He had inspected St. Brendan's when he bought the warehouse, hoping to restore both buildings. He had seen at least a dozen gargoyles along the church's various roof levels. He couldn't remember seeing this thing. "Was that gargoyle always there?"

Bittan paused. "It is a *chimère*." She gave the word the French pronunciation.

Michael nodded slowly. Of course. Gargoyles were rainspouts. "Chimère." Beautiful word for such an ugly thing. He must have seen it before, and called the creature up from his subconscious when he was knocked down.

He stared at its closed stone eyes.

"How did they think up monsters like this?" He shook his head and pulled the window closed. He wished it had a blind.

Bittan stared past her reflection to the chimère. "Perhaps they were once true beasts," she said softly.

BITTAN CLOSED THE DOOR BEHIND MICHAEL and finally allowed the trembling to overtake her. The rage and remorse formed a ball in her chest, threatening to choke her. She strode to the window Michael had just closed and shoved it open.

"He was running away," she whispered harshly. "There was no need to kill him."

Leuk's fierce yellow eyes slowly opened and looked at her. For a moment he was not her mother's wrathful guardian, but the conduit to a deeper past filled with gods, sacrifices, and magical beasts.

Once, as a small child, she had seen a man grab her mother by the shoulders and shake her. Before her mother could stop him, Leuk had swooped down. Clasping the man by the shoulders, the chimère had carried him over the cliff, only to drop him onto the jagged rocks below.

Her mother's anguished scream still echoed down the years.

Bittan slid to the cold tile floor, grateful for the fire in her shoulder that connected her to this life, this here and now. The god's presence washed through her, vast and lonely, leaving behind only silence.

What was she to the chimère, that he had transferred his deadly loyalty to her?

Leuk's arrival should have meant that the god had chosen her for his priestess, as he had chosen her mother, and her mother before that, for unbroken generations. But the god remained silent. She was left to grieve for her mother, to wonder at the manner of her death and to deal with Leuk in a world that no longer believed in him.

She looked up at Leuk, hating him almost as much as she pitied him.

DAYLIGHT PUSHED WEAKLY THROUGH THE RAIN CLOUDS, reflecting off the polished wood of the kitchen table. Michael stared at the grainy newspaper photo, his coffee mug poised halfway to his lips.

The man in the picture was clean-shaven, but the eyes were the same. His name was Jerome Beck, well-known to police for breaking and entering. Beck had been found on the roof of a downtown building by a teenager stealing a smoke.

Every bone in Beck's body had been broken, as if he had fallen from a great height. The medical examiner couldn't explain the puncture wounds in Beck's shoulders.

Michael set the mug down with a thump, scalding himself. The spilt coffee spread slowly towards the newspaper.

In his mind, he saw again those great wings beating the night.

He grabbed the newspaper, strode out of his apartment, and banged on Bittan's door.

He heard a movement on the other side and realized she was standing there, watching him through the peephole. For a moment, he thought she wouldn't answer.

The door opened just as he was about to knock again. Judging by the dark circles under her eyes, she hadn't slept either. In her jeans and oversized sweatshirt, she looked like a child.

"What is it?" she asked.

He met her gaze and revised his opinion. Not a child. A woman on the brink of despair.

Silently, he handed her the crumpled newspaper. Bittan took it to the kitchen and placing the paper flat on the counter. As she read, her face slowly drained of colour.

Michael went to the window to stare at the chimère. It looked smaller in daylight, just a stone reminder of a superstitious past.

What was he thinking—that a piece of stone had come to life and killed a man? But he *had* seen something. And something *had* killed Jerome Beck. He turned so he could watch both Bittan and the chimère.

Finally, she turned dark eyes on him. Her lips were pressed tightly together. He almost went to her, until he remembered Beck.

"You saw it, too, didn't you?" he asked. His voice was harsh and accusing, strange to his ears.

She shivered suddenly, as if in fear. Of him? Or of being found out?

"Didn't you?" he insisted.

"You fell," she said, her gaze dropping away from his. "You imagined—"

"You—" He reached for her, hard hands on her arms. The rough handling drew a gasp of pain from her and Michael released her.

Then her eyes widened in alarm, and he whirled, placing himself between her and whatever had startled her. It took him a moment to discover the empty niche in the belltower.

"Oh, dear Jesus," he said. "Where is it?" When Bittan didn't answer, he looked around. The apartment was empty.

Michael swore and ran to the kitchen window. Craning his neck, he glimpsed Bittan running past the alley, towards the church.

"Bittan!" he yelled, but she disappeared from view. Had she seen the chimère go into the church? What was her connection to that thing?

Michael turned and ran out, only pausing long enough to snatch up the baseball bat from his apartment.

Once outside, he scanned the sky. The ceiling of clouds pressed down, dripping rain, but he saw no winged creature. He ran to St. Brendan's. The church's central portals stood resolutely closed. He tugged on the rusted rings that served as doorknobs, but the massive doors refused to budge. On either side of the arched doorway were two smaller doors. Both were locked.

Stepping back, he looked up at the gothic facade of the church. Maybe she hadn't gone in. Maybe she was running from the chimère, not to it.

A sudden vision of Bittan lying broken and bleeding on a rooftop flashed through his mind, and he shuddered. Then his glance caught on a thin shadow on one of the portals. A narrow door sat in the portal itself. It had no external doorknob and normally fit snugly into the bigger door, but now it was slightly ajar.

He edged the door open and slipped inside. With a roof between himself and the sky, his shoulders stopped itching. He couldn't be sure Bittan was inside, but all his instincts screamed at him to make sure.

Far above his head, shadows lost themselves in gloom. He studied them carefully before leaving the relative security of the entrance. He made his way down the nave, past the remnants of broken pews, to the back of the altar. Fallen plaster and broken glass crunched beneath his feet, and clouds of dust stirred up by his passage billowed up to choke him. He found the staircase leading to the belltower and looked up.

Shafts of watery daylight penetrated the gloom through narrow slits in the stonework. Dust lay thick on the wooden handrail, the narrow, stone staircase, and the rotting ropes hanging down the central shaft.

"Bittan!" Michael called, his voice muffled by a century of dust. He waited.

This is nuts, he told himself sharply. Go back to the apartment, call the cops, the fire department—the army. Whatever that thing was, it would take more than Michael Esteban, architect, to corner it.

Then he recalled Bittan's face, etched with loneliness and despair. Whatever fear drove her, it was connected to that thing.

A thing that could lift a grown man by the shoulders and drop him on the roof of a penthouse.

No way was he leaving her alone with it. Holding the baseball bat as if it were a shield, he began the long climb up the belltower.

"MICHAEL!" BITTAN SCREAMED, but he was too far away. She ran down the street towards the condemned church, splashing through puddles and calling his name frantically.

Too late. Michael slipped inside without even glancing her way.

Was Leuk inside, too?

She had fled the apartment in a panic when she saw the empty niche, terrified Leuk would attack Michael. She had hoped . . . she didn't know what she had hoped. She only knew that for Michael's safety, she had to be far from him.

But now Michael was in the church, alone with Leuk.

She could not accept the weight of another death. Especially not Michael's.

She ran the last four blocks at a sprint and came to a stop in front of the church, breathing hard. It presented a closed face to her, as if it knew she did not belong there.

The drizzle settled on her sweatshirt like tiny beads of crystal before being absorbed by the cloth. Where had he entered? All the doors were locked. Then she saw the narrow door set into the massive portal. It was open.

She stared at it for a moment. She had never been inside a house of worship before, let alone one that honoured the Christian god.

A small shiver raced up her spine as she finally stepped over the threshold.

Inside, dust floated in the streaks of daylight leaking through boarded up windows. A series of stone pillars held up the roof, drawing Bittan's gaze upward. The vaulted ceiling loomed with shadows.

"Michael?" she called softly, reluctant to disturb the silence. A musty, damp stone smell caught at her nose. Beneath that smell was a redolence of prayer, and something else. Incense?

Foreign smell, foreign god. She did not belong here.

Suddenly she recalled the braziers her mother had lit to honour the god, the flowers she had scattered over the coals to send up the scent of beauty.

Longing caught at her, threatening to send her stumbling out of the church, into the rain, away.

The god might yet call upon her . . . she might yet serve him. . . .

Bittan looked at the peeling frescoes on the walls, the broken plaster statues, the vacant windows where once had been stained glass, and fear filled her again, dislodging the longing.

She went to the altar. Behind it, off to one side, was a door. It opened to her touch to reveal a short hallway. Two doors led off the hallway to small rooms, empty of all but dust and debris. A third door revealed a stone staircase. She stood at the foot of the stairs and looked up. It was the belltower. Starting halfway up, regular openings on each side of the tower and at different levels allowed the bells to be heard all over the neighbourhood.

One of those openings was now Leuk's home.

Bittan looked at the stairs and considered what she was about to do. There was still time to leave. She could go back to her apartment and pretend she had not set foot in this place. It was no longer consecrated to the young god. There was no real betrayal involved.

Her gaze followed the stairs to where they disappeared in shadows.

"Michael?" she called, but the great stone tower threw her voice back at her, a supplicant unheard.

Taking a deep, shuddery breath, she began to climb. Her hands grew grimy and slick from the dust on the wooden handrail, but she clung to it nevertheless.

She passed nothing but ropes dangling down the centre of the tower from what was presumably the bell's housing, lost in the shadows above.

Had she made a mistake? Had Michael not come to the tower, after all?

Just as she was about to call his name, she heard something shuffling above her.

Was it the sound of a shoe brushing against stone?

Or a stone wing unfurling?

"Leuk!" she screamed, and propelled herself up the stairs.

"Bittan? Get out of here!" came Michael's voice from above. She looked up to see his pale face peering down at her over the handrail. "It's up—"

Bittan screamed as Leuk swooped down on Michael from behind the wooden bell casing. But Leuk had trouble maneuvering in the cramped bell-tower. First one wing brushed against the wall, then the other, sending stone dust filtering down the well.

"Leuk, no!" She ran up the last flight to the catwalk.

Whatever bells the casing had once contained were now gone, leaving only tangled, dangling ropes. Across the chasm, through the wooden struts, she saw Michael against one corner of the belltower. On either side of him were narrow openings through which daylight seeped, dripping with rain.

Michael pressed his back into the corner and clutched the baseball bat in front of him with both hands. His shirt was ripped and dark with blood.

"Oh, Leuk, no." Bittan looked up at the dark space above the bell housing and saw two amber eyes staring back at her.

The pale oval of Michael's face turned towards her. "You know that thing?"

She forced her trembling legs to move, edging around the catwalk towards him.

"His name is Leuk," she said, trying to keep the sob from catching in her voice.

As she drew closer, she began to distinguish Michael's features. They looked as hard as Leuk's.

Above her, Leuk shifted, sending stone dust drifting down on them. Was he waiting to see what she would do?

"What is it?" demanded Michael. "What's it doing here?"

Bittan reached his side. Leuk would not attack while she was this close to Michael. Ignoring the wary look Michael threw her, she pulled the shirt away from his chest and peered at the wound. It was a deep laceration, going diagonally from pectoral to rib.

"What is it?" repeated Michael, catching her hand with one of his.

Bittan kept her body between Michael and Leuk. "His name is Leuk," she said again. "He protects me."

The baseball bat dropped fractionally as Michael stared at her. "Protects you from what?"

"From danger. From love." She shrugged and winced as the movement hurt her shoulder. "His duty is to the god—he keeps the priestess safe and pure for the god."

"Pure . . ." Michael looked up at the waiting chimère, confused. "You mean a virgin?"

Bittan shook her head. "No—it is the heart's purity the god demands." She could see in his face the struggle to reject her words and their implication. But he could not refute Leuk's presence.

"Call it off, then, if you're a priestess! Why did you let it kill that man?"

Bittan's tears rose finally, turning the world a shimmery silver. "Leuk is not mine to control," she whispered. "He was my mother's protector. She was the priestess, but she died, and he was left behind."

"Doesn't that make you the priestess now?"

Bittan looked away from him and up at the chimère. "I . . . I do not know." Her voice dropped to a whisper. "The god does not speak to me."

Michael stared at her, horror struggling with pity in his eyes. "Bittan," he finally said. "Either you're nuts, or I am." He pushed her away, and she let her hand drop to her side. He could not understand, of course. The god he knew was safely contained between walls.

Leuk moved, and they both cast wary glances upward.

"Call on this god of yours," said Michael. "Is he your father?"

Bittan looked at him. "No. The priestess takes a lover—"

And suddenly, she understood. Understood why the man had been angry, all those long years ago. Understood why her mother had screamed with anguish and grief at his death. He was Bittan's father, and her mother had loved him. Had Mother tried to send him away, to save him? Was that why Leuk had dropped him from a cliff? Not because the man had grown angry with the priestess, but because she had loved him?

As though reading her mind, Leuk swooped down, reaching taloned hands for Michael.

"Look out!" Michael shouted and raised the bat to swing at Leuk.

Bittan stepped in front of Michael.

Leuk's wings swept back in an effort to stop his momentum. The great stone body slammed into the catwalk railing, breaking it, just as Michael's bat smashed down on one wing. A loud, unearthly cry filled the belltower as the wing tip broke off and fell six stories to land with a crash.

The chimère teetered on the edge of the catwalk, balancing on one foot and clasping the remaining handrail with one clawed hand. The damaged wing spread out to one side.

Mother had sent her away to school and encouraged her to stay away. She had tried to keep Bittan from the god.

At last, Bittan confronted the questions she had avoided since Leuk's arrival. What role had the chimère played in her mother's death? Had Mother's death been a final rejection of the god, or had the god abandoned *her?*

Bittan's grief spiraled out of control as she suddenly realized she had lost everything: father, mother, and the god. "Leuk!" she screamed in sudden rage.

The chimère's wings spread as Leuk steadied himself. He stepped onto the catwalk with clawed feet and turned towards her.

"Enough!" cried Bittan. "It is finished!" Fresh tears blurred her vision.

Then Leuk's huge amber eyes fixed on hers, and she felt herself falling, falling into their depths, losing her sense of place and time, forgetting the dust and the fear and the loneliness. She was in the presence of the god, a great fierce presence that filled her and emptied her and comforted her and terrified her.

The god laid the covenant before her, the same covenant that had bound her mother, and her mother before that. The god demanded all of his priestess, her life, her love, her child. He gave of his terrible, unfathomable love, opened the doorway between the worlds, but allowed no human love.

This could be mine, she thought.

Then she became aware of Michael's presence. She felt his strength as he stood before the god, afraid but unyielding. She reached out for him, for his solidity, his humanity.

As suddenly as he had come, the god was gone, and she reeled on the catwalk, awash in bitter regret and overwhelming relief. She would have fallen but for Michael's clasp on her waist.

She leaned back against his bloody chest, and his arms wrapped around her. He trembled, and she turned to wrap her own arms around him, to comfort him. She, at least, had always known of the god's existence.

After a moment, Michael spoke. "Where is he?"

The god? No, he meant Leuk.

Bittan glanced up, but Leuk was not among the shadows above the bell housing.

She looked out the opening at the bright red warehouse wall next door and down at her kitchen window. Moving jerkily, she stepped up to the opening in the belltower and leaned out to look down on the cobblestone alley.

At the foot of the tower were chunks of rough stone, as if a statue had fallen from a great height.

Help

Matthew Costaris

HE COMES UP FROM BEHIND AND HELPS HER. She has only enough time to make a slight whimper, and then she is dead. He lets go of her, but the blood has already stained his hands. He'll have to scrub extra hard tonight to get it off. When he's done he looks at himself in the mirror and sees the blood staining his hands and shirt. He feels sad. There is a little blood under his eyes but his tears wash it away. When he is completely done with the woman, he looks at her hair. She has pretty hair. It's just like Mom's, and he hopes this woman mill meet Mom when she gets up to Heaven. Maybe she and Mom will even be friends. He leaves the woman then and goes back into her house to find her husband.

Her husband isn't going to get any Help.

BACK IN HIS HOUSE HE WATCHES TELEVISION. He likes watching comedies— they make him laugh. He likes to laugh. He and his mom used to watch comedies together when he was little. They would laugh together and eat popcorn and drink pop, and he always had a good time. He misses Mom. He always had fun when she was around and Dad wasn't. They used to go to the park sometimes and play on the teeter-totter or swings. She used to push him, because he never learned how to pump. Now that she's gone he can't go to the park anymore. Last time he went alone everyone looked at him funny because he was so much bigger than the kids, and then someone called the police and he had to leave. That never happened with Mom. He hasn't been back since.

He misses her the most when he is in bed and has nothing to think about except maybe all the people he's Helped. Sometimes he feels bad after he's done Helping them because it's always so messy and they always look so scared.

He tries to do it as quickly as possible, but sometimes he has trouble doing it and the people are hurt by him even though he's just trying to Help them. He wishes it wasn't so messy.

He doesn't want to think about this anymore because like Mom used to say, *it isn't good to go to bed with sad thoughts in your head.* So instead of thinking about the people he's Helped he thinks about happy places. He pictures Mom and him at the beach having a picnic.

He falls asleep with a smile.

HE'S HELPED A LOT OF PEOPLE IN HIS LIFE. They're always different. Sometimes he Helps children and sometimes he Helps adults and sometimes they're men and sometimes they're women. A lot of them are women, and this makes him sad. He wishes that the women could have been happier. They all remind him of Mom, even if they don't look like her. They have more pain in their bodies than anything else, and this is why he has to Help them. He wishes he didn't have to Help them, but it is the only way. He hopes they all realize how nice he was to send them up to Heaven. In heaven there won't be anyone to hurt them and maybe they will all be friends with Mom and they'll wait for him to get up there so they can have a big welcome party. And they can watch all the movies they want. He just hopes they let him up to Heaven. He hopes God realizes he is Helping all those people even though it does get a bit bloody sometimes.

It would be easier if he had Mom with him. Then he wouldn't have to be alone in the house all the time. It gets scary sometimes when he's all alone and there aren't any comedies on television. When it gets really dark and he's in bed all alone, the shadows look scary. He knows it's stupid, but he can't help being scared. Sometimes he even goes to bed crying and telling all the ghosts and monsters to leave him alone. But they never do. Sometimes when he has a nightmare it's about Dad. Those ones are even scarier than his monster dreams. If only he weren't alone.

He isn't really. But he doesn't count *him* as company.

He hates Dad.

HE REMEMBERS THE LAST TIME he and Mom watched a comedy together. It was a really funny one—he doesn't remember the title—but he remembers that they were eating popcorn together. She got a special type with extra butter, and it tasted really good. They were halfway through the movie when Dad came home. He was angry and he smelled bad and he started yelling at Mom right when he walked in.

"What the hell are you doing?" Then he shut off the movie even though it was only halfway through.

"Please, Arthur," Mom said, "We're just trying to watch a movie."

"I don't care what you're doing. I don't want you wasting all your time watching movies with that retard."

"Don't call Chris that name." Mom's face turned bright red then, and it looked like she was going to cry. He wanted to stop it from happening.

"No! Leave her alone!" That's what he tried to say, but the words got all scrambled and they came out sounding funny. But that didn't matter to Dad; because he still got angry. Dad walked over to him and breathed his bad breath all around. Dad was really angry. "What the hell did you just say to me?"

No words would come out, so instead he pushed Dad out of the way and yelled as loud as he could.

Dad pulled back his fist, and he was about to punch when Mom grabbed his arm.

"Don't hurt him! He didn't do anything!"

Then Dad turned around and started punching Mom in the face over and over and over again until her face was covered with blood. She was screaming and crying. He tried to stop Dad, but he couldn't get close enough to do anything. Finally, Dad left and went to his room.

Mom was bleeding on the floor, and he went over to her. "You'll be alright, Mom. We'll go to the bathroom and clean you up then you'll be better and we can finish the movie. Maybe I'll even make some extra popcorn and we can share it. Mom?"

He looked at her. There was blood all over her face and shirt, and he wanted to cry when he saw it. Mom never did anything to anyone, and she had to live in pain all the time because of Dad. She didn't deserve this. He hated to see her looking so sad and helpless.

He Helped her that night after Dad left the house. He did it quickly, and he hoped it didn't hurt. He cried so much that he thought he had lost all the water in his body. He didn't want to do it, because then he would never get too see her again. But when he saw her face after Dad hit her he realized that it wasn't fair. She shouldn't have so much pain, so he Helped her. Now she could be happy in Heaven forever. After it was done he kissed her cheek and said goodbye, even though his voice was hard to understand because of all the crying. Then he left her and went outside.

To wait for Dad.

HE OPENS HIS EYES, AND HE'S COVERED IN SWEAT. He hates it when he has to remember sad times with Mom. He wishes he could just remember the happy times, but he can't because any time he thinks of Mom he thinks of Dad and he doesn't have any happy memories of Dad. He thinks about Mom once more, and he pictures her in Heaven smiling down at him. Then he stops because he has work to do. He gets out of bed and washes his face and brushes his teeth the way Mom always used to tell him. Then he gets dressed. He has trouble getting his socks on, but finally he pulls them on.

He walks downstairs and goes into the kitchen. He picks up the sharpest knife he can find and goes straight to the basement door. He tries not to think of what he's about to do, but it's difficult not to. He opens the door and turns on the light and walks down the creaky steps. Dad's sitting in his normal spot.

He can hear Dad babbling already. It's hard to understand what he's saying, but sometimes sentences come through. "God, please don't" and "Please, it hurts so bad" and "Leave Chris alone."

He steps towards Dad and wipes away the spit on his chin with a napkin. Dad's eyes are glossed over and completely red. He's wearing the same clothes as he has been for the past ten years. Ever since the night Mom went to Heaven.

After he Helped her something special happened. When Mom started going up to Heaven, she grabbed his hand and smiled. He felt something in his entire body. It felt like something was filling him up, and he couldn't stop it. Then she whispered the words "Use it" and died. That's when she'd given him his Power. Just like a hero in the comics.

He looks down at Dad and tries to feel sadness. But he can't. Every time he sees his face he thinks of how mean he was and remembers how he'd hit Mom and him and make them stop watching their movies. Dad deserves this. He wonders what is going through Dad's head right now. Which memory he's living through. He wonders if it's the time he broke Mom's arm for no reason at all and then laughed and acted like nothing happened. Or the time he crushed all of their comedy videos and threw them away.

It's fair this way. At least now Dad can finally realize how bad he is. He thinks of all the people he has used his Power on. Stuck in the memories of everyone they've hurt for the rest of their lives. It's the only way to really get back at them. Mom knew that, and that's why she gave him his Power. He'd done the same thing to the man tonight. He'd seen him beating up that woman on the street before, so he Helped her first. Then the man got what he deserved.

The Power is all in his hands. Once touch does it all. One hand on the face, and the bad people are changed forever. They will never be normal again, because all they can ever do is relive all the times they hurt someone through the eyes of the victim. Then they can finally see how much pain they cause.

He hears his dad mumbling again and decides not to take any more time. It's been more than ten years now, so he figures Dad's had enough time to think about what he's done. He would leave him this way forever if he could but that's going to be impossible now, so this is the next best thing.

Without thinking about it anymore, he lifts up the butcher knife and Helps Dad.

It's over in a second.

HE'S WATCHING THE TELEVISION AGAIN, but there are no comedies. He flips through all the channels three times, but he can't find anything funny. Then he sees a commercial, and he starts to feel really sad. In the commercial a mom and her son are walking through a park holding hands. It's really pretty and they are smiling and they look so happy and he wishes he could have done that with Mom once more.

He starts crying, and once the tears start falling they seem to go on forever. He tries to stop, but then he thinks of Mom in Heaven and him all alone in this stupid house with no one at all and he can't stop. He hates his life, and he wishes it could just end. It isn't fair. Why did he get stuck with *his* dad when the kid in the commercial got to stay with his mom and go to parks and smile all the time? Why couldn't that have been him in the commercial? Any time he sees someone in pain he tries to stop it, but no one has ever tried to stop his pain. He's Helped so many people in his life. But there's no one to Help him.

He's thought about it for a long time now, and he's finally decided. He can't stand it anymore. He hates living the way he does, and it's time for it to finally end. He wants to see Mom again.

He reaches over and picks up the telephone; he dials.

"Nine-one-one; what's the problem."

"Uh . . ." he pauses. He's getting nervous. He goes over what he is going to say.

"Sir?"

"My neighbour has a dead body in his basement and he killed him and it was his dad. The body's in the basement right now. He lives at 98, Evelyn Street, and he's outside the house right now with a gun and he's going to kill someone." Click. He hangs up. Then he walks over to his closet and takes out his gun and walks outside. It takes a few minutes, but soon the police are in his driveway. They step out of their cars with their guns in the air. He points his gun and they start shouting at him to put his hands in the air but he doesn't listen.

He shoots forward without aiming at them, and his plan works. He doesn't hit anyone and he never planned to but they don't know that so they start shooting at him. He feels a bullet go through his leg, and then another goes through his chest. He thinks of Mom and smiles as everything goes black.

Help has finally come.

FEAST OF THE GODS

Drew Karpyshyn

THERE'S AN OLD AZTEC LEGEND about a time long before the slaughter by the Spaniards, before the building of the temples, before the people of the land were even born. It seems that after creating the world Quetzalcoatl, Serpent Ruler of the Sky, was pretty damn impressed with himself. So the Winged Serpent King summoned his brothers and sisters, his children and nieces and nephews—all the other Gods—to a great feast to celebrate his magnificent accomplishment. And of course every God had to bring a gift to honour their King.

Now the Aztec Gods weren't stupid, they knew what Quetzalcoatl liked. He had no use for gold or gems or jewelry—Serpent Gods weren't into that materialistic shit. Even music or art or poetry would only get you a polite nod of appreciation. Sometimes he'd smile at a joke or a real good story. But, truth be told, every God knew the way to Quetzalcoatl's heart was through his stomach, and if you wanted to get into the Serpent Ruler's good books you better show up at the party with a casserole dish under your arm.

So, on the top of the tallest mountain in the Andes, in the feast hall of the Sky King's Celestial Palace, the Aztec Pantheon gathered for the world's first potluck dinner. Each of the Gods brought something to the table, each hoping to come up with the dish that would forever earn them a place in the Sky God's favour.

The first God to approach was Centeotal, a nephew. "Great Quetzalcoatl, I bring you this dish which grows most abundant on the fertile earth. It is called corn."

The Serpent God unhinged his jaw and swallowed the corn, cob and all. "Not bad," he mumbled, picking a kernel from between his teeth, "but a little bland."

Tlaloc the Rain God offered him some water to cleanse his fanged palate as Huixtocihuatl approached.

"Try this, my King," she said as she offered him a handful of granular white crystals. The King flashed his forked tongue and licked the stuff from her hand. "Good," he sputtered, "but it makes me thirsty—very thirsty!" Instantly the rain God refilled his cup with water, and the Sky Serpent took a long, long drink.

"It is called salt, Great Ruler," Huixtocihuatl said.

"Salt," the King nodded. "It is good. I think it would go well with the corn." The other deities nodded in agreement with his wisdom—salt and corn. "Genius," they muttered. "Goddamned brilliant. That's why he's the King."

Each God approached in turn and offered a dish to Quetzalcoatl, hoping to win his favour. The King tasted many foods for the first time that day, some good and some not so good. Some so sweet they made him purr like the contended puma, some so bitter he scrunched up his face and ruffled his eagle's wings. And so it went until Tonacatecuhtl approached. The other Gods grumbled to themselves, for Tonacatecuhtl was the God of Food. "This isn't fair," they whispered, "he's got the inside track."

And indeed it seemed this was true, for Tonacatecuhtl brought forth a variety of dishes. "What is this?" Quetzalcoatl asked, surveying the bounty with a greedy eye, "I only required you to bring me one item."

"Ah, my King," the crafty Tonacatechtl replied, "these are all dishes made from the same thing—I call it cacao."

"Very well," the King responded, drooling at the corners of his mouth, "I will allow it. Let me begin with the drink."

"The is cocoa, oh Winged Serpent." The King took a sip and smiled. "And this I call chocolate." The King bit into it and smiled even more. "And this powder I call cocaine." The King took a blow, and he flapped his wings so hard he rose from his seat and hovered there for a second before settling down back down on his throne, smiling so wide his head nearly split. And all the other Gods had to admit that Tonacatechtl had bested them yet again. All save Chantico, the Goddess of the Volcano, for she had a sly smile on her young face.

She approached the King and dropped a withered lopsided little orange sphere into his hand. The King looked down with disdain. "Surely, Chantico, you cannot expect me to eat . . . this . . . after the wonders of cacao?"

Chantico bowed. "Forgive me, great King, but my home is, as you know, a place of fire and sulfur. I have no fertile plains to grow corn; I have no oceans from which to extract salt. I do not have the lush jungles which produce cacao. This is all I have. It is called haberno."

The King shrugged and popped the little pepper into his mouth. For a second all was still, the Gods standing in silent shame at the humiliation of Chantico in presenting such a sorry gift to the Sky God himself, each thankful they had not had the misfortune to follow the miracle of cacao. And then something happened.

Quetzalcoatl's expression of contempt changed to one of bewilderment, then surprise, and then pain. He shook his head from side to side and made a noise like the scream of the wounded panther. His slitted serpent's eyes began to weep tears of steam, and red smoke curled up from his nostrils. He threw back his head and howled in agony, bellowing orange flames into the sky. The Great God leapt from his throne and flew about the room, circling crazily on wings flapping so fast they were but a blur. He screamed, belching forth fire in his fury, scorching and burning the other deities in his torment and setting the Celestial Palace alight in his madness.

The other Gods panicked, overturning tables and chairs as they leapt and dove to stay out of his way. In desperation Tlaloc opened up the Heavens and unleashed the torrents, flooding the feast hall, drowning the Gods in a wall of water, washing away the chairs and party tables and nearly the guests themselves. The Serpent Sky King unhinged his jaw and swallowed the sea which fell from the ceiling, then he drank up the ocean which had wiped out his party and would have spilled forth from the palace to cover the whole Andes. Quetzalcoatl gulped and guzzled the cooling waves down into his gullet until all was dry again.

The other Gods lay in a tangled heap, singed and soaked, angry and afraid. Quetzalcoatl, attempting to restore his dignity and grace, sat down again in his throne and regarded the ruins of his palace with a solemn majesty as the other Gods rose slowly to their feet to stand in a tight little knot in the middle of the carnage. "Bring me Chantico." A wisp of smoke escaped his lips as he spoke.

Chantico suddenly found herself all alone in the middle of what remained of the feast hall, pushed forward from out of the crowd of cowering Gods who trembled beneath Quetzalcoatl's impending wrath.

The Serpent Sky God fixed his gaze on her, his eyes still weeping from the torment of the haberno. And then he smiled, and asked for another.

THE NEW PARANOIA ALBUM

Aaron V. Humphrey

BENSON CALLED ME ONE DAY. "You see the new Paranoia album yet?"

I continued restringing my guitar, phone tucked under my chin. "They got a new one? I thought they broke up a year ago. Hyacinth Atchison was working on a solo project, Ellwood Ruggels was drumming with Eric Clapton's new band, and Delphina Nunn was raising a family and starting a coven. And Chauncey Pest's dead."

"All I know is what I see, man. I don't hear any of that industry stuff, what the people do, like you and David. I just hang at the record stores, and when a new album comes in, I buy it. Hey, is Delphina Nunn really a witch? I thought that was just a rumour."

"You sure it's not an import?" I asked, ignoring his question. "If you look at it closely, it's not some underground band from the UK or New Zealand or Japan or something? Or France. I heard there was a Paranoia in France."

"Just come see it, man."

"Shit, Benson, not today. I got stuff to do. I got a song in my head just begging to be written down. And I'm waiting to hear from Frequency Button about that demo tape I sent them."

"Okay. See you, then." And he hung up.

Damn Benson, anyway. He knows me. He knows that Paranoia was my favourite band. He knows that I'm gullible, and I can't pass up an opportunity to find a new album of theirs, even if it's bogus. He and Roxene probably came up with this last night at David's apartment, stoned to the gills, and they're sitting there giggling and wondering whether Dougal's gonna fall for it.

Well, he is. Damn Benson.

IT ONLY TOOK ME A FEW MINUTES to get from my apartment to Oracle Sounds on 109th, the best alternative record store in Edmonton, and, as soon as I walked in, there it was. The new Paranoia album. Big displays, and Oracle doesn't do big displays for anyone less than U2 or Smashing Pumpkins. Awesome cover art. Looked like that sci-fi stuff from old Journey records, but better. And it was out on vinyl. Shit, nobody released vinyl anymore. Yet there it was. It had one of those sleeves where the title isn't shown anywhere except on the spine, so after a fruitless search while I determined this, I gave up and looked on the spine: *Exorcism under the Stars*. I flipped it over, looking at the song titles. Quintessential Paranoia stuff. "Marconi's Devil." "Middle of the Street." "Generals and Minors." No authors given, but it looked like there was pretty thick stuff inside, so I said to hell with it and bought it.

I drove home with the album on the passenger seat, looking at it from time to time at stoplights. The cover art looked like a 3D distorted version of the Mandelbrot set, like a warped teddy bear covered in tiny black tentacles. I started having second thoughts. This could all be a big disappointment. Chauncey Pest was dead, after all. His songs were always the best. And if Delphina was serious about the family shit, then the other two would be hard-pressed to make up the difference without her. The big push might be over-compensation on the part of the record company. This could be like that Fleetwood Mac album after Lindsey Buckingham left. If this album's crap, I won't even listen to it twice. I don't need to lose my idols.

I got home and ran in the door just in time to catch someone hanging up on the answering machine. I put down the record and listened to the message. It was Dolphus from Frequency Button, and he'd left a number, thank God. I called him back and heard what I'd heard from so many other bands over the past few months. Sorry, but we have our own songwriters, and we're just not really looking for new songs these days. I thanked him and hung up.

I then had to face the album. I couldn't put it off any longer, even though I knew if this sucked it would ruin my whole day. I pulled a letter opener off the rack on the wall, slit the plastic, and peeled it off. I pulled out the sleeve, slipped the record out and onto my turntable. I cranked it up, not caring what my neighbours would think, and went to sit on the beanbag chair that was at the focal point for all the sound in the room.

Then the music started.

I surfaced as the needle lifted off the record at the end of side 1, tears streaming down my face. It was good. It was better than good, it was the best they'd ever done. How the hell? I got up and flipped it over, and this time I had a chance to glance at the record sleeve before the music started again. All the songs were written by C. Pest, copyright 2003 Silent Stalker Music. Every single one. Normally Hyacinth had one or two, and there was at least one song where the whole band got credit. But Chauncey had written the whole album single-handedly, if these credits were to be believed.

I listened to side 2, and it was, if possible, better. I glanced down at the sleeve again as the last song faded away.

Then I saw the musician credits, and my spine froze. Hyacinth and Delphina on vocals and guitars, Ellwood on drums. And Chauncey Pest was there. Lead guitar, synthesizers, programming.

He was dead. He'd died on the tour for their last album. I'd heard the interviews. "It wouldn't be the same without Chauncey," Hyacinth had said. "Paranoia is done." So what the hell was this?

I sat, numb, for ten minutes. Then I got up and flipped the album over to listen to it again.

I LOST TRACK OF HOW MANY TIMES I PLAYED THE ALBUM through before I eventually gave in to the needs of my body. All I know is that it was mostly dark, which happens pretty late in the summer and this far north. So scratch about ten hours or something. I went the bathroom, made and ate a peanut-butter sandwich in the kitchen, and fought with the urge to listen to it again.

Jesus Christ, what had happened to me? A good album could definitely make me lose track of time when I immersed myself in it—Godley & Creme's *Ismism* or Shriekback's *Oil & Gold* did that to me every time—but playing it for ten hours straight?

That was flaky even for me.

Remembering the song that had been battering at the inside of my skull that morning, I turned on my Mac. I'd gotten this nice songwriting package for it a few years back. It was probably way behind the state of the art, but it worked for me. The sound reproduction wasn't the best, but it got the melody across, and I got a chance to polish it up before taping it.

As I ran the song through my head again, though, I could already see places where it could be improved. I'd been having trouble coming up with a title, but suddenly "Surfacing" seemed the most appropriate. So there should be some kind of synth effect in the background, with a gradual crescendo . . . that verse would have to go, but I had some ideas for a bridge which would work better . . . and the guitar line could use a little livening up.

By morning, "Surfacing" was polished. It was more ambitious than most of the songs I'd done before. I usually left lots of room for the individual band to personalize the arrangement. This one was already arranged for a fairly standard four-piece. I picked up my guitar and started tuning it, wondering if it was time for me to get off my butt and record something of my own, like Roxene had been telling me to do for years. I'd always said that I'd seen too many people ground down by the business to want to get into that, but if my songwriting was coalescing like this it might be time to see if I was right, or if I was just scared.

I started cataloguing the uncommitted musicians I knew. Roxene could sing pretty good, maybe not lead quality but with some backup she'd do okay, and she could play guitar almost as well as I could. Benson hadn't drummed in years, but he had a killer sense of rhythm and I figured he could probably get into it. They weren't always the most reliable sort of people, but we could work on it. I could handle the synth and maybe a little guitar. I couldn't think of any immediate possibilities for the fourth part, another female vocal/guitar slot, but I probably knew most of the people in town who knew musicians, so it would-n't take long. Maybe I should ask Hyacinth Atchison, I thought half-seriously.

Wait a minute. What was I thinking? I went back over my hypothetical band, and the arrangement of "Surfacing." Two female vocalist/guitarists, a drummer, and a bass/synth player. Who was this starting to remind me of? And the lyrics I'd come up with—the frustrated rhyme in the bridge was a classic Chauncey Pest trick.

That album had affected me more than I thought. It was like I was a milk carton that had been left next to an onion—the next thing I wrote sounded like Paranoia. Which wasn't necessarily a bad thing, because "Surfacing" was still probably one of my best songs. But, however much I liked them, I didn't want to start up a Paranoia clone band.

I went to take the record off my turntable. My hands, however, went through the now-familiar motions of raising the clear plastic dust-cover, lifting up the needle, setting it down on the first track. . . .

Just as I heard the opening chord of "Marconi's Devil," I got enough control over my hands to wrench the needle off the record. I heard that most horrible of all sounds—a vinyl record being scratched—and snapped off the tone arm in the process. I stood there breathing heavily, holding the arm in my hand, watching as the record spun around, the new scratch, from rim to label, winking into view once per revolution. I bent over and turned off the power. I didn't play much vinyl anymore, but already I was thinking of who I could get to fix my turntable, and maybe I should get another copy of the record now that this one was scratched. . . .

I'd been up too long, I decided. Benson always told me that I was too isolated from humanity, and about now I was ready to believe him.

Carrying the new album, I hopped into my truck and headed back across the river, wondering as I did so if I was a public health hazard yet.

I WAS TOO DISORIENTED TO REMEMBER that David wouldn't even be up until after noon at least. He was a night person, which I normally wasn't. Nobody I knew was at the *Slur* magazine office, and eventually one of the two people that was there got around to asking me why I was standing there looking around like a zombie.

"David? No, he was just leaving as I was coming in," she told me. "Hey, hear the new Paranoia album yet?" But I'd already turned and started shambling down the stairs.

David and Roxene lived not far from the office, just a block or two off Whyte Avenue. Luckily Roxene was up to buzz me in. "Geez, you look like a wreck," she said. "Sort of like Dave if he stays up too late into the afternoon." She left me to crash on the couch while she went out for some food.

I woke up with more energy, if not a much clearer head, to the smell of one of Roxene's delicious stir-fries and the sound of Tom Waits's "Rain Dogs." The music sounded wrong, somehow—too minimalist, too deep—but I decided this was just Paranoia afterimage. Here I was probably safe from them, since David had always thought they were overrated and Roxene just didn't like them. The food was a very welcome idea, though, since I'd only had one peanut-butter sandwich since yesterday morning. David emerged, and the three of us ate in companionable silence.

"So what brings you in here, Dougal?" David said after we'd eaten and complimented Roxene on her cooking.

"I'm not sure where to start," I said, stirring my coffee. "With the Paranoia album? The song I wrote last night? Ripping the tone arm off my record player?"

"Start with the song," Roxene said.

"This the new album?" David interrupted.

I nodded. "I was hoping that you'd know something more about what's up with that."

David shrugged. "You mean the Chauncey Pest thing? I think it's just a publicity stunt—an ill-advised one, too. Everyone's been expecting some press release saying that it was just a tribute to how they were all trying to recapture

Pest's spirit, or something. But not a word from the band. Nothing. Just the record, and those impossible credits."

"Maybe it's like the 'Free As A Bird' thing the Beatles did, with that old John Lennon track," I said.

"Maybe," David said dubiously. "Have you heard it?"

I laughed roughly. "Have I heard it? I listened to the goddamn thing for ten hours last night before it let my brain go. And even then it took over the song I'd been meaning to write. I'm not even sure how much of it's mine."

David raised an eyebrow, but Roxene seemed to understand. "So you broke off the tone arm."

"Not intentionally. I should—well, maybe I should see if you know anything about getting the arm replaced. Not that it's urgent," I forced out.

"These days it'd be easier to replace the whole thing, and that's not exactly easy. But I may know a guy who can fix it. He likes tinkering with that kind of stuff."

"Look—" I took a deep breath. "Don't tell me. Don't give me his name, or his number, not even if I call you later."

David looked very puzzled, but he said, "Whatever. Anything else? Do we get to hear that new song?"

"I—maybe I need to get a little distance from it. Right now I feel like someone—Chauncey Pest, probably—stole my idea and wrote a song based on it. But if I start thinking it's any good . . . well, maybe it's time for Roxene to brush up on her guitar playing."

"Oh, Dougal, that'd be wonderful," Roxene said.

"Don't get your hopes up yet, though. I know, we're not going to go through that whole argument again. Yes, I have been thinking about it, but I don't feel like myself these days, so I'm not sure if it's my idea. But being a songwriter isn't what it's cracked up to be. Maybe twenty-five, thirty years ago, but these days anyone who gets any respect at all writes their own songs, you know? Except for teen pop, 'adult contemporary' pap, and country. And I'm not interested in writing any of those." I sighed. "Why the hell did I ever think I could make a living at this? I can't even tell if my own songs were any good, and maybe that was one reason nobody wanted to record them. Another month, and I'm going to have to go back to flipping burgers or phone sales or one of those crap jobs."

I took a deep breath. "Sorry, don't know where that came from either, and I didn't mean to unload it all on you. But that feels more like me."

"Hey, it's okay," said Roxene. "We all feel that way sometimes. I've always liked your songs, you know that."

"Yeah, just hang in there," David said.

I stayed a little while longer, my brain beginning to feel less Paranoia-shocked, with the help of Roxene's selection of 100 percent gravel-voiced background music. Finally I decided I could go back home, since I was safe from the Killer Record. I wished I felt foolish about the whole thing, but I remembered my hands, doing someone else's bidding, and it gave me the shivers.

As I left, I said to David, "Listen, let me know if you hear any more on this Paranoia thing, eh? And if you see Benson, give him a kick in the shorts for me."

THE NEXT FEW WEEKS turned into a battle between my rational mind and some obsessive creature that had taken residence in my skull and just wanted to listen to the new Paranoia album one more time. And then one more time after that, and that, and that. . . . As time went on it even seemed to start sounding like Chauncey Pest's voice. I would find myself dialing David's number and have to hang up before I could ask him about the guy who could fix my turntable. Or I'd be looking at repair shops in the Yellow Pages. Or driving to another record store to buy the CD, or even the cassette version of the album.

So I started to take some precautions that in retrospect must have seemed strange to those few whom I had contact with. If I could've just broken *Exorcism under the Stars*, it would've been simpler, but I couldn't make myself do it. One side was scratched badly enough that I might be able to listen to it safely, but the other was still new. So I made sure not to replace the tone arm. I disposed of the old one so that I wouldn't get it fixed, and I avoided contact with people who might have been able to reattach it.

After one incident a week later, when I found myself halfway to the elevator with my record player under my arm, Chauncey Pest's voice hissing in my mind, I decided it might be a good idea to move out to my Uncle Ian's acreage for a while; he was on the road six days a week anyway, so I hardly saw him. After being there for a little while I even forced myself to disable my truck to make it harder to get into town. I determinedly listened to other music, trying to convince myself that there wasn't something missing. I removed the modem from my computer so I couldn't download the songs off the internet. And I tried very hard to keep from doing any serious songwriting—I might end up rewriting the album from memory.

David kept me updated, by snail-mail, on what was happening with Paranoia. The album was a phenomenal success, the *Dark Side of the Moon* of the new century, and even more so. This was despite an almost total lack of radio airplay, which was caused by some DJs' obsession with the album; I read several stories about prominent radio personalities getting sacked for refusing to play anything else. The radio stations played earlier Paranoia songs instead, but the massive re-releases of their prior albums didn't really sell. And the band simply refused to make any videos.

They did, however, go on tour, the *Exorcism* tour. Given the controversy that had surrounded the album almost from the outset, the concert tour seemed to be alleviating trouble rather than adding to it, although a few places, more paranoid than others, chickened out and cancelled. Hyacinth Atchison was quoted as being "disappointed, but also relieved," in one of the only interviews any of the band gave during this period. She seemed almost embarrassed about the success of their album and described it as "an experiment that worked too well."

An experiment that somehow put Chauncey Pest into my head. I don't know when I started believing that it was actually him, not just my subconscious, and not a splinter of my own personality. How many other heads was he in?

Then came a slim envelope in the mail with a pamphlet for a performance in Calgary in a month, a single ticket, and a note from Roxene that read, "Maybe it's time to face it up close."

I ALMOST TORE UP THE TICKET, but Roxene's comment was telling. I couldn't live as a recluse for the rest of my life. So I started to put as much thought into preparation for the concert as I had into Paranoia avoidance. I called Dave, and he gave me the number of his friend Gideon, who came to fix my tone-arm— he looked askance at me when he saw the nature of the damage, but kept his comments to himself.

When he was gone, I put on the scratched side of the record and braced myself. I put all my willpower into actually *listening* to "Marconi's Devil," not just immersing myself in it. The "pop" that came around every couple of seconds was a big help there, like a metronome, out of synch with the song's beat, keeping my awareness from slipping away.

I put the analytical side of my mind in gear, and started dissecting the songs like I had so many others before. A nice little high-hat fill there, not too intrusive . . . the bassline seemed scattered, but actually had an eleven-beat cycle if you listened closely enough . . . Hyacinth and Delphina were actually switching their roles in the harmony between verse and chorus.

And so on. The fact that I was familiar with Chauncey Pest's tricks from previous albums helped, too, because it gave me things to watch for, to hook onto. I even caught some of the elements that had leaked into "Surfacing" and made a note to see if they were truly necessary by the time I could look at the song more objectively.

At the end of side 1, I was still myself, enough so that I could methodically put a scratch down the middle of the other side of the record before flipping it. Chauncey Pest's voice whimpered at this deliberate damage, as opposed to the earlier accident, but at this point I wasn't taking any chances.

My daily regimen was listening *once* to *Exorcism under the Stars*, focusing on the scratch-pops, and then putting it away. A couple of weeks later, I happened to catch a rare broadcast of "Marconi's Devil" on the college radio station (played by a new DJ, who didn't last much longer), and I still managed to keep myself from getting absorbed into it.

Still, knowing how much more overwhelming and seductive concerts can be—I'd bought quite a few records on the strength of concerts and been disappointed in them later—I invested in a good pair of earplugs. When I had them in, I couldn't hear normal-volume music (for me, normal volume was what others would call loud) except as that indistinct buzzing that I found so annoying coming from the apartment next door. I even gave it a couple of tests at what *I* consider loud—which was probably halfway between normal and concert—and it wasn't overwhelming. I decided I was ready to handle it.

Just going to the concert was a struggle. Chauncey Pest did not want me to get into my truck and drive to Calgary. I took this as a good sign, that what I was going to do would actually help. I had to concentrate on listening to the voice, so that I knew which thoughts were mine. On the highway, when my mind kept drifting, I kept finding myself slowing down, or veering towards exit ramps. But I made it.

I KNEW THE CONCERT WOULD BE A ZOO, and it was. Still, it wasn't as bad as it could have been, because most of the audience were almost Paranoia-drones by this time, unable to focus their minds even when the record was playing before the opening act. What was Chauncey Pest whispering inside their brains?

And I pitied the opening act, some local band, who thought that opening for Paranoia would make their careers. They were soundly booed and didn't even finish their set; the crowd quieted when the album was put on again.

I had been wondering if this was some kind of mind-control experiment, but I had decided against it. Putting it out on a record album wouldn't be very effective, if you wanted to take over the world. Pumping it into the theme for the Olympics or something would work better. No, this must be just what Hyacinth Atchison had said: an experiment that had worked too well.

I noticed the crowd start to grow quiet, the lights changing, and I quickly fumbled the earplugs out of my pocket and into my ears. I felt a bit self-conscious about doing so, but I needn't have worried, since not even my nearest neighbours were paying any attention to me. All eyes were on the stage.

I remembered the last Paranoia concert I'd been to, a couple of albums ago: one of the best I'd ever attended. By that point it had already become tradition to open with "Under the Axle," and the crowd had cheered when the opening notes of Chauncey Pest's bassline started to boom out. Obviously they couldn't do that here, with Pest gone. . . . Then the bass *did* start to boom out, but it was for "Middle of the Street" instead. So much for tradition, I thought, although with the success of the new album it made sense.

I tried to catch a glimpse of the bass player, whoever he was—he *did* sound like Chauncey Pest. He should be standing alone on stage—but all there was was a pool of dark. Then the lights came up on the rest of the stage, the rest of the band appeared, and the song started up in earnest. Bringing the music analyzer up to the forefront was an effort, because ever since the first bass notes Chauncey Pest's voice had become more persistent than ever. I had to admit that this song had a lot of the same elements as "Under The Axle" and would probably serve just as well as a concert-opener. If they ever toured again, of course; after this "experiment," they might really call it a day.

I checked for the bass player again, but there was still only that dark spot in the middle of the stage. I could see some shadowy form, but not make out any details. I shivered, and Chauncey Pest growled in my head. I wasn't sure if he was angry or scared.

They stuck mostly to the newer songs, of course, but the response to the old favourites was extremely muted. The audience started a restless murmur, and any applause was desultory, until the band went back to the new album. Almost the reverse of any concert I'd been to. But I hadn't expected a normal concert in the first place.

I was glad, though, when they started into "Right Behind You." This had always been one of my favourites, since it got me to buy my first Paranoia album, and it had aged well. It wasn't until the middle of the second verse that I remembered the bridge, where, for the only time on any of their albums, Chauncey Pest did the vocals. Would this shadowy bass player . . . ?

And then it was time for the bridge. The distinctive snarled voice, with a hint of a British accent, saying, "You'll never be rid of me. . . . I know what you want to be . . . don't try to be rid of me . . . I'm the one who can make you live. . . ." The frustrated rhyme, the first of many. The shiver of menace. And I could feel it working through the crowd around me, startled out of their mesmerism just for a second. Then they started into Ellwood's pounding drum solo, and everything seemed to go back to normal. *Real* normal.

In my head, though, Chauncey Pest just kept snarling over and over, "You'll never be rid of me . . . you'll never be rid of me. . . ." And the sense of menace lingered. I had to restrain an impulse to clap my hands over my ears, knowing it wouldn't do any good. Whatever they had done, it may have worked on others, but not on me. Pest's voice took a gleeful turn.

At the end of the song, the audience cheered with a quality unlike any of the others that night—not the mindless adoration for the new songs, or the tepid tolerance of the others, but the sincere appreciation of listeners for a good song. The band came to the front, did their bows—an old Paranoia tradition—and then went offstage. I didn't realize until later that the shadowy bass player had already gone. And no matter how much the crowd cheered after that, there was no encore.

I HAD TRIED EVERYTHING I COULD to wangle a backstage pass, but apparently on this tour Paranoia was living up to its name, because even all the favours Dave could call in hadn't come up with one. So, instead, after the concert I snuck around behind the stadium and hid under a concrete staircase near their jet-black tour bus. Chauncey Pest was still muttering and chuckling in my head, and I was beginning to think that he would never completely fade away. I wasn't sure what the band members could do to help me, but it was the only thing I could think of to try.

It took hours, and the Calgary air cooled off rapidly. It got harder and harder to stay where I was. Why didn't I go back to my truck and turn on the heater? Or even to the bus shelter I'd passed on the way? It was becoming harder to ignore the voice now. I had almost given up when I saw the door open and they came out.

Delphina Nunn turned to be just as short as she was rumoured to be. I could see Ellwood Ruggels and Hyacinth Atchison as well, but no sign of their mysterious fourth player. Whether it was Chauncey Pest or not.

I hesitated, unsure of how to approach them. There seemed to be no security guards around, but with the band's refusal to grant backstage passes, I didn't trust that. The voice whispered to me, "Don't risk it," and I stiffened my resolve.

Just then, Delphina Nunn suddenly looked up like a hound that had just scented the fox. She turned slowly around and then said softly, looking straight at me, "You can come out now." Her voice had the husky London accent I had heard in the few interviews they'd done on TV.

I couldn't move. "There's no way she's talking to you," the voice whispered. "Just stay quiet, and they'll go away."

"It's alright," she said. "We know why you're here." When I still didn't react, she said, "We can get him out of your head."

I still couldn't move. "Can't you see what they're doing?" Chauncey Pest said. "They're trying to make me go back!" I could almost feel his breath on the back of my neck, right behind me.

"Can you hear him?" Delphina said. Her voice was barely a whisper, but it carried perfectly to my ears. She took a step forward.

Now it was a battle just to stay still, to keep from backing away, and running, and getting as far away from Delphina Nunn as I could. As we could.

"We would make a good team, you and I," Chauncey whispered. "I'm the one that can make you live. . . ."

That line, so familiar from my repeated listenings, brought me back to myself. It's not really Chauncey Pest, I said to myself. Or if it is, it's only a part of him. It is what I let him be.

"I am myself," I whispered. "I have my own music."

I thought back to the first real song I had ever written, back in high school. I'd gotten my first keyboard for Christmas, and after I finished banging out all of my favourite songs by ear, I noodled around for a while, until a melody came to me. I was playing it before I realized it, and I started singing the first words that came to mind. Later I wrote it down, but I never gave it a title, because nothing seemed good enough.

It wasn't a great song—I wince to look at the lyrics these days—but it was precious to me. I could still remember every note of the melody, and every awkward teenage word. I summoned them up, and I sang them.

I took a step forward. This was my own voice. This was who I was, alive, not dead. Chauncey Pest's voice started to fade, turning panicky. I took another step. And another. I emerged from the shadows, and Delphina Nunn was right in front of me. She put her hand on my forehead, and Chauncey Pest's implorings stopped in mid-word.

I guess that rumour about Delphina being a witch had some substance to it, I thought. She took my hand, and together we walked slowly all the way up to the bus.

"I could tell the exorcism was not complete," she said.

"Exorcism?" I asked. The name of their tour had seemed a quite natural one, given Paranoia's goth tendencies and the album title, but now I realized it was more than just figurative.

"Later," she said. "You have beaten him back, but he will return, when you let down your guard. Now, when you are strongest, we must finish the job." She turned to the others. "Tell them to set up the equipment again."

"Not again," Ellwood muttered. "Listen, Delphie, next time let's just leave it all on stage until *after* we've checked for these blokes backstage."

And so I was treated to my own impromptu Paranoia concert. They only did three songs, but all three were the most Chauncey Pest–intensive ones. Their fourth member appeared as soon as they started on "Middle of the Street." I finally got a good look at him, and I almost wished I hadn't. It was Chauncey Pest, and yet it was not. It was like I could see him through one eye but not the other, like one eye was adapted to the dark and one was still blind.

As the performance progressed, I felt a lightening in my skull. The pounding bassline of "Under the Axle" felt like it drained a shadow from my heart, and the bridge of "Right Behind You" was a sharp sting like a needle draining a blister. At the same time, Pest's "essence" grew firmer, denser, more real. But still not quite completely real.

And at the end of the song, he, or it, disappeared, like his spotlight had gone out. The voice in my head was gone.

I glanced over at Delphina, who was sheened with sweat. "Now can you tell me what happened?"

A frown flickered across her face. "You cannot tell anyone of this." When I nodded my assent, she said, "We had intended never to record again after his death. But we were all together in London last Christmas, and it seemed harmless enough to get together for a little jam session. At first there was a space where he had been, but as we continued, that hole suddenly seemed to be filled. We moved into my studio, which I had designed specially to be . . . receptive to certain energies, and there he manifested fully, not as he had in life, but as his essence.

"The songs were good—they seemed to come from none of us, so we credited them to him. We thought we would explain it as a cache of his songs we had discovered after his death and were recording in his memory. But something happened when we recorded them. His spirit went into the records. Especially the vinyl records our record company released, initially as a publicity gimmick.

"It took us awhile to realize how his spirit was spreading itself through the world, through the songs, to any who listened to it. Maybe that was what he intended all along, or maybe it was an accident. But we could not leave it as it was. His spirit was spread too far, and it could not survive. We had to reclaim it. And so the tour, intended to reverse what we had done."

"But it didn't work on me?" I asked.

She shook her head. "In some souls, the ones who were the closest to his in essence, he took deeper root than others. We have met others as well. Our album has turned your life upside down, and for that we apologize. Had we known—but that is in the past. All we can do is help the present.

"It gets harder every time. But there's not much more left. A few more cities, and that should get most of it; everyone who was most seriously affected should have made their way to a concert if they could have. Though there may be a few that weren't able, and we may have to seek them out."

They struck their equipment again, their roadies with a air of tolerant exasperation with the quirks of their employers. I managed to get them all—well, the three of them—to sign my concert program. "I—well, we—wrote a song," I said. "It's called 'Surfacing.' What do you think I should do with it?"

They exchanged glances, and then Hyacinth shook her head. "I don't think we'll be playing together again. This may not happen next time, but we can't take the chance. I mean, we could certainly take a look at it—maybe Delphina could record it—but it won't be recorded by Paranoia. Do with it what you will."

HYACINTH ATCHISON'S SOLO ALBUM came out a few months after the end of their tour. It sounded as different from Paranoia as it could be and still be her; to my ears, a distinct effort to avoid Chauncey Pest–isms. I knew the feeling, having recently done much the same to "Surfacing."

Which I still haven't gotten around to recording, but Roxene, Benson, and I have done a few jam sessions out at my house, and we might be able to work something out.

I still like to listen to the last Paranoia album once in a while. It really does have some good songs on it.

Eye of the Storm

Marcie Lynn Tentchoff

THE WIND BLEW DOWN THE JAGGED SLOPE, across the beach and through the trees that circled round the barren rock foundations of Asylum Light. It howled through the holes and crevices in the stone like some hungry, haunted night creature. Rain slapped against the lighthouse roof and walls with an almost musical rhythm.

Within, a woman lay asleep, down-filled sleeping bag zipped tightly to her chin, thin cotton blankets bundled round her head. Her sleep was sound, despite the slenderness of the foam pad that was her bed, but her dreams were filled with gale force winds and tossing, whitecapped waves.

The booming of thunder, the rattle of sand and pebbles thrown against the walls by the wind were soothing, lulling, normal, expected sounds. No reason to stir.

The gentle tapping against her windowpane was something different, alarming. She woke.

Tap . . . tap, tap. Not at the near window, though. Down below, far below, near the lighthouse door. No wind-tossed branch stood so close to that entrance. No random pebble could make so domestic a noise.

Who? A misguided mariner seeking sanctuary? Foolish, if true. The lighthouses along this coastline were all empty, mechanized, and inhospitable. Officially there should have been no one to answer such tapping. The door was locked, the lower windows boarded over. And yet . . . perhaps the darkness, the storm, made those telltale signs less obvious.

The tapping sound came again, and she crept out of the sleeping bag, shivering in the cold air. Scooping up a thick coat from the floor beside her bed, she wrapped herself up tight and pushed through the stacks of musty smelling, leatherbound books to the staircase.

The steps were icy beneath her bare feet. At each curve of the circular wrought-iron stairway she ducked low, beneath the level of the windows. If there was someone out there, watching, she could not afford to be seen.

The bottom floor, like her sleeping level, bore evidence of her presence. A small kettle, already filled and ready for her morning cup of tea sat beside a camp stove. One counter was laden with one or two weeks' worth of tinned food, and more huge books were scattered about the floor.

She glanced around, sighing in frustration. The next scheduled maintenance inspection was not due for months yet. There'd been no reason to erase the signs of her presence.

Tap, tap, tap! On the door now, and less gentle. More insistent.

Clutching the coat closed at her chest she tiptoed to the door, peering through the peephole.

At first she saw nothing unusual. Swirling wind, star-filled, wave-swept darkness. Then, suddenly, with an odd, fluid jerk, the scene before her moved backwards a step, and she realized that she had been gazing into a dark, blue-black, sparkling eye. The face surrounding that eye was pale as sea foam, with smiling, bluish lips. A lock of dark hair, shot with a streak of lightning silver, almost concealed the other eye. It was a male face, calm, and somehow cold as the night air around it. As if he could see her looking at him, the man reached up, tipping an imaginary hat. He bowed slightly, still smiling.

This was no sailor driven to seek shelter from the storm. His hair, his dark, fluttering clothing, seemed dry despite the rain. He showed no signs of seasickness, nor of the weariness of a man who has been wrestling with tiller or wheel.

Still, there was no taint of inspections, rules, evictions about him either.

And suddenly, for no good reason save that she could not place him, she unbolted the door, thrusting it open with the slight twist of her hand, which she knew would pop the rusted padlock.

He stood on the doorstep, smiling faintly. Rain pooled around his feet, winds swirled about, but not into him. Absently she noticed that there was no boat moored at the small dock in front of the lighthouse, and no sign of one anywhere else in sight.

"Ahoy the lighthouse." His voice was dark, rich, sardonic, even when raised against the noise of the wind. "May I enter, or is it always your habit to leave people out in the night for the elements to batter?" His midnight cloak swirled about his body, and flapped once. Thunder boomed.

Rain was beating into her face, trickling down her coat to pool on the tile floor. She blinked the water out of her eyes and reached up with one nail-bitten finger to rub at the bridge of her nose. "Well, it is, really. No-one's supposed to be here, and when they are, I make sure I'm not. But, you're also not what I was avoi—hrm. You're not what I was expecting. At all."

She peered up at him and quirked one eyebrow at the odd cut of his clothing, his billowing cloak. "Actually, you remind me of . . ." She blinked again, then smiled a small, dusty smile, stepping back a bit from the doorway. "Enter freely, and of your own will."

That tore a laugh from him, a true, warm one, at odds with his mocking smile. His left eyebrow mirrored hers in its arch skywards. "My thanks, lady. I didn't expect a line like that from you. It comes as a surprise. A pleasant one." He bowed himself into the lighthouse.

She turned from him, busying herself at the camp stove as her hair dried in sticky tendrils about her face and confusion warred with curiosity within her. It had been a very long time since she'd had a guest. Perhaps her company manners were out of date, or atrophied?

"Tea?"

"Tea?" He seemed to savour the taste of the word, rolling it round inside his mouth. "Yes. Tea. Please." He glanced about the messy room, then lowered himself, gracefully, to sit crosslegged on the floor. His cloak spread out from him, making movement in the small room even more difficult.

"So," she said, setting the kettle onto the burner. Her back was to him, but she still felt no uneasiness. Only an odd, intrigued wonder. "Who are you? And how did you get here? Do you have a boat out there somewhere? Did it go down? Or . . . do you always go about knocking on lighthouse windows in the middle of a storm?"

She met his eyes in time to see him flinch slightly at the last word. Her nose wrinkled as she looked him up and down, considering. "In a very nice cloak, by the way."

He sighed softly, his eyes on the flames that flickered, blue and gold, up the kettle's side. "If that's a truly meant compliment, thank you."

He paused a moment, as if for thought, then frowned at her. "Don't you think it's a touch impolite of you to pester weary travellers for their name and business? After all, if I've just been in a shipwreck, or if I've been marooned here for long, languishing days I can't possibly be expected to answer interrogations until I'm warm, safe, and comforted. And even if that's not the case, are the questions wise?" He spread his arms wide, showing swaths of dark, slightly damp silk beneath the cloak, winds swirling within his eyes. "They might lead me to ask you who you are, and why you're living here, in a locked, deserted lighthouse, where no one, man or woman, should legally be."

"Ah." She readied two mugs, one a chipped spare. "I suppose that's a point. But I can give you my name, at least. It's Laura. As for why I'm here . . . I'm a student. Of a dim, old, underrepresented branch of the Arts." She poured out boiling water, her lips curling upwards. "Can you think of a better place for uninterrupted studying than an old lighthouse? No loud parties, distractions, or nosey neighbours. No guests to eat up time better spent reading."

She glanced at him pointedly and watched the tip of his nose turn a faint, regally embarrassed pink.

"Should I be apologizing?"

She shook her head swiftly, feeling warmth flooding her own face. "No. After all, you didn't stop by to borrow a cup of sugar. Not in this." She gestured out the rain-battered windows.

As she watched, his blush faded into an almost terrifyingly pure paleness. "No. Not sugar."

There were tea leaves floating, swirling in the chipped cup. She frowned down at them. "So, why are you here? I've given you my name and my reason for being here. Enough to get me into trouble if you decided to. And you've told me nothing." She shoved the mug aside, picking up the unbroken one as she turned to face him straight on. "Or do you need to?" Her eyes narrowed. "Do I know you?"

This time both of his brows shot up, then as swiftly down again, his entire posture stiffening. "Oh, I don't think so. It's not as though we could've been formally introduced somewhere, at a party, or in a university classroom." His eyes flicked towards her books, then back to her face. He stared at her intensely, then let his breath flood out in a soft keening whoosh. "Oh, may all the gods damn it. Perhaps we were. In a way. You've studied more than you should have, I think."

Then, slowly, he relaxed, leaning backwards against one rounded wall. A soft laugh gusted from his lips. "You know a lot of things, but you won't tell anyone. You avoid interacting with people. You avoid everything. I've watched you, Laura. I've been watching for months now. You lurk here, as far away as possible from the rest of humanity. You hide in this tower—no, worse than that—you hide in your books." His brows furrowed as he reached to page through the nearest book, then through another. "Latin. Who reads Latin anymore? Bearded, tweed-clad professors?" He glanced at her, lips curling, then back at the books in front of him. "And Sanskrit. And what's this one? Archaic Greek?"

He let the books fall back to the floor, snorting a bit at the loud, echoing thump. "Laura, you spend your days studying dead, obsolete languages, living in an old, obsolete structure . . . and believing in obsolete concepts, like . . . well . . ." He flicked his fingers inwards, towards himself, then aborted the gesture, raising his eyes to meet hers as the wind howled mockingly.

"Maybe." She frowned at him as she handed over the unchipped mug. "But the fact that something's old doesn't make it automatically inaccurate. Or ineffective. Or even outdated. True wisdoms don't fade into nothing simply because they've been set aside for newer beliefs. And you . . ." She slid down the wall, letting one hand caress its aged, solid stone, and sat facing him, head tilted to one side as she once again studied his clothing, his manner, his very form. "You don't exactly go out of your way to look modern, or normal. You don't try to blend in."

He shrugged. "True enough. I've never seen the point, since I don't really interact too much myself." His sudden grin bordered on menacing. "Face to face, at least. But I'm . . . what I am. And you are a student. What makes sense for me is unusual for you. You live in the past. You prefer the company of relics to that of other people." He crinkled a perfect, if too pale nose. "And that makes you just a bit obsolete yourself."

Laura thumped her mug down in front of her, sloshing tea onto the already damp tiles. "If you've come here just to insult me, you might as well leave now."

He raised one hand, shaking his head so vigorously that his dark, bright hair completely covered his right eye. "No! I . . ." He reached absently upwards with one hand to drag the flowing locks aside, then left it there a moment, tugging nervously on one strand. "I'm not trying to be insulting. Really, I'm not. I'm just trying to say—poorly, perhaps—that you must be lonely here, all by yourself amongst old, dead things."

She smiled then, one corner of her mouth twisting cynically upwards. "What? And you've come knocking to offer me yourself as a companion? A real, live cold shoulder?" She shook her head, still smiling a bit, though now at the bitterness she heard in her own voice. Her eyes studied the chip in her mug as though it was her only safety, her only harbour in the storm. "That's cold comfort, my friend, if you're right, and my beliefs and studies have no place anymore."

She shrugged. "But that doesn't matter. I doubt it even matters to you, or not enough for you to be here, anyway. There's no way that . . . that someone like you would waste time trying to talk a solitary student into behaving properly. Or fitting in." She swallowed hard, her throat suddenly dry despite the tea, then raised her eyes again, searching his face for some sign of intent, of purpose. "So why are you here? Really, I mean."

He had turned away from her, seeming to stare through the wall, out towards the ocean. His words came out in a soft whisper, as if spoken to himself, or to the sea. "I'm lonely. . . ."

Almost, she moved towards him, but then, over his whisper, over the sound of wind and wave, she heard it, soft, but clear. A cry for help. From outside the lighthouse.

Startled, she stood and moved towards the door.

"Don't."

The bleak tone in his voice wrenched her gaze back to him. He was still sitting on the floor, his cloak moving, as of its own accord, to wrap him protectively tight. His eyes were lowered, his face settling into lines somehow both defensive and formal. "Those folk out there are my rightful prey. Unwary, perhaps wholly unwarned, they come to me. They shall sail, and bail and sink, and I shall feed."

"No." Her back was to the door before she had time to think, one hand grasping the door knob even as her body half-blocked his access to it. "No, I'm sorry, but I can't just let people die."

"There's nothing else you can do." His voice was harsh in her ears. "Even if you were somehow to rescue them, you would be found out, your hiding spot discovered, your hermitage made public. Let them go." He rose, his grace momentarily forgotten even as his speech assumed the patterns of days long past. "As I must go to them." He looked down at his half-consumed mug of tea, then held it out to her. His hand was shaking slightly; she saw it in the rippling waves held bound within the cup. The waves pitched higher as it was pressed into her own grasp.

"You'll not want me here anyway. Not now." He reached to gently push her hand from the door handle, turning it with his own. "But . . ." He paused, the door half open now, as rain splattered in again, and wind gusted through the room. He would not meet her eyes. "You implied you might know who . . . what I am. You accepted that somehow, and other things most folk can't. You have to accept, as well, that this is what I do."

His cloak blew out behind him, one last bit of ink-dark night in the warmth of her kitchen, then he was past her, out and free.

The door slammed shut behind him.

Laura looked down at the mug. She lifted it to her lips, drinking down the remainder of her guest's tea in a few swift, still-warm swallows.

"So," she whispered softly. The room seemed colder now that he was gone.

The cry for help came again, both fainter and more urgent. Laura shook her head briskly, set the mug aside, and wiped a mixture of sweat and tea from her hands. Turning, she strode purposefully across the room to the stack of books, then bent and searched till she found the volume she wanted. One handwritten page, another. . . . She flicked through them, more and more swiftly, murmuring topic headings under her breath as if they were curses.

Ah. This one. She'd been reading through it only a few days past. Perhaps that, in itself, had been what had attracted her guest, even if he'd not realized it at the time. With painfully careful slowness she recited the words of the invocation, her mouth forming itself with some practice around the syllables of a long dead language. Her fingers worked their way through a dance of gestures that had been debunked, ignored, or forgotten by every sensible person of the modern age, while trickles of light sprang from the curling tangles of her hair and shone out of her eyes.

Starlight. Moonlight. Power harnessed and channeled and unleashed inside the lighthouse walls, beaming outwards.

Sea strength, tide strength, bound and written. Books and knowledge and memories of things that real folk, sane folk knew could not exist or did not matter. Obsolete.

Protection. Comfort. Calm and healing. A tower standing high above the spray, manned by something, something living and caring and steadfast. Always steadfast.

In her mind she saw it, the small ship taking on water through a serious leak in the hull, the crew bailing incessantly, hopelessly, the captain at the helm, trying . . . striving against the storm to steer his ship towards the small dock. She gestured and saw the helm turn more easily in his grasp. She sang a few brief, soft, rejuvenated words and felt a layer of water solidify to patch the hole in the ship's hull. Then Laura whispered the ship towards her, the beam of light both beacon and pathway. She calmed the ship's stout fibreglass heart as easily as she calmed the sea about the hull, and she watched as the vessel glided up to the dock and was tied fast by the weary, amazed crew.

Later, as she climbed the cold stairs to her sleeping room, she heard knocking at the door, then a harsh, rusty rattle, as someone shook it, testing the lock.

The bolt was in place again, the padlock secure.

By the time she had crawled, exhausted, into her makeshift bed, her head buried deep in the blankets, the sounds from below had faded to a dim, wistful rhythm, almost indistinguishable from the rain.

She wondered if the storm would forgive her, if he would return.

She was, after all, lonely.

It's Beginning to Look a Lot like Ragnarok

Vincent W. Sakowski

A TASTE FOR THUMBNAILS

IMAGE: BATHROOM. Modern. Tiles shining. Porcelain glowing. Fans humming. Fluffy towels that look and feel great, but absorb water about as well as a sheet of steel. Would make a great set-up for a commercial. There's a couple included, and they're real. Well, sort of: GQ and Vogue, late twenties, slick and pointy, ripped abs, dyed hair, Fake Bake, and all.

The time: morning. Even though there are no windows. No clear, bright sunshine. No fresh air. Even if there were windows, the bright sunshine and the fresh air wouldn't be there. Not invited. Not missed.

Not a situation comedy? Hardly. Or does that remain to be seen? Depends on one's sense of humour, of course.

Rather simple actually. Morning ritual before they part ways for the remainder of the day. Both naked, showered, squeaky, but absolutely unaroused—never time for that. Such a spontaneous action could kill one or the both of them.

Vogue has just finished waxing her underarms and legs and is disposing of the unsightly strips. They're reusable, of course, but she always buys new ones. She can't conceive of going through all the trouble of washing them, or even worse is the thought of ever having to touch them again. Their mere presence makes her empty, stapled stomach heave.

GQ ignores the flash of her grimace and speaks to her for the first time today: "Pass me my electric razor would you, my dear."

"Only if you pass me the nail clippers first."

They smile smugly in unison. Nothing like a bit of humour to start their day right.

They exchange the desired items, careful not to make any fleshly contact. No need to tempt Fate and be scratched or bruised through some carelessness. Their Teflon coating can only take so much abuse.

Razor on. Buzzing. Fistful of angry bees. Second snap. Clippers chattering in their place. Raised high. Jaw locked. Fingertips on his face. Skin pulled tight.

"You're not serious. You've had that beard for years. You finally have it trimmed just right: manicured to perfection. It doesn't even irritate me any more. And despite—"

"I feel the need for change. . . . Something in the air, perhaps? So, keep your concern. I may need it later. Don't mind me. You have your nails to trim, and the clock *is* ticking, my dear. So focus."

Hairs fall. Nails fly. Transformation all around. Just see the results.

Aftershave. Expletives: but barely evoked in his mind, never uttered aloud. Still: pain. Sharp. Electric. Burning. Looking for something . . . some release. Glances in the nearby garbage pail. Pauses. Frowns. Picks it up. Holds it out to her.

"I think you've lost a nail. I've counted, and there are only nineteen crescents, not twenty."

"Really now. It's not the end of the world."

"Listen, *dear*. After you fell asleep last night, I saw the Norse God Loki building a long ship from people's discarded hair and nails. When he finally had enough and the ship was completed, Ragnarok began. And Ragnarok is the battle at the end of the world. Granted, this was only a re-enactment on television, but it seemed quite plausible to me. So don't tell me that the world isn't going to end because you lost this nail. *Find it!*"

He pauses; breathes, but with little depth. "Now, I have to go or I'll be late." Hands the pail with his clippings, then crosses over to his clothes. "Take great care with those, and yours, after you have them all, of course."

"But if I don't have them all and the world is going to end, then what does it matter if you're late? There won't be anything to be *late* for."

"*Just find it!*"

"And if the world is going to end, do you really want to die wearing those socks with that suit? *And those shoes?* What's come over you this morning?"

"I have no time for this." And he is gone.

Search: an exercise in futility, but she continues nonetheless.

Sighs. "Now I'm going to be late, too."

In haste. Abandonment. But a reminder: Garbage Day. Rushing. Rubber gloves. Disinfectant spray. Bags from each room. Takes them to the foyer. Back upstairs, her own layers are applied. Quickly. Methodically. Machine-like in her efficiency. Finally, out the door. Security system armed and quadruple locks in place. Then, by the garage: lid up. Bags dropped. Lid down. Wheels the bin to the sidewalk.

"I can't believe I'm doing this."

But being privileged only means so much sometimes.

Turns back to the garage. Feels a presence: *Derelict*. Suddenly, in her face. Silent. Sultan of Scatology. Smoldering, yet smiling. Teeth: rotting. Breath: reeking. Eyes: deep, dark, indecipherable. Long, greasy, stringy salt and pepper hair and beard. Bursting burlap sack over his left shoulder. Hairs and nails poking through its entire surface.

"Good morning, my dear. I was wondering if you could spare some—"

"Is your name Loki?"

"Do I look like a Norse God to you?"

"I don't watch that much television. I have no idea how a Norse God is supposed to look, but I couldn't help noticing that sack of hair and nails. Are you building a long ship with them?"

"This is the suburbs, my dear. No open water for tens of miles. . . . Will you be my friend?"

"Is that really necessary?"

"It would be nice." The derelict flashes a brown, hourglass toothed smile.

Vogue steps back, grimacing. "Let me think about it."

"Uh huh. . . . Bad day, my dear?"

"I've just discovered that my husband's an asshole."

"Only this morning? You have my sympathies."

"Thank you."

"But not to worry—"

"Yes, yes, I know. The end is near, and if I can be of any help—"

"Why, that's very gracious of you."

"Think nothing of it." Vogue lifts the lid of the garbage bin. "Top bag on the left. Knock yourself out. And here—" She digs in her small purse and holds out a fistful of change, just in case. He snatches it away and pockets it before she even realizes it's gone. "But I must be going."

"To work?"

"How much time do I have?"

Hefts the sack. "Not too long."

"Then definitely not. . . . Today is just full of epiphanies, isn't it?"

"And so much more."

"Well, good morning then."

"I will remember you; this day."

"I'm counting on it."

And with that, she strides away and gets in her car. Vogue is gone. For good.

"That is one strange broad. . . . It won't be long. . . . What a laugh. . . . But then again, let me take a look at what she's left for me. . . . It might just be . . .

THE END

෨෪

THE DANGERS OF BLACK SOCKS

BUT, FIRST, SEE THE MAN: GQ, late twenties, slick and pointy, with his ripped abs under his two-thousand-dollar suit and his hundred-dollar shirt. Abs like those shouldn't be covered, but he is on his way to work, after all. Plenty of time to admire them later in his mirror at the office, perhaps while his male secretary is blowing him. (Hey, when you close your eyes, a blowjob is a blowjob. And when your eyes are open, and you don't mind what you see—well, perhaps you need to have a talk with your wife.)

If he ever gets there, that is.

The idea persists—dominates his thoughts while his car remains gridlocked on the "freeway"—but not about his abs, or the office, or his secretary. Rather, this is something worthy of a good water-cooler discussion: he just can't shake the idea of the end of the world—although, in a Ragnarok kind of way.

He slams his fist on the dash. "Damn you Public Television for planting that evil seed of knowledge in me last night!"

However, in consolation, while the seed is planted, growing, he is still aware that his day planner is completely filled. Too many commitments. Besides, he could easily be mistaken of course, so why cancel all of his appointments, until he has some more solid proof?

Nonetheless, it doesn't help that his wife lost one of her fingernail clippings this morning: only mere hours after he sees the Norse God Loki completing the construction of his long ship from discarded human hair and nails. And then, after the last plea for donations, Ragnarok followed. Naturally.

"Why did you have to do that, woman? And then to top it off—those cracks about my wardrobe? This hasn't been a good morning."

Still gridlocked. Then, in the mirror: brown blur barrelling along from behind. Shock. Focus. Definitely a man approaching.

Is traffic moving that slow, or is that guy moving so fast? GQ wonders.

Passing by: *Derelict*. Singing. Slumming along. Long coat whipping out behind. Bursting burlap sack over his shoulder—hairs and nails poking through its entire surface.

"Hey!"

Eyes over the shoulder. Briefly. But he keeps on going.

"*Hey!*"

Opens the door. Starts to get out.

The derelict stops. "I'd put on the emergency brake if I were you."

Car rolls forward. Stalling in the process.

GQ sits back down in time and stomps the brakes before he hits the car in front of him. Pulls up the emergency brake. Meanwhile, the derelict continues to cruise.

"Wait! Loki, is that you?"

The derelict stops once again. Spins around as GQ runs up. Agitated. Severely. "Do I look like a Norse God to you?"

"I'm not sure. The guy playing Loki last night looked different, *a lot different*, but I know he was just an actor."

"Wow. I applaud your wisdom."

GQ points at the sack. "Are you building a long ship with that?"

"That's really wacky, my boy. You sound as weird as your wife."

"*My wife?* You spoke to my wife?"

"Just a little bit ago. She was going on about the same thing. I tried to explain to her—"

"Yes! Yes! Yes! I told her all about that stuff. I saw it all!"

"In a vision? Wow. I wouldn't have expected that from—"

"No. No. No. Like I was trying to say before: I saw it all on television."

"Oh, yeah, right. Well, that's not so remarkable then, now is it?"

"But it was on Public Broadcasting!"

"Point taken. But I really must be going." Steps away. Then, turns back. "Oh, and by the way, thanks for the beard."

Grabs at his chin. Awakening. "Oh my! Wait! How much time do I have?"

"You and your wife are like a couple of broken records. . . . You *do know* what a record is, don't—"

"*How much time?*"

Scowls. Hefts the sack. Then smiles. "Oh, I'm sure you'll be fine for a while. Why don't you just go to work."

"Ragnarok's approaching, and I should just go to work?"

"That's just all the horns blaring around you because your car is holding up traffic, my boy."

In desperation: "Can't I give you a lift or something?"

"In this gridlock? It's faster walking. See you around. Oh, and by the way, nice socks." Winks. And with that, the derelict is gone.

Hell's orchestra honks around him. Finally, with his head down, GQ returns to his car and moves forward the five feet that opened up for him. Uncertain and afraid, but also aware that he is late for work. *Very late.*

"Is that a coincidence or what?" He pauses. Thinks. *He said it was okay to go to work, and, if he was Loki, then I should be fine. Who am I to argue? Or, if he was just a derelict, then I really have nothing to worry about . . . except maybe my sanity. . . . Work it is then.*

Now: almost lunchtime. Arrival. Everywhere: eyes. Peering. Probing. Senior Partner approaching. But GQ makes a few quick moves. Deftly creates a diversion with two secretaries, and makes it to his office relatively unscathed.

"See me in my office." Barks at his secretary, who obediently follows, pen and pad in his hand.

"Lock the door."

The secretary, well aware of his duties, does so, then crosses over to the full-length mirror and discards his stationary. On his knees, he adjusts himself so that his boss will have the perfect angle to admire all.

The things a person has to do to get ahead in this world. The secretary sighs. Unbuckles and unzips his boss's pants. Lowers them and his boxers. Makes a few final adjustments, before swallowing GQ whole. While maneuvering, he notices his boss's socks. He grunts, laughing.

"Watch the teeth, buddy. I've had a hard morning."

"Show I shee." And he continues.

Meanwhile, GQ pulls up his shirt and admires his waistline. Some consolation. *If it is the end of the world, at least I'll meet my maker with perfect abs.* That has to say something.

Ridiculous, the secretary thinks. *Sometimes I just can't believe he's my boss. I could never dream of doing something so shocking, so . . .*

Laughing. Choking, while GQ is ejaculating.

Choking.

Laughing. Hands on his throat.

Choking.

Dying.

Dying?

Truly.

I can't believe this is happening. Their thoughts echo.

GQ in panic. *Mouth to mouth? With that much semen on his lips? Guess again . . . Heim . . . lime . . . or something. Just like on television. Yeah!*

Ribs crunch, implode, but he is unsuccessful.

Starts to run, but he is caught in the doorway to his office. Pants around his ankles, GQ stumbles into the foyer. Changes his mind. No need to be charged with fleeing the scene of a crime. But *what* crime? Death by lethal sperm injection?

"Help me! A doctor? Someone? *Anyone?*"

Everyone thinks he's joking, but nobody's laughing. Blasé. Totally.

In consensus: *How rude and inappropriate. What is this, a sitcom?*

But, after he pathetically and desperately goes about the foyer with his pants still around his ankles, they conclude he is insane. Most leave before he takes hostages and starts knocking them off.

Finally, the Senior Partner appears and takes control. Leads the remaining few, including GQ—after he pulls up his boxers and pants—back to "The Scene of the Crime." Too late, it seems.

"Something either severely surprised or frightened him, and instead of swallowing properly he choked and ended up with a lung full of semen." The Senior Partner concludes with a slow shake of his head.

Army of eyes on GQ. Accusing. Assaulting.

A voice from behind: "Now that's what I call a cumshot!"

Silence.

Titters.

Laughter.

Scowling, the Senior Partner doesn't bother to quiet the crowd. He makes a couple of quick nods and gestures, getting his key people in motion to take care of this situation.

"Come with me." He walks away without looking at GQ, but GQ knows to follow. Eyes forward, he gets into step behind the Senior Partner. Avoiding all eye contact, he tries to shut out the disgusted glares and whispered rebukes. He still can't believe this is happening to him, but there is no escape . . . not unless Ragnarok is going to happen any time soon.

They enter his spacious office, and the Senior Partner sits behind his desk, reclining. GQ stands opposite. Afraid to do anything more. Police and ambulance on the way.

"Don't worry, I know who made that cumshot crack. He's packing his things as we speak. We simply cannot tolerate these kind of outbursts . . . from him or from you—"

"From me? *Me?*"

"Now don't get me wrong, this is not sexual discrimination. I'm all for gay rights—big business—*good business* for us right now, in fact. In any case, an ass-hole is an asshole and a blowjob is a blowjob, correct? Especially if your eyes are closed. Were they?" Throws his feet up on his desk. "Maybe don't answer that. . . . Let me get straight to the point."

"You're worried about a scandal?"

"Hell no. We've covered up worse messes than this; although, word will leak out, I'm afraid. No real open scandal, but rumour and innuendo, which is even worse in some ways. In any case, I'm not especially concerned about that. Your sexual escapade is not really at issue. Well, not the main issue. Taken on its own, I couldn't give a rat's ass, or even two or three. Hell throw in some squirrel nuts, but—Anyway, the real point is, this last incident was simply the frosting on the cake—that extra green on the convenience-store wiener. Until today, I was willing to let things slide for a bit, allow you time to adjust in your new position with us, but then this morning—or, I should say, it was almost noon, I caught a glimpse of—"

"I can explain!"

"Not just your tardiness, but we have a certain image to maintain, and we can't allow for such . . . *indulgences*, particularly when they are so, so . . ." Feet drop. Leans in. "I mean, my God man! What were you thinking about when you were getting dressed this morning?"

"I—"

"Don't answer that. There's nothing you can say. I'm so disappointed in you. I thought you had a better sense of fashion than this. Black socks with *that* suit? *And those shoes?* Where was your wife when you were getting dressed? Didn't she see what a mistake you—"

"She—"

"I don't want to hear it!"

"So I'm being let go?"

"Yes. And you can go now—the back way. You are familiar with the back door, aren't you?"

". . . This is it?"

"Your things will be sent. Now please go. . . . And you may want to consider getting some help, or switching to someone else—with your wardrobe *and* your psyche—because whoever you may be with doesn't seem to be doing much good for you."

GQ leaves. In silence. Help still on the way. Told not to worry about "the incident," *for now*, anyway. It'll be taken care of—part of his severance package.

Behind the wheel. Eyes dead. Eventual resurrection.

"But Loki said . . . *that bastard! He tricked me!* I should have known better. Lots of time to go to work, *my ass!* He set me up! I wonder if my wife is in on this? I'll find out . . . if it takes my whole life and fortune, well . . . most of . . . uh, some of . . . in any case, I will find you, Loki, and you too, my dear wife, and I will make you both pay before Ragnarok begins. It's going to be the end of the world alright! Yes indeed. We shall definitely see. . . .

THE END

ᘏᘓ

THE BED BUGS BITE

IN THIS HOTEL SUITE: shadows and silence reign. Curtains drawn tight. A/C off. Everything on autopilot. Waiting for the next guest to arrive and bring life.

No.

Hold on.

Life does exist here, but for now it is asleep. In hibernation. Just barely.

Waiting.

Then: footsteps.

Arrival.

Presence.

Well, sort of.

Vogue manages to get the door open with her arms overloaded. Quite the feat, but she's done it before. Never dreams of hugging anyone, but she can wrap her arms around enough packages, doubling her body weight, and still be able to sign on the dotted line at the same time.

Illumination is lacking, so she reaches for the light switch. There is a slip, but in a phenomenal display of speed and dexterity she hits the switch and saves the bag of breakable bobbles before it meets its untimely demise. Sighing in relief, she slides past the door and steps over to the bed. As the door snaps shut behind her, Vogue lowers her bundles of joy onto the quilted surface with practiced ease.

She spins, kicking off her stilettos, slapping them against the wall. Then, underhands her massive carrying bag into a chair across the suite. Again she sighs. Again she spins. Several times. Smiling. Laughing. A little maniacally? Perhaps. Perhaps insanity has settled in her lobes. But she's enjoying herself, so who's to criticize? Who's to know or care that she's maxed out most of her credit cards in just one morning? (Well, possibly her husband for one, but he hasn't found out just yet, nor does he count in her books anymore, anyway.) Besides, she's got mondo overdraft to boot, so it's cat's-ass-living-the-sweet-life until Ragnarok approaches.

Then she could be screwed, of course. But she's not worried. Not about her credit, in any case. About Ragnarok itself? Well, Vogue figures she's gotten in good with Loki so far, but she doesn't know if that in itself is such a good idea. From what she's gathered, Loki's the "Bad Guy," and the bad guys *usually* lose in the end—on TV and film, anyway. And she doesn't know much beyond that. Normally, she would embrace her ignorance—actually, she's usually unaware of her ignorance—but Ragnarok seems like a pretty big deal. So, she's even put some of her non-existent funds to good use and bought a couple of books on the subject. Vogue would have preferred the videotape versions, but they would have taken too long to arrive on special order "for preferred clients only." And she's not sure if she has the time to waste learning to read once more. But again, is it the only way to escape the inevitable? It's a possibility, especially with so many outside forces at work beyond her understanding.

Vogue picks up one of the books and scans the cover, then flips through the pages looking at the picture for any clues. Pictures are good, as long as they are not too abstract, because using one's imagination can be difficult, and *difficult is not good*. And using one's imagination can be pretty scary, and too much like work, and *work is not good*, either. Not *that* kind of work, anyway.

Fortunately for her, the illustrations are fairly straightforward. Depicting Vikings. Doing what Vikings do. Trading. Killing. Conquering. Laying with their women. Telling stories to each other about trading, killing, conquering, and laying with their women. And yes, there are images of their gods: trading, killing, conquering, laying with their women, and doing all those other things that gods do in a Viking kind of way.

She drifts. Lying back, book in hand, she soon falls asleep. Exhausted. There's only so much shopping a woman can enjoy in a morning. Actually, there is no known limit, except for what time provides.

She dreams: of herself. Of her husband. Of Ragnarok. Of more. But she understands little of what she sees and experiences. Flashes of their future? Could it be? So much darkness . . . but they're just *dreams*. Never taken stock in them before, but then again, they've never been so vivid before. So detailed. So realistic. All around her: sights, sounds, smells, pressing in against her. Seizing. Squeezing. Nibbling. Gnawing on her mind—her whole being.

She wakes. Bound to the bed. Wrists and ankles wrapped around by the sheets. Somehow secured. She struggles for a minute to no avail, then tries to scream. Before a sound escapes her lips, however, the pillow beside her flips over her face, smothering her. Panicking, she struggles harder, but, surprisingly, she soon learns her mistake and lies still. The pillow presses down for a moment longer, but then it flips back beside her.

Her purse lies open. Beckoning. Something that enormous must have something useful inside in it—in theory, anyway. The previous lesson already forgotten, Vogue tries to ease her hand towards it. The purse appears to open wider for her and draw nearer—almost within her reach—a nail file glimmers, shimmers.

Closer.

Laughing.

Laughing?

Not her laughing.

Laughing at her.

Around her, the room echoes with guffaws. She stops her straining and struggling. Listens. Her eyes dart all around the suite, but she sees no one. Yet everything has changed. Or has it? Vogue can't remember if she ordered a theme room or not. A little too realistic for her liking in any case: tapestries of ancient battles cover the walls; spears, swords, and shields line the perimeter. Across from her a fire blazes. Before it lie an empty plate and a long knife on the dirt floor.

Dirt floor?

I didn't pay all that money for a dirt floor, did I? Whimpering, she continues to look and listen, trying to pinpoint the laughter.

It's coming from the bed. Reduces to soft snickers, and, in its own way, does some "listening" of its own. Waiting to see what her next move will be. The bed doesn't have to wait too much longer.

"Who's there?"

Vibrating, the bed answers. "Just the two of us."

"And who's that?"

The bed shifts beneath her. "Who's that where?"

Exasperated, she cries: *"Who's that under my bed?"*

"No-one is under the bed, Mama Bear, and the bed is not *yours* to begin with."

"Is that you again, Loki?"

The bed sighs and the woman sinks.

"You really have no clue what a Norse God looks like, do you?"

Lower, the bed enfolds her.

"Will you stop playing tricks on me? I helped you out, remember?"

The bed pauses. Hardens.

"Don't you know that Loki is the Ultimate Trickster, Baby Bear—it's what he does—well, when he's not killing, conquering, laying with women, doing what Vikings do, or, well, whatever. And I must point out that you have never helped me at all. *Ever*."

"Stop this already, Loki, and just tell me what you want."

"First of all—stop calling me Loki."

"What do you want me to call you then?"

"You're talking to a bed, Goldilocks, what do you think?"

"I'm not thinking much at all. For all I know, I'm still sleeping and dreaming . . . *and I didn't want a dirt floor!* So give me a break already. Let me wake up, or let me go. I'm not going run away."

"Hmmm . . . so much to consider. . . ." The bed inflates, but the sheets do not loosen.

A voice erupts from across the suite. "Enough of this idle bantering, Veikur Rum!"

Vogue turns her head to see a beautiful, buxom, naked woman with long blond braided hair reaching down to her waist. Lying there, Vogue is both deeply envious and strangely aroused, admiring the perfection in her form, searching for some flaw. Finding it fast. As she glances below the waist once again, her envy and anticipation are turned into gloating and revulsion. So much for perfection. The beauty stops at the meridian. From the waist down, her figure is rotting and putrid. Dead flesh hangs in sinewy strips. Every movement brings a watery, squishing sound and an escape of septic gases. Slowly, purposefully, she moves towards Vogue, leaving a trail behind her like a massive slug.

She cries out as the Valkyrian female draws nearer. Her body trembling, tickling, then burning and bruising as her body is bitten—her clothes being eaten away.

Weeping. "Who are you?"

"Hel, his daughter."

"You mean Loki's daughter, right? What's your name?"

"I just said, *Hel*."

"You mean your name is Hell?"

"Not *H-E-L-L!*...*H-E-L!* Why do I *always* have to go through this with everybody? Aren't you listening—"

"Okay! Okay, already! What does Loki want with me now?"

Sitting on the bed, squishing and farting, Hel coldly caresses Vogue's cheek. Somehow soothing and scaring her at the same time. She trails her frigid fingers down her neck. Feels Vogue's pulse quicken.

"He wants you and your husband to be the last two people in Midgard to restart humanity after the end of the world."

"And where exactly is Midgard? Do I need my passport or any shots first? And . . . did you just say that only the two of us are to survive?"

"Yes."

". . . And it *has to be* with my husband?"

"Yes."

"But Loki knows what an asshole my husband is."

"Yes. Everything has its price."

"So it seems. . . . Can't we negotiate?"

"No. You're to join with him shortly."

"What exactly do you mean by *join?*"

"Just meet with him."

"And then?"

"And then you go into hiding until Ragnarok is over."

"That's it?"

"That's all."

"And you needed to tie me, and . . . and all of—well, just to tell me this?"

"Not at all. He only wanted me to pass on the message to you. The rest was all my idea."

"Don't forget about me! I helped, too," Veikur Rum chimes in, but Hel ignores it. She leans back and reaches across Vogue for her bags.

"Now let's take a look at what you've bought to help you make it through Ragnarok."

"And have ourselves a little fun in the bargain," Veikur Rum adds, and Vogue's bindings tighten once again.

"Isn't Loki expecting me? Shouldn't I be on my way? Won't he be upset that you've kept me as it is?"

They hesitate. Retreat. Regroup. Reconsider. Hel settles in her seat. Minor eruption underneath.

"Perhaps. . . ."

"We're dead anyway, soon enough." Veikur Rum rumbles and starts to nip at the woman again.

"Just for tying me up—that's harsh." Vogue doesn't really sympathize, being totally unfamiliar with the experience of being sympathetic. However, she is starting to think on her feet, so to speak. And she wants to get away relatively unscathed.

Hel explains: "No. No. Almost all of us are to die—it's our Fate. After Ragnarok, very few will remain alive." She nods, contemplating. "Yes, we must satisfy honour. Fate is calling us."

Remembering her dreams, realizing there may be some truth to them, Vogue changes her mind and decides to stall.

"Well don't you have call display or message manager? Don't answer. Just ignore it. That's what I do. I don't think I'm ready for this yet. Let's put Fate on hold for a while."

"Loosen her bonds, Veikur Rum. It's time for her to be on her way."

Whimpering and groaning, Veikur Rum complies.

Vogue sits up and rubs her wrists and ankles. Still desperate, she asks: "But what about Free Will?"

"Do we look Catholic?"

". . . uhhh . . ."

"Don't answer. Just get dressed." Hel stands and shifts away, her lower body burping and oozing.

"But Vayker Room here ate my clothes."

"Sorry." Veikur Rum rumbles, but not too apologetically, still enjoying the feel and the view.

Hel gestures, dismissing her. "I'm sure you have something in your bags."

"I suppose," Vogue pouts, "but I really think you owe me."

"Perhaps," Hel smiles darkly, "we shall see what you deserve in . . ."

THE END

⚬

SHAVING THE WEASEL

SLOWLY, CAREFULLY, the derelict lowers his bursting burlap sack on to the beach. He's spent too much time collecting discarded human hair and nails to have them spill all over the sand now. Satisfied that his bag is safe, he sits down beside it on a nearby log and watches the waves lap up against the shore.

Waiting.

Knowing he won't be alone for long.

Soon, he hears their approach from opposite directions. Man and woman. GQ and Vogue. Slim and stylish . . . well *usually* anyway, but not today. Sure, they're still slim and Teflon coated, possessing abs of envy and buns of stainless steel. But they are also haggard—dirty and sweaty from running around store to store, trying to find the right things to get them through Ragnarok. But they've never had this kind of experience before, so, mostly, they've bought a lot of crap. During their sprees, knowing the clock is ticking, neither made their usual pit stops to check the hair, the makeup, the dandruff flakes, the creased clothes, and the runs in the nylons. Or to change those cursed black socks. In any case, Teflon may be a breeze to clean, but it gets filthy just as easily given the opportunity. So for many reasons—including the awareness of their lack of cleanliness—they are also angry.

At themselves.

At each other.

At *him*. They both yell, "There you are—I've been looking all over for you!" Then they run, shopping bags slapping their thighs, converging on him.

He sighs. "I figured you folks would be by sooner or later." And he doesn't bother to look up at them. Scratches at some mud caked on his pants. Flicks away the dust.

Scratches.

Flicks.

Not expecting to be so blatantly disregarded, the two stand above him, chests heaving, eyes darting around dubiously. Searching.

Finding . . . *nothing*. Certainly not what they were expecting. Well, they were expecting Loki, here, at the only nearby body of water: a shallow river in a park at the edge of the city. And they figured that by finding Loki, they would also find each other, but something is missing.

"Where's your long ship?" Vogue asks. "I thought you'd be almost finished by now. Isn't that your last sack? What about Ragnarok?"

Attacking from another angle, her husband shouts: "You said I had *lots of time!* You set me up! I lost my job! My only wish was to see you pay before Ragnarok begins—but now it seems Ragnarok is nowhere in sight and I'm unemployed! What am I supposed to do now? I'm hungry. Thirsty. Filthy. My teeth feel like they're coated with—"

"You would go and lose your job, wouldn't you? Well, if there's no Ragnarok, at least I won't have to be stuck with you to rebuild humanity." Vogue glares at her husband. "I want a divorce."

"What are you talking about?"

"You know what a divorce is—almost all of our friends and family have—"

"No. Not that. The being stuck together part and rebuilding humanity. How are we supposed to do that when we've both been snipped?"

"Well, it's a long story, but this morning I went on a bit of a shopping spree—"

"Shopping spree?"

"—and I got a hotel suite—"

"A suite? For one person?"

"—and I was laying down reading about the Vikings, and I fell asleep. I had all these dreams about you and me and Ragnarok—"

"Who's credit cards did you use?"

"—and then I woke, or I thought I woke, and Loki's daughter, Hel—"

"His daughter's name is *Hell?* Man, who are we dealing with?"

"Not *Hell*, you idiot, *H-E-L*! I understand why she complained so much now. Anyway, she explained everything to me—"

"Did you get a refund for the room since you left after staying for only a couple of hours?"

"Don't you want to hear about what Hel had to say, or about my dreams? I think they were prophetic, you know like on that mini-series that was on last weekend—"

"You kept your receipts, I hope."

The derelict clears his throat. "Why don't you two stop arguing, sit down, and relax." He pats the log on both sides. They hesitate. Both about to speak. Then they drop their eyes and their seats soon follow, with their bags still held before them. "Did *I* say Ragnarok *wasn't* approaching?"

". . . No. . . ." They glumly answer in unison.

"Just because you don't see a long ship moored here, it doesn't mean that it isn't somewhere else, now does it?"

Again, they reply: ". . . No. . . ."

"Well then, you two have a date with Destiny, don't you? Humanity is in your hands, or perhaps more appropriately, it is in your loins, and I don't need you two bickering over such trivialities. Right?"

". . . Right. . . ."

"That's better. Now do you two want to go to that cave in the hill over there?"

"*A cave?* Do we have a choice?" Vogue pouts.

The derelict only answers with a smile.

GQ whines. "We have to spend Ragnarok in a cave? For how long?"

"Until it's over."

"You're still being vague."

"You think I don't know that?" He flashes a brown, hourglass grin, which neither returns. "Now take your things and get going. I'll have to seal you in pretty soon."

"*Seal us in?*"

"It's for your own protection. Besides, what else did you expect?"

"You're going to seal us in a cave? How do we know when Ragnarok is over? How do we get back out? How are we to survive? More importantly, how do we even know this isn't just some trick on your part?"

Vogue cuts in: "I really think I should tell you about my—"

But the derelict ignores her interruption and speaks over her.

"Everything you need is in the cave. Go ahead. Take a look for yourselves. But if you two want to stay out here instead while Ragnarok is running amok, then be my guests and you can die with everyone else. Let me know right now though, because if you want to stay out here then I have to find another couple to rebuild humanity—*fast*—So what'll it be?"

"... The cave. ..." The couple agrees, albeit reluctantly for a number of reasons, but neither wants to die so soon—not when they have so much to live for.

Getting up together, the trio walks away from the water towards the cave's entrance; husband and wife each holding on tightly to their purchases. A mass of huge boulders is suspended above the opening, ready to block it at the pull of a rope. The derelict stops.

"I forgot my sack. Go on ahead. I don't want it to get wet." He pats them both on their shoulders. Simultaneously they cringe but remain silent. "Oh, and thanks again for your contribution, I couldn't have gotten this far without you."

"How stupid do you think we are?" GQ scowls.

"Is that a rhetorical question?"

"What does *rhetorical* mean?"

"Just get going, I'll be right behind you. Besides, you know I'm going to be sealing you anyway, soon enough."

Slowly complying, knowing that this is where their Fate lies, the couple enters the mouth of the cave. Nearby, there is a gas lantern—which fills them with hope and despair: hope in that it appears Loki did leave provisions for them, but despair because neither of them have ever operated a lantern before. Sure, they can ask him when he comes back, but what about *after* they are alone together? What other complex mechanisms may they be forced to learn how to use? They can only continue to hope that Loki provided something a little simpler for them to operate. GQ takes hold of the lantern. Continues into the darkness. Eyes open for a flashlight. His wife is at his side but neither reaches out for the other.

The derelict returns. Sack over his shoulder, he pauses at the entrance and takes hold of the rope.

"I really should go in and make sure they're alright first, but—" He shrugs indifferently and pulls the rope. The massive boulders come crashing down, covering the cave's entrance. As the rocks and dust settle he steps away and shakes his head: "That is one gullible couple. Oh well, I suppose there is no other way."

Inside the cave, they hear the rocks tumbling behind them. Both know they are here to stay for quite some time. Rather than trying to find their way back to the entrance, they feel their way around the cave. Soon they find a wooden table with a large flashlight on it, among other items. After dropping their bags, GQ wrestles the flashlight away from his wife and thumbs the switch.

On the table there is a brief note, which reads:

> Hey folks:
> Perhaps we'll meet again in Valhalla (ha ha). You should have enough to get by, but take it easy. Batteries—like most things in life, and in this cave—don't last forever. Let's see how long you two last together.
> Score one for Midgard.
> Cheers,
> Loki

Sighing. Shining the flashlight in his wife's frowning face, GQ takes a step back.

"Boy, have we been screwed."

"You think so?" Vogue snaps. "Now will you get that light out of my eyes?"

He turns off the flashlight. Both are happy not to see the other. They remain standing, eyes adjusting somewhat to the utter darkness.

"Well Ragnarok or no Ragnarok we've got a long haul ahead of us. I wonder if Loki left us anything to dig ourselves out?"

"How long do we wait though? Shouldn't we be certain Ragnarok has come and gone—if it's going to come at all? Although, from what Hel was telling me—and why didn't you listen to me in the first place about my dreams?"

"You have plenty of time to tell me now, don't you?"

"If they even matter anymore. . . . How did we get in this mess in the first place? You and your wanting to get some culture. . . . Damn you and Public Broadcasting straight to Valhalla!"

"It doesn't matter anymore. What matters is how me make it through . . .

THE END

༃

SUCKING ON THE MARROW OF LIFE

SPITTING OUT THE SMALL BONES, GQ reaches for another rack of rat heating over the gas lantern in the middle of the cave floor. Charred on the outside, raw on the inside. Even after all this time, he still hasn't got the hang of barbecuing. Too blue collar for him, and Vogue has never been a cook. (Why get your hands dirty and cook when you can dine out or have it prepared and delivered?) Besides, being in the cave all this time, it's not like Loki left them any spices besides a red-and-yellow plastic salt-and-pepper set, or anything other than the lantern to cook with. They almost starved before they finally relented to eating their first rat, oh, so long ago. So now, they eat what they can, when they can.

Across from him, Vogue sits with her legs crossed, avoiding his gaze in the shadows.

"Did you know a rat only needs a hole a quarter inch wide to fit through?"

"Kinda like something else, hmmm?" Vogue picks at the meat on her stick.

"No need to be snippy." He blows on the rat. "It's not like size matters anyway, when you're not getting any to begin with."

"What's the point—with your vasectomy and my tubes tied? No children to repopulate Midgard."

"I asked, but you never said anything back then either. Besides, I assumed Loki took care of those things—"

"Nice assumption—"

"Just like he took care of this. . . ." Pulling the skinned rat off the skewer, GQ stabs her in the heart, until the stick pokes out the back of her blouse.

"*Owww!* Would you stop doing that already?" Vogue pulls the skewer out and throws it on the stone floor. The wounds close over before much blood is spilled. Still: "You've just ruined another blouse. It's not like I have that many to chose from."

"You're still alive, aren't you?"

"Yes. Just like all the other times you've tried to stab me, choke me, smother me, bash my brains out."

"And don't forget about trying to kill me too."

"How can I forget when you're sitting here nagging me all the time? Just quit it already, I'm so *bored* with all of this: living in the dark, sleeping on a stone floor, the stench, your endless bits of trivia, eating rats, bugs—"

"But we're immortal. . . ."

"Big deal. We've known that for decades, and what good has it done us? We still get hungry. Still feel pain. Still can't get out of here."

"Well, why don't you open up already, and we'll find out what Fate has in store for us?"

"Despite what I saw in my dreams in that suite all those years ago, I still can't bear the thought of having sex with you anymore."

"But that's *exactly* what we're supposed to be doing. What about our Fate? Did it ever occur to you that maybe if we started having children, Loki would come back for us, and set us free?"

"Of course not! If Ragnarok is over, he's dead. We have to find our own way out . . . *somehow*. . . . Or maybe there will be someone—"

"You *know* there is no way out. The only entrance is blocked with stones too large for us to move, and we have nothing to break them down with. 'Everything you need is in the cave'—*my ass!*"

"Stop whining already. Maybe Ragnarok isn't over yet anyway. Who knows how long it's supposed to last?"

"I still think we need to have sex."

"I didn't want to thirty years ago, when you still looked half decent, and when you didn't smell so . . . so . . ."

"You think you stink any less than I do? We've been out of soap, cologne, and toothpaste for more than twenty years. It's not going to get any better. . . ."

And so the two argue and argue, still try to murder each other on occasion, and slowly go insane until . . .

THE END

ᘐᘎ

MISADVENTURES IN A THUMBNAIL UNIVERSE

WATCHING THE SUN SET, Loki and Hel sit on a log on the sand a short distance from the cave that holds GQ and Vogue. A low fire at their feet. Loki pokes at it with a length of driftwood, while Hel scruffs her brother Fenrir behind the ears—the massive wolf's head in her lap. His eyes closed, he growls lowly, contented. Loki is still dressed as the derelict, with the bursting burlap sack of hair and nails beside him. He has a *long* way to go yet before he has enough to build the long ship, but he's in no hurry, especially since he knows that he will be killed at Ragnarok.

"How long are you planning on keeping them in there?"

"I don't see any reason to release them, especially since they're not living up to their end of the deal. So, I'll just keep sending a rat or two their way to keep them going, driving each other crazy."

"But what about their children—if they *ever* have any? You did take care of them, too, didn't you?"

"Of course. I made them fully functional just before they entered the cave."

Hel shakes her head. "They're about the worst possible parents I can imagine."

"Considering you're the goddess of the underworld, that's saying a lot."

"It is, isn't it? Still, that's been your plan all along, hasn't it? No children, they go insane together in a cave for eternity, their own special room in Niflheim, so to speak. And if they do have any children, Midgard will be reborn with the worst possible offspring."

"Pretty funny, don't you think?"

"Always like having the last laugh, don't you, Father?"

Loki grins, makes no reply, and stabs the smoldering driftwood into the sand. He pulls out a chipped and rusted Swiss Army knife—with only eleven tools, including the main blade—so nothing too fancy. He digs his thumbnail in the groove of a smaller blade and snaps it open. Holds up his thumb. Inspects the scratched and broken cuticle; the dry and cracked skin; the caked dirt underneath the yellow half-moon of the nail. Raises the small blade and sets in to scrape the dirt away. Maintaining a disguise or not, he can only stand so much grime after all.

Hel nudges him, and he almost stabs his hand. Somewhat irritated, he turns his head.

"What was that for?"

Hel points at his still-raised thumb.

"I thought you knew better than that?"

"What're you talking about?"

"What? Don't you know? Haven't you ever watched Public Broadcasting with all those science programs?"

"Yes. It's funny. That's kind of what got GQ into trouble in the first place. So . . . ?"

"So . . . see that dirt under your thumbnail?"

"Of course. That's what I was going to scrape away until you shoved your elbow in my side."

Hel raises an eyebrow. "Well, think of all the millions and billions of people I probably saved . . . ?"

"Start making sense, or it's going to be more than my nails I'll be cleaning out." But there isn't much of a threat in his voice, or in any other part of his body.

"That dirt is made up of molecules, and those molecules are made up of atoms. Perhaps every one of those atoms is a whole universe, filled with planets and stars and people. Perhaps we are—our whole universe—just one of those atoms that make up the molecules in some other 'old man's' thumbnail sitting on a log on a beach somewhere else. . . . Ever consider that?"

Hel holds a superior smile, but she is also happy to pass on this "knowledge."

Loki considers her words for a moment and answers: "No. Can't say that I have. Nice story . . . though I wouldn't be telling that to anyone else in Niflheim or Asgard if I were you. Not a very Norse idea." Holds up his thumb again, and places the blade under the nail. "Still, maybe you're right, but it's still just dirt to me." And he draws the blade across, creating a tiny shower on the ground before him. "Besides, if their universes are anything like ours, they aren't really worth keeping anyway." Blows the bits of dust. "Now I've got nine more nails to do, not counting my toes if I feel like doing that much today. So why don't you just sit back, relax, and enjoy the sunset, rather than worry about any other possible universes, or that couple, or . . .

RAGNAROK

More Painful than the Dreams of Other Boys

Derryl Murphy

MIKE GORDINI LEANED AGAINST THE HOOD OF HIS PATROL CAR and watched the world go by, marveling at the sight of families all together, children being towed along by parents, patient and otherwise. Kids here were so helpless, so unable to control themselves and their lives, and on the second day of his new duty it was still taking him by surprise.

His new partner, Simone Perez, came out of the Korean grocery and tossed him his Coke, then walked around and climbed in behind the driver's seat. Mike opened his door and sat beside her, found himself staring at her and wondering at how she looked; pretty, he thought with surprise, even though a few wrinkles showed and some grey hairs were creeping in around the temples and up top. The ring on her finger told him someone else likely thought she was good-looking as well, but he hadn't had the guts to ask about that yet. Weird enough that he was here with her, in this strange section of the city.

She turned her head back from shoulder-checking, caught him staring at her. She smiled. "What?"

Mike could feel the heat in his cheeks. He turned his head and looked out his window, pretended he was watching for perps as he cracked open his soda. "Nothing," he answered, then took a sip.

"Nothing my ass. I can't say I know what you're feeling, Mike, since I grew up here. But I've met a couple of people who came out of Templeton, and they've told me how weird it is for the first little while. I can only imagine."

He grunted and took another swig; watched this city of age go by, and wondered at it.

FOR THE REMAINING THREE HOURS OF THEIR SHIFT, life remained uneventful, the presence of their car serving as a check for anyone thinking of pulling any stunts. Twenty minutes before the end of their shift, all available units were called to an address near the Line with Templeton.

Simone looked over at Mike. He felt a lurching in his stomach, knew he wasn't ready to get that close to the Line so soon after having to cross over. But he forced a smile and nodded at her, then turned on the lights as Simone shrugged her shoulders and stepped on the gas. But before they'd gone a block, a second call instructed them to come in to the precinct to see the captain.

"Come in, both of you," he said, when they got to his office. "Close the door and have a seat."

Captain Munro was even more amazing to Mike. Almost no hair, a huge gut, wrinkles and age spots lining his face, he was everything that Mike had always thought he would never be. Was this how he'd end up on this side of the Line?

"There's been a murder," said the captain. "Derek Hayes."

"Jesus," said Simone. She looked over at Mike, but he just shrugged. The name meant nothing to him. "Very rich guy, sometimes seems like he owns—owned—half the town. To say nothing of all his other interests around the world."

"Ah," said Mike, nodding. He looked back to Captain Munro. "So what does this have to do with us?"

"Well," said the captain, "mostly it just has to do with you, Gordini, although Perez will continue to back you up. Hayes was found dead inside Templeton; beaten to death."

Mike leaned forward. "*Inside* Templeton. What, you mean just over the Line?"

Munro shook his head. "Nope. He was down on fifty-fourth, near the clocktower."

"Holy shit," said Simone.

Mike leaned back and nodded, feeling a little nervous now, then asked, "Why are you telling us?"

The captain steepled his fingers and for a long moment stared over them at Mike. "The mayor had a little chat with the chief," he finally said. "Hayes, as you might imagine, was a go-to guy for political contributions, and already his lawyer and his corporate partners are making noises about wanting this solved now. So the mayor wants someone from our force in there to make sure that the investigation goes the way it should. To say nothing of the fact that we don't know if we can trust whatever they have for investigators over there."

Ice-water shock ran down Mike's spine. He closed his eyes for a second to regain control, heard Simone say, "No way, Captain. We can't do that!"

"Who said anything about you, Perez? You'll be staying here on this side, giving backup when the time comes." He looked back to Mike. "You understand what's up?"

Mike nodded, too stunned to speak. He'd only been out of Templeton for just over three months now, and after training and then only two days on the street, here he was being asked—no, told—to go back in. "I'll age," he managed to croak.

"You have an advantage, Gordini, you know that. You're only just out, so it isn't going to hit you as hard. And even though you were forced to leave, I'm told that the way things work your recent departure should actually help retard the process."

"It gets worse each time you go back, though." He winced at how whiny the plea sounded.

Munro's deep voice sounded hoarse now, but he ignored Mike, just carried on. "We'll provide for you, of course. The only way you can go in there is as a full detective; there's no way anyone would accept just a beat cop working on this case. And we're only asking that you do the most basic investigations while in Templeton. Most of your work will be done on this side of the Line, with our full support."

Mike leaned his elbows on his thighs and sat there, quiet, first looking at the captain and then at Simone. Munro just leaned back in his chair, arms crossed, but Simone was staring hard at Mike, almost glaring. Finally he shrugged, looked at her with what he hoped was an apologetic face, and said, "I'll do it. I can't turn down this chance to prove I can handle it."

Simone stood up, threw up her hands. "You stupid prick. You've only been on the job a couple of days. What the hell do you think you need to prove?"

"That's enough, Perez," whispered the captain. Even that quiet Mike could hear the threat in his voice. "You're going to get a bump up as well, go back up to detective."

Back? thought Mike.

"It's not about a promotion, captain," protested Simone, but he waved her off.

"You have a suit?" he asked Mike, whose thoughts jumped back to the situation at hand.

"Yes, sir. In my locker."

"Right. Go downstairs and get changed. I'll meet you at Sarge's desk with your new badge and the keys to your car. You too, Perez. Make it fast."

Mike stood, saluted, and left the office, Simone right behind him. In the squad room, a dozen faces all turned to look at them, but no one said a word. A telephone rang, but everyone ignored it at least until the two of them had crossed the room and were through the door to the stairwell.

THE CAR WAS A RATTY OLD BUICK, probably the worst one in the garage. But at least it was his own, and he thought it went well with his shiny new badge and his brown, slightly dilapidated secondhand suit, slacks hanging by mismatched suspenders while they waited for a chance to be taken in. Simone sat in the passenger's seat this time, sullen, staring out the window, looking quite snazzy in her beige outfit.

He reached the edge of Templeton in about fifteen minutes, pulled the car to the curb and just sat there, staring at the Line and gripping the steering wheel tight enough for his knuckles to go white. Several squad cars sat at the edge, as well as one ambulance, but the officers were just milling around, nobody willing to step over. Looking through the thick fog of the Line, he could see only the vague shapes of buildings; no one over there liked to approach it unless absolutely necessary.

"Ready?"

Simone turned and looked at him. "Fuck no. But it's your decision, isn't it. And since I'm your partner . . ." She gave a weak smile. "Let's go."

Mike stepped out and pocketed his keys, then flashed his new badge at the first cop to approach him. The officer, a guy he recognized but didn't recall ever meeting, shook their hands and led them over to the sergeant standing at the edge, hands on his hips and staring down at the road.

"Sergeant Dickson," said the patrolman. "Gordini and Perez are here, the detectives we were told about."

The man reached out a big meaty paw and shook Mike's hand, then Simone's. "Detectives. You got a radio?"

Mike blinked. "Uh, no," he said, pretending to pat himself down. "Got my sidearm, got my badge, didn't think to grab a radio."

"Dewey, grab the man a radio so he can go in!" Another patrolman ran and pulled a portable radio from a car and ran it over. Mike took it and hooked it to his belt, trying to hide the bulge under his jacket.

"Ready?" asked Simone, squeezing his elbow.

"Guess so," he finally said, and turned and, after a brief moment of hesitation, crossed the Line.

Instantly he felt tired, run ragged, but soon that feeling was overwhelmed as he crossed out of the haze, was replaced by something approaching claustrophobia. Everything was as he remembered, but his short time out in his new life had served to change his perspective.

To his right he heard the click of a lighter being closed, smelled the sweet smell of the tobacco that they sold on this side of the Line. "I was wondering if they were gonna sucker you into coming."

Mike turned, smiled in spite of the turmoil he was feeling inside. "Hiya, Danny." His old partner, Danny Glaus, stood leaning against a light pole, taking a drag on his smoke, looking up at Mike. He wore a light blue short-sleeved shirt with suspenders, a black beret with "TPD" emblazoned on it, and jeans with runners. His heavy black baton hung loose from a holster on his pants.

He walked up and shook Mike's hand. "You a detective already? Way to go."

"Thanks." Mike looked down at his former partner. "It was an incentive to get me to come back across."

Danny took one more drag then flicked the smoke away, nodding. "Thought as much. Never struck me as anything like a game of cops and robbers anytime I talked to someone from over on *your* side." The accent was deliberate, Mike knew.

Danny tossed a stick of gum to Mike, who caught it and grinned. Cinnamon: made Danny feel a little more grown up, rather than chewing the bubble gum so popular on this side. He unwrapped it and started chewing, felt some memories rush back with the shot of flavour gently burning his tongue.

After putting a stick in his own mouth, Danny walked around to the driver's side of his car, face grim. "Climb in."

Mike stood and looked at the car for a second, feeling a bit flustered. He either didn't remember the car being this small, or else himself being this big. Feeling like a clown at the circus, he opened the door, slid the seat back as far as it could go, then squeezed himself in, knees halfway up to his nose and his back bent at a peculiar angle. It was then something of an operation to reach out and close the door.

Danny fired up the little two-stroke engine, and the car jumped away from the curb, rattling and roaring as it went, little bouncing-head dinosaur doing a sympathetic shimmy from its suction-cupped location on the dash. Inside, it smelled of tobacco and cinnamon, a strangely sweet aroma after having lived on the other side of the Line.

Mike thought about asking questions regarding the crime scene, but between the noise and his currently squished diaphragm, he decided it would be prudent to wait. Instead he watched the town go by, remembering the sights, looking at billboards advertising new toys or imported G-rated flicks, viewing with wonder the tiny buildings that had once seemed a normal part of his life.

He turned and looked at Danny out of the corner of his eye. His former partner still looked thirteen, something that seemed a bit weirder now that he'd gone to the other side of the Line and seen kids that age who still acted like kids. Danny had been this age for most of his life, grown into it and then just hit a holding pattern, some parts of his mind and emotional makeup maturing, but still remaining basically a kid. He took his job with the Templeton Police Department seriously enough, although Mike remembered so many of the days where it had all seemed a game to them. And it had been, really just playing at cops and robbers, no domestics or rapes or murders ever happening, ever needing to be dealt with.

And now there was Derek Hayes, lying dead near the clocktower. No game this.

There weren't many cars on the streets, but that was normal for Templeton. Instead, Mike watched as they roared past bicycles and skateboards and scooters and pedestrians, even some smaller kids riding metal or plastic trikes. It was close to the end of the day, so he imagined most of them were coming home from work or school right now.

A billboard on the side of one of the buildings advertised two old Shirley Temple and Jackie Coogan movies playing at the art house theatre, a retrospective from when they had first quit acting and moved into directing, sharing that bill with adult directors on the other side of the Line—a procedure no longer in vogue. Coogan was dead now, had crossed over and aged a couple of decades ago. But Temple, Mike knew, lived still, hiding in her suite uptown, tucked away like a miniature version of Garbo, unwilling to face or deal with anyone in the town that carried her name.

He watched several heads turn sharply as they went by, and he knew he was seeing looks of shock on some of the faces as they realized what the passenger in the cop car was. He'd never seen such a sight himself, all the years he'd lived in Templeton, so he could imagine just how bizarre he looked.

Danny cut the motor and let the little car roll to a halt in the middle of the road. Mike managed to pry open the door with a moderately paralysed hand and then practically fell out of the car and to his knees, thinking this was a great way to start as he stood and brushed dirt and gravel from his pants.

There was a crowd standing near the yellow tape, about three dozen kids, looking anywhere from five to fifteen years old. As he approached they all stepped back, almost as one, staring up at him. It was an unsettling feeling, combined with everything else that was happening; he knew he'd gotten taller since leaving Templeton, but looking down at them and seeing just how much most of them had to crane their necks to look back up at him, the changes he had gone through hit home that much harder.

"Through here," said Danny, lighting up another smoke and lifting the tape to walk under. Mike just waited until he was through, and then he stepped over it.

He recognized the building they were at; it was an apothecary on the main floor, run by Sandy Hancock, and then some low-rent apartments up above. A uniform Mike only half-recognized nodded at them and held open the door to the pharmacy and Danny led the way in, Mike stooping just a bit to clear the doorjamb.

Inside he found he could stand up straight, as long as he was careful around the light fixtures, which were just the right height to clip him a good one. He looked to make sure he had a good fix on where all of them were and then turned his eyes and his mind to the business at hand. There were several cops inside, three guys and a girl who knew enough about forensics to do the job when needed, and he nodded at each one briefly before following Danny.

At the end of the aisle Danny turned, then pointed to the counter. "Over there."

Mike stepped up to the counter and leaned over to have a look. Lying on the floor were two bodies, which was a surprise: Sandy Hancock, face up, eyes wide open and back of her skull bashed in; and, sprawled on top of her, curled up in a fetal position, an adult male with even more dents and furrows in his skull. Derek Hayes. Blood was spattered everywhere.

"Eeuuw." He could feel two urges, fought to keep them both down: the desire to puke and the complete fascination with seeing two dead bodies.

"No kidding," said Danny. His voice seemed a little shaky. "Here's where you get to start. We've already dusted for prints and taken photos, and Doc Baird is ready to move the bodies, but we wanted you to have a look first."

Mike moved around to the other side of the counter, bent down and looked at the man's wounds without touching anything. "Find a weapon yet?" He was already feeling out of his league here. The closest he'd come to a murder investigation was when he was a cadet, a visit to the crime scene after the body had been removed so that they could watch the forensic team do their work.

"I've got guys checking alleys and garbage bins and the like," said Danny. "Nothing yet."

Mike popped his head up and looked for the head of the forensics team. "Any interesting prints, Jim?"

Jim peeled off a glove and scratched his head. "I don't know, uh, Mike. We've got a bunch of adult and kid prints here, but I don't know what to make of it. I mean, it was so weird having *him* here," he gestured at the body, "it just goes beyond making any sense to me that we might have had another adult in here, too."

"So do you figure these prints are all his, or do some of them look like they might not match up?"

Jim shrugged his shoulders. "Oh yeah, Mike, like we're experts at this." With a start Mike realized that Jim looked frightened, that they all did. "Nobody I know's ever been murdered before. We play good guys and bad guys." He paused to catch his breath, shuddered. "But nothin' like this. We don't know how to do this stuff."

Mike stood and walked over, put his hand on Jim's shoulder. "Sounds like you did good finding the adult prints. If you can get them together for me so I can take them back over the Line when I'm done here, that would be great."

Jim nodded and smiled up at him, looking every inch the ten-year-old boy that he was. "I've already lifted and marked them all and have them ready to go. Just ask Marie for the baggies when you leave."

"What else do you have for me, Danny?" he asked, walking back to where his former partner was lighting up yet another cigarette. A sure sign just how nervous he was feeling.

"Up the stairs, but I haven't had much of a chance to look yet." He turned and headed through the back door and on up, Mike following close behind.

It wasn't too tight a fit, but it was small and mildly claustrophobic, and when they came to the top of the stairs he saw that this room must have been where Sandy combined her office and living quarters, small even by Templeton standards. He quickly walked over to the half-open window and knelt down on the floor, eyes closed and breathing in fresh air until he felt his shoulders lift a bit.

"The bed," said Danny.

Mike looked and grimaced. He couldn't help himself then, all his years in Templeton came bubbling up to the top. "Oh, yuck!"

Danny smiled. "Yeah, that's pretty much what we all were thinking." He pointed his smoke at the fresh stains on the sheets. "Doc had a quick look up skirts and in pants, and what you're thinking is right. Sandy Hancock and Derek Hayes were bumping uglies, man and child, right here in Templeton."

"Son of a bitch," whispered Mike. "You hear stories on the other side of the Line, and I know sometimes they've caught some pathetic fucker thinking about crossing over, but I never heard about both sides being in on it. That's sick!"

"Besides being illegal. Most of us think the same, Mike. There's still some people who don't think it's sick, though."

Mike shrugged. "I think you can safely rule out everyone who's under, say, ten or twelve. This beating seems a little much to have been done by a little kid. Plus, Derek was not only an adult, he looked to me to be a pretty big guy. That would be a tough fight for anyone, most of all a kid."

"Unless he was caught by surprise."

"The only thing that makes that guess difficult, Danny, is that he was on top of Sandy. We'll go back down and ask Jim if he thinks he was moved, but I doubt it. So that means that he got it after Sandy, which makes the element of surprise that much less likely."

"Oh." Danny took another drag, then stubbed out the cigarette in an empty ashtray. "Sounds like you're learning lots as a grownup."

Mike smiled. "I have to. It's a big and ugly and exciting and dangerous place. Not that I've really had a chance to use any of that training yet."

"Good a time as any, hey?"

"Guess so." Mike leaned down to push up off the floor, caught a glimpse of something and stopped, stumbling back to his knees. "What the hell is that?" he asked, now lying down on the floor and reaching under the bed.

Danny was down on his knees beside him, leaning over and looking. "What? What do you see?"

The bed was big compared to others he knew of in Templeton—no question why, now—and so Mike even had to get his head partly under the frame before he could reach it. He could have just picked up the bed and moved it out of the way, but he reasoned to himself that the work involved would have been greater, this room being so crowded they would be moving furniture every which way to make space.

He rolled onto his back and then sat up facing Danny. In his hands was a small ornate yellow and orange box, a thick blue rubber band wrapped around it to hold the lid in place. Written on the side in black felt pen were the letters "SH."

"Sandy Hancock," said Danny.

"You still have a keen grasp at the obvious, my friend," responded Mike, grinning. He frowned then, set the box down on the floor, realizing he wasn't completely prepared for handling the crime scene. "Got any gloves?"

Danny jumped up, looking eager to help. "Downstairs," he said, running out to pilfer some from someone on the forensics crew.

He returned and handed a pair of latex gloves to Mike, but they were made for extra-small hands, and kept pulling at the hairs on the back of his hand. Finally, Mike snapped the glove off and handed both over to Danny. "Easier if you do the honours."

Gloves on, Danny peeled back the rubber band and lifted the lid, leaning over so he could see inside. "Me too," said Mike, pushing his shoulder. Danny grinned and tilted the box so they could both see.

Cotton balls. "Pull them out, gently," said Mike.

Danny did so, and about halfway down he felt something hard and cylindrical. He pulled it out and held it up to the light: a finger-length glass vial with a black stopper on top, dark green liquid inside.

"Holy shit," said Mike. It was barely a whisper. "Anything else?"

Danny pulled back some more cotton, and then very carefully removed a small syringe. "Drop it back in," said Mike. He pulled out a larger evidence bag, and Danny slid the whole box inside.

"Is this the real thing?" asked Danny. His eyes were wide.

"Looks like Slow," said Mike, standing up. "If it is, maybe we have a motive for the murders. I have to get back to the other side of the Line now. I've been over here too long, and there's going to be plenty of work to do if this is what we think it is."

Danny stood with him, lit another smoke. "You know," said Mike, pointing at the cigarette, "That stuff'll stunt your growth."

"Har har," replied Danny, sticking out his tongue. "Mr. Funny himself has returned."

Mike took a bow, turned towards the stairs.

"We miss you, y'know."

He stopped, didn't turn around.

"I remember when I first noticed that you weren't going to stay a kid forever, when you started to age. I felt real cheated that day."

Mike turned back to face him. "It wasn't my fault."

"Maybe, maybe not," said Danny, trying unsuccessfully to blow a smoke ring. He'd always thought smoking made him look cool, and Mike had never had the heart to tell him how wrong he was. "You chased that one bad guy pretty close to the Line that one time I remember. I still wonder if that had anything to do with it wearing off."

Mike shrugged, looked down at the floor. "It just happens sometimes. I'm not the first kid to all of a sudden grow up."

"No, but it's the first time it happened to a friend of mine. It's hard to see you grown up like this, knowing that you're living in another world and you're never going to be able to play or run, to be like a kid ever again." Danny wiped a tear from his eye. "And now you come in here for this stupid murder, you're going to get even older! All this time, being stolen away from you. . . ." His voice trailed off.

He didn't need to be reminded of any of this. After a long moment, Mike finally lifted his head. "I can't stay any longer, Danny. Are you giving me a ride back to the Line, or am I going to walk?"

"Jesus." Danny stubbed out his smoke on the heel of his shoe and then brushed past Mike, heading down the stairs before he could say anything else.

After arranging for the body to be sent back across the Line and collecting everything he thought he needed for the investigation, Mike squeezed back into the car and rode in silence. As he was climbing out, Danny reached over and put a hand on his arm. Mike didn't look back, just sat there, looking at the fuzzy outline of figures on the other side.

"Try to remember to have fun sometimes, okay?"

Mike shook his head, trying to pretend there were no tears fighting their way up and out. "Doesn't work that way once you grow up, Danny. You know as well as I do." He stood up and shut the door, still looking across the Line.

Danny gunned the noisy motor, yelled, "I don't *ever* wanna know that, Mike. Don't take this the wrong way, but I hope I don't see you again." Car belching black and blue smoke and roaring like a walrus on a motorcycle, he spun around and drove off, leaving Mike to cross the Line on his own.

He still had the gum in his mouth, he realized. Old habit from when he used to live as a kid. It was as tasty as cardboard now, so with two last open-mouthed chews he spit it onto the road, and then stepped across the Line.

It hit him harder coming back, the weight of new years bearing down on him not only from above, but from around and inside of him. Any spring in his step he may have felt before was definitely lost now, and for only the second time in his life—the first being when the growth spurt had told him he would no longer be a kid—his bones were aching. He practically staggered out of the fog onto the other side of the Line.

Hands grabbed both his arms, voices called for coffee and a place to sit. Next he knew he was leaning against a seatback on the passenger's side of a patrol car, and Simone was there, leaning down and pressing a cardboard cup of coffee into his hands. "I don't drink that shit," he said, trying to smile.

"It's an acquired taste," she responded, making as bad an effort to return a smile. "You grow into it."

He took a sip, grimaced at how bitter it was, then marveled at the warm feeling he got as it settled inside of him, at the fact that already he felt more awake and alive. "Jeez, this ain't half-bad," he said, taking another sip and grimacing again.

"Welcome to middle age, Mike," said Simone, putting a hand on his shoulder and squeezing.

ALL DAY MIKE HAD AVOIDED LOOKING IN A MIRROR. He'd let Simone drive back to the precinct so he could avoid using the rearview and had kept his head down when walking through glass doors.

But now that he was at home, leaning back in his overstuffed chair and drinking a strangely unsatisfying Coke, the urge to look had finally overtaken the fear. He took one more sip and then wandered into the kitchen, pouring the remainder of the soda down the drain, and then walked down the short hall to the bathroom. Once inside, he closed the door and stood facing the mirror for a good while without turning on the light, just letting the darkness accompany his worry while he thought about the case.

Derek Hayes had gone across the Line to engage in some deviant pedo action with Sandy Hancock, and, if Mike was right about the little vial of liquid he'd found, he'd been doing it regularly. Tomorrow Mike expected to visit the lab and be told that the stuff was Slow, a drug that gave a buzz like nothing else on the streets, but that usually killed the people who took it.

A side effect of the drug was its ability to counter the effects of crossing the Line, which meant that when it first hit the streets a few decades ago there had been a huge underground market for it. But the market had dried up among all but the worst of freaks with its eighty-or-more percent death rate, enough even to scare off most of the sick fucks who wanted to cross the Line into Templeton to screw little kids. But for those people who were able to use Slow and not drop dead after the first hallucination, the trips over to Templeton could be a possible bonus; an hour, maybe even two or three, safe from the aging effects of the Line. As a kid, Mike had never thought about the possibility of predators crossing the Line and doing their thing with impunity, but he found that his new self came up with that thought very quickly.

He shuddered, then turned on the light.

It was too bright, but after squeezing his eyes shut for a few seconds, he was able to open them and slowly raise them to the mirror. A small cry escaped his mouth, but he clenched his fists tight, regained control, and continued to look.

There were wrinkles on his face, mostly at the top of the bridge of the nose and in the corners of his eyes, as well as two large smile lines grooved deep in his cheeks. A few light brown spots flecked his face, and he needed to shave his definitely pudgier chin. His hair was still mostly brown, thank God, although there were a few wisps of grey, and besides looking a bit thinner it also seemed that his hairline was higher up his forehead. He reached down and grabbed a small mirror that sat on the counter, held it behind his head, angled it so he could see that, yes, he did have a small bald spot on the crown.

Looking at his hand as he put the mirror back down, he saw that his fingers were fatter and hairier, something he had not expected. He put his hand on his stomach, felt the belly, and slowly unbuttoned his shirt, letting the mass of flesh and fat spring free with a last flick of his fingers. Then he finally undid his pants, unsure even if he could pull them on again in the morning. His gut bulged, loose and defiant, daring him to find a way to shake it off.

"Christ." He shut off the light and went to bed, shedding clothes in the hall, utterly dejected, lost in this new body.

THE PHONE RANG AT 7:30, waking him from an unsettled sleep. It was Simone.

"I talked to the captain, and he gave me an idea about how much more you're going through. So I'm coming by with some sweats, and then we're going out to get you some coffee and breakfast and then some new clothes."

Mike rubbed his eyes. "Thanks, but I have to get down to the lab."

"Captain's orders. Have a shower, and I'll be there in ten minutes." She paused. "Besides, the captain will meet us with all the results, probably while we're eating."

"Right." He leaned over and hung up the phone, then slowly pulled himself out of bed. When he was essentially vertical he realized he had to pee like nobody's business, so he hurried into the john to relieve himself. After what seemed a crazily long time standing there—he was amazed that his body could hold that much piss—he flushed and then turned on the shower, climbed in while it was still too hot and danced around inside while he worried at the faucet, finally setting the temperature right only after alternately scalding and freezing several parts of his body.

When he was done he brushed his teeth in front of the misted-over mirror, ran a comb through his hair, then headed to the bedroom to put on underwear and a housecoat, stooping down with some effort to pick up last night's clothes on his way. Then he sat on the edge of his bed and just waited.

Five minutes later there was a knock at the door. He closed his eyes for a moment and then opened them and went to answer. Simone stood there, grocery bag in one hand, smiling. She wasn't dressed for work.

"Captain gave me a few hours off. I get to spend it helping you acclimatize." She shoved the bag into his hands. "Here. It ain't high fashion, but it'll do for the diner. Go get dressed."

"If you have some free time, shouldn't you be spending it with your family?"

Simone rolled her eyes and pushed her way past Mike. Sitting down at the kitchen table, she said, "I said the captain gave me free time. To be with you, not to piss away my day pretending I still have a life."

The look on her face told him to not bother asking any more questions, so he went to his room and changed. Basic grey sweats, loose sweater, then his own socks and sneakers. "Where to?" he asked as he opened the door to the outer hallway.

"The Ritz Diner. I'm having fried eggs and hash browns and coffee, lots of it." The two of them climbed into her car, and she started it up. "You?"

He thought for a second. "Pancakes, side of sausage, OJ, coffee." His stomach rumbled. He was hungrier than he'd thought.

They got a booth near the front of the diner. Mike watched Simone prepare her coffee—two scoops of sugar and one creamer—and copied her, found that it was more palatable that way. After the first jolt hit his system he leaned back and closed his eyes, almost smiling, picturing himself having a day off where nothing was weighing on his mind.

"You gonna stay with the case?" asked Simone.

He cocked one eye open, stared at her. "What do you mean?"

She shrugged her shoulders. "You've already done what the captain asked you to do. You crossed the Line, checked out the evidence, there's not much more you need to do, if you don't want. I know that the captain has other people on the job now, folks who'll stay safe on this side of the Line."

He shook his head. "Are you saying I'm *expendable?* Now that I've done my bit and took away fifteen or twenty years from my life, now I don't need to stick around anymore?"

Simone leaned forward and put a hand on his arm. "Cool down, Mike. I was just asking. The captain didn't say nothing about you being pulled from the case. He just wanted me to make sure you were okay. I'm your partner, even if it's only been a couple of days. It's my job to look out for you."

Mike looked out the window, watching a mother and her three young children walking by. "You have kids?"

She took her hand away. "Used to. Jason was thirteen when he was hit by a bus, two years ago."

Mike grimaced. "Jesus. I'm sorry."

Simone shrugged. "That's okay. I think it's one of the reasons I took to you so easy. He would still have been younger than you were when you were forced to leave Templeton, had to come across, but I could see a lot of the same qualities in you that I remember so well in him."

"I was still a kid." He smiled.

"You were," she said, nodding. "Newly minted adult, still keen about life. Even though just a few months before you'd had to leave your childhood behind."

"Not anymore." He frowned, pinching at the skin on his forearm and watching it droop rather than snap back into place. "Nothing new about any of this."

They were both silent for a moment, and then Simone continued. "Anyway, I took a leave of absence for a while, and when I came back I requested to be put in a patrol car. Just didn't have the head for thinking seriously about cases right about then."

That rang a small bell in the back of Mike's brain. "That's right. Captain promoted you *back* to detective. I was going to ask about that, but I guess I forgot."

Their breakfasts arrived then, and for a few moments the two of them just ate. Finally, halfway through his third pancake, Mike could feel himself starting to fill up. He leaned back again, took one last swig of juice, then cleared his plate to the side and leaned his arms on the table. He was about to speak when the door opened and in walked the captain, heading straight for their table. Mike scooted over to make room for him.

"How are you feeling today?" he asked, signaling the waitress for coffee.

Mike shrugged. "A little better now that I'm up and about. Have to go get some clothes and get looking decent again, though."

Captain Munro eyed him for a few seconds, then reached into his pocket and pulled out a wad of bills, peeled off a bunch of twenties. "You'll be needing to shave, too," he said. "Just yesterday your face was like a baby's butt. When you buy your clothes get yourself a decent electric razor as well." Mike made to protest, but Munro put up his hand. "It's not on me, it's on the department. We got you into this, so we may as well help equip you." He turned his attention to his coffee then, squeezing in two creamers and a heaping spoonful of sugar.

After a sip and a grimace he rummaged in his other pocket, pulled out a couple of folded-up pieces of paper and handed them over to Mike. "It's the preliminary results from the lab on that vial you found," he said. "They faxed this to me at home this morning."

Mike grabbed a napkin and wiped away the juice and coffee rings, then flattened out the report. He tried reading it over two times, but finally had to lean back and push it across the table to Simone. "I'm not sure I follow, sir," he said. "I mean, they had us read lab and forensics reports when we were in training, but nothing had detail like this."

Simone looked up from the papers. "Jesus," she said. "This is for real?"

Captain Munro nodded and then turned his attention back to Mike. "That was indeed a vial of Slow that you found at the apartment, Mike. But there's a difference in the chemical makeup, and, while they're still trying to confirm their initial impressions, they are pretty sure that the stuff retains its ability to counteract the Line but is no longer so lethal. If it's even lethal at all."

Mike took a second to let this news travel around inside his head. Then he asked, "How come we don't already know about this stuff? Why isn't it on the streets big time?"

Munro shrugged. "Beats me. Maybe it's just hit, and only the special people have it. I talked to the folks on the drug squad, and they're just as surprised as we are. They've got people out snooping around right now, but we're going to have to do our own checking as well."

"Where do we start?"

The captain fixed Mike with a stare. "I know you're still new at this, detective, but try and remember that you were also a cop on the other side of the Line. Try and *think* like one."

Mike scratched his chin, feeling the unfamiliar stubble growing there. "I guess I should go make myself look pretty and then go talk to Mrs. Hayes, for starters. At least I assume there's a Mrs."

"There is. I've already made an appointment for you to see her, at 11:30." The captain slid another piece of paper across the table to him. "Here's her address. It'll give you plenty of time to fix yourself up." He turned and looked back at Simone. "And Perez, your day off just ended. Get yourself dressed like a detective again, so you can ride along."

TWO HOURS LATER, Mike was shaved and wearing a new, although cheap, suit, and they were back in the car after stopping at Simone's apartment so that she could get changed. "Makes me sick," said Mike, "thinking that Hayes and

Sandy were getting it on like that. There's no place for that sort of thing, anywhere in the world."

Simone scratched her head. "It's a weird situation, though, Mike. Here on this side of the Line, pedophilia is illegal. But how does it work over on the other side?" She looked uncomfortable, but pressed ahead. "I mean, do the kids over there make it with each other?"

Mike shook his head, feeling more than a little weirded out by the question. "Nuh-uh. No way. If anything like that happens to you, you know you're a candidate for crossing the Line and not coming back. And since no one wants to do that, even the teens don't go the distance."

"What do you mean, 'Go the distance'?" Simone gave him a half-smile. "Are you telling me that there's heavy petting in Templeton?"

"Well, I wouldn't call it that," replied Mike. He felt himself squirming a little, hating where this was going. "Just that sometimes a couple of the older kids might get together for a date, because they like each other. Hell, there's a few who even live together, although that tends to bring funny looks from everybody else. Never lasts too long."

"So where . . ." She paused, appearing to gather her thoughts. "So where do new kids come from? I mean, I know that Templeton isn't overpopulated or anything, but it's always been there, it seems. If they lose kids every once in a while, like what happened to you or worse, what happened to that girl, Sandy, then eventually some kids have to replace them, or else Templeton becomes a ghost town."

Mike shrugged. "They just show up."

"They just *show up?*" Simone looked disgusted.

Mike was feeling defensive now. "Hey, don't blame me for not knowing. I never thought about it when I was a kid. Never had any reason to, did I? When you live in Templeton, every day's a new day, y'know? The big questions don't need to be dealt with, not too often, anyways. Kids go about their lives, do what they want or sometimes even need to do, but usually life is just one long game, even when they're doing what they call work." He rubbed his eyes. "I don't even remember where *I* came from. As far as I know, I was always there."

"Always there? Jesus." Simone pulled the car over to the curb and stepped heavily on the brake, slamming Mike forward in his seatbelt. "We're here."

Mike unbuckled himself and climbed out onto the sidewalk, choosing to ignore her mood for the moment. It wasn't a topic that made him particularly comfortable, thinking about what little he knew of his past.

The house was smaller than he had expected, a simple grey bungalow set close to the street. Only the four-car garage and the professional landscaping gave it away. The front door of the house was already open and a man in suit and tie was standing, waiting for them. "Lawyer," muttered Simone.

"Detectives," said the man as they arrived at the door. "I'm Colin Singh, Ms. Hayes's attorney. Please come in."

He closed the door behind them and then asked them to follow him. It turned out the house seemed a lot larger from the inside, and soon Mike was feeling somewhat adrift. Soon enough, though, they were brought to a small office. Singh sat behind a large metal desk. "Please sit down, detectives." He gestured, and they sat at the two chairs placed across from him. Before either could start, he raised his hand and said, "Ms. Hayes will be with us shortly, but will not be answering any questions at this time. If you wish to formally question her, please deliver a subpoena to my office so that we can arrange an interview."

"Then why are we here?" asked Simone.

"First, because you need to know that Ms. Hayes is not terribly interested in knowing who killed her husband."

Mike blinked in surprise. "Um, can I ask why not?"

"You were the boy," came a soft voice from behind.

They turned their heads, then all three stood as one. A young woman in simple dark blue slacks and matching blouse had entered the office, walking around them to stand beside the lawyer. She was petite, very slender in her hips and her bust, almost childlike. Which, Mike assumed, was likely the point.

"You were the boy," she repeated. "The one who came over from Templeton."

Mike nodded, unsure where this was going. Simone put a reassuring hand on his forearm. "I was . . . I am."

"This is Ms. Hayes," said Singh. She sat without offering to shake hands, and the rest of them followed suit.

"I'm sorry this had to happen to you," Ms. Hayes continued. "Enough innocence was lost without you being added to the mix."

Mike swallowed, wondering if he would have the nerve to ask the obvious question. But he didn't have to; Simone beat him to the punch. "Ms. Hayes, I know we're not supposed to ask you questions, but we need to know. . . ." Her voice trailed off, and she sounded very uncomfortable.

"I'm twenty-two," was the reply. "We married when I was sixteen." Her voice turned bitter and cold. "Apparently I was too old for him. It worked better if his partners didn't age."

Singh held up a hand. "That will be enough questions *and* answers." He looked pointedly at his client. Then he opened a drawer and pulled out two small wooden boxes, slid them across the desk. "This is why Ms. Hayes doesn't want to know."

Mike reached over and grabbed the boxes, knowing full well what it held. Sure enough, more Slow. One held two small vials of the stuff; another dozen were in the other. In little fabric pouches tucked alongside the vials were fresh syringes as well.

"Where did you find these?" asked Simone.

"In Mr. Hayes's office," said the lawyer, putting his hand on his client's arm. "Don't worry, as soon Ms. Hayes found them she called me. Aside from doorknobs and drawer handles, these were the only things she touched. His office, across the hall," he pointed, "is otherwise unmarred, and ready for your experts to search. Any other rooms you wish to check, you'll need to come back with a warrant."

"And what do we need to do in return?" Mike closed the box that only held two vials and slid it into his pocket, knowing damn well this was against procedure. The other wouldn't fit, so he just tucked it under his arm.

"Nothing. Your bosses will be made aware of things shortly. I don't know if you'll find names in there, but chances are good there's a path to them. I imagine there are some people who won't want their affiliation with Mr. Hayes known after this comes out."

"*If* it comes out," said Simone.

"That's a big word," agreed Singh. "But between the three of us and your bosses, Ms. Hayes and her husband were not living a very happy marriage these past few years. As soon as the will is cleared up, she has plans to liquidate assets and leave the country for good."

"We should probably rule you out as a suspect, first," said Mike, trying to look apologetic as he glanced at Ms. Hayes.

"Already taken care of," countered the lawyer. "Ms. Hayes was out of town, with friends. Here are her travel tickets, receipts, and a list of phone numbers." He handed Mike a manila envelope. "I'll also tell you now that she had no hand in her husband's business, took no notice of any people he chose to entertain, and, as you'll see in the envelope, was away for almost two weeks. She has no knowledge of any people who may have visited during that time."

Mike riffled through the contents of the envelope, then put them back to be checked later. "Are we done here then?"

"Mr. Hayes's office, detectives. One of my associates will wait in the hall for you to finish and then show you out." He nodded his head at the two of them; Ms. Hayes gave a slight smile and then turned to look out the window. "Good day."

The other office door was open. This one was much larger, more sumptuous than the first. The desk was oak, and immense, and expensive prints or even actual paintings inhabited the walls. Several thousand hardcover and leatherbound books sat in floor to ceiling shelves, and curios and knick-knacks and antiquities covered desk and shelf space everywhere else. The office was larger than his wife's, but it felt smaller, much more crowded.

"I'll call forensics to come and do the dirty work," said Simone. She pulled out her cellphone and rolled her eyes. "Shit. Battery's dead. If I'd known I was actually going to be working today . . ." She handed Mike a pair of gloves as she walked by. "I'll call from the other office, in case there are prints on his phone. Be right back."

Not really knowing what he was looking for, Mike put down the box he had under his arm and carefully lifted papers and books and opened drawers, hoping something might catch his eye.

Not the eye; the nose.

In the small tin garbage can sitting on the floor beside the desk, a familiar smell. Mike squatted down, slowly pulled out pieces of trash, sniffing each one before piling it on the floor beside him. Simone had come back in and was also searching. Now she stopped what she was doing—grabbed the chair and pulled it over, sat and watched.

Halfway through, Mike stood, grimacing as his knees popped and cracked. "What's with the knees?" he asked, groaning in pain.

"Middle age," replied Simone. "Usually your body gives you enough time to get used to the fact that you aren't as supple. This aging overnight business brings all sorts of nasty surprises, I imagine."

"Ow ow ow." Mike walked around the office, stretching out his legs and rubbing a new sore spot in the small of his back. "I wanna be young again." He knew he sounded whiny, but right now he didn't give a shit.

"Don't we all." Simone picked up the can and put it on top of the desk. "What were you onto with this?"

"I dunno." Mike came back to the desk and picked up the can, waving it under his nose. The smell was still there, faint but familiar. "Something . . ." He rummaged around a bit more, came out with two cigarette butts and a rock-hard piece of well-chewed gum, held them up to his nose. "Jesus."

"What?"

Mike looked at Simone, still holding the butts and the gum. "I have to cross the Line again."

She made a face and grabbed his arm. "Hell no, you don't! Once was enough, dammit, and you know it! If you cross again, you'll be just about ready for retirement when you come back. *If* you come back; if your heart can handle the stress."

He fumbled in his pocket, looking for baggies for the evidence, instead found himself pulling out the second little wooden box. He stared at it for a moment, then looked into Simone's face. "I can do it." He tossed the full box into a desk drawer and then turned and stepped quickly to the door, gloves still on, box in one hand and cigarette butts and gum in the other.

The lawyer waiting in the hall led the two of them out, assuring them that no one would enter the office until the forensics officers arrived. When they reached the car Simone turned on him. "You can't be thinking that; you can't. Beside being fucking illegal, it's dangerous. We still don't know enough about this shit."

"Just get me to the Line," said Mike, finally getting the evidence into some baggies and pocketing them. He fumbled through the box, pulled out a vial and syringe, stuck the needle through the lid and drew the green liquid up. "Same location as last time."

"Then tell me what you know." She swung hard on the wheel, taking a corner fast enough to throw Mike's shoulder up against the door. He eyed her for a second, then waved the syringe in the air before recapping it.

"I know who did it. But I don't know why, and I can only place him and Hayes in the same room. No real proof."

"Yet."

"Yet. Someone has to cross the Line to get a handle on the rest of this, and it sure as hell ain't gonna be you, or the captain, or anyone else who's never been there before."

Tires screeching, Simone brought the car to a stop by the Line. A couple of well-dressed men were standing across the street; one look at the car and both turned and walked away. The street was otherwise empty.

Mike undid his tie and wrapped it around his arm, pulled it tight until his veins were bulging. "Hope to hell this works." Twice he stopped short, little baby pinpricks that made him wince more in fear then in pain. But finally he worked up the nerve, plunged the needle into a vein.

The rush was almost instantaneous. Back arched, Mike squeezed his eyes shut, falling into the flood of images pouring across the blackness. He felt his body shudder once, twice, three times, and then he reopened his eyes.

"Mike?"

He turned to look at Simone, reached out and touched her face. "Jesus. You're beautiful." He leaned over and kissed her on the lips, hard, then grinned and opened the door. "Gotta go," he said brightly. "Got me a murderer to catch."

This time the Line had nothing on him. There was no added weight of years, no sense of desperation and sadness fell over him. He had a bounce in his step, felt stronger and more alive than he had even as yesterday's fresh-faced rookie.

He was also seeing weird shit float by his eyes every once in a while, but with a little bit of focus he was able to mostly ignore that. It wasn't too hard. The feeling of youth and vitality was enough that he didn't even care about the hallucinations; he was able to concentrate on just feeling *great*.

There was nobody around on the Templeton side of the Line. Nobody liked to come too near it if they could manage, so this was no surprise. It was raining lightly on this side as well, a drizzle that melded into the Line and quickly soaked him to the skin.

It didn't matter. Mike started off towards his destination, feeling young again.

After a few blocks the rain began to let up, and soon Mike noticed that he was being followed. A bunch of kids, twenty or more, the youngest only about six, the oldest in his teens. Mike waved to them, but there was no response. They just followed along, faces blank, apparently intent on keeping up.

The police tape was still across the door at the apothecary. He pulled it away and opened the door, flicked on the lights and stepped in. The kids stayed outside, still watching through the windows.

He had no idea what the hell he was looking for. He started with the garbage can beside the counter, saw that Jim and his forensic crew hadn't touched it. Out went the contents onto the counter top, papers and empty packages and, yes, two cigarette butts.

"It'll be the package with the green lettering," came a voice behind him.

"Sonofabitch!" yelled Mike, jumping in the air and spinning around. "Don't *do* that! My heart's racing fast enough as it is, without you sneaking up on me like that."

Danny lit up a smoke, pointed the cigarette at the box he was referring to. "It's kind of a sedative, kind of a hypnotic. I can't remember everything Sandy told me about it, but it worked pretty good. Best the stupid fucker could do was lift his hands in the air and cry like a baby."

The rush from the drug left Mike's system then, just drained right out and through his feet to the floor, it felt like. Now he felt fear and an almost unbearable grief, ice in his veins and a cold knot in his stomach, and his hands were shaking. He tucked them in his pockets. Hell of a comedown this drug gave.

Mike tried to talk, his voice caught. He tried again. "You *did* kill him."

Danny nodded. "Hell, yeah. Him and his kid-fucking buddies, coming across the Line with their safe new drug, screwing little girls and little boys."

"So tell us. Let the law deal with this."

"I am the law." Danny blew a puff of smoke into the air. "Don't you remember?"

"The law doesn't execute people without a trial, Danny. Not on either side of the Line."

His former partner walked over and with a hop pulled himself up to sit on the counter. Mike flinched back, then steadied himself; they were now eye level with each other. "This wasn't an execution, Mike, this was a warning shot. Already, all the pedos who are in on this are thinking twice about coming across the Line."

Mike thought back to sitting in the car, just before he'd injected the Slow into his system. "I think I saw two thinking about coming across just before I came in, standing at the corner and then buggering off when we showed up. Doesn't sound like it's working."

"Oh, it's working alright. Just needs a little more time to get through all the thick skulls and remind these bastards that the big head should do the thinking." Danny stubbed out his smoke and stood the garbage can back up, dropping it in. "And you'll note you weren't going anywhere without being noticed today," he continued, pointing to the crowd of kids outside. There were even more now, close to fifty, it looked.

"What about Sandy?"

Danny closed his eyes for a second, then shook his head. "She killed herself. Once she was done giving Hayes his drugs upstairs she was supposed to come down and tell me. She did, but not before she injected something into her neck." He wiped a tear from his eye. "Stone dead in seconds, it seemed. When I yelled and tried to stop her, that attracted Hayes, who came downstairs like a great big drunk moose, all dizzy and giddy at the same time."

Now Mike was all confused. "Then how do you explain her skull being all caved in?"

"Because I was pissed off!" Danny slammed his hand on the counter. "Because she was a stupid bitch for getting herself into this, for killing herself, for getting herself pregnant!"

His eyes widened and his hand went to his mouth. "I wasn't supposed to say," he whispered, tears welling up in his eyes.

"Oh no," whispered Mike.

Danny leaned over to lie down on the counter top, face pressed into the glass. The tears grew, quickly became huge, desperate sobs.

"She would have had to leave Templeton." Mike leaned over and slowly rubbed Danny's back, looked down on his tear-stained face. "Having sex with Hayes, maybe that started up her period. Between having to leave and being pregnant, she couldn't handle it. She killed herself."

Danny nodded, still sobbing. He was holding his beret now, crumpling it in his hands as if he was trying to squeeze away all of the pain.

"That explains the extra working over you gave Hayes. With your baton?" Danny nodded. "But why did you go and visit him in the first place? And how?"

After a few shuddering breaths Danny sat back up and leaned into Mike's chest. It felt strange to Mike as he wrapped an arm around his old friend, reminded him that he'd never had an adult to hold him like this when he'd lived here. "He had a stash of Slow on this side of the Line. I tried to warn him to stay away," gasped Danny. "But he just laughed, and told . . . and told me that he had a friend who might like to visit *me* soon."

"Jesus."

Danny nodded. "He knew that Sandy was pregnant. Said he'd take care of that his own way. And then he warned me not to use any more of his Slow. Too expensive to waste on a kid, he said."

Mike nodded. "Who are the rest of the pedos? Do you have any names?"

Danny reached into his jeans pocket and brought out a crumpled piece of paper, straightened it out as best he could and gave it to Mike. "Four that Sandy knew of. Sometimes Hayes would mention these guys. Only first names, though." He slid out of Mike's arm and back down to the floor, sniffling and wiping his nose with his sleeve. "Sorry."

Mike tried to smile. "It's okay, Danny. We might find something in his office. Thanks for the list."

"So what happens now?" asked Danny, trying to brush away more tears.

"I dunno," shrugged Mike. "It's not like I can bring you in or anything." He thought for a second, then said, "I think I'll just have to tell my captain the truth, see where it goes. It sounds like this is ugly enough they're gonna want to keep it a little more quiet."

"Yeah, maybe." Danny was staring at Mike now, his eyes growing wide.

"What?"

"You took Slow to come across the Line, right?"

"Yeah. Got it from Hayes's stash. Which is gonna mean bad trouble for me when I go back across."

"Did you bring enough to go back across?" His voice was barely a whisper.

Mike leaned back against the counter, fear and exhaustion both swamping him at once. "You don't have any more?"

Danny shook his head. "You took the last vial from Sandy's room. All the rest I know of are on your side of the Line."

"Think, now." Mike pinched the bridge of his nose and tilted his head up, eyes closed. "I am *such* an idiot. Simone has a cellphone, but her battery is toast. She didn't have time to go get her charger."

"Did you bring a radio?"

He patted his pockets, already knowing that he'd forgotten the thing. "Slow doesn't exactly promote forward thinking, it appears."

"We have a phone back at the station. Connects us with your headquarters."

Mike held up a hand. "I know, I know."

"We can call."

"What, and tell them I took an illicit drug to come across the Line and decide to cover up a murder my best friend committed? I'd call if it was just me, but I can't get my partner in trouble."

They were both quiet for a minute. Outside the sun was now shining, and it seemed that most of the kids had left; only a few were still standing around.

"Did you bring your car?"

Danny nodded.

"Take me back." Mike grinned, but he was feeling scared, and he knew it probably showed, no matter the front he presented. "I guess I'll put in for early retirement. Maybe I can even qualify for full pension after only three days on the job."

"Mike, no."

"Danny, I can't stay. I can't." He squeezed his friend's shoulder. "You know it, and I know it. If I stay too long I start to age anyway. May as well be old in a place where old people are welcome."

A long pause. "Right, then." Danny's voice was catching. "Let's go."

The drive back to the Line seemed too short. Neither of them talked, or even looked at each other, Danny concentrating on the drive and Mike just looking out the window at the buildings and kids as they went by.

At the Line he climbed out, groaning even more from the pain of the ride. He went down on one knee then, and they hugged, tight, knowing this was really going to be the last time.

He stood at the Line for a moment, looking up high into the haze, then back at Danny. "I'll miss you."

"Try and enjoy your retirement." They both tried to smile.

Mike shrugged. "Maybe I'll use my old age to go knock a few heads, make sure nobody's thinking about crossing over ever again."

"It ain't perfect, but this is still some pretty goofy shit," came another voice, quiet but definitely amused.

Mike turned back and watched as Simone staggered across the Line, carrying a syringe and the second vial of Slow, half empty. She handed them to him, turned and winked at Danny, then said, "You kiss real nice, Mike. Hurry up and take that stuff; it's probably not enough to hold back all the years, but it's better than nothing." She brushed some hallucinatory thing away from the front of her face, and then sighed. "You kiss like a kid. Felt nice."

Mike, not sure how long her hit would last, put a hand on Danny's shoulder and forced a grin, then loaded up the syringe, found a vein, and with only one false start stuck himself.

Taking Simone's hand, he left Templeton. The extra years bearing down on him were not as heavy as before, and the Slow kept some spring in his step. He closed his eyes, and tried to remember what it had meant to be a kid.

AFTERWORD

SHORT STORIES ARE PROMISES. Promises of new talent and skill, promises of new delight and joy, promises of new art and craft. The story itself is a promise, that a tale will begin and end, an idea develop, words will be run together with skill and care. Short stories also promise so much more beyond the immediate page; they are small works waiting to be gathered into bigger works, collections and anthologies, or to be themselves developed into novellas and novels. And short stories are so often promises of new talents to come, promises of visions and voices that are different and fresh, somehow young, only just beginning, promising long lives and many stories more to tell.

This anthology of speculative fiction covers a broad range of tastes and styles, showcasing a tremendous scope of talents that incidentally make up this country's literary landscapes. From the weirdness of a lonely lighthouse to the immensity of a prairie sky, from the fragmented novelty of Catherine MacLeod's "Postcards from Atlantis" to the pure gothic otherness of Richard Gavin's "Leavings of Shroud House: An Inventory," *Open Space: New Canadian Fantastic Fiction* delivers a gathering of distinctly Canadian, distinctly original voices—truly a book of promises.

Original anthologies such as *Open Space* are collections of promises, gifts from the future to the now, voices and talents we can only hope to meet again. Promise.

John Rose
Toronto, April 2003

CONTRIBUTORS

West Coast writer **Colleen Anderson**'s poetry and fiction have appeared in over seventy publications. She edits books for US and Canadian publishers and writes in numerous genres: poetry, children's stories, nonfiction articles, erotica, fantasy, horror, and anything that comes to mind. Some of Colleen's writings have appeared in *Descant*, *Amazing*, *On Spec*, *Talebones*, *Star*line*, *ChiZine*, *Twilight Tales*, *Tesseracts3*, *Northern Frights 4*, *Dreams of Decadence*, and *The Mammoth Book of On the Road* (Caroll & Graf). Her chapbook of speculative poetry, *Ancient Tales, Grand Deaths and Past Lives*, is available from Kelp Queen Press.

Shane Michael Arbuthnott was born and raised in Saskatoon. He is twenty-two years old, has written one novel, *Dreams of Stone*, for which he is currently trying to find a publisher, and is working on a second book. His story, "Of Wings," was begun while backpacking through Scotland in 2001 and finished once he came back home. About "Of Wings," which is his first publication, Shane says: "This story is for my uncle, who is more extraordinary than he knows."

Mark Anthony Brennan is a member of SF Canada with stories published in such magazines as *Descant*, *On Spec*, *Challenging Destiny*, *Hadrosaur Tales*, *Foxfire*, *Crux*, and *Andromeda Spaceways In-Flight Magazine*. As a journalist, he is a regular contributor to the lifestyle magazine *In Focus*. He is also the fiction editor for the online magazine *SDO* (www.sintrigue.org). Mark lives in Comox on Vancouver Island with his wife and three children.

Leslie Brown lives and works in Ottawa, Ontario, as a technician for the National Research Council. She has previously published four stories in *On Spec* and has received much support and direction from that publication. She is also part of Lyngarde, a writers' group based in Ottawa.

Matthew Costaris is fifteen years old and has had work published in various venues, including Gothic.net, *Metropole, Horrorfind,* and *Writer's Digest's* special *Writing for Kids* publication. He welcomes email and would love to know your thoughts on his contribution. Send comments to mcostaris@hotmail.com.

Cory Doctorow (www.craphound.com) is the Campbell Award–winning author of the novel *Down and Out in the Magic Kingdom.* His collection of short stories, *A Place So Foreign and Eight More,* was just published by Four Walls Eight Windows, and his next novel, *Eastern Standard Tribe,* will be published by Tor in January 2004. Though born and raised in Toronto, he lives in San Francisco, where he works for the Electronic Frontier Foundation and coedits the popular weblog Boing Boing (boingboing.net).

Marcelle Dubé grew up in Montreal and lived in Victoria, Winnipeg, and Belgium before finally settling in the Yukon. She now makes her home at the foot of Mount Lorne, sharing the land with coyotes, lynx, and the occasional bear. Her fascination with gargoyles and their relationship—physical and symbolic—to old churches led to "Chimère." Her stories have appeared in *Storyteller* and *The Last Whole Moose Catalogue.*

Richard Gavin began writing horror in childhood. Since that time his writings have appeared in nearly one hundred publications around the world. He has received Honourable Mention in *The Year's Best Fantasy and Horror* and is the author of the online comic "Palace of Shadows" (with artist Michael Ramseur). In 2004, Rainfall Books will release *Charnel Wine,* a collection of Richard's macabre short fiction. Richard lives in Ontario, where he is seldom seen during daylight hours.

Aaron V. Humphrey is a full-time computer programmer living in Edmonton, Alberta. His stories have previously appeared in *Tesseracts7, On Spec,* and *E-Scape.* His interests include music, books, theatre, heraldry, simulations, blogging, languages, and amassing data. He has twice completed the NaNoWriMo challenge.

Ahmed A. Khan was infected with the writing bug at an early age. He has lived in India, Kuwait, and Canada, in that order. His works (both fact and fiction) have appeared in magazines in India, Kuwait, Pakistan, the USA, and Canada and in webzines such as *Anotherealm, AlienQ, Pif, Cyber Oasis, GateWay*

S-F, Jackhammer, Millennium SF, Strange Horizons, The Phone Book, etc. Recently, one of his SF stories has been picked up to be included in the academic book *Preparing for FCAT Reading / Grade 8 Science Content.*

Drew Karpyshyn is the author of two novels: *Temple Hill* and *Baldur's Gate II: Throne of Bhaal.* He is also a writer/designer for the acclaimed video game developer Bioware and has worked on a number of award-winning titles, including *Neverwinter Nights* and the *Baldur's Gate* series, and on the forthcoming *Star Wars: Knights of the Old Republic.* Drew currently lives in Sherwood Park, Alberta, with his beautiful wife, Jennifer. When not typing away at his computer, he can likely be found on one of the local golf courses, still struggling (vainly) to make his PGA Tour dream a reality.

Born and raised in Ontario's Niagara region, **Nicholas Knight** now lives with his wife in the lower mainland of British Columbia. His stories can be found in *Hour of Pain, Midnighters Club, Sideshow, The Witching Hour, Mystery in Mind, Underworlds, Whispers from the Shattered Forum, Futures Mysterious Anthology Magazine*, and *Black Petals*, among many other print and online publications. He can be contacted at knight@darktales.zzn.com.

Claude Lalumière (www.lostpages.net) is a Montreal author, critic, and editor. His other anthologies include *Witpunk* (coedited with Marty Halpern) and *Island Dreams: Montreal Writers of the Fantastic.* His fiction can be found in *Interzone, The Book of More Flesh, On Spec*, and others. His criticism appears in many venues; most notably, he's a columnist for *Locus Online, Black Gate*, and *The Montreal Gazette.* In 1989, he founded Nebula—a Montreal bookshop devoted to the fantastic, the imaginative, and the weird—which he ran until he sold it in 1998.

Murray Leeder is the author of the *Dungeons & Dragons* novel *Plague of Ice* (as by T.H. Lain) and of *The Nectar Deceptions*, published by Adventure Books, as well as of short fiction that has appeared in such anthologies as *Circus* and *Realms of Shadow.* A lifelong resident of Calgary, Murray has just completed an undergraduate degree in English and is now puzzling over what to do next.

Nova Scotian **Catherine MacLeod** has published short fiction in the magazines *On Spec, Solaris*, and *Talebones* and in the anthology *Tesseracts6.* When not writing odd prose at odd hours, she feeds her tastes for 8-ball, country rock, and noir.

Derryl Murphy is hard at work on his first novel as well as some more short stories, is a fiction editor and art director for *On Spec*, and spends his free time playing soccer or laughing hysterically at *SpongeBob SquarePants* with his boys. Among other things.

John Park was born in England and moved to Vancouver in 1970 as a graduate student in chemistry at UBC. While there he published his first story professionally and attended the Clarion writers workshop. In 1978 he took a temporary position with the National Research Council in Ottawa. Still residing in Ottawa, he is now a partner in a scientific consulting firm. His stories have appeared in magazines *(Galaxy, On Spec,* and *Tomorrow)*, anthologies (*Far Frontiers, Cities in Space, Northern Stars, TransVersions*, and several *Tesseracts* volumes), and in French and German translations

Janet Marie Rogers is a writer, visual artist, and performance poet living in Victoria, BC. She is Mohawk from Six Nations territory in southern Ontario. Janet writes passionately about her heritage and includes her culture in her performance work. Her literary work can be found in several anthologies from Canada, the USA, and New Zealand. Janet has recently completed the first phase of a screenwriting program at the Banff Centre for the Arts in Alberta.

John Rose owned Bakka, the Toronto science-fiction bookstore, for twenty-two years. He took it over in 1980, watching as it grew into one of the premier specialty bookstores in Canada. He established a strong connection with the writing community and maintained support for local writers, many of whom worked at Bakka. His publishing interests began with the repackaging of several Canadian science fiction novels and the publication of an anthology of short stories commemorating the thirtieth anniversary of Bakka. In 2003, Rose sold his interest in Bakka to pursue a career in publishing.

A writer of fiction, poetry, and plays, **Vincent W. Sakowski** is the author of the anti-epic novel of the surreal *Some Things Are Better Left Unplugged* and the novella *The Hack Chronicles*—both published by Eraserhead Press. He lives with his wife, Robin, in Saskatoon, SK, where he was born and raised. He is at work on his latest novel.

Jes Sugrue was born in Ottawa but now lives, parents, and teaches in Victoria, BC. Her publishing credits include postcard fiction in *The Writers Publishing*

and nonfiction in *Canadian Living* and *Island Parent*. She meets weekly with a writers' group for support, critique, and "Wild Mind" time, attends the annual Victoria school of Writing, and has been a delegate to the BC Festival of the Arts for both Poetry and Writing for Children. She is currently working on *Life Bites*, a collection of dark young-adult fiction, and on her second novel, *Pearl's Gate*.

Marcie Lynn Tentchoff, an Aurora Award–winning writer, lives in Gibsons, BC, with her family, numerous cats, and a truly obnoxious cockatiel. Marcie's work has appeared in such periodicals as *On Spec, Weird Tales, Dreams of Decadence*, and *Talebones*, as well as in various anthologies. She is poetry editor for *Spellbound*, a fantasy magazine aimed at readers aged nine through fourteen.

Born and raised in the woods of northern Ontario, **Steve Vernon** has crossed this country by hitcher's thumb, making a living as a professional fortune teller, a writer of horror, a poet, and an oral-tradition storyteller. You'll find Steve's latest stories in *Scriptures of the Damned* (Double Dragon) and *Wicked Wheels* (Cyber-Pulp). Steve now resides in Halifax, Nova Scotia. In the summer you can find him on the waterfront, in Nathan Greene Square, next to the caricature artist and the sandstone carver. Look for the palm-reading sign and say hello.

Melissa Yuan-Innes is currently working on a novel about Sam and his family, tentatively titled *The Ape in the Mirror*. Some of her stories can be found in *Weird Tales, Andromeda Spaceways, Full Unit Hookup*, and the anthology *Island Dreams: Montreal Writers of the Fantastic*. Lights! Camera! Action! at www.melissayuaninnes.com.